Jane Freeman  Morning Herald column she writes numerous feature articles on everything from television and the arts to lifestyle, travel, finance and unusual things to do with throw rugs.

FLIPSIDE

JANE FREEMAN

BANTAM BOOKS
Sydney • Auckland • Toronto • New York • London

FLIPSIDE
A BANTAM BOOKS

First published in Australia and New Zealand in 1999
by Bantam

Copyright © Jane Freeman, 1999

National Library of Australia
Cataloguing-in-Publication entry

Freeman, Jane.
Flipside
ISBN 0 7338 0174 9.
I. Title
A823.3

Bantam books are published by
Transworld Publishers,
a division of Random House Australia Pty Ltd
20 Alfred Street, Milsons Point, NSW 2061

Random House New Zealand Limited
18 Poland Road, Glenfield, Auckland

Transworld Publishers (UK) Limited
61–63 Uxbridge Road, Ealing, London W5 5SA

Random House Inc
1540 Broadway, New York, New York 10036

Cover photograph by IPL Image Group
Typeset in Sabon 11/14pt by Midland Typesetters, Maryborough,
Victoria
Printed by Griffin Press, Netley, South Australia

10 9 8 7 6 5 4 3 2 1

For Simon and Sally,
who are always amazing

CHAPTER 1

Clare Calloway flicked impatiently through *Manifesting Your Man: A Guide to Finding (and Keeping!) Mr Appropriate,* until she reached the section on home dates.

THE HOME DATE: Never forget that every time Mr Appropriate comes into your home, he will be imagining what it would be like to live with you forever and ever. For better or worse, men still see women as the homemakers and so you can bet donuts to diamonds that he'll be subconsciously assessing you in this area whenever he's over. Is the floor covered in cat hair? Is there a blunt razor and the wrong kind of fuzz in the bathroom? Are the towels fresh and fluffy? These may seem like pesky little details to you but be warned. The cumulative effect of such trivial things could make the difference between Mr Appropriate seeing you as just another Saturday night fling, or as the mother of his children. And it would be heartbreaking if that exciting new man slipped through your fingers just because you neglected to wipe around the kitchen sink once a day, now, wouldn't it?

Disgusted, Clare threw the book across the room. What a lot of unadulterated, appalling, unreconstructed twaddle. She should have known better than to buy any book that referred to 'Mr Appropriate' in the first place.

On the other hand, maybe there was something to it. Self-help books were like a box of assorted chocolates, Clare told herself Gumpishly. You had to keep going because you always believed that the next bit of advice or the next chapter or even the next book was going to be the one to satisfy you.

And, come to think of it, Leo had made a scathing remark the other day about the vintage condition of her chopping board. And he often pointedly picked the cat hairs off his black jackets. Maybe he was trying to tell her something.

Reluctantly, she walked over and picked up the book and dusted off the fluff, cat hairs and a stray curl of plastic tampon wrapping. Just to be on the safe side, she decided, she should do a tidy-up before Leo arrived. Well, at least hide that old chopping board. Or at the very, very least, hide *Manifesting Your Man*. It would be disastrous if Leo stumbled across that.

Quite apart from the fright the title would give him, he regarded the reading of self-help books as a sign of soft-headedness. Which, Clare was prepared to admit, it possibly was. Still, a woman needs to have some kind of hobby. Consequently, she was forever having to conceal her latest handbook to life improvement, and she still recalled with shame his jeering when he stumbled across her copy of *If I'm So Wonderful, How Come I'm Still Single?*

Of course, Clare didn't even know whether Leo was coming over tonight. He was due back today after spending three weeks in the country where they were shooting his first feature film. No doubt he'd have spent the time hanging around the set, wearing black and hoping everyone noticed that The Writer was present. Clare hadn't heard from him but that didn't mean that he wouldn't suddenly turn up. Leo had the thrilling habit of appearing without warning, rushing noisily through her door demanding food, wine and her, in no particular order. It was all extremely breathtaking, when it wasn't irritating – like when she had eaten garlic at lunch or hadn't got around to shaving her legs for three days.

She realised with a start that it was seven o'clock already. Peeling off her suit and leaving it thrown carelessly over one of the living rooms chairs (now what would *Manifesting Your Man* have to stay about that!), she flung herself into the shower where she furiously sorted through all her shampoo bottles. Clare was convinced that if she could only find the right shampoo her hair would miraculously become thick, shiny and luscious. And as all the shampoo bottles happened to promise the very same thing, she was a sucker for a new brand.

As she scrubbed away, concentrating on the hairline and back of the head, as recommended in some magazine article she'd read when she was thirteen, she wondered whether Leo had missed her. He'd been away for weeks, with only a couple of cursory phone calls in that time. It didn't seem promising, especially given that they'd only been going out for six months. They should still be at the (admittedly, tail end) of infatuation and obsession, according to *Manifesting Your Man*. On the other hand, one of the things that was appealing about Leo was his detachment. Not, Clare reassured herself, that she indulged in any of those clichés about wanting to join a club that didn't want her, but there was no denying that doglike devotion simply didn't interest her. It never had.

In between shampoos she exfoliated until she glowed pink all over and then bashed away savagely at the callouses on her feet with a pumice stone. They were the price she paid for wearing fabulous shoes, she supposed. Still it did seem unfair that men went around with baby-soft feet while women were hobbled by horny skin, bunions, corns and hammer toes. Who said that foot binding had gone out of fashion?

She started to make a mental list of all the things she had to do to the flat before it would be deemed present-able to the assessing eye of Mr Appropriate − vacuum, dust, wipe, polish, deodorise, air ...

Pity they never went to Leo's place, she reflected, shaving herself in as many places as she could reach. Leo shared a house in the bijou inner city Melbourne suburb of Albert Park. He always made the excuse that it was much easier to come to her flat, where they had the place to themselves, than to battle it out for the poky bath-room with Geoff and Scott. Clare wouldn't mind it if he had to do the housework for a change. Solo housework was another one of the penalties of living alone, she mused, along with nights when you felt like you were the last puppy left after the rest of the litter had found a home.

Clare mostly loved living by herself, but sometimes it did occur to her that it was a dangerous game. Too much solitude left a very fine skin separating normality from hermit-like eccentricity. She found herself doing odd things, like dancing naked to overnight video shows or heating up green chicken curry for breakfast or video taping really bad midday movies and then watching them at night while she ate tubs of non-fat, non-dairy diet ice cream.

Living with other people must at least help to keep you sane and normal, she thought. Like her sister, Isobel, for example, who was doing the married with two kids and a house in the 'burbs thing. You'd never catch Isobel dancing naked in the living room or eating buckets of some weird concoction that seemed to be made of absolutely nothing. Clare wondered idly if she kept living alone whether she could, in the end, go entirely around the twist and whether anyone would notice.

Realising that she was still standing under the hot shower, she hastily turned off the water. Patting herself dry with a (not very fresh, definitely not fluffy) towel, she slathered on anti-cellulite cream, and followed it with her most expensive body moisturiser. She earnestly tried to think erotic thoughts as she trimmed her toenails because she worked on the theory that it was always better to get oneself in the mood, rather than relying on the man to start from scratch. She'd read somewhere that this could cut foreplay time by fifty per cent and make it much more likely for the woman to achieve orgasm before the man either developed RSI or decided to come anyway and then pretend to do one of those 'Oh, I didn't mean that to happen, I'm so sorry, gosh, I'm feeling sleepy, aren't you?' routines. Not that sex with Leo needed many more added fireworks. In fact, the problem was that although the sex was explosive, so were the arguments.

'Maybe that's *why* the sex is so fantastic,' Isobel had pointed out dryly. Clare, of course, stubbornly refused to concede the point. Right now, Leo was far better than early nights and man-sized pyjamas and hoping to bump into Mr Wonderful while buying Lean Cuisine for one at the supermarket.

She was running out of time. She blow-dried her hair and carefully made up her face in an unobtrusive way, because Leo was always saying how much he hated women who plastered make-up on their faces as if they were rendering brick veneer. She brushed her teeth twice, swallowed some parsley oil capsules to ensure her breath was fresh and had her usual five-minute battle to get her diaphragm and cervix in alignment.

By the time she was finished all that, she felt more like a good lie-down than a sex goddess. But there was no time to rest. Instead, she stood in agony in front of the wardrobe, trying to decide if it would be better to opt for casual elegance ('Oh gosh, I wasn't expecting to see you, Leo, I was just having a quiet night, stretched out on the couch in silky pyjamas with contemporary jazz music on the stereo ...') or black and skimpy with no knickers underneath ('I've been waiting for you, tiger, come and get me, you lust-crazed beast ...').

In the end she went for black and skimpy and a pair of sexy high-heeled shoes. She might as well get started on some new callouses as soon as possible.

Then she looked despairingly at her flat. When she said 'her' of course she used the term loosely. She was probably the proud owner of the front door, while the bank rejoiced in the rest. After years of vaguely thinking that one day she would get married to someone who understood money and made quite a lot of the stuff, Clare had realised with a jolt when she turned thirty that she had no savings and no husband ready to say, 'Here darling, let me wrap you up in my Armani dinner jacket/ six figure income.'

So after two years of saving she'd scraped together enough to put a deposit on this tiny flat. It was in an art deco building in inner city St Kilda, only two blocks from the sea. The drawbacks were the tram tracks running right outside the front door and the fact that she only had one bedroom, a sitting room and a kitchenette. But there were polished floor boards, creamy walls, wooden blinds on the windows. Like living in a little treehouse but with more reliable plumbing.

Clare scurried about plumping pillows, dustbusting the cat hair, lighting aromatherapy candles and arranging the right lighting. She would have preferred to put on a CD of Savage Garden singing slushy romantic pop tunes, but Leo regarded pop as slightly infantile, so she put on some jazz instead. The things you do for love. Then she headed into the kitchen to whip up some food in case he wanted a snack.

As usual, Barchester, her elderly ginger cat, was sitting in the kitchen doorway demanding mutely to be fed, his feet primly together and his tail wrapped around the whole package for the sake of tidiness.

'No time to talk now, Barty,' she said, scooping him out of the way. 'I'll chuck some dried cat food in your dish but there'll be no canned stuff tonight. I don't want the place to reek of cat food.'

When she'd taken the quiz test in *Your Problem Zones and How to Challenge Them*, Clare had confronted the fact that cooking was one of her weak spots (along with gossip, lack of commitment, failure to floss every night and a habit of peeking curiously in other people's bathroom cabinets and surreptitiously smearing dabs of their expensive French moisturiser on as hand cream).

If she'd had time she would have stopped for something from the deli on the way home but surely nothing much could go wrong with a quiche? She'd just grab pastry out of the freezer, throw in eggs, cream, bacon and onion and generous handfuls of the three different types of herbs she could scrounge out of the back of the cupboard.

Clare began thrashing together the eggs and cream, relieved that someone had told her recently that you really didn't have to take any notice of the use-by dates on food stuffs, they were just there as a rough guide.

Tossing in random sprinkles of herbs, she wondered what mood Leo would be in after watching the making of his first movie. Exhilarated? Satisfied? Contented? Somehow she could not imagine Leo contented. Ever. He was always so – hungry.

Clare had met Leo Robertson on the set of a successful television soap where she was interviewing one of the show's starlets for *Verve*. *Verve*, the magazine 'for the woman who had everything', had condescended to offer Clare a job two years ago and somehow, despite her best intentions, she was still there.

At lunchtime, she'd sat next to Leo on a bench seat, while she tried to resist the delicious (and enormously fattening) catering van fare. She often wondered how actresses managed to stay so enviably thin when every film set she'd ever been on had been catered for like a luxury cruise liner. She'd noted with some cynicism that Leo made a point of informing her that, while he was a writer on 'Down Town', he was *really* a feature film writer and already had several scripts in development.

Although she wasn't immediately attracted to him, she'd accepted an invitation to dinner that night. Before she knew it, he was staying over at her place several nights a week.

Isobel thought she was crazy. 'Why can't you pick someone who actually cares about you for once in your life,' she had tutted over her armfuls of babies, washing, groceries and freshly folded nappies.

Clare's friend from work, Fiona, told her straight out that Leo was self-centred and self-satisfied. 'I can see that he's cute,' she'd said, 'but really, just how many hours do you want to spend listening to someone jabber on about their personal creative process?'

But Clare found his obsessive streak exciting. She once watched him write a draft of one of his film scenarios and had been amazed to see that he started sweating as he scribbled, even though it was a cool evening.

'Incredible,' she'd murmured, looking up from her book to touch the big beads of sweat standing out on his forehead. 'Your brain is working so hard you're sweating.'

'Yeah, knocks the socks off digging coal,' he'd told her mockingly.

She was intrigued by his whole prickly, pugnacious attitude to life. Coming from a working-class background, Leo passionately resented the spoilt, middle-class privately educated brats who colonised the film industry. Everything about Leo was aggressive, from

9

his determination to be famous to the way he persuaded Clare into his bed (or rather her own). And yes, Clare admitted to herself, as she roughly chopped up some gamy bacon, she found it exciting. She joked to Fiona that she had finally found her Lady Chatterley's lover.

Barchester gave an impatient mew and jumped up on the bench to see what Clare was doing.

'You know you're not meant to be up here, you old renegade,' she told him tolerantly.

The cat ignored her and began washing his face. Barchester had been acquired in one of the dry spells 'between relationships', when Clare believed she'd never meet another decent man so she may as well roll with the punches and become an embittered, cat-loving single woman.

Of course there had been other relationships, but nothing that stuck around. Now Barchester was getting old, Clare was thirty-four, unmarried and her main achievements in life were buying a flat and securing a job on a glossy women's magazine with a small circulation and massive advertising revenue. It was hardly the glittering future she'd once imagined for herself back in the days when words such as Pulitzer, Oscar, Booker, BAFTA and Nobel did not seem altogether out of her reach. But then neither did a man who was handsome, funny, honourable and fabulous in bed. How long can you go on telling yourself that you are just being discriminating?

She leant on the kitchen bench, gazing vacantly down into the glutinous mess in the bowl, asking herself for the hundredth time whether she was 'in love' with Leo (whatever that meant, as Prince Charles once so pithily said). She certainly lusted after him, she was fascinated by him, but she thought she could see his foibles clearly. Not least of all his obsession with his career. Still, she reassured herself dubiously, at least it was a career with pizzazz. Imagine how much worse it would be if he was a chicken sexer or a derivatives trader. There were some topics no woman could bear to listen to for hours on end.

But for two years now a small and rather whining voice in her head had been reminding her that, if she was ever going to have children, it had to be soon. Leo gave no sign of being someone who wanted to invest in anything as ordinary as children and a stationwagon with a dog grill. He was poised on the brink of success and would probably be leaving for Los Angeles this time next year. But then there was no denying the primitive fact that, at the thought of seeing him again, her heart was thudding with excitement.

When the quiche was in the oven (she figured cooking would probably get rid of the lumps), Clare settled back on one of her new cream mock croc couches with her laptop and some *Verve* work. Might as well let him find her writing. That'd remind him he wasn't the only one with a burgeoning career.

As she'd been rushing out the door that afternoon, The Colonel had dragged her into her office for a 'little chat'. 'The Colonel' was Clare and Fiona's nickname for *Verve*'s editor, Helen Hogan. She was a desiccated, tough old prawn, but Hogan had a force of personality that left everyone else bobbing in her wake. She also ran *Verve* as if it was her personal fiefdom.

While Clare had shuffled impatiently from one foot to the other, The Colonel informed her blandly that this month she would have to fill in on the 'Dear Marion' problem page, as the regular writer was off having another face lift.

'Marion' had never been glimpsed around the *Verve* office but her picture on the page showed a handsome grey-haired woman in her early fifties, clad for some mysterious reason in a white coat (perhaps the *Verve* readers were meant to assume that the agony aunt also had some kind of unspecified medical degree).

Clare hated it when The Colonel made her do these trivial fill-in jobs. After all, she was a feature writer, not some general dogsbody doing work that wouldn't even have her name on it.

'I am a valuable professional resource. You shouldn't squander me,' she'd admonished The Colonel.

The Colonel fixed her with her knitting needle sharp glare.

'My dear, as they say, there are no small jobs, just small writers. Now, if you'll excuse me, I have more important things to do than discuss *your* importance.'

Clare winced at the memory. She should have known better than to try to take on The Colonel – again. The Colonel had personally founded *Verve* decades ago as the mature sophisticated woman's lifestyle guide. She envisaged it as giving the last word on everything from the clothes the *Verve* woman put on her perfect size-10 body (the *Verve* woman never puts on weight, even after her two children), to the right ash blonde hair colour and what to do if it all falls out in the process (it's amazing what you can do with a Hermes scarf). When it came to the magazine and its readers, The Colonel wasn't just an editor, she was a totalitarian dictator.

Clare poured a glass of wine and reached reluctantly into the green folder containing this month's chosen 'Dear Marion' letters.

Dear Marion, she read, sipping chilled white wine.

I'm desperate to know what to do about my partner who is having an affair. At least, I suspect he is. Although I will not go into the tedious and tawdry details, all the evidence points that way but he will not admit it when I confront him. Should I cut my losses and leave him now, or try to force him to come clean so we can start again?

Yours hopefully, 'Betrayed'

Clare switched on her laptop and waited impatiently for it to boot up.

Dear 'Betrayed', she then typed rapidly, striving for the right tone. 'Marion' was meant to be kindly but sophisticated, an aunty with edge.

What a grim situation to find yourself in. My guess from your letter is that you still love your partner and want your relationship to continue, with the proviso that he will admit his infidelity. Let me point out the error of logic in your thinking. If you are willing to take him back despite the adultery, then it's not important whether he has or hasn't, you are taking him back either way. Am I right or am I right?

So forget this punitive carping about the past and cut to the chase. What you want to know is will he stay faithful in the future? Concentrate on that from now on. And let me suggest that you sharpen his mind a tad by agreeing to have a lawyer draw up some kind of contract which will set up certain financial ramifications if he strays again – presuming you are living in a legally binding relationship. Lastly, remember that men are indeed the weaker sex. Victims of their hormones, they often need our compassion. All the best to you both!

Pleased with her efforts, she looked up and saw that the time was already ten o'clock.

Well, Leo was often late. Once he had rung her doorbell at 1 am, and when she had rushed out thinking something must be wrong with Isobel or her kids, he'd calmly strolled in and said he'd come to stay the night. 'I'm not a motel,' she had shrieked, shoving him out the door.

Something was burning. In the kitchen Clare snatched open the oven door to discover the quiche, now a piece of blackened wood cracked and crumbling at the edges. Well he can just make do with cheese and crackers, she thought. She mashed up the burned quiche and put it in Barchester's bowl, where the cat regarded it disdainfully.

'Don't eat it then. Why the hell did I get a male cat? You're all self-centred,' she muttered at him.

The phone rang and she almost sprang across the room to answer.

'Hello? Oh Mum, it's you . . .'

'Hello dear,' boomed June Callaway in her big, rolling voice. 'I just thought I'd ring to catch up. I haven't spoken to you in ages.'

Clare slumped down on the little seat beside the phone. The last thing she needed right now was another exhaustingly dull encounter with her mother. Even worse, she had visions of Leo arriving and finding her on the phone talking to her mum. About as sexy as spencers and bed socks.

'Yes, I haven't spoken to you since last week,' she reminded June. 'You do know it's after ten.'

'That's hardly late these days. Your father and I often don't get to bed until midnight. Particularly when the mah jong club is meeting.'

'Mah jong! Honestly Mum, I don't know what you see in it. I thought you and Dad would spend your retirement doing university courses or going on archaeological digs with a very big first-aid kit. Instead you play mah jong.'

'Yes we do,' June said comfortably. 'I spoke to Isobel today, everything's fine with the children. She really is so wonderful with those two.'

'Isn't she,' Clare said shortly. 'I'm going over there for dinner on Friday night. Isobel's roped me in again.'

'That'll be lovely for you. Do you good to get a decent meal inside you. Isobel is such a lovely cook.'

'Yes,' said Clare moodily, looking at her quiche in the bottom of the cat bowl. 'Iso is a marvellous cook.'

'And so clever! The things she does that your father and I would never have dreamed of. You know she has made car seat covers with special pockets in the back where she can put toys, snacks and drinks for the children for long car rides?'

'Yes, I know. Very clever,' Clare said.

'She's so practical,' June said emphatically. 'Really practical. She could patent those and start selling them. Make a fortune.'

'She should think about that. I'm sorry, Mum . . .'

'And with those children, she really has the patience of an angel. I don't think I've ever seen her lose her temper. It's wonderful the way her life has just come together.'

'Yes Mum, I hear what you're telling me. Now I really have to go, as I said. I'm expecting an important call. Something for work.'

'Oh, I won't keep you, someone exciting I hope?'

'Sure, er,' Clare groped for a name. 'Andie McDowell, all the way from her ranch in Montana.'

'Oh she's lovely. Such a nice girl, managing to combine her movie star career with having all those children and that beautiful home.'

'Yes and a lovely house husband who knows how to cook too,' Clare said. 'Look Mum, I'll call you next week.'

She put the phone down feeling, as usual, as if her whole life was a fib and a failure. Strange, the way her mother always managed to make her feel so small.

Not that this was anything new. Clare and Isobel had grown up as allies in a household where their unenthusiastic parents had practised a form of apartheid, keeping grown-ups segregated from children. June Callaway used to say 'Girls, run outside and play where I can't see you' only slightly more often than 'Stop that giggling, your father has had a long day in the shop and doesn't need to hear from you.' The sisters told each other later in life that their parents must have conceived children by mistake when what they really wanted to do was grow a few bonsai plants. Isobel, the oldest sister, had responded by trying to be very good. Clare had responded by being moderately bad. The effect on their parents had been the same – they scarcely seemed to notice.

Clare wandered restlessly around the flat, pausing to clean her teeth again and then touching up her lipstick. In the bedroom she examined herself in the full-length mirror. Shoulders too broad, breasts too small, hips too wide. Legs not too bad, especially in black stockings.

Her recently blow-waved hair, which an hour ago was artfully tousled, was now drooping again. As usual, she longed for Isobel's magnificent hair. Isobel had scored all the looks in the family – the thick glossy hair, the bright blue eyes and creamy skin – leaving Clare with the conviction that she'd better cultivate her personality and her peroxide or be left out of the race altogether. She always longed to have hair like Isobel's so she could just pile it up on her head in some elegant Helena Bonham Carter style and forget about it. Instead she ruffled more mousse through her own fine hair and then regretted it immediately. Leo would probably try to put his tongue in her ear and end up with a mouthful of styling chemicals instead.

Grimacing, she went back to the sitting room and poured another glass of wine. At this rate, when he finally showed up, she would be tanked. He could at least have had the courtesy to ring her and explain when he was arriving. Or even *if* he was arriving. Perhaps he was so exhausted from hanging around the film set watching men with big tool belts do nothing much in a very busy fashion that he had decided to spend one more night in the country.

Seeking distraction, she pulled out the second 'Dear Marion' letter.

Dear Marion, it said.

I have fallen in love with my best friend's husband. Naturally I haven't told him about my feelings yet but I believe he feels the same because of the way he behaves, sometimes touching my hand when he passes me a glass of champagne or kissing me on the mouth when we say goodbye after a dinner party. I don't know whether I should decide it's every woman for herself and pursue this man, or whether I should opt for sisterly solidarity and tell my friend about her husband's feelings. What do you suggest?

Yours in anticipation, 'Lancelottie'

Clare reached for a handful of cashews from the bowl she'd casually placed on the table ('Oh yes, I always have bowls of fresh, delicious and expensive produce just lying around'). Cashews were horrendously high in fat but she was starving. She gulped more wine.

Dear Lancelottie, she tapped.

What an absurd question. Of course you should leave your 'friend's' husband alone, if she really is your friend. Or even if she isn't for that matter. For a start there's your own self-respect – how would you feel about nuking someone's marriage? Then there's the man in question. Why on earth would you want to shack up with someone who cheats on his wife with her friends and, even more disgustingly, paws their hands when he's passing over some wretched glass of bubbling spumante? Sounds like a shady character to me.

Save your passion for someone more deserving of

it. Some men just aren't worth losing a good friendship over. In fact, some men aren't worth losing a night's sleep over. So, my dear, forget Mr Handyman and find yourself a good chap with integrity. You'll be able to spot him because he'll be tall, dark, handsome and he'll know the meaning of a fraternal peck on the cheek when it comes to YOUR friends. And he'll be out there when you least expect it. Or so they tell me.

She had forced herself not to check the clock while she wrote her reply, thinking superstitiously that if she stopped peering at the time, he would show up.

But by 11.30 pm, there was still no sign. Furious, bored, hungry and deflated, she wondered if she should call his home number.

Of course, it would look bad for her to call him, then he would feel like he was being hunted. Men needed to feel they were winning the prize otherwise they started to wonder if it really was a prize after all.

Clare dragged her copy of *Manifesting Your Man* out of the freezer and rifled through it until she found the section headed 'Hard to Get'. She'd decided to play this relationship by the book, for once, and *Manifesting Your Man* was an international bestseller so the writers must be doing something right. Either that or they'd managed to claw their way on to Oprah which indicated some sort of talent, anyway.

Leaning against the kitchen cupboards, shifting her weight from leg-to-leg to take the strain off her feet in her high heels, Clare read avidly.

HARD TO GET: No one wants to do something as corny

and manipulative as 'playing hard to get' but this whole life-altering exercise is about finding and keeping Mr Appropriate. And the plain unvarnished truth is that men are like cats. They don't like to be chased. And they just seem to spontaneously jump on the lap of anyone who doesn't like them. So when it comes to handling your own man, keep these rules in mind. Treat your man as a cat. Never pursue, let him come to you. Don't overfeed him with your company – less is more. And never undervalue the power of a good, firm stroke, you'll be amazed at how he responds. Make sure that you have plenty of other things going on in your life so you're not hanging around him (if you don't have other things going on in your life, then get to work to make sure you do. In a worst-case scenario, you'll have to fake it). Finally, don't be too readily available. As the old show biz adage goes, always leave 'em wanting more.

Shoving the book back in the freezer, Clare wondered if she'd been too readily available to Leo. Maybe she should have invented some phantom rival to keep him on his toes – say, 'Max', a wealthy wildlife documentary filmmaker who lived on a vast property in the country with his beloved Rhodesian ridgeback dogs when he wasn't in South America wrestling with crocodiles in a torn shirt through which his suntanned muscles bulged erotically . . .

Or maybe, Clare thought, her heart beginning to lift, Leo had simply lost track of the time. He was quite capable of sitting down at his Apple Mac for five minutes, and lifting his head a couple of pages later to find that two hours had slipped by. She had to remind herself that he was creative. She had read three of his film scripts and thought they were wonderful – taut, urban thrillers with black comic undertones swirling below the surface.

She knew he'd be famous one day. She could even lose herself in daydreams about the Oscars. She'd be sitting next to Leo and when he won the award for Best Original Screenplay, it would be Clare that he bent down to kiss first, followed by some touching tribute from the stage along the lines of, 'To my beautiful, patient (Valentino-wearing) wife, Clare. You are the angel of my life, and of my work. I would be nothing without you.' Such a declaration in front of millions of television viewers and assorted Hollywood stars would be better than getting married in magnolia-tinted raw silk with one of those sassy little veils.

Clare shook herself out of this luminous vision and stalked around the flat one more time with Barchester scuttling nervously out of her way.

Nothing. In a sudden spasm of fury, thrusting *Manifesting Your Man* firmly out of her mind, she reached for the phone and dialled Leo's number.

His answer machine picked up and started playing the theme music from *2001: A Space Odyssey*. God she hated novelty answer machine messages, they were about as amusing as those signs on the back of cars saying things like 'Plumbers do it with tools'. Might as well cut the crap and stick up a sign saying, 'I'm a jerk who never gets any.'

She was just about to slam the phone down when she heard someone lift the receiver at the other end.

'Speak . . .' Leo's voice said sleepily.

An unseen hand clutched at Clare's heart, squeezing

21

meanly. The bastard was home and he hadn't even bothered to call her, let alone come over to see her. And now he was asleep! Not absorbed in some creative frenzy, but having a bit of a kip while she foolishly paced around her flat in a mini-skirt and fuck-me heels.

She knew what she should do. *Manifesting Your Man* would be quite firm on this point. She should quietly put the phone down, leave her answer machine on for the next three weeks, and when she finally returned Leo's increasingly frantic calls she should mention casually that she'd been having a holiday in the Caribbean with some mysterious new 'friend'.

She knew all this but instead she found herself saying querulously, 'Leo, is that you?'

'Uh, Clare, hi babe,' he said sleepily.

'So you're back.'

'Sure, got in this afternoon. Had the most outstanding time. Look, babe, I'm in bed asleep. Totally wiped out. I'll call you tomorrow.'

'Oh please, don't trouble yourself. It's not as if you'd want to come over and spend time with me.' Clare winced. It was as if she had suddenly become possessed by some domestic demon who was speaking through her in a shrill, peevish voice. Instead of sounding cool, detached and lightly amused, she heard her own voice whining like a mosquito.

'What do you mean?' Leo was more alert. 'C'mon Clare, I've had a really tough three weeks on the film set and I just felt like an early night.'

Clare tried to clamp her lips shut but the demon insisted on speaking out. 'You didn't even give me a call to let me know whether you were coming over here or not,' she heard herself say, to her horror.

'I certainly didn't call you and say that I was,' Leo snapped. 'What's going on? Why am I the bad guy? I've just been away working for three weeks, come home and gone to sleep in my own bed. What's the crime here?'

Clare felt annoyingly like she might start crying. Pure drunken self-pity, she thought, savagely squinting back tears.

And then, to make matters worse, the demon started up again. Her own voice griped, 'It's just that I knew you were coming back so I thought, given that you've been away for nearly a month, you might trouble yourself to come over and see me. God, I thought you might even *want* to see me. Obviously I was living in some kind of fantasy.'

'Three weeks, not a month,' Leo said. 'And I still don't know what's going on. I mean, we're not married or anything. We're two independent people with our own lives. That's what we both like about this relationship, isn't it? We get on and do our own thing and when it suits us both we get together. You know I love that about you, babe, the fact that you're so independent, you're so into your own life. That's why we're so great together.'

Clare knew she should just put down the phone, but her hand remained clamped around the receiver. 'Great for you, maybe. You just roll up here when it suits you and don't even bother to call when it doesn't,' her voice grumbled. Clare wondered if the only way to stop this nightmare was to bite her own tongue out.

'Look,' Leo was really angry now. 'You're starting to sound like some crabby girlfriend laying down the rules of the relationship. I was working, now I'm sleeping, we'll see each other soon when it suits us, there's nothing more to it than that. What is the matter with you?'

'*What is the matter with you?*' Clare mimicked childishly. Then, for good measure, she threw in, 'You selfish creep.' With a mighty effort of will, Clare clamped her lips shut and slammed the phone down. Then she yanked the plug out of the wall, not just in case Leo tried to call back to have the last word, but so the demon couldn't pick up the receiver and call Leo to continue her complete humiliation.

Then she ran her fingers through her hair, unable to believe that she'd actually had that conversation. Whatever had possessed her to sling accusations and behave like a five-year-old? More than likely she'd never hear from him again and she would have no one to blame but herself.

The CD had worked its way through the stack and now the flat was filled with nothing but silence, oppressive silence so thick that it seemed to be ringing in Clare's ears. Miserably she slumped down on the couch and dragged off her shoes. After months of presenting herself to Leo as an independent, cool-headed, career girl, she'd just blown it all in one hysterical phone call.

And clearly, she thought desolately, it hadn't even occurred to him to want to see her. He was still thinking about his bloody film. But then, with Leo it would always be his work. She would only ever get second-hand, half-distracted, half-hearted attention. How could any woman compete with the distant shimmering prospect of Hollywood?

Years ago she had developed the habit of occasionally imagining how many people would go to her funeral. It was like a litmus test of how well she was doing in life. At times the turnout had been impressive – when she was in school, for example, she could imagine the other girls weeping hysterically as the pretty, white coffin was carried past. At uni too she thought there would have been plenty of mourners to watch the ideologically sound pine box go by. The old boyfriends alone would have taken up a couple of pews.

But if it happened now (tasteful light oak, brass handles) she reckoned that, apart from her family, she could only count on a handful of people from *Verve*. And most of the latter would be too busy worrying about how they looked to care about Clare's demise. Now even Leo wouldn't show up. She felt as if there was hardly anything tethering her to the planet at all, no one to care what she did or didn't do. She could cut the string and float away like a balloon and no one would even notice. Tears of self-pity pricked her eyes again.

She slumped back and reached wretchedly for the last 'Dear Marion' letter in the folder.

Dear Marion, it said in neat, feminine handwriting.

A work colleague whom I admire and like very much has asked me to go to a wedding with him in a few months' time. Although he seems nice and funny and attractive and kind and cares about animals and fossil fuels and small children etc, I do have qualms about mixing my personal and professional lives in case it leads to awkwardness. On the other hand, I really like this man. He's a senior partner with his own holiday house on the south coast. And a Bentley. Please advise.

Yours 'Crossroads'

Dear 'Crossroads', Clare pounded out.

Do not accept on any terms. Your mother was absolutely, dead-set right when she told you that men are only after one thing and we all know that it's one thing that does not work in the workplace. Frankly, he is an insensitive jerk even to suggest that you go to this boring old wedding with him. I'm thinking you might even have a case to sue him for sexual harassment in the workplace. That way you could make a few bucks on the side and spend them on a good bottle of wine, a book and a quality vibrator which beats the pants off a man any time.

Frankly, he's a creep to compromise your work relationship just because he is selfish enough to want to have the convenience of having you attend some dreary social occasion on his arm, and then he'll no doubt use the same arm to make a horrible nuisance of himself on the way home so you will never want to look him in the face again and will probably have to leave work and be unemployed for a long time and unable to meet your mortgage repayments and lose your house and end up as a bag lady living under some fucking bridge somewhere. Take it from me, sweetheart. Piss the bastard off!

CHAPTER 2

Clare woke the next morning with a thumping headache and the nightmarish memory of the previous evening's indiscretion with Leo. Keen to get away from both these things as quickly as possible, she tumbled eagerly back into unconsciousness, slept through the alarm and consequently missed the early train. She reached the hotel ballroom after everyone else had already been seated.

Perfect, she thought sourly as she tiptoed through the door. She was about to scuttle into a room full of rivals and potential employees, looking sweaty, flustered and windblown.

Eventually finding her seat, Clare mouthed furious apologies at Fiona, who was seated next to her, then quickly scanned the room to see if she recognised anyone. Or, more importantly, if anyone recognised her.

Booking herself in to this Women in Media Breakfast was part of a resolution to get serious about networking. She'd decided recently that if she was never going to sink into the serenity of the domestic millpond, she'd better start getting serious about swimming energetically with her career. If it wasn't too late. After she'd bought her own ticket, she'd spent days cajoling Fiona into accompanying her so she wouldn't be stranded there by herself.

At the podium, the guest speaker was already in full-flight. From her table, all Clare could see was an exquisite shell-pink suit topped by a swelling of stiff blonde hair which looked out of all proportion to the emaciated body and the tiny, perfect features.

It was Gillian Sinclair. A former television goddess, Sinclair was living proof that once you reach a certain level of fame, it's no longer necessary to earn it. Like one of those ceaselessly moving executive toys, fame becomes self-perpetuating.

Despite the fact that she no longer worked in television, Sinclair still haunted magazines covers, talking about her latest diet, her new husband or her decision not to have a face lift. This last one was especially cunning, because when she *did* get around to the face lift, she would create even more interest and even more magazine covers.

A former current affairs reporter, she went on to host a daytime talk show called 'Wives' Tales' which had probed the depths of such important questions as 'Adultery – When is it Okay?' and 'Divorce – How to Have Your Cake and Split it Too'. When the ratings dropped after ten years, Sinclair took the inevitable axing with some dignity (there was only a handful of magazine stories in which she complained that the network had insensitively sacked her in the same week she'd found a lump in her breast that the doctors said might have been cancer if it hadn't been benign). She then went on the celebrity speakers circuit and made a bomb.

'Since my own days on television,' Sinclair was trilling, 'I have been struck by the progressive debasement of the industry. Ladies, take a look at news or current affairs these days. It seems there is no longer a lowest common denominator in the quest for ratings, nor a story that the media will agree to leave alone, simply because that would require the kind of good manners that the media doesn't have these days. It's as if good taste has gone out the window in a relentless, sensationalist quest to grab the viewers.'

Fiona grimaced at Clare. 'Huh, not the sort of thing she was saying two years ago when she earned that big-hair salary by fronting one of the trashiest shows on TV,' she whispered.

'Amazing how dollars can momentarily distract one from one's never-ending striving for niceness,' Clare murmured back.

Fiona was peering at Clare over her coffee cup. 'Are you okay? You look like you haven't slept for a week.'

'I feel like it. That bastard Leo didn't show up last night after all.'

'Oh,' Fiona said. 'Shame about that.'

'You don't mean it,' Clare shot back.

'Sure I do. I hate it when you lose a night's sleep for no good reason.'

The waiters slithered silently around the hotel ball-room, slipping plates of smoked salmon bagels and gourmet sausages in front of the guests, along with baskets of fresh pastries and muffins.

Clare remembered with a pang her solemn vow after last night's chardonnay and cashew orgy that she wouldn't let a single calorie pass her lips all day. Still, everyone knew that eating high-fat food was the best cure for a hangover. (Didn't McDonald's use that as one of their advertising slogans? They should, she thought.) And besides, she reminded herself, a woman needed to eat small meals regularly to stoke the metabolic rate and outfox the devious female fat cell.

Clare would have got a PhD in the science and practice of dieting if there was any such thing (or if she lived in America where there probably *was* such a thing). Sure, she knew dieting was absurd, counterproductive and neurotic. She'd read *Fat is a Feminist Issue* too – and *II*, for that matter. But somehow she couldn't help herself. She dieted as reflexively as she breathed, although she was smart enough to be embarrassed by her own preoccupation. Still, she figured everyone had to be addicted to something, and it could be worse. She might have been addicted to alcohol and that was incredibly fattening.

Then she remembered guiltily that she hadn't had time to go to the gym this morning and she put her knife and fork back on the table. The gym was part of her morning ritual: weekday or weekend she had to relentlessly thump the Stairmaster or trip the treadmill in a quest for that Nirvana known as the Fat Burning Zone.

But this morning it was all she could do to get ready for work. The teal-green suit with the new knee-length skirt and cropped jacket was perfect, but she had dithered over which set of earrings made her look professional and yet creative, and whether stiletto heels labelled her ironic and witty or just pathetic fashion victim.

What the hell, if she'd paid all this money to come to

30

a breakfast meeting, she may as well eat, she reasoned, reaching for a piece of dry wholemeal toast. And, given how much the tickets cost, she may as well have a second cup of coffee and hang the potential cellulite. Besides, she was miserable. Everyone knows that if you're miserable you need carbohydrates. It's a biochemical thing.

Fiona had no such dieting dilemmas. As usual, she was trowelling butter thickly onto a muffin without a flicker of guilt. Plump and pretty, Clare often imagined Fiona as a robust dairy maid in some rollicking eighteenth-century novel by Henry Fielding, all wavy, light-brown hair, rosy cheeks and hands on hips.

Fiona was Clare's closest friend at *Verve*, mainly because she had the endearing trait of treating the whole world as a joke, not least of all her own job.

'I used to have such high ideals when I was doing my communications degree,' Fi would sigh with mock solemnity. 'I never thought I'd be using my hard-hitting investigative talents writing the annual feature on "High Tech Hair Removal" or "How to Make Your Rented Holiday Home Look as Stylish as You Are".'

About the only things Fiona took seriously were her three miniature schnauzers whom she adored fiercely and babied absurdly. All three slept on her bed every night, no matter who else was in it. 'They were there first,' she maintained, 'and they'll be there when the bloke has gone. Why should they be chucked off?' Needless to say, it was not an attitude that impressed sexual partners. But Fiona wasn't perturbed. She seemed to regard men as a bit of a hoot as well.

Judging by the carefully modulated crescendo in her voice, Gillian Sinclair was reaching the end of her speech.

Clare paid attention again as Sinclair was pleading prettily with the audience to save journalism from being crushed by a sweeping tide ('Gosh, a landslide and a flood,' Fiona muttered) of hidden cameras, outraged consumers, shonky electricians, fad diets, lingerie and any other story that the producers could use to justify showing the bare bottoms of either gender.

'As women, it is our task, even our duty, if I might use an old-fashioned word, to maintain the standards,' Sinclair warbled. Her helmet of thickly lacquered hair stayed curiously centred despite the fact that she was earnestly scanning the room from right to left.

Someone up the back hissed and a ripple of laughter crossed the ballroom.

'It may be shockingly non-PC,' Sinclair said in that complacent tone of voice which declares that being non-PC was very naughty and daring but rather free spirited as well, 'but I do believe that there is such a thing as a "woman's touch". Something that sets the tone, something which shows how things should be done. That is what I call a woman's touch, and just as you see it in the private sphere, we can also see it in the professional.'

'And you can also see it in sexual harassment cases,' someone heckled. This was rather cheeky as, years before, one of the sensationalist tabloid newspapers had run a 'True Confessions' piece about a youthful cameraman who claimed he'd been boisterously propositioned in a lift by Sinclair after she got tipsy at an end-of-ratings party.

Resolutely deaf, Sinclair ploughed on.

'So, in conclusion, ladies, let us strive, as journalists and as women, in fact as Women in the Media, to make journalism the important and, yes I'll dare to say it, inspiring profession we all know it can be. Thank you.'

While the applause dribbled across the room, Clare muttered bitterly to Fiona: 'And she gets paid to do that.'

Fiona clapped lustily. 'Just shows what a TV career can do for you. She can make a couple of speeches a week, throw in a bit of behind-the-scenes goss from the old 'Wives' Tales' days and earn more money than you and I make in six months.'

Clare sighed. 'Which wouldn't be difficult.' She stopped flapping her hands together and started to hack into a bran muffin (no butter, of course).

'By which I take it that The Colonel turned down your application for a pay rise?' Fiona asked sympathetically.

'Well, she didn't so much turn it down as laugh openly in my face. I think her words went something along the lines of, "There's plenty of people who want this job if you don't." Then she finished the discussion by advising me to Be Grateful for Small Earnings.' (The Colonel had the disconcerting habit of talking in magazine headlines, so any conversation with her was always liberally sprinkled with dreadful puns.)

Fiona held up her coffee cup so the waiter could refill it. 'Bad luck for you. But she has a point. Look around this room and I'll bet half of these women are freelancers. They'll run you a big line about loving the freedom and autonomy, but they'd give up laptop dancing tomorrow to claw their way on staff somewhere and have a regular weekly pay packet.'

'Maybe, but would they yearn to work at *Verve* where you spend your life telling "The Woman Who Has Everything" what's out or in for this year and whether it's more stylish to serve bitter or dark chocolate after one's dinner parties?'

Fiona stirred three teaspoons of sugar into her coffee. 'It's a living,' she shrugged. 'No one thinks it will win you a Pulitzer. Although, on the other hand, that piece you did last issue on "Aubergine is the New Black", now . . .'

Clare waved a croissant at her menacingly, and then decided to eat it (jam but no butter). Fiona was right – as usual. But she'd been rather counting on a pay rise to clear her current crop of credit card debts. Suddenly even more depressed, she began ladling butter on top of the jam.

By the time the waiters started collecting up the fruit platters, Clare realised she'd better knuckle down to her networking before it was time to go. They were sharing their table with four women who worked for the same serious broadsheet newspaper. After scanning Clare and Fiona's nametags, they'd studiously ignored the inter-lopers at their table and talked among themselves.

Clare figured that they probably didn't have any time to waste talking to women who wrote for a lifestyle mag-azine. They were too busy solving a crisis in Angola or achieving equality for Muslim women, when they were not scribbling poignant stories about their first-person experiences of breastfeeding in Middle Eastern war zones.

She mentally shrugged. What did they have to take themselves so seriously about? After all, they weren't getting job offers from New York or Paris. They prob-ably weren't fast-tracking to becoming editor either. And they certainly would have no idea how to wear aubergine.

'So, tell all. What happened last night?' Fiona asked.

Clare chose another apple and cinnamon muffin and neatly cut it into quarters because it looked like fewer calories that way.

'Oh, nothing. Literally nothing, as in he didn't show. I sat there and wrote the "Dear Marion" answers then I went to bed.'

'And what?' Fiona probed.

'What do you mean, and what? I went to sleep. Or, being more than slightly tipsy, I suppose you could say I passed out.'

'C'mon, Clare. This is me talking. I know something else happened.'

Clare gave up. It was no use trying to dodge Fiona when she was doing her gypsy mind-reader routine. 'I rang Leo just to see if he was home,' she confessed. 'I know I shouldn't. I even re-read *Manifesting Your Man* to remind me of all the reasons why I shouldn't, but then I did anyway. And when he answered, I started to shriek at him like a banshee. It was embarrassing. And I hung up on him.'

'So has he called back?'

'Nope, and I don't think he's going to.'

'All the better,' said Fiona. 'I think you're well rid of him. He never realised how lucky he was to have you.'

Clare cut the buttered muffin into eighths and thrust a piece in her mouth. She hated it when people told you that something bad was for your own good.

'Maybe,' she said. 'But Fi, that's another relationship down the drain. I'm thirty-four and I think I want to have children. That gives me, say, four years max to find someone, fall in love, persuade them to do the same, settle down and then coax my aging body into getting pregnant, not to mention the chances of miscarriages and birth defects. It's ridiculous. I'm starting to turn into one of those women that's so desperate to hold babies that I snatch them out of their mother's arms. And you should see what I do if I actually *know* the parents . . .'

'Well I don't think Leo was going to turn into Daddy Dearest, was he?' Fiona pointed out cheerfully.

'I suppose not. But I'm just fed up to the back teeth with having to even think about it. It's so unfair,' Clare wailed. 'Men never have to worry about it. They can have kids till they're ninety-seven. They never have to hurry.'

Fiona grinned. 'Oh well, maybe it's the price women pay for being able to have children in the first place. At least we don't have to suffer from womb envy and start inventing weird reproductive technologies just to know what it feels like to make a baby.'

'Yeah, I bet men are just longing to get into those haemorrhoids and stretch marks and labour pains and incontinence. They can't wait . . . What about you?' Clare asked. 'Don't you ever think about having a baby before it's too late?'

'I've got three of them, remember?' Fiona joked. 'And before you think about babies, you have to think about having a man around. I'd need to find someone who would love the dogs. Plus I'd want him to be happy doing stuff like lying around on the couch watching TV and going camping for the weekend and eating cornchips for dinner. Somehow I think this particular man will be hard to find. And I'm not sure that I have the energy to look for him.'

Fiona had been single for years. Clare couldn't understand how she put up with it. Despite reading *Why Do I Think I'm Nothing Without a Man* (twice), Clare still hated those times when she was between men and her life felt dull and arid. Even the misery of worrying about whether Leo would ever call her back was marginally more exciting than going home to an empty flat night after night.

She snatched a final croissant off the tray before the waiter whisked it away.

'I can't help envying people like Isobel who have it all worked out,' Clare said through a mouthful of crumbs. 'She's got the husband and she's got the two kids and now they're trying for a third. It must be bliss to have it all settled. I don't think she understands how tough my life is in comparison.'

'Staying home and looking after children is no picnic either,' Fiona pointed out.

Clare shrugged. 'People are always saying that. But how difficult can it be? All she has to do is supervise one baby and a toddler who thinks the best fun in the world is to go outside and sit on the sprinkler.'

Clare waved aside Fiona's embryonic protest and continued. 'My theory is that the reason women bang on all the time about how difficult it is and what a tough life they lead is because they want to fool their partners. They don't want men to realise they're actually having a great time lazing around at home or nipping down the street to the deli for a couple of lattes and a babyccino. I'd love to spend my afternoons tucked up on the couch with a good book while the kiddies have their afternoon nap.'

'And I'm sure Isobel thinks it would be a dream to come strolling home from work, have a long bath and a tub of green chicken curry from the deli before putting on the latest video,' Fiona said. 'After all, staying at home with someone who thinks sitting on a sprinkler is great fun must be incredibly mind-numbing. And this idea that women with young children sit around sipping coffee all day is ridiculous. My friends who have young children spend their days wiping up spilt cordial and making macaroni jewellery. And when they get away from the kids they're folding the washing.'

Clare grimaced. 'So maybe I was being unfair. But Iso does always go on about it, as if she's solving the Middle East peace crisis instead of trying to run one household. Anyway, I'm going over there tomorrow night. Phil has invited the next-door neighbours from hell in for dinner and Isobel asked me to come along to try and make the whole thing more bearable. I haven't met Margaret, the nightmare-next-door, but Isobel says she's a fright. Phil plays golf with the husband so he insists they have them over for dinner every so often. I guess I'm going over to provide a bit of light relief.'

'At least you'll have a good dinner. Iso's such a good cook,' Fiona said.

'Mmm,' Clare agreed moodily. 'Still, it's a bit tragic when the best thing you have to do with a Friday night is go over to your sister's place for dinner. I have no life. And now I can't even take Leo with me.'

'But you can talk to Isobel about the latest Leo crisis. She's always good for pragmatic, sisterly advice,' Fiona suggested. 'Although I do have this theory that Iso just likes inviting you to her dinner parties to add a bit of glamour, "my sister, the soon-to-be-famous glossy magazine writer".'

'Hardly. More likely I'm there to entertain the kids. Here comes Clown Clare ...'

'You should love that if you're so keen to make babies,' Fiona pointed out tartly. She added under her breath, 'And now that's over, let's find someone to talk to before these snooty bitches fall backwards off their chairs trying to get away from our trash magazine talk.'

They went off in search of the magazine enclave. Inevitably, despite the earnest efforts of the organisers to get everyone to *mix*, the function had divided into niches, with newspaper writers (glasses, bad suits) gathered in one corner, television reporters (blonde, bobbed) in another and the magazine writers (chic, white shirts, red lipstick) in the third.

Clare was soon busily crying 'Hello!' and pressing her cheek up against various other cheeks so no one's lipstick was disturbed.

The women's magazine market was so tiny it made networking a little like getting together with the extended family at Christmas time and trying to make new friends.

Of course, there were the differences between the magazines. *All Woman* was pure fashion, and prided itself on giving readers the absolute last word from the overseas collections about what they would be wearing in Fall/Winter in two years' time. Then there was *Verve*, aimed at the thirty- and forty-somethings who had grown out of *Cleo*, *Cosmopolitan* and *marie claire*. Somewhere further down the food chain were all the so-called 'women's magazines', the tabloid weeklies that pounced like piranhas on scandals involving hairy tennis stars of either gender and/or the royal family. The tabloid writers didn't tend to mix with the fashion magazine writers even at a function like this. The latter were busy telling each other that it was quite possible to treat fashion as a serious socio-cultural phenomenon. The former were louder, larger, more colourfully dressed and determined to show that they wouldn't tolerate the word 'downmarket'. And they always had the latest on Brad Pitt.

Clare read the tabloids avidly but dreaded that one day she would end up working for them. When she was in a pessimistic mood, she would envisage her career spiralling downwards as she aged, through the tabloids, then publicity, followed by writing press releases about new breakfast cereals and finally, at fifty-five, doing the 'What's On' column for the local paper and struggling to eke out her meagre salary so she could afford to buy her monthly copy of *Verve* and dream of the good old days. But, of course, that was only when she was feeling pessimistic. The rest of the time she was sure that she would be miserably reading free copies of *Verve* for the rest of her life because she'd still be working there.

Fiona beckoned Clare over to where the glossy magazine writers were talking shop. She could see the various beauty editors had already gathered together to surreptitiously eye the depth of one another's crows feet. And the fashion writers said lovely things about each other's recent shoots in New York or Hawaii, while feeling secretly relieved that they, at least, had long ago realised that they didn't have the figure for the particular Chloe dress.

'Clare,' Fiona said. 'You've met Toni Mawson from *Me Myself*, haven't you?'

'Not yet.' Clare smiled and held out her hand to the anxious-looking woman standing beside Fiona. *Me Myself* was the latest women's magazine on the market, a hybrid between a fashion magazine and a cosmetic surgery manual, with the emphasis, of course, on fashionable cosmetic surgery.

Toni Mawson had straggling dark hair and a face that looked like all the features had tried to pool in the centre. A fringe partly hid the vast forehead, but nothing could save the broad slab of cheeks and the spreading chin. Unsmiling, she gave Clare one of the limp, fingers-only handshakes that some women favoured for unknown reasons. Presumably they think it's more feminine to flop like a fish, rather than take a firm grip. Clare, who thought otherwise, gave Mawson's hand a vigorous shake to show her how it was done.

'Pleasetomeechew,' Mawson said, her eyes sliding sideways as she looked for someone else in the crowd she should be talking to.

'So how's *Me Myself* going?' Clare asked politely.

'Not bad,' Mawson said tersely.

Clare glanced suspiciously at Fiona, who looked blandly innocent. Nevertheless, Clare had the strong feeling that Fiona had called her just to rescue her from a solo conversation with this morose woman. 'And what were you doing before you joined the mag?' Clare asked, somewhat desperately.

It was the question that unlocked the floodgates. For the next fifteen minutes they were deluged in the woes of Toni Mawson's career – how she was really a serious

41

feature writer who had worked on very prestigious broadsheet newspapers. That was, until she left to write her novel, an ambitious, esoteric work which traced the fortunes over hundreds of years of one family, all suffering from a rare genetic disorder which made them incapable of speaking. It turned out that Mawson was only working at *Me Myself* to get enough money to live on until an enlightened publisher stepped forward to publish her novel. Then she'd be out of *Me Myself* faster than you could say 'rhinoplasty', after which she would apply for a writer's grant to write the next book in her proposed trilogy.

Mawson was still droning on about the semiotics of silence in the post-modern literary form when Clare looked at her watch and gasped loudly.

'Oh my goodness me, look at the time. Fi, we'd better get back. So sorry to rush off like this, Toni, but we've got an editorial meeting at lunchtime so we really must dash.'

After they had pushed through the hotel's enormous revolving door, Clare pinched Fiona's arm. 'Unfair! You just called me over so you wouldn't be stuck with that woman by yourself.'

'That's what friends are for,' Fiona said gleefully. 'Besides, it seems to have done you a power of good, I've never seen you so anxious to get back to the office.'

CHAPTER 3

The *Verve* office said everything you would want to know about the magazine. Naturally, it was housed in a boutique office block, just off the self-consciously chic shopping strip of Chapel Street, South Yarra. The office itself was over-designed in look-at-me silver, cream and black. It had fresh-looking plants that were actually made of some amazingly realistic rubbery substance. It smelt of dozens of clashing French perfumes.

Around the open-plan office, the writers hunched over their tiny work stations, which they were forbidden to 'personalise' in case they disturbed the concept of the incredibly expensive New York designer to whom The Colonel paid a handsome sum to touch up the office every two years.

Clare rather despised the magazine, finding it snobbish, superficial and self-satisfied, when it was not trivialising issues that actually mattered, like little children being forced to make Persian rugs or animals used to test cosmetics. However, she kept those views to herself when The Colonel was around.

The Colonel adored *Verve*: it was her child, her lover and her masterpiece. She had even bestowed a name on 'our typical reader'. She called her Suzanne ('Definitely with a "z"') and often issued pronouncements on what Suzanne would or would not like with the same kind of mystical, revelatory air that Moses must have had when he strolled complacently down from Mount Sinai.

'Suzanne definitely wants to read more tips on how to look slimmer but she doesn't want to hear the pedestrian word "diet",' The Colonel would say. Or, 'Suzanne has no time for stories on how to get a promotion. Leave that to *Cosmo*. Suzanne already knows how to get a promotion, she just wants to be told which is the right restaurant to celebrate it in afterwards.'

Clare's job was writing the feature stories that The Colonel decreed Suzanne wanted to read, consumed apparently between cementing that fabulous business deal, giving birth to her third child (by Caesarean so she could schedule it) and finding the perfect caterer to serve New Comfort Food at her next dinner party.

On good days, Clare felt this job was a stopover, a way of making money until she could move on to something else.

All her life she had held the vague belief that there must be a profession that was right for her, something she had come to think of as The Right Thing. More than a decade after finishing her university degree (arts, majored in English and history, edited the university newspaper, second lead roles in the drama society), Clare was still waiting for The Right Thing to materialise. It was like seeing a flicker of movement out of the corner of her eye. She knew it was out there, wasn't it? She just didn't know how to get to it.

The trouble was she was creative – maybe, she told herself sometimes, even too creative. She knew she had artistic talent, it was simply a matter of finding how to tap it.

She tried advertising copy writing but her style was hampered by everyone droning on about what The Client wanted, The Client inevitably being some fat middle-aged man in a business suit who wouldn't know a decent advertising campaign if it poured a beer over him in a pub. And really, having to think deeply and imaginatively about tampons and cracked, dry lips just made Clare want to giggle.

Then she'd dabbled in television, scoring a job as an assistant to a television producer in London. For a while she thought this would be The Job, imagining herself graduating from assistant to producer. She'd work on fine costume dramas for the BBC and then move up to her own feature films. Finally she would be standing behind the podium at the Oscars after her witty little film about the conflicted lives of women in the nineties had been snatched up by Miramax and become a worldwide hit. Her only problems would be where to keep the Oscar (the doorstop idea was amusing but hadn't someone else already thought of that?) and what to do with all the money she would make from her unexpected international box-office smash.

But apart from daydreaming about what she would wear to the awards ceremony, she found the actual process of making television tedious. All that standing around while men in bad jeans fidgeted importantly with wiring and lights. And while her brain was teeming with fantastic, new, innovative projects, she had to work on soap operas, cooking shows and a daytime chat show that was really an excuse to sell bizarre pieces of exercise equipment and ineffectual hair-removing implements.

She'd chucked her TV job on the day she found herself explaining one of her innovative program ideas to the producer and he had told her, tetchily, to pull her finger out and use it to type the script changes for the next day.

As she had slunk away, she realised what she was, a tiny and unimportant cog in a large machine, designed to sell things as surely as her slogans were in the advertising industry. She didn't go to work the next day, but as she sat on the couch at home watching 'Hello London', she felt rather proud of the script changes she'd made. The daytime television host had probably never before found himself advising his lady viewers that the best way to lose weight was to get off the couch, turn off the bloody television and walk over to the phone to cancel their cable television subscriptions.

After that Clare thought publishing might be her forte, until she got a job as a dogsbody in a small publishing house and found out that the whole thing was another exercise in marketing. Pinpoint the niche, find the writer, plug the gap with product.

So much for her visions of long, deliciously witty lunches where 'her' writers punctuated the courses with loud cries of 'But I couldn't have done it without my editor – Clare. She has made this book the international bestseller it is today! And she thoroughly deserves her lovely $500,000 dollar bonus!'

Lately she'd realised with a faint thrill of panic that she was still no closer to unearthing The Right Thing than she had been when she left university at twenty-one.

Maybe, there really was no Right Thing. Or maybe The Right Thing was having babies, like Isobel always said. You think you love your cat, Iso constantly told her, but you're going to love your children seven thousand times more. Or maybe, Clare thought, biting down ferociously on the top of her pen, thinking about babies all the time was just an excuse for not confronting the failure of her career.

Clare had fallen into her current job when a friend heard there was an 'editorial assistant' vacancy going at *Verve*. The job turned out to be working in the photographic studio helping people in and out of clothes for stories such as 'Well Shod Fillies' or 'The New Debutante'.

After months, Clare progressed up the ladder until The Colonel actually permitted her to write stories or, she noted sardonically, write the first draft of stories which The Colonel then rewrote with a lavish hand. After all, no one understood what Suzanne wanted to read as well as The Colonel.

Clare still had furious rows with The Colonel over this. (The rewriting, that is, not whether The Colonel thoroughly understood the *Verve* audience, because Clare freely conceded the latter.) But the fact was that *she* was the creative one. To have a withered-up, bossy old hag trample all over her cleverly crafted features made her furious.

Fiona constantly had to drag her out to the downstairs

cafe for iced tea to calm her down. 'Look, by next week the mag is going to be at the bottom of someone's Burmese cat litter tray anyway,' Fiona would say. 'It's not worth getting het up about what happens to your copy or which jobs you get.'

'Oh, I know that,' Clare would grumble. 'But that doesn't change the fact that the story has my name on it. I want it to be my work. It drives me nuts when that old bag of bones comes in and just changes the whole thing. And then says something patronising and awful like Many Hands Make Right Words. I don't see why she doesn't just write the whole magazine herself.'

'Because Suzanne likes to imagine an office full of chic women wearing the new season's lipsticks and tapping away on dainty little laptops,' Fiona said. 'The Colonel just gives us jobs so she can pander to that fantasy.'

It was indeed a fantasy, Clare thought now, looking around her at the off-the-rack suits and biro-stained fingers. She leant back in her office chair, closing her eyes for a moment against the tangerine glare of the computer screen and the blast of the overhead fluorescent lights.

Certainly, the day had got off to a lousy start. And when they'd arrived in the office from the Women in Media breakfast, Clare had eagerly checked her voice mail and found, unsurprised, that there was no message from Leo. If men really were like cats, he was probably off somewhere sulking or killing small birds.

But things had begun to improve. She'd thrown herself into work, starting with a gruelling but successful series of phone interviews for her vasectomy story. For half an hour, she heard how splendid it was, after having the requisite two children (one son included), to trot off to a skilled surgeon for the snip. 'And the super thing is it all looks exactly the same afterwards. They don't actually chop any of it off!' one wife had told her triumphantly. Now all she had to do was stop The Colonel from headlining the story 'The Kindest Cut of All'. Clare rather thought she might be able to win the day with 'A Snip in Time'.

Then she'd scored a major coup. Clare had heard on the grapevine that Barbara 'Thumper' Arundell, the sixties fashion model, had dramatically discovered recently that the woman she had always thought was her aunt, was in fact her half-sister, the product of a discreetly hushed up premarital liaison by their long-dead mother. After some sweet talking with Thumper's agent, Clare had persuaded the reclusive ex-supermodel and her newly acquired sister to appear together in print for the first time. She was sure that The Colonel would be thrilled. She stretched. Her headache was just about gone.

'You look like a cat that's swallowed a whole cage of canaries,' someone said behind her.

The sound of a man's voice talking about cats irresistibly reminded her of Leo. Clare swivelled her chair around and smiled up at the deputy editor, William Gilstrap. He was the only decent man around the office. In fact, come to think of it, he was the *only* man around the office.

When she had first joined *Verve*, Clare had eyed William with the interest she felt compelled to direct towards any single man aged between twenty-five and forty-nine. Okay, he was a little short and balding and his forehead bulged just the tiniest bit between the fringes of hair on either side of his head. But it was a broad and serene forehead, and he had those smiley eyes with the puppy-dog droop that worked so well for Paul McCartney. And, according to everyone in the office, he was definitely straight and definitely non-attached and definitely had a sense of humour.

But she soon discovered why he was single. William was that saddest of men, in Clare's eyes: the brother figure. He was sweet, he was funny, he hugged superbly, he even remembered birthdays, but there wasn't the faintest whiff of danger about him.

'He's the kind of man that the women's magazines are always telling us to marry, the Mr Nice Guy,' Clare had said to Fiona. 'The trouble is the magazines never tell you how you are meant to feel *attracted* to those kind of men. They have no ... zing.'

'So you want zing, you want danger, and you want someone who's going to be there in the labour ward, massaging your feet and saying, "Sweetheart, I know you can do it"?' Fiona smirked.

'Without the zing I don't think I'm ever going to be in the labour ward in the first place,' Clare had retorted.

Now, smiling at William, she thought again what an agreeable man he was. 'I'm just contemplating my victory with Thumper Arundell and the mystery sister. Do you think The Colonel will go for it?'

William perched himself on the edge of her desk, stretching out his legs.

'She'll be ecstatic. I can't wait to see her face in conference when you tell her.'

Clare patted his arm affectionately. He was always so supportive. In the early days, she'd even been out for drinks a few times with Will, but she'd been obliged to gently signal to him that she was not interested in Taking It Further.

She did this, rather cleverly, she thought, by sending herself red roses at work, hinting at mysterious romantic weekends and telling him she was too busy to have dinner because she was starting an Adult Education Course in Sensual Gourmet Breakfasts for Two. He soon got the message, although she suspected quietly that he still pined for her a little.

The real mystery was what Will was doing working at a women's magazine in the first place. The attraction for The Colonel was clear. She chose a male deputy editor because then her deputy hadn't a ghost of a chance of ousting her from the main job. The Chairman was never going to give the *Verve* editor's job to a man. But what Will was doing there was another question.

Late one night after many drinks, Will had confessed shyly to Clare that it all went back to his mother. (What didn't, she thought dourly, listening to him pour his heart out over a pint of Guinness). Will's father had disappeared when Will was no more than a tadpole-sized blob *in utero*, so he'd been raised in an intensely feminine environment, living with his mother, grandmother and one uncle, who would probably have admitted he was gay if only he hadn't been so terrified of what William's grandmother would tell their staunchly Baptist church community.

William claimed to be one of the few men he knew who genuinely liked women. Sure, most men would say they liked women but, according to William, scratch the surface and you'd find they had bitter reservations about the other sex. They'd tell you that women yakked all the time, or stored up old grievances like camels, or tried to suppress normal male tendencies when it came to things like beer or breaking wind, as if women were nothing more than a battalion of domestic Nurse Ratchetts.

Not so William, who enjoyed everything about women. Including their encyclopaedic memories and their mental tics over things like toilet seats, toothpaste tubes and people who chewed with their mouths open.

'Maybe you're gay,' Clare had suggested when he told her this.

'I wish I was,' he said sadly, drawing unhappy faces on the top of his Guinness. 'At least then I might have the chance of meeting a life partner. Every woman I meet is terrified of commitment. Women don't seem to like closing down their options these days.'

'Or maybe they're just terrified by the fact that you're deputy editor on a women's magazine. It's not really a guy thing,' Clare pointed out.

'I just feel comfortable in an all-female environment,' he said. 'I love the smell of the face powder and the roar of people making unkind remarks about each other's hairstyles.'

'Unfair! We're actually a very supportive environment,' Clare had protested.

'Just kidding. But the fact is that it feels like home to me. Plus The Colonel wanted a male deputy, which meant I was able to get higher up the ladder much faster than if I'd stuck at somewhere like *Time* magazine. God knows what it will do to my long-term career prospects but I don't really care. At the moment I'm having fun and I'm making great money.'

She was flung back to the present by him rapping on the desktop. 'Hello? Planet *Verve* to Clare?' he said. 'Are you with us?'

'Just thinking about the sister story again,' she said.

He dropped a sheet of paper on her desk. 'Here's the proof page for your costume jewellery piece. Helen's decided to go with the headline, "The Fake's Progress".'

Clare grimaced. 'I should have guessed.' She stood up quickly and started gathering notebooks and papers. 'I'll walk you into the meeting.'

Every Thursday lunchtime The Colonel decreed that the whole 'team' get together. She said it was so she could keep track of what everyone was doing and allow for mutually beneficial feedback from colleagues. One big happy team-building exercise. Clare figured it was more so The Colonel could administer public floggings and keep everyone in line.

Fiona was already sitting at the large table in the conference room with the arts pages editor, Veronica, who was tall, cool and blonde and would have been Grace Kelly gorgeous if her parents had had enough money to fix her prominent jaw. Next to her sat the other full-time writer on the magazine, Michele, still sweet-faced and a great believer in Laura Ashley clothes despite having worked at *Verve* for six years.

'Ah, more gladiators to the Colosseum,' Fiona greeted Clare and William with her old joke as they walked in.

William paused to hold the door open for Gina, the office secretary who was invariably the most expensively dressed and impeccably groomed woman in the office. Today she was wearing a long-line Nehru-collar suit in cream. Clare looked at her enviously. She knew if she'd been wearing such an ensemble it would have been covered in spilt coffee and train-seat grime before she even reached the office. Gina, on the other hand, looked like she'd just stepped out of the changing room of some hideously expensive designer boutique.

'Sandwiches and coffee,' she announced loudly, plonking the tray she was carrying on the table.

The staff reached over eagerly. Editorial conferences took a lot of caffeine.

Last to arrive was Robin, the chief designer on the magazine. She was a fey, quiet woman, who used to talk about nothing else but fonts and photos and hadn't seemed to have a life outside the office. Then she'd amazed everyone by announcing at the age of forty that she was getting married. A year later, she was seven months pregnant and had taken to wearing black lycra clothes that proudly emphasised the prow of her belly.

Clare had watched the growing bulge with fascination. While Isobel shrouded her pregnancies in oversized men's shirts and yoked dresses, Robin wore hers like a shout. To be honest, it made Clare a little uneasy. She could never imagine her own stomach achieving that shape in a million years. And she'd even seen Robin's bulge quiver at times. All just a little too *Alien*, Clare thought, shuddering quietly to herself.

As she was idly scribbling daisies on her notebook, William leaned over and murmured, 'Do you have those "Dear Marion" answers? Helen wanted the first draft on her desk this morning so she could see if the tone was right.'

'Damn,' Clare muttered. 'I did do them last night but I forgot to print them out. I've got them on the laptop.

I'll just rush out and print them up and be back in two seconds. I haven't checked them yet, but she rewrites everything anyway so what does it matter?'

William looked uneasily at his watch. 'You'd better hurry.'

It was well known that The Colonel would not walk into the meeting until everyone was settled with mugs and notebooks in front of them. Clare and Fiona frequently speculated on how she managed this – perhaps Gina had a secret buzzer under the table which she used to signal her boss? Now, everyone waited and reluctantly chewed on the cheese sandwiches until Clare hurried back into her place with the 'Dear Marion' folder in her hands.

Almost as soon as her bottom hit the chair, The Colonel stalked in. 'Right, now that everyone is here . . .' she said, pointedly, perching on the edge of her seat at the head of the table.

'Unfortunately Sabrina is not feeling up to scratch today so we'll have to do without her.' There was a faint snicker at this. Sabrina was the beauty editor and she was regularly 'not feeling up to scratch', usually because she was staying home to slather on some new sample product and see if it had any effect on her fine lines and wrinkles. Occasionally, of course, she had to stay home because one of the new products had managed to bring on a rash or a tiny pimple. Sabrina would never be seen in the office looking less than perfect.

The Colonel pushed on. 'We'll start with the whip around and you can share what you are working on. Keep it quick, people. Remember the motto, Short and Happy.'

She leant forward over the table so she could eyeball each of them intently while they talked. The Colonel may have been one of the most successful female magazine editors of this century (certainly one of the longest-serving), but she was not someone you wanted to be eyeballed by. About five feet tall on a good day, her squirrelly little face was topped by a bouffant helmet of grey hair, inspired by Princess Margaret.

While she listened to the staff talk about their stories, she fiddled with her exaggeratedly large sterling-silver pen. It was a gift from the staff when she celebrated her Silver Jubilee as *Verve* editor. They never actually found out if she saw the joke behind the over-sized pen but it managed to look menacing, as well as bizarre, in her wizened, little paws.

William sat between Clare and The Colonel, where he made notes and occasionally offered comments intended to steer his boss or soften a particularly Draconian position. Usually in vain.

They were talking about stories for the upcoming issue. Because the magazine worked at least three months ahead they were already talking about early summer, which meant chemical tans, new ways to tie sarongs and summertime liposuction, even though it was still wintry outside.

Veronica, the arts editor, had approval for her choices for the books, music and theatre pages so she got off relatively lightly, with just a quick tap on the wrist for daring to suggest that one day a story on the continuing craze for karaoke bars might be amusing.

'We don't do karaoke at *Verve*, we've never even heard of it,' The Colonel snapped.

When it came to Clare's turn, everything seemed to go swimmingly at first. The Colonel was pleased Clare had finished the first draft of the 'Dear Marion' page and tucked the folder in among her papers, saying she would look them over.

And, as predicted, The Colonel was delighted with the news about Barbara Arundell and her sister Viv. 'Thumper' Arundell was, without doubt, one of Suzanne's absolute icons, The Colonel declared. Such a stylish woman. Not to mention the four husbands, her excellent cosmetic surgery, an incredible shoe collection and two salukis. She was a perfect *Verve* woman. And if you threw into the mix the gothic story of the woman she'd been raised to think of as her aunt turning out to be her half-sister, the whole package was delectable. 'Excellent, excellent. We can slot her in for January as a human interest summer read. Now Robin, what are we thinking with pictures here?' asked The Colonel.

'Oh,' Clare cut in. 'There's just one little thing . . .'

'I'm talking to Robin now,' The Colonel snapped.

Clare bit her bottom lip and looked beseechingly at William. Meanwhile, Robin was thinking out loud.

'Well, there's the home shots of course. Shots of sisters looking happy in the kitchen, shots of sisters looking sad with old wedding pic of Mum,' she said dreamily. 'And for the main pic I'm thinking that, with Thumper's amazing white hair, let's get the sisters outdoors, somewhere sunny. Maybe standing in a field with strong contrast between the intensely green grass, the blue sky, and these women in white. That way it will work even if the sister isn't much to look at. Run it double page.'

'Perfect, absolutely perfect,' The Colonel crowed.

'They can even take the damn dogs. And if we made it a wheat field, we could go with the headline "Thumper Crop" and talk about a relationship coming to fruition. Although I'm quite keen on "Sister Act" as well . . .'

'Well there is just this one tiny problem,' Clare tried again.

'Problem?' The Colonel said irritably, swinging her chair round to face Clare.

'Well, uh, it's not exactly a *problem*,' Clare prevaricated. 'It's more like a condition.'

'What do you mean?'

Clare quailed inside under The Colonel's arctic glare, but ploughed on.

'It's just that Arundell won't let anyone take her photograph these days,' she faltered. 'I mean, she has her own pix taken by her favourite photographer and touched up by him personally. She's already had some taken with the sister and those are the only ones she'll allow to be published. Apparently she's too far gone to risk the camera. Not that we'd say that in the story of course,' she added hastily.

'Absurd,' The Colonel growled, using both hands to grip her pen so fiercely that it looked as if she was attempting to snap it in two. '*Verve* has airbrushed the best in the business. And the worst. I hope you told her it was out of the question. We do things the *Verve* way.'

'Ah, not exactly,' Clare said reluctantly. 'In fact I sort of agreed to it. I mean, I knew how keen you'd be to get her, and her agent said she's absolutely adamant about this. So I thought just this once . . .'

'You thought too much,' The Colonel said grimly.

'Which is a continual problem with you, Ms Callaway. You're not a team player. Once again you've rushed ahead without finding out what the magazine wants to do. You've taken on more authority than you're equipped to handle and the result is we may lose the story altogether because of your arrogant mishandling of the situation.'

Clare blushed at this public drubbing. The only thing worse than being mortified by The Colonel was being mortified in front of a whole group of colleagues. 'I think I took the best way out. I just didn't see any way around it,' she protested, despite the fact that Fiona was furiously making 'shut up' faces at her across the conference table.

'You didn't, did you? Well you should have consulted someone who's seen a lot more and a lot further than you ever will.' By now, The Colonel had worked herself into a rage.

'Stop sitting there feeding your face with my sandwiches and get out there, get on the phone and sort this mess out. It's your job to convince the agent. And if you're not capable of doing it, then you had better find something else for October. Because I'll be holding you responsible if the story falls through.'

'That's hardly fair. If it wasn't for me we wouldn't have Arundell in the first place,' Clare said vehemently.

'All's Fair in *Verve* and War,' The Colonel barked back. 'Now stop answering back and get on the phone.'

Keeping her eyes down so she wouldn't see the sympathy in Fiona's face and burst into humiliating tears, Clare struggled to her feet.

But as she did so, the edge of her folder caught the

saucer, spilling an almost full cup of coffee over the conference table.

Everyone jumped and started rescuing their papers from the spreading tide of coffee. Even The Colonel, seeing a rivulet of coffee heading for her grey Armani suit, sprang backwards off her chair, involuntarily letting her silver pen fly out of her hand.

Clare, who'd taken one look at the widening puddle of coffee and decided she could only salvage her dignity by pretending she hadn't done it, then saw with dismay that the sacred pen had bounced off the wall and landed on the carpet. She would either have to pick it up or look foolish by stepping over it on her way out the door.

Still puce with embarrassment, she bent down to pick up the pen in one sweaty hand. But as she began to straighten up, she felt a strange sense of constriction around one ankle. She realised with dawning horror that one of her stiletto heels had jammed in the hem of her new teal-green skirt. With the shoe stuck in the skirt, there was no way she could stand up. Even worse, in trying to straighten up, she'd tipped herself off balance.

Inexorably, awfully, unbelievably, she began toppling forward in slow motion. 'This is not happening,' her mind said firmly as she watched the chair legs and William's brown brogues moving slowly past and the mushroom carpet swaying up to meet her nose. But it was. When it was all over, she lay sprawled flat on the floor, with one shoe still hooked in her hem and her papers spilled all around her.

Wishing fervently that the floor would simply open and swallow her up, she wondered dreamily if she could just pretend to have fainted. Maybe they'd call an ambulance and she could be carted off to hospital still with her eyes closed. She might never open her eyes again.

There must have been a buzz of exclamations, surprise and a flickering dawn chorus of sympathy and mirth but Clare didn't hear it. In fact, she felt foggily that she could just lie there forever and ever.

A voice penetrated her mental haze. 'Ms Callaway,' it said loudly. 'Ms Callaway.'

Clare began to come reluctantly back out of the dark, humming nightmare place.

'I think I'm fine thanks, Colonel,' she murmured feebly, still keeping her eyes closed.

'Ms Callaway,' the penetrating voice said again.

'No, really. I might just stay here for a while.'

'Get up this instant,' the voice flicked like a whip. 'You are lying on my Silver Jubilee pen.'

It was William who scraped her off the floor and Fiona who took her to the cafe downstairs to have a cappuccino before she tackled Barbara Arundell's agent.

'I've never felt so humiliated,' Clare moaned. 'This has got to be one of the worst days of my life. I think I even called her "Colonel". Did I?'

'Forget it,' Fiona said briskly. 'Think how much worse it would have been if you'd been wearing a miniskirt. As it was, you managed to pour some coffee on The Colonel's suit and then hump her pen. What's so bad about that?'

Clare laughed in spite of herself. 'God, that woman is unbelievable! "Ms Callaway, you're lying on my Silver Jubilee pen!",' she mimicked.

Fortified by two cappuccinos, she dragged herself back up to the office to call Arundell's agent and try to persuade him that new photos had to be taken or there was no story.

'We've done Joan Rivers and Ivana Trump. And Gillian Sinclair. We can make anyone look good,' Clare told him, unable to keep a pleading note out of her voice. 'And of course Ms Arundell and her sister will have full approval rights over every photo.'

'Well, yes, but that is standard at *Verve* with personality profiles,' the agent pointed out.

'Uh, yes, it is,' Clare dithered, 'but with Ms Arundell there will be more than full approval rights. I mean, we'll get the pictures to her promptly and she's welcome to try to change the tonal colour of the, well, the sky or whatever she wants.'

She could hear the agent sighing down the phone. 'Look Clare, we've been all over this. Barbara will only consent to the supplied pix being used. We'll just skip it altogether if *Verve* can't come to the party.'

'Would it make any difference if I got Ms Hogan to call you personally?' Clare asked desperately.

'No difference at all. In fact, please don't sic her on to me. Frankly, Barbara was only ever half-hearted about it in the first place herself. Just between us, I think she liked Viv a hell of a lot more as an aunty than as a sister.'

Clare breathed out. 'Let me know if you change your mind,' and put the phone down.

How much worse could this day get, she thought leaning her head on her hands. Now, instead of finding the magazine a great story, she'd actually lost one. She wanted to moan out loud. And of course Leo still hadn't rung.

'Clare, get in here,' The Colonel rasped from inside her office.

Clare painfully climbed to her feet and trailed into the office to confront The Colonel across her big wooden antique desk. The Colonel motioned one little paw towards the uncomfortable metal chair on the other side of the desk and Clare gingerly sat down, keeping her back very straight. She hated to think how furious The Colonel would be when she knew that Thumper had got away.

'Thumper turned us down,' The Colonel said flatly.

'Uh, yes,' Clare admitted, too depressed to even wonder how The Colonel always knew these things.

'That gives you till Monday to get up a replacement yarn for that double-page spread.' The Colonel leant back in her big leather chair and pushed her fingers together into a little steeple. Clare had once read in a book called *How to Body Language Your Way to a New Career and a New Life* that this particular gesture was the sign of dominance.

The Colonel went on implacably, 'Clare, your attitude to your work has been shall we say, disinterested for months now.' (Uninterested, Clare said smugly to herself). The Colonel barged on heedless of her grammatical crimes. 'I've read these "Dear Marion" answers and they're totally unusable. I'm not sure what you were thinking when you wrote them, but frankly you sound as if you were on drugs. They're complete rubbish. So I'm taking you off "Marion" and giving you one chance to rectify the damage you've done by your presumptuous mishandling of this Arundell story. Find a replacement story. And if you can't come up with something, I suggest you start looking for another job instead.'

Clare glanced up sharply, visions of her mortgage and her little flat whirling dizzyingly around inside her head. Suddenly her hard-won sliver of security seemed as insubstantial and unreliable as soufflé.

'Are you serious? You're saying I might lose my job?'

'Not if there's a story idea on my desk by Monday,' The Colonel said coldly. 'Think of it as an opportunity, not a threat. Clare's Last Stand.'

Clare knew she should come back with some professional and yet reassuring response but all she could do was stand there forlornly while she envisaged herself packing her belongings into a rent-a-ute and taking them . . . where? Back home to June and Jack?

Clare's last stand indeed, she thought, groaning inside. There was no way she could afford to lose this job. Now all she had to do was figure out some way to satisfy The Colonel.

And, after today's performance, that should be about as easy as getting a full body wax. In the week before the Sydney Gay and Lesbian Mardi Gras.

CHAPTER 4

Isobel Ashton watched Alexander crawl miserably down the play tunnel.

He hadn't wanted to get inside it so Isobel had stuffed him in one end like a reluctant ferret down a rabbit hole. Then, by rushing around to the other end and calling him in sprightly tones, she encouraged him to come scrabbling along the canvas pipe, his plump, little face contorted with imminent tears. Any minute now he would be howling like a hyena.

'That's right darling, *what* a clever, clever boy you are,' she cooed through clenched teeth as he stumped furiously along on his knees and hands and into her waiting arms.

If she had hoped to stave off the deluge, there was no such luck. He began to scream in outrage. Isobel could feel the other mothers gazing at her in disapproval. Their little Emmas or Thomases or Rebeccas tottered happily around the mats, under the enthusiastic guidance of those perky young women in bright yellow T-shirts who made up the staff of Babyrobics ('the work-out centre that puts your baby in first place').

Isobel had come to dread these sessions at Babyrobics. Instead of happily playing on the luridly coloured pieces of equipment, Alex preferred to regard the place as a roomful of mediaeval torture equipment. But she would be damned if she was going to give in to him.

Apart from the fact that his membership cost the equivalent of a short family holiday in Tahiti, all the baby books emphasised how essential it was for children to develop gross motor co-ordination skills at an early age. He may be only eleven months old, but his whole academic future might depend on these crucial months and it was her job to do the best she could by him. Otherwise, she told Phil only half-jokingly, he'd be suing them for inadequate early learning stimulation before they had finished paying for his first university degree.

Isobel did manage a wry smile when she saw the mothers keeping a competitive eye on the progress of one another's babies. She'd played that game with her four-year-old daughter, Ellen. She called it the Baby Stakes – all the mums vying with each other to see whose child would walk first, talk first, request 'Sesame Street' instead of 'Barney'. They all knew there would only be so many university degrees and jobs out there when all these Georgias and Jacks grew up. They had to do their bit to make sure it was their offspring, and not someone else's, that snatched the brass ring, not to mention the six-figure income, home with a water view and his 'n' hers matching BMWs.

Isobel hoped she'd got over the worst of the Baby Stakes by the time Alex came along. If nothing else, Ellen had taught her that babies will relentlessly do whatever they have come into the world to do. But of course that didn't mean she shouldn't give Alex the same opportunities she'd given Ellen. It was only fair.

'Shush Alex,' she muttered, jiggling him around on her hip, while the women glanced away, probably pained by the sight of a child with such low income-earning potential.

Isobel could feel rage swelling up inside her, which she tried to hide from Alex. These days, it seemed even one little frustration could make her irrationally furious. Or feel like bursting into tears. It seemed to be always one or the other, like some farcical see-saw.

She jigged Alex around even harder. 'Would you like to do some tumbling on the yellow playmat, little man? Would you like that, hmmm?'

Alexander signalled his conviction that he definitely would *not* like that by clinging violently to her hair and increasing the decibels of his screams.

'Now, who's a naughty boy, then?' Beatrice, the head coach, appeared at her side.

A chunky woman of indeterminate age, Beatrice had a ferociously tight perm and the kind of cut-glass British modulation that was even out of fashion on the BBC. She addressed her pupils in the tones generally reserved for caged parrots. It was usually remarkably effective.

'You mustn't give in to him, Mrs Ashton. He's just being a naughty, naughty boy. Who's a little pixie, then?'

Isobel half-heartedly came to Alexander's defence.

'Maybe he's just tired, he didn't sleep very well last night, so he might not be in the mood,' she muttered feebly, as a pair of strong arms, biceps contracting like pistons, reached for the baby.

'None of that, Mrs Ashton,' Beatrice scolded, bearing Alexander away to the climbing frame. 'We don't hear negative words here at Babyrobics. Babyrobics is all about "can do". Now,' she addressed Alex playfully. 'Alexander want to go on the climbing gym?'

Alex's indignant crimson face peered at his treacherous mother over one of Beatrice's bulging shoulders. He obviously knew he was in the grip of something bigger than both of them, and his sobs increased in volume.

The truth was that Isobel was the tired one. She had been up and down with Alex all night, spending hours plodding back and forth in a darkened house, trying to lull him back to sleep. There was an understanding between Isobel and Phil that, if the children woke during the night, it was her job to see to them. This was because Phil worked during the day as a partner in an accounting firm and needed his sleep. On one occasion, Isobel had ventured to suggest that she worked during the day too, except her work happened to be looking after a baby and a toddler. Just possibly it might be as important for her to be as alert, looking after two kamikaze children, as it was for him to be awake during his meetings. Phil had looked at her kindly, like an Everest mountaineer listening to someone complaining about having to tackle a flight of stairs. 'But I'm the one earning the money so I really need to be as sharp as possible during the day. We're dependent on me keeping this job,' he'd pointed out calmly, as if that put an end to any arguments. Which it did.

Things continued as before, with Phil sleeping peacefully, oblivious to any noise, and Isobel springing up to soothe Ellen after a nightmare or trudge the floor, patting Alex's back while he complained in the only way he knew how about sore gums or a painful belly or all the other pinches and sorrows of a new life.

Sighing, Isobel followed Alex over to the climbing frame where Beatrice was shifting his fat, little hands and feet around the bars as if he was climbing up the ladder.

'Who's a good little boy?' Beatrice crooned encouragingly while Alex kept howling.

'Oh well *done*,' Isobel echoed dutifully.

Alexander wasn't fooled. He rolled one eye balefully as if to tell Isobel that she was going to pay for this later.

'Now, who's going to climb up to the top of the little ladder?' asked Beatrice brightly.

Not me, Alex clearly thought, digging his hands and toes into the frame and hanging on like a limpet, meanwhile escalating the volume of his protests so the other mothers again looked over in horror.

'Now – then,' Beatrice grunted, tugging at the clinging child. Isobel, flushed with embarrassment, moved in to help just as the teacher gave one last forceful tug on the baby.

With that final pull, the plastic climbing frame lifted clean off the floor and Beatrice, still clutching Alex, stumbled backwards, tangled up in the frame, scrabbling for a purchase on the slippery vinyl playmat.

'Oh God,' Isobel muttered, lunging forward to catch Alex before he hit the ground. She managed to get a hold of the flailing baby as Beatrice and climbing frame staggered around the mat. Isobel grabbed Alex, now like some infant superman in mid-flight, and began frantically hauling him back into the safety of her arms.

But by then Alex was yelling so hysterically that he'd made himself sick. While still managing to emit that siren-like wail, he vomited his breakfast of Rice Bubbles copiously over Isobel, Beatrice and the climbing mat.

Mortified, Isobel clutched the squalling smelly Alex and looked with horror at Beatrice, her yellow T-shirt and her carefully groomed iron-grey hair splattered with baby vomit. Isobel could even see bits of Rice Bubbles caught in the curls.

Dead silence descended on the room, apart from Alex's sobs. Then, without warning, Isobel too burst into tears.

An hour later, Isobel was pushing the fractious baby around the Glen Iris High Street, her skin still crawling with shame. Beatrice had coolly offered her the Babyrobics bathroom to sponge off her shirt, but she could still smell baby vomit.

She and Alex had then slunk out the door, accompanied by Beatrice's artificially bright assertions that of *course* Mrs Ashton and dear little Alex were welcome at Babyrobics next week. It was just a matter of being firm with the naughty little fellow. And all this from a woman with partially digested breakfast cereal in her perm.

Isobel still had to shop for the dinner party she was cooking that night, not to mention picking Ellen up from kindergarten and cleaning the house. As she pushed the heavy stroller along the crowded pavement, Isobel felt the cold wind like a slap against her hot face. She couldn't believe she'd burst into tears in public like that.

Isobel never cried, certainly not in public. She scolded, she slammed cupboard doors occasionally. She had even once been seen to lose control and say the word 'damn' in front of Ellen – but she never cried. Now she couldn't get away from this vision of herself standing there, vomit spilling down her linen shirt, her eyes red and her nose runny. Crying might look beautifully dewy-eyed in films, but it's a wretched, snuffling, gulping, piggy-eyed sort of business in reality which just makes you look ugly and out of control. And Isobel hated being out of control.

She tried to distract herself by contemplating the evening ahead but even that filled her with foreboding. For a quiet man, Phil was a surprisingly enthusiastic host – probably because he never had to cook. Last week, in a fit of conviviality, he had invited their next-door-neighbours, Margaret and Kevin, over for a meal. Then Isobel, petrified by the thought of having to face up to Margaret on her own, had roped in Clare. Now she had to cook a dinner for five on a Babyrobics and kindergarten day, which always left her limp as a rag anyway.

Thinking of the work involved – not just cooking, but scrubbing the bathrooms, brushing the dog, running the vacuum over the house, arranging flowers, putting out clean towels and washing Ellen's grubby fingerprints off the dining room wall – Isobel felt exhausted.

Friday was her ironing afternoon and now that would have to be pushed back to Saturday which mucked up her whole weekend. This was the weekend when she always did her home-made tomato sauce, enough jars to last them for the rest of the year. And Phil would be the first one to feel put out if he had to wander around the house looking puzzled and lost because there was no ironed shirt waiting for him on Monday morning.

Isobel felt so peevish about the whole thing that she stood at the deli counter for five minutes unable to decide between camembert and brie for the cheese platter. She began to feel convinced that there was no difference between the two anyway, it was just a cynical fraud played by marketing managers in the cheese industry to see how gullible people could be.

She was woken from her reverie by the sound of a crash as Alexander, to his immense satisfaction, smashed a bottle of rosemary-infused, cold-pressed olive oil all over the floor.

'Good thing your daddy had a fabulous night's sleep last night so he can earn all the money to pay for that,' Isobel told him crossly.

Alexander grinned beatifically.

Driving home to her pretty little Edwardian bungalow in the pretty leafy eastern suburb of Glen Iris, Isobel felt another flush of shame over her pathetic outburst at Babyrobics. She could just imagine the other mothers muttering to each other, 'Not *coping*, poor thing,' and scrutinising her child for signs of neglect. Worst of all was the mother spotted at the video shop taking advantage of their 'Ten Kids' Vids for the Price of Five!' offer.

It would be the same tone they used to talk about post-natal depression or those unfortunate women who hadn't managed to breastfeed. 'Hormones, of course, can't be helped,' they said, while secretly preening because it had not happened to them. It was the steeple-chase of the Good Mothers which ran parallel to the Baby Stakes. The winner was the mother and baby combo that came out chicest, smartest and, at the end of a couple of decades, with matching MBAs.

By the time she got home, Alexander needed a sleep but it was only half an hour before she had to pick up Ellen from kindergarten. She debated whether she should leave him in the car and drive around aimlessly until Ellen was ready to come home, or whether she could risk trying to transfer him from cot to car without waking him up. Desperate to sit down for a few minutes, she decided to go inside and risk the cot.

Drinking her fifth cup of coffee for the day, she sat at the kitchen table, listening to Alex's half-hearted squawks from the nursery room. (Don't give in to manipulative crying, the baby books had instructed her. If the baby learns he or she can control you, you will soon regret your weakness.)

She was tempted to eat one of the fun-size Mars Bars hidden at the back of the pantry but for her latest resolution to cut back on fattening food. Isobel had always had one of those enviable bodies that undulated in all the acceptable places and laid low in between, but she was getting just a fraction broad about the rump. If she wasn't careful she might commit one of the cardinal sins of womankind and *let herself go*.

But the more she resolved not to eat one of the chocolate bars, the more she felt burningly aware of the packet up in the cupboard, calling to her.

She wrapped her hands firmly around the mug of black coffee and switched her thoughts to how much she enjoyed this room, the main reason she'd urged Phil to buy the house in the first place.

It was a big open-plan kitchen painted in sunny lemon, lime and cream, which overlooked a family room with floor-to-ceiling windows onto the large garden. Big woollen rugs in bright beach-towel colours were splashed over the polished wooden floor and one corner was taken up by an enormous toy box that Isobel had painted midnight blue and stencilled with gold stars. The whole scene shrieked family, togetherness, cosiness – all the things Isobel was determined to cultivate in their lives.

From where she sat at the big kitchen table, she could see Daisy, the fat golden retriever, nosing around under a bush outside, expecting with blithe optimism that she would discover something to eat. It was the same attitude she had towards her food bowl, which she checked at all hours of the day in case it had magically refilled when her back was turned.

That's me, Isobel thought sadly, scuffling around for anything to shove in my mouth to stem the boredom.

But did she really care if her hips didn't fit some mythical fashion template? Having babies had made her realise her body could do things that were a lot more interesting than carry around a bikini. She'd learned with amazement that the body she had taken for granted for years was capable of creating and nurturing another human being from microscopic speck to baby. She still felt overwhelmed by that biochemical miracle. She became gushy about Alex's magnolia soft skin and his ecstatic smile. And it was incredible watching the children develop with the speed and brain power of tiny Einsteins. All of it probably a lot more important than worrying about the size of one's thighs.

Besides, Isobel thought wryly, she didn't have to worry about her body. She didn't need to attract men any more, she was a married woman. Her problem was more how to stay attracted to one man for a lifetime.

She gazed blindly out the window and thought about that for a while. A whole lifetime. She did adore Ellen and Alex. But it would be this house, this man, forever.

Sometimes she wanted to scream. Last night she'd decided that if Phil didn't stop making that slurping noise when he ate, she was going to brain him with the salad tongs. Then he'd come in and cut his toenails sitting on the living room couch. When she'd protested, he'd pointed out in a baffled kind of way that he did pick up all the clippings, what was her problem? 'My problem,' she'd hissed, 'is that you're just getting a little too *comfortable* in this relationship.' He'd looked at her like she was speaking Aramaic and promised tolerantly to clip his toenails in the bathroom from now on. And then she felt like a bitch for worrying about something as trivial as toenails in the first place.

Isobel absentmindedly filled her coffee mug again. Maybe she should have explored her options more, worked different jobs, slept with different men, lived in another city, gone to Istanbul to watch the sun rise. Instead she had this kitchen, this life, and the saddest thing was she couldn't even talk about these feelings to Phil, who was supposed to be her best friend. She knew that if she even mentioned her frustrations, he'd be impossibly hurt. He seemed perfectly satisfied with the way things were, while Isobel felt like she was a train running on a track that went around one bland circle. Or perhaps she'd been watching too much 'Thomas the Tank Engine'.

She used her hands to push herself up from the table, and went over to reach for the Mars Bars. Only three left, and if she polished them off she'd be able to tidy the empty packet away into the bin.

If you had told Isobel ten years before that one day a chocolate bar (or three) would be the highlight of her day, she would have scoffed. Back then, she had a vocation, the dream she'd had since the age of six when she'd been given a dress-up nurse's uniform for Christmas and she knew what she wanted to be was a nurse. Later on her dream became not just to be a nurse, but a matron, running the hospital and holding hundreds of lives in her capable (and yet beautifully kept) hands. She'd march around the wards, looking organised and crisp and benevolent. Rather like being a nun without having to go to the bother of poverty, chastity or obedience.

Of course, for Isobel, obedience wouldn't have been a problem anyway. As far back as she could remember, she had always tried to be the good girl, anxious to please her teachers and parents and to live up to the standards set by her comprehensive library of Enid Blyton books. Her urge to be good was as random and unfathomable as a yen for gambling, alcohol or daytime soap operas. It just was.

Not that her parents made much of a fuss about her efforts. If she came home with an 'A' in her spelling test, they would smile at her vaguely and say, 'That's nice dear', which was exactly the same reaction Clare would get if she produced some pathetic, trumped-up story about having to see *Last Tango in Paris* for her school sociology class. June and Jack Callaway were always too busy running the family pharmacy (Callaway's Family Medicine) to take much notice of their daughters.

In the sixties, June was a career woman before career women had truly arrived. Isobel often thought that if June had been born thirty years later, she would now be fast-tracking towards running a major corporation, wearing power suits and Italian leather shoes. The idea of a husband and children would not even have registered as a bleep on her radar. Not that it had been a bad marriage. Jack was as obsessed by the business as his wife was. He tended to the potions out the back while she managed the fractious customers out in the shop. Their joint dedication to a common cause had given them a semblance, and even perhaps a reality, of total harmony. If they could have worked seven days a week they would have been in heaven.

By her late teens, Isobel had given up on ever winning her parents' attention, let alone their approval, and transferred her obedience (plus her poverty and chastity) to nursing college and then to the hospital where she was given her first job.

She'd met Philip Ashton in the casualty department where she bandaged his hand after a nasty accident with a wood-work tool.

She neatly and precisely cocooned his hand and its four stitches in a snowy white elastic bandage. By the time she'd fastened the clip, he had shyly asked her out for a cup of coffee some time if she wouldn't mind.

Phil told her later he'd been struck dumb by this vision in institutional blue, her shining, dark hair pulled gracefully back under a cap, her long eyelashes almost coming to rest on her cheeks as she gazed earnestly down at the neat bandaging.

Isobel, disillusioned by the cockiness of the male medical staff, liked Phil's diffident air. She even liked the fact that he had cut his hand when he was making a toy for his young nephew.

Phil had seemed everything Isobel had thought a husband should be. He seemed like a real man. He had a serious and rather impenetrable job in accountancy. He worried about leaves blocking the guttering and he could fix fuses. When she cooked for him, he ate gigantic plate-fuls and came back for seconds. When he watched sport on television he would absent-mindedly stroke her hair until she felt hypnotised like a rabbit. (These days he didn't stroke her hair while they watched TV. Usually she was too busy bustling around doing the ironing or cooking with an air of unconscious martyrdom.)

Back then even his family felt familiar to her: safe, middle class. His mother put lavender sachets in her closets, his father wore singlets under his business shirts.

She loved imagining Phil holding their first baby in his big hands and smiling his gentle, infectious smile. Two years after they met, he presented her with a modest diamond solitaire and they announced their engagement.

On the wedding day, Isobel (in ivory silk) followed Clare down the aisle towards the altar where Phil (grey tails) was waiting, sweaty-faced and furiously blinking away the tears in his eyes.

Once more, Isobel thought as she absent-mindedly ate the last Mars Bar, she had been a good girl. She'd headed straight into marriage and, in due course, produced healthy babies in the appropriate gender mix. Now she directed her energies into being as perfect a mother and wife as she could be.

Staying home to look after Ellen and then Alexander because she didn't want to put them in full-time childcare (Why have children if you are going to hand them over to strangers to raise them? she and Phil had asked each other), she took this new job as seriously as she'd taken nursing.

She was determined to give Ellen and Alex a model childhood very unlike her own, and to this end had amassed an impressive library on parenting techniques and numerous enthusiastically written tomes on stimulating your child's creativity, self-esteem, intellect, academic ability and bowels.

Financially, they could cope on one salary, especially since Phil had become a partner in his firm. Besides, it turned out that Phil found the idea of being married to a hospital matron just a little laughable. 'You don't have enough of the dragon in you,' he told Isobel, kissing her on her perfectly shaped little nose.

When the phone rang she snatched it up, realising with a start that it was almost time to meet Ellen.

'Oh Mum,' she said breathlessly. 'I was just dashing out to pick up Ellen from kindie.'

'Oh well, dear, I won't keep you then. I just wanted to check how things were going with Ellen's new kindergarten.' June's voice had the slightly magisterial tones of a lady judge or the kind of school librarian who stays in the same job for twenty-five years. Isobel figured it was the result of years of reassuring customers that, yes, that haemorrhoid cream would really be just the thing and there was no need to be embarrassed whatsoever.

Surprisingly for such reluctant parents, June and Jack were enthusiastic grandparents. Particularly June, who regarded Ellen and Alex as if they were the most interesting and talented children to have ever tottered off a grandmother's ample lap. The Callaways had sold their shop two years before. Clare reckoned their obsession with their grandchildren was just a sign that even the mah jong club couldn't fill up *all* their retirement days.

Isobel thought more hopefully that maybe they were finally realising what they'd missed out on when they'd been too busy behind the cash register to notice Clare and Isobel growing up.

Isobel fumbled for her house keys, tucking the phone receiver into her neck where she kept it in place by wrenching her head over at an uncomfortable angle.

'Just fine, Mum, thanks,' she muttered, searching for the keys. 'She's loving it. I'm sorry I can't stay and chat but I really have to rush off to pick up Ellen.'

'Of course dear. I was just thinking little Ellen looked a bit peaky last time we were over. You know they now make the most marvellous multivitamin tablets for children. Taste just like lollies so they just gobble them down. Just the thing for when little ones are feeling a bit off-colour.'

'I think she's fine, she's just naturally pale-skinned,' Isobel snapped, marvelling at how her mother had the capacity to rub her up the wrong way after just three minutes on the phone.

'If you say so, dear, but you really should take a look at these pills. We always used to recommend them to mums with young children.'

'A sale is a sale,' said Isobel disagreeably.

'And there's nothing wrong with that,' agreed June blithely. 'I know for a fact that Jenny Jamieson uses them for her children. You remember Jenny, Pam's eldest daughter? She was the one who married that investment banker and they built that gorgeous two-storey place and now they've just bought their own holiday place on the coast. And she swears by these pills.'

Isobel found the keys at the bottom of the fruit bowl.

'Mum, I'm sure Ellen's healthy. Even if she doesn't have a holiday house and vitamin pills. I'd rather she just ate good, healthy, home-cooked meals,' she said firmly.

'And have you heard about Clare?' June went on busily, as though Isobel hadn't spoken. 'She interviewed Gerard Depardieu last week. Isn't that wonderful? What a life she leads.'

'Yes, she does lead a very interesting life. Look Mum . . .'

'I always said Clare would do something fascinating. She was such a bright and bubbly little thing, never stopped talking for a moment.'

'Yes, yes, she was lovely. Still is,' said Isobel, feeling a pang. Her mother frequently managed to make her feel drab and uninspiring. There was always someone else with a more exciting job or a bigger house or better tended children. Perhaps June thought these examples would galvanise Isobel into trying harder. And perhaps she was right. 'Look, sorry Mum, I really have to dash. I'll give you a call tomorrow . . .'

'Oh well, yes, you must go. You'll be late and I hate to think of little Ellen standing there worrying about where you are. Love to Phil.'

Isobel slammed the phone down and headed up the stairs to grab Alex. There was no way now that she could gingerly get him into the car and glide off while he stayed sweetly asleep. It was going to be ten minutes of Alex bellowing and Isobel rushing to get there on time.

She pulled up outside the kindergarten just one minute after three o'clock. The Fast Track kindergarten was housed in a weatherboard cottage, painted in pale blue and pink and surrounded by a huge garden, the whole

81

effect looking like something Hansel and Gretal might have found in the woods.

Isobel yanked the stroller out of the boot and unfolded it. Alex, whose protests had quietened to snuffles with the help of a fruit stick, was then loaded on board and Isobel began to cleave her way through the sea of mothers, infants and prams that were spilling out of the door of the kindergarten.

As she was anxiously looking around for Ellen, a petite young woman with smiling dark eyes and an urchin hair cut tripped over to her. This was the kindergarten teacher, who went by the unlikely name of Miss Skandi. Isobel thought Skandi's elfin appearance was perfect for the fairytale atmosphere of the kindergarten.

'Ah, Isobel,' Skandi said brightly. 'I was looking out for you. Could I have a word in my office?'

'Is everything all right with Ellen?' Isobel asked, frowning, and following the fairy woman into her cubby hole of an office, where there was room for a small wooden desk, painted a cheerful pillarbox red, and two folding deck chairs with blue-and-white striped covers.

'Nothing to worry about. Do sit down,' Skandi waved her arm at one of the folding chairs and perched herself on the edge of the desk. 'It's just that one of our assistant teachers did happen to notice today that Ellen has head lice.'

'What?' Isobel almost shrieked.

'Head lice,' Skandi repeated loudly as if Isobel was deaf. 'Nothing to be concerned about. It seems to go in waves through kindergartens and primary schools. You just need to pick up some head wash from the chemist and a fine tooth comb. Should clear up in a jiffy.'

Isobel felt the Mars Bars shift uneasily in her stomach. Of course she knew head lice could happen when small children congregated in the one place, but surely not to *her* child. She had visions of a magazine ad which had shown a blown-up picture of a head louse, like some prehistoric monster, crouching on the child's head. The thought of something like that creeping through her Ellen's baby-fine hair made her feel physically ill.

'But, I don't understand, is there head lice going through the kindergarten?' Isobel asked, prepared to feel indignant. Phil and her were paying a minor fortune to send Ellen to the Fast Track kindergarten so she could get a head start for school. The idea that the place was crawling with communicable parasites hardly seemed to fit the size of the cheques that Isobel had to write every term.

'Well, uh, not so far,' Skandi said delicately. 'In fact, Ellen is the first one we've noticed it on. But there may be others, so we'll be getting the nurse in to do a check through the whole kindergarten. In the meantime, if you can just treat Ellen, and obviously Alex and all the towels and bedding as well, that would be a great start to controlling it before it gets out of hand.'

Isobel nodded dumbly, realising she'd now have to go back up to the High Street and find a chemist to sell her head-lice shampoo. And on top of all the work she already had to do for dinner, she'd have to wash both kids' hair as well as towels and sheets. And weren't you meant to iron the mattresses and pillows as well? She wanted to put her head down on the red wooden desk and start crying again.

Ellen chirped away happily as Isobel loaded both children into the car, unaware of her mother shrinkingly eyeing the top of her head, looking for small crawling bugs. She avoided the gaze of the other mothers, hoping no one knew that her own child was Ground Zero for the plague.

'An' we did finger painting. An' we did paper cutting. An' we did make pictures of dragons because of a story that Miss Skandi told us,' Ellen babbled on happily.

'Did you sweetheart?' Isobel pulled out of the parking space, and then squinted back at Ellen in the rear vision mirror. She *looked* perfectly normal.

'An' we did a sleep too an' I nearly did a poo in my pants but not really.' Ellen informed her.

'Well, that's interesting to hear.'

Then Isobel remembered with a chill that Margaret was coming to dinner tonight. Margaret, whose daughter Katie was the same age as Ellen and also went to Fast Track, did part-time work for the kindergarten as their book-keeper (or 'business manager' as Margaret liked to put it). Isobel wondered glumly if Margaret would already have heard all about the head lice. She could just imagine what her voluble neighbour would have to say if she found Ellen had been the one to start some kind of kindie epidemic.

At least Clare would be there tonight, Isobel thought with relief. She could always be relied upon to keep the conversation bowling along and draw a lot of the attention towards herself. And it sounded like she had had another bust up with Leo so there would be even more drama to talk about.

For once, Isobel thought, thank God for Clare and her theatrics.

CHAPTER 5

By six o'clock that night, Isobel had forgotten everything she'd ever said to Clare about the cosy joys of a contented family life, the comfort and ease of flannel pyjamas and fluffy slippers and newly washed babies and a loving man putting on the kettle for tea.

Instead she just felt increasingly desperate. Perhaps tonight she would simply snap and run out the front door and never come back. At least it would save her having to explain Ellen's head-lice problem to Margaret.

It was bad enough trying to summon up enthusiasm to cook dinner, although it was a simple menu of roast beef followed by a lemon tart she had, somewhat guiltily, picked up from the local cake shop.

But she also had to cope with Ellen winding around her feet, whining that she wanted to play *The Lion King* game, and why couldn't Mummy come and play now? It wasn't that she didn't adore Ellen, who was a miniature version of Phil, with the same dark wavy hair and easygoing nature. But sometimes it did occur to Isobel that she might have overdone it when she decided to fill almost every waking hour of Ellen's day with stimulating and wholesome interactive activities. Isobel watched other people's children playing quietly by themselves and felt envious. She wondered if Ellen's refusal to do so was a sign of a deficiency in imagination which needed to be remedied. Perhaps drama lessons? Or creative modern dance? But on the other hand, if she *didn't* play with Ellen it might stunt her daughter's creativity.

Tonight at least she had a good excuse for not hunkering down on all fours and scampering around on the newly vacuumed carpet. She had to get the potatoes into the oven. And then she needed to get the kids into the bath, leave the head-lice wash on for at least ten minutes (according to the bottle) and then comb their hair out afterwards.

In desperation, she plugged a video into the VCR.

'But it's not *dark*, you always say no videos till it's *dark*,' Ellen pointed out piously.

'I know, sweetheart, but Mummy has to do something special in the kitchen, so this is a treat just for today.'

Isobel saw with relief that Ellen, mesmerised as ever by the flickering screen, was sinking to her haunches in front of it. A giant purple dinosaur advised her chirpily to love everybody and always wash her hands before meals.

Isobel reached for the potato peeler, only to hear Alexander start screeching from his playpen in the corner. He was no longer amused by his alphabet flash cards and wanted his dinner.

She rushed over to pick him up, then toted him back to the stove where she quickly stirred the cheese sauce for the cauliflower.

When the phone rang, she tucked the receiver under her chin, stirring with her left hand and bouncing Alexander around in her right arm.

'Everything okay?' Phil asked.

'Of course, just dandy,' Isobel bellowed over Alexander's hungry protests. 'Well, there is one thing, but I'll tell you when you get home.'

'Anything you want me to pick up on the way back?'

'No, everything's fine,' she shouted. 'Just get home as soon as you can. There's a lot to do.'

Phil agreed and rang off hastily, probably anxious to get away from the deafening yells of his son.

Isobel knew that, despite his assurances, Phil would stroll through the door at his usual time. Phil believed that having people round for dinner just meant fewer leftovers the next day. He had no idea of the extra work for her, Isobel thought with frustration. It would never occur to him that she had to scurry around scrubbing the bathrooms and bench tops, and queue up in specialty shops for cheese, freshly ground coffee, hand-made chocolates and candles. For Phil, those things just magically appeared.

She should have got used to it by now, she thought, resting the spoon on the edge of the saucepan. She went to the fridge and scrabbled around for the chicken for the kids' dinner.

When they were newly married and both working, the chore war was their major bone of contention. Phil readily agreed they should take turns doing the vacuuming and the bathrooms, it was just that he was often too busy to do his turn. But, as he reasonably pointed out, what did it really matter? Things could wait till next week (when it just happened to be her turn). There was no need to get *obsessed* by the housework.

He'd smiled when he saw her fluttering around lining the shelves of their first rented cottage with clean brown paper.

'There is a lot of my mother in you,' he'd said, comfortably reaching for the television remote control.

The thing that had driven Isobel absolutely mad was that Phil never seemed to see all the other things that needed to be done, like cleaning the refrigerator or washing the kitchen floor.

When she mentioned this, he would point out, again reasonably, that if she wanted something done, she just had to tell him to do it. He would do anything for her.

'But I don't want to *tell* you to do things,' wailed the newly married Isobel. 'You're my husband, not my child. We should be equals, partners. Besides, I spend all day telling people what to do at work, I don't want to come home and do it here as well. I feel like a sergeant major.'

The chore war resolved itself when Isobel became pregnant with Ellen and gave up work. Phil just assumed she would have time to do all the housework, not to mention organising their lives.

So she was the one in charge of paying bills and booking holidays. She told herself it was just more efficient if she organised everything, anyway. It would take forever if she left things to Phil. And she soon got used to reminding him to take out the rubbish or mow the lawn. He didn't even have to remember his own mother's birthday any more, just scribble his name on the card she held out to him.

But before Isobel wound herself up into a pitch of indignation, she reminded herself, as she always did, that everything in their life was paid for by Phil's money and his hard work. He was the one who slogged off to work on the train every morning, which sometimes made her feel guilty. Mind you, she thought, would he really have liked to stay home trying to deal with the imperious demands of two children?

She leaned wearily on the edge of the bench for a moment. How was she ever going to cope with three of them if they did have another baby? As it was, she scarcely kept up with things. When she'd first got married she'd established a card file system which gave her an annual calendar of chores, so she always knew when it was time to wash the dining room curtains or clean the light fittings. She was guiltily aware of falling behind. The venetian blinds were meant to have been wiped down about a month ago. If she was exhausted by pregnancy, or had a another baby at her feet, she would really fall behind. Still, she reflected, given the current hit and miss nature of their sex life, maybe a pregnancy wasn't that likely . . .

With a start of horror, she realised that the cheese sauce was burning. She flung it into the sink swearing in the ersatz fashion ('Jeepers' and 'Blast') she had developed to protect Ellen from bad habits. Now Alex needed changing and feeding, the guests were due in an hour and she still hadn't managed to do the potatoes, have a shower, bath the kids or set the table. And she didn't want to think about having to iron all the mattresses.

Alexander was in a clingy mood and refused go back quietly in his playpen and Ellen, the television addict, was bored with her video and was demanding macaroni and cheese for tea before her bath.

'No darling, you've got yummy, yummy broccoli and chicken tonight,' Isobel said.

'Yeaghgh, I *hate* that . . .'

'No you don't, honeylamb. It's delicious. Now sit up at the table and use your fork properly. No fingers. And stop squeezing your bread into those nasty little balls. Eat nicely.'

By the time Phil walked in the door ('How was your day, sweetheart?' he sang out happily as he wandered in at 7 pm), she was beginning to grimly tick things off her 'no time for that now' list – shower self, polish door knocker, shine wine glasses . . .

Phil gave her a peck on the cheek. As Ellen was wrapping herself around his grey-suited legs chanting, 'Daddy, Daddy, you be Zazu,' Alexander reached for Phil's glasses with destruction in mind.

Isobel thrust Alex into his arms and snapped, 'Mashed chicken and vegies in the microwave and Ellen has got head lice so I have to get her into the bath for ten minutes. Bring Alex up as soon as you can.'

While Phil gaped after her, Isobel rushed Ellen upstairs into the bath.

Ten minutes later, she rushed back down to take over feeding Alex. She knew that when Phil was in charge there was a lot of giggling but very little food actually going in (did he *really* think that 'Here comes the aeroplane' stuff worked?). So she grabbed the bowl and sent Phil upstairs to comb Ellen's hair and get her dressed.

Then while he bathed Alex, she flew around the house,

doing dozens of things at once, from setting the table to whipping cream and putting a ribbon in Ellen's hair. Strange, she thought, how she often ended up rushing madly about doing hundreds of things while Phil was placidly concentrating on one task, like trying to find the television remote control . . .

When the doorbell rang at 7.30, Isobel was in their bedroom pulling a black long-line tunic top over her head which she hoped would skim kindly over her ripening hips. She followed it with a swipe of pink lipstick and a despairing look at her hair. She should have washed it this morning, but being so thick it took hours to dry, so she had settled instead for pulling it back up on her head in a ponytail which she now decided looked absurd for a dinner party.

Too late. Rubbing mashed carrot off her trousers, she headed for the front door. On the way, she passed Ellen's bedroom where Phil was still coaxing Ellen into her pyjamas. Isobel sighed when she saw that he had chosen the pink elephant pyjamas that were Ellen's favourites last year.

'Oh, not *those* ones,' she hissed impatiently at him. 'They're as old as the hills. Put her into those nice red ones your sister gave her for Christmas. In the cupboard behind you.'

Phil smiled at her. 'Yes baaass,' he said, while Ellen protested loudly that she really, really, really wanted to wear the pink elephants.

Stumbling down the stairs, Isobel thought wearily that she would give her right arm to be lying on a couch with a book and a glass of wine and nothing in front of her but blissful empty hours.

Instead she flung open the front door, a big smile plastered on her face and ominous thoughts of half-cooked roast potatoes in her head.

'Hello Isobel. You do look comfortable in that outfit. Those elastic waists are wonderful, aren't they?'

Margaret stood on the doorstep holding out a bottle of wine. 'I've brought a bottle of my brother's home-made wine over. I'm sure you'll find it interesting. Kevin's just coming up behind me with the girls,' she said.

She bustled into the family room, leaving Isobel waiting on the doorstep for Kevin and looking dubiously down at the infamous home-made wine, which, according to Phil, was positively lethal. Still, at least Margaret hadn't heard about the head lice. Isobel could guarantee that she'd have mentioned it the minute she opened the door if she had.

Margaret and Kevin had been living next door when Isobel and Phil moved into their new house six months before. Margaret had popped over in the middle of moving-day mayhem, clutching a bran loaf as a welcome-to-the-street present.

'My goodness, what a lot of things you have,' Margaret had observed brightly, holding out the block of cake. 'I always think it's best to get rid of a lot of the old junk before you move house to save yourself some bother.'

It was not a promising start, but Isobel was a firm believer in the ideals of neighbourliness, and she had been pleased to discover that Margaret had two children, Kate and Grace, who were about the same age as Ellen and Alex. Readymade friends next door, she thought. It was so important for children to have a kind of *village* atmosphere.

But while the children could play together happily for a few hours, Isobel felt sorely tried whenever she spent too much time with Margaret. She was one of those infuriating people who was an expert on everything. Isobel couldn't count the number of hours she had spent listening to her neighbour complacently hold forth about anything from the paediatric health implications of soy milk to the pitiful reluctance of many parents to come to grips with the IT age (unlike Margaret, of course, who was proud of doing all her kindergarten book-keeping on her laptop).

'I know she means well,' Isobel had lamented to Phil, 'but it's not even as if you can hold a reasonable discussion with her. She never *listens*. She just says, "Yes, of course. And I've always thought . . ." and then goes on to directly contradict what you've just said.'

'Yes, of course. And I've always thought that it's very handy when we want to leave the kids over there if we're going out on a Saturday night,' Phil said, grinning mischievously. 'You shouldn't let her get to you. I just let it wash over me like a wave of babble.'

'Yeah, right,' Isobel muttered. 'Easy to do when you're standing by the barbecue with Kevin saying things like, "Great day for it." Look, I know you're right. And it's important for the kids to have friends nearby so I really do work at it. It's just that sometimes I want to yell, "Well, I was a nurse, you know, I do know a few things".'

Phil had told her good humouredly that she was taking small things to heart and the two couples had become occasional friends, not least of all because Phil and Kevin played golf together. In fact Isobel suspected that Phil secretly felt sorry for Kevin (who was the kind of man who said, 'What can I do you for?' and thought it was funny). Phil had a theory that one day, like the blind suddenly being restored to sight, Kevin would wake up and realise that he had married a monster. And one who didn't believe in getting rid of superfluous hair.

Kevin finally appeared, walking slowly because he was leading Kate by the hand and carrying baby Grace. He was a handsome man with an impressive head of silvery hair. He could almost have passed himself off as a successful politician, if it wasn't for his unnerving habit of giggling loudly and often. Isobel supposed it was some kind of nervous tic.

She was quite fond of him, however, and gave him a warm peck on the cheek. She'd just settled everyone in the family room and Phil was dispensing drinks when the doorbell rang again.

'That will be my sister, Clare,' Isobel said with relief. 'Did I mention I'd invited her? I know I talk about her all the time so I thought it would be great for you to meet her.'

She hastily scooted out to the front door and yanked it open.

'Thank God you're here,' she hissed, pulling Clare into the hall.

'What's the matter with you?' Clare asked.

'Everything. Alex vomited in Babyrobics, I ate the Mars Bars, Ellen has head lice. But don't worry about any of that now, just come in and help me out here. Every time she comes in, she's worse than the last time.

She just told me that I really should get my rugs professionally steam cleaned because I'd be amazed at how effective it was at getting rid of that doggy smell.'

Clare laughed. 'She sounds like a riot. Lead on Iso, I've had a lousy week too, so things can't get any worse.'

After fending off Ellen's joyous welcome, Clare was able to get her first glimpse of Isobel's 'nightmare-next-door'. Margaret was squat and unashamedly plain, wearing no make-up except for a frosting of beige pancake foundation, and leaving her straight, liver-coloured hair tucked behind her ears. As usual, she was wearing one of her floral shirtwaister dresses which, for this formal occasion, she'd teamed with open-toed shoes and orange-beige stockings instead of the famous massage sandals Iso had lampooned.

In turn, Margaret turned her sharp eyes on Clare and didn't seem impressed by her mini-skirt, knee-high leather boots, cropped knit jumper in fuchsia-pink and a matching beret (it had been a bad-hair day).

Soon there was a two-tier party in the family room. On ground level, there were the squawks and squabbles and shrieks of the four children tumbling around the floor, while above their heads the adults valiantly pretended to carry on a coherent conversation.

It was continually broken off while one of the parents refereed the violence below. 'No *don't* put Ellen's ear inside there, Kate.' 'Grace, please don't sit on Alex, he doesn't like it.' In the end, out of sheer desperation to get away from the kiddie chaos, Clare announced she was putting herself in charge of the music for the evening, and spent fifteen minutes rifling through Iso's CD collection, trying to find something that wasn't John

Farnham, Phil Collins or the soundtrack from *Titanic*. In the end, she gave up and put on Frank Sinatra. Retro was at least marginally better than Celine Dion.

When the children were finally settled in bed, the adults sat down at the table, wine glasses in hand, while Phil carved the roast which, Isobel saw to her relief, was still pink on the inside.

Isobel relaxed a little and looked contentedly round her dining room, which was small but cosy. The walls were painted a deep rose pink and the table, inherited from Phil's grandmother, had a warm, walnuty golden glow. Isobel and Phil sat at the head and foot of the table, with Clare on one side, facing Margaret and Kevin on the other. Isobel realised now that this was a mistake. It gave Margaret the chance to pin Clare with her gimlet gaze.

'Of course, I instantly said to her that if there was any child at this childcare centre who was biting, it was certainly *not* my Katie,' Margaret was saying. 'Katie is much too well adjusted for that. And I frankly think it was just one of the other mothers trying to pass the blame, probably from one of the boys.'

'I don't think she was actually accusing anyone,' said Kevin. 'And for my money, I don't think the occasional bite is such a terrible thing. Why do we spend all this money putting fluoride into the water if kids can't use their teeth for a bit of innocent recreational fun?'

He giggled suddenly, making Clare jump. Isobel flinched, thinking guiltily that she should never have inflicted all this on Clare. Especially not if she was having a bad week anyway. Isobel wondered what could be going wrong in Clare's life now – boyfriend problems?

Career crisis? Failing the fat-pinch test at the gym? She knew that anyone of these, and a whole lot more, were capable of sending Clare into a flat spin.

Frowning at Kevin, Margaret was charging on regardless. 'Everyone knows that male children are much more aggressive than the girls. Hormones, of course. But then everyone says to me that Kate and Grace are the most beautifully mannered children they have ever met.'

She leant confidingly across the table towards Clare who was attempting, with some difficulty, to cut through a roast potato. 'I personally put it down to good parenting. And it was no accident. I insisted that Kevin come with me to a parent training course as soon as we knew Kate was on the way so we could be ready to give her an expert start.'

Isobel tried desperately to steer the conversation away from children, but not before Margaret assured Clare that she really must have children.

'I'm really surprised that you haven't settled down and had them by now,' Margaret said through a mouthful of lamb. 'After all, we all know that women's fertility starts to decline over the age of thirty. You're risking all kinds of complications by leaving it so late, anything from infertility and birth defects to an increased risk of breast cancer according to the statistics.'

Listening to this lecture, Clare wondered exactly where this woman thought she got off. After all, for all Margaret knew, Clare might be infertile. She might have had an abortion last week. She might have lost her womb in a horrible childhood accident and it was the grief of her life. It was none of her bloody business *when* Clare chose to have children. If at all.

She plastered on an artificial smile. 'Oh I'm afraid children are just not a priority for me at the moment,' she said sweetly. 'My partner, Leo, is just making his first feature film and my career is really taking off at the magazine so there are just so many other exciting and important things going on in our lives. We really just haven't had time to even think about children.'

'Yes, of course. And *I've* always thought that you just don't understand what real love is until you have a child,' Margaret said.

Isobel winced again. The evening was turning into a prolonged nightmare. She'd never forget the look on Clare's face during Margaret's long and detailed discussion of the importance of breastfeeding children up until the age of three. Unless it was the slightly raw potatoes that were making her look so queasy.

'Not everyone wants to have children,' Isobel finally pointed out, placing the lemon tart on the table. It really did look quite pretty on the white china plate, dusted with icing sugar.

'Yes of course. And *I've* always thought that no one who has children ever regrets it.' Margaret raised her eyebrows. 'Is that from Rogalsky's in High Street? They do quite a nice job.'

She ignored the look on Isobel's face and went on with her diatribe. 'Obviously the decision to have children has to depend on how well you're doing financially. These days children are expensive, especially when you take into account that they need the best quality childcare, then private schooling to get into tertiary education,' she ticked them off on her stubby fingers. 'Not to mention tutoring, school trips to Europe and support through university. We see this is a major financial commitment for the next twenty years or more.'

Isobel briefly stopped slicing the tart and thought, horrified, that in twenty years time, she would be fifty-six, almost old enough to get the pension . . .

Margaret helped herself to a slice of pie and dolloped on cream lavishly. 'That's another reason why I'm glad I have my part-time job at the kindergarten. Not only does it keep my brain alive, but it's helping provide financial security for my children's future,' she said smugly.

Blushing at the mention of the kindergarten, Isobel was relieved when she could escape to the kitchen where she let her pent-up steam mingle with that escaping from the freshly boiled kettle. Keeping her brain alive! Really, the woman was insufferable!

But she had to admit that Margaret always got to her when she started bleating about money. It was a subject that had never been particularly important to Isobel before she had children. Money was just something that went in and out like the tide. That was until she gave up work and discovered what it was like not to have any.

Well, it wasn't true that she didn't have any. She and Phil had a joint bank account and Isobel was free to draw on it at any time, as long as she could explain to Phil where the money was going. Not that he begrudged her a new pair of shoes or a trip to the hairdresser's; it's just that he never really forgot who earned the money. And of course he hardly needed to spend money on himself thanks to the unfairness of a world where an executive businessman could still get by with a seven-dollar haircut.

It was the sort of thing you never thought about before marriage, she mused as she spooned ground coffee into the plunger. The luxury of occasional extravagance. When she was earning money, she could always justify any purchase by saying, 'Well it is my money.' Now she knew that Phil, while he rarely said anything, did think she could be more careful. Why buy the cold-pressed olive oil when the plain label brand would do perfectly well?

When she talked to Clare about all this, Clare always argued with her. 'But it's your money too,' she'd point out. 'If you weren't staying home looking after *his* kids, he would have to be paying for full-time childcare, not to mention housekeeping, laundry, secretarial work ... Imagine how much all that would take out of his pay packet. You earn everything you spend and more.'

Yes, all very fem cred, Isobel would reply, but theoretical. Of course Phil *knew* she was working hard, but did he really *believe* that work was just as valuable as his? How could he? In his eyes, it didn't pay the mortgage. She secretly suspected that Phil really thought he was doing her a favour by 'allowing' her to stay home while the kids were young. 'A lot of blokes these days expect their wives to go back to work,' he said casually to her once. And even if (when) she went back to work part-time, she could just see her money being used for 'little things' like food and electricity bills, while Phil's 'real' money went into paying the mortgage.

She paused, coffee tray in hand, wondering if Phil ever wished he was the one staying home. Especially in the depths of winter when he plodded out the door to catch the train while she and the kids waved goodbye from inside the warm house.

'Oh there you are,' trilled Margaret, as Isobel pushed through the door from the kitchen. 'We were just saying you must have got lost out there. Or perhaps you're just exhausted by putting together that little meal. Very tasty it was too.'

Phil looked at Isobel with faint desperation.

'Coffee!' he said with excessive heartiness. Isobel could guess that conversation had not been flowing smoothly while she was in the kitchen. 'Clare, what will you have?'

'You ought to be careful if you do want to have children,' Margaret chipped in. 'With coffee, I mean. Do you know that as little as just one cup of coffee a day can affect your fertility?'

Clare raised her eyebrows. 'As I said, I'm really not concerned about that at the moment. If ever. Not everyone is cut out for reproduction. In fact, Phil, you can make it a double for me.'

'And sperm as well,' Margaret pressed on. 'You men are so naughty with your sperm. You should take notice, Phil, if you and Isobel are serious about having that third baby. You men hardly ever consider the damage you're doing to your sperm – coffee, tight underwear, alcohol, processed food, laptop computers. I've always kept an eye on Kevin to make sure . . .'

Isobel sprang to her feet and grabbed a dish off the tray. 'I nearly forgot. Shop-bought biscotti, anyone?'

Later that night, after Margaret and Kevin had marched out into the night carrying their sleeping children, Isobel and Clare were in the kitchen tidying up. Phil had gone to bed, explaining that he had an early-morning client meeting.

101

'You're right. You're more than right. She is totally unbelievable,' said Clare, who was stacking the dishwasher.

'I know,' said Isobel, glumly pulling on the rubber gloves. 'And you've just met her once. I see her all the time. If she's not popping in here, I run into her at kindie. It's torture. I'm sorry, I should never have dragged you over.'

'Nonsense, it was quite fun in a freak-show kind of way.' Clare waved the wine bottle over some glasses, raising her eyebrows. 'We may as well finish up the bottle of wine. I thought I'd just crash over here tonight if that's okay with you.'

'Sure,' said Isobel. 'As long as you don't expect me to drink any more of that toxic home-made wine. It tastes like he makes it with rat poison.'

'No, this is the one I bought. Quite safe.'

Isobel started to put all the empty glasses into the sudsy water.

'So what's going on with you? What did you mean about having a lousy week?' she asked.

Isobel secretly thought Clare's worries (boyfriend, job, cellulite) were ephemeral in the grander scheme of things. The complications of working on a glamorous women's magazine must be a doddle compared with making life and death decisions over a child's spiking temperature, or walking the floor at 3 am with a teething baby.

But looking after Clare came naturally to Isobel. From the moment Clare was born, June had instructed Isobel in taking care of her baby sister. By the time Clare was five, June happily left Isobel in charge. Sensible Isobel knew the shop number off by heart and could be relied upon to call if things went wrong. Meanwhile Clare was allowed to be the baby. Soon June decided that Clare had artistic leanings, and she was enrolled in the appropriate drama and clay sculpting courses (which, apart from anything else, helped solve part of that pesky problem of what to do with the girls between school and bedtime). While Isobel was doing science subjects, Clare was steered into the humanities.

Isobel loved Clare and wanted to take care of her. She also had to admit she secretly enjoyed being a kind of agony aunt for Clare. She loved being able to offer sensible advice and bolster up Clare's sometimes frail self-esteem. If only, thought Isobel, I was able to be quite so efficient when it came to dealing with my own problems.

Now Clare grimaced. 'When I said lousy, I really meant to say utterly disastrous. The week from hell. First of all, Leo didn't show up on Wednesday when he got back from the shoot so I rang him when I was pissed and made an idiot of myself. Then this really big story for the magazine fell through and The Colonel was furious. She told me that if I didn't come up with a replacement story I'd lose the job.'

'What! She can't be serious,' Isobel turned to face her, hands still plunged in the sink.

'I'm afraid she is,' Clare said. 'The old witch. I had this thing set up with Thumper Arundell, you know, the sixties supermodel. She's discovered she has an aunt who turns out to be her sister. I mean, Thumper's mum had a baby when she was seventeen or something and the grandparents offered to raise it as if it was their own child. So this woman that Thumper thought was her aunty turns out to be her sister. It would have been a great yarn but I lost it. Which means now I might lose my job altogether if I can't come up with a replacement story.'

'Well it's not as if you love that job anyway. Even if you lose it you can get something else,' Isobel reassured Clare. 'But you don't have to lose it, all you have to do is find another story. It can't be that hard. Maybe we can brainstorm some ideas over breakfast tomorrow.'

'Maybe,' Clare said listlessly, drying plates.

Isobel hesitated. She never knew quite how critical she could be of Clare's boyfriends when the relationships were on the downward slope, just in case Clare got back together with them after all. Isobel's nightmare would be to declare some bloke a loser, just to have Clare go and marry him in the end and so drive a lifelong wedge between the sisters. She had to tread carefully. 'As for Leo,' she said finally, 'you know how I feel about him. I can't understand why you're always attracted to men like that.'

'Why can't I just find myself a nice man,' Clare parroted.

'You can laugh but why not? There's nothing wrong with loving someone who loves you back, you know. You deserve someone much better than Leo. In fact, it wouldn't hurt you to spend some time by yourself.'

'Well that's easy for you to say, with your husband and two kids and the cosy house behind the picket fence,' Clare mocked.

'But I didn't get here by constantly falling in love with men who had egos bigger than this house,' Isobel reminded her.

'Oh yes but you know what they say about egos,'

Clare said, grinning. 'Directly proportional to the size of the . . .'

'Oh, rubbish,' Isobel said, flicking soapy suds at Clare.

Clare took another swallow of red wine. 'So how are things going, anyway? I hardly had a chance to see Ellen and Alex before they went to bed.'

Isobel stared gloomily down into the sink. 'The kids are great. Ellen seems to be really fitting in well at her Fast Track kindergarten and next year Alex will start spending two days a week at Baby Steps, that new child-care centre for accelerated pre-schooling. That means I get a bit of time to myself. Which means I'll almost be able to keep up with all the housework. So that's really helpful.'

Clare grinned and was just about to poke fun at the idea of a fat eleven-month-old baby going into 'acceler-ated pre-schooling' when she noticed that Isobel was behaving very oddly. She had ducked her head and made an alarming choking noise. Clare realised with a shock that Isobel was crying.

'Gorgeous, what is it? What's happened? Is it Phil? Oh my God, he's not *leaving* you is he? Not with two children and that hungry dog to support?'

Isobel, hunched over the sink, did a strange twisting movement of her shoulders.

'Oh God, Iso, you're really serious,' Clare said.

'Sometimes,' Isobel mumbled, 'I wish Phil *was* leaving me, at least that way something – anything – would happen in my life. I feel like I'm on one of those airport baggage carousals, just seeing the same things go around and around and around. Alarm clock at 6.30, Phil asking, "How did you sleep, sweetheart?", kids, meals, shopping, Phil asking, "How was your day, sweetheart?", TV, bed, sex on Sundays . . .'

Clare was astounded. She knew Isobel had her down days, but every woman did. Being a little depressed on a regular basis was no cause for excessive alarm – just two blocks of family-sized fruit and nut chocolate and a good lie-down.

It had never occurred to her to think of Isobel as a serious candidate for Betty Friedanesque home maker angst. Despite Isobel's anxieties and complaints, Clare had always believed she thrived on being a mother.

Isobel ran her family's life like an efficient military campaign, a kind of Stormin' Norman of the suburbs. She was the kind of mother who froze the children's drinks the night before a family outing so they'd stay cold all the next day. She made freshly squeezed juice icy poles and sugar-free muesli cookies for the family to snack on. She name-tagged everything, including the baby's nappies. (In fact, Clare always joked that if anyone ever decided to microchip human beings, Isobel would be hustling Ellen and Alex to the top of the queue and yanking back the neck of their hand-knitted, pure wool jumpers.)

Maybe it was the baby thing again. Isobel and Phil were trying for a third baby. The women who lived in the leafy eastern suburbs often had three children. It was a badge of the non-working upper-middle-class woman. It went along with the bobbed, frosted hair and appearing at kindergarten in the morning in tennis gear.

Now, watching her sister snuffle miserably into the washing-up water, Clare felt alarmed for Isobel. To be frank, she also felt alarmed for herself. After all, it was

106

Iso's *job* to be the stable one so Clare could be the little sister who was always on an emotional rollercoaster. It had always been that way. Surely Isobel wasn't going to bugger up the family dynamics now.

She threw her arm around Isobel's shoulders and squeezed her in a way which she hoped was bracing and yet sympathetic. She steered her away from the sink so they could sit down at the kitchen table. Reaching over to the bench, she snagged their wine glasses and the half-empty bottle of red.

'Look, gorgeous,' Clare said, peeling off Isobel's rubber gloves and pushing a full wine glass into her hand. 'You know I've always thought you had the most fantastic life. You don't have to trudge off to work every day, you don't have to panic about who's going to pay the mortgage. You have two lovely kids and Phil who is the sweetest man. I think you're incredibly lucky.'

Isobel managed a watery smile. Why do people always think you'll be more happy with your rotten life just because theirs is worse?

'Most people's lives look pretty good from the outside,' she said, sniffling. 'It's just that I feel like I'm treading water. We did the marriage thing, we got the house, we did the pregnancies and now . . . what? I know it sounds like some sort of ridiculous midlife crisis but I'm terrified this will be all I get for the rest of my life. Like Mum, time will flash past and one day I'll be looking back and say, well, at least I kept a well-stocked kitchen.'

Clare snorted derisively. 'Which she never did. She was always at work. Remember, her idea of adventurous gourmet cooking was to sprinkle a packet of French onion soup across the T-bones and then bake? Probably still is, if we ever got invited over to their place instead of having the big family dinners at your house. Really, I'm not even sure Mum cooks at all any more. Last time I dropped over there she was about to stick a tin of beetroot in the blender and call it borscht.'

Clare adroitly guided the conversation into the sheltered waters of family reminiscences or, to be more precise, slagging off their mother. She was sure it would help Isobel to buck up. There's nothing more bracing for siblings than figuring out ways in which they can attribute all their problems to inadequate parenting. (And then in later years reversing the process by figuring out ways in which their own offsprings' problems occurred in spite of such excellent and well-intentioned parenting.)

But it clutched at Clare's heart to see Isobel looking so woebegone. Clare regarded her own worries as having much more tragic cachet than Isobel's. After all, she was the one who was still single and childless while Isobel was complaining about whether Phil ever realised that the oven wasn't self-cleaning. But now she looked so genuinely sad and defeated that Clare picked up her hand and gave it a little sideways shake.

'You should see what it's like out here in the real world, you would really hate it. You should realise how lucky you are,' Clare chided her. 'It's true what they say, all the single men are gay, married or living at home with their mum so she can do their washing. Sometimes all three. And then there's work. Imagine plodding off every day worrying abut deadlines and what your boss wants and whether you'll get sacked next week or, maybe even worse, whether you won't get sacked and you'll end up doing the same dead-end job for the rest of your life. You should count your blessings. You're safe.'

'Oh Clare, if only you knew,' Isobel stopped to toss back another mouthful of wine. 'You really have a lovely life – freedom, great sex, no strings attached. Count your blessings, because one day you're going to find yourself putting up with nappies and kindergarten duty and three loads of washing a day.'

'Can't be half as bad as putting up with going on dates with men with bad breath and bow ties just because otherwise you think you'll end up a lonely bag lady with too many cats,' Clare said. 'Not to mention the nagging of the biological clock.'

'Rubbish,' Isobel replied briskly, back in her big-sister role. 'I refuse to listen to that time-is-running-out stuff again. You have years in front of you. Meryl Streep had her last child when she was forty-three. Susan Sarandon had her first baby at thirty-eight and her last at forty-six. *And* she had endometriosis. When you do have children, you'll regret not making the most of your liberty while you still had it. Remember what they say, be careful what you wish for.'

Clare started giggling.

'What's so funny?' Isobel asked.

'I'm just thinking that we always have this conversation,' Clare snickered. 'I say how terrible my life is and how good yours is. Then you say, no, no, my life is boring and your life is so great. We always do this, don't we?'

Isobel smiled a bit sadly. 'I guess we do.'

'You know,' Clare said, 'the only way we're ever going to really know who is telling the truth is if we could live each other's lives. I mean really live them. I could be you and you could be me. Then we'll see who's telling the truth.'

'That must be a common fantasy, stepping into someone else's life for a while,' Isobel said, filling her glass again.

'So why don't we give it a try?' Clare said suddenly. 'It would be fun. You can be me for a couple of weeks and I'll be you and then we'll really see what's what. In fact,' Clare began to almost bounce on her chair with puppyish excitement, 'I reckon I could even sell it to The Colonel as an off-beat story idea for *Verve*. You know, we swap lives and then we both write about our experiences. I see what it's like to be a home maker, you can work in a groovy magazine and wear uncomfortable shoes. Maybe I can even offer it to her as the replacement for the Thumper story. That way, I could save my job.'

'Why would The Colonel or anyone else care if we swapped lives?' Isobel objected.

'Are you kidding? It would be great, a kind of lifestyle experiment. *Très Verve*. It could be something like, "So you think the grass is greener on the other side of the fence? *Verve* puts it to the test." The Colonel could call it "Putting on the Life Switch" or "From Here to Maternity".'

Isobel laughed. 'Or what about "How the Other Half Loves"?'

'Or "Sister Pact",' Clare topped her.

'Oh no,' Isobel moaned, clutching her stomach.

'Well, you can laugh, but I think this is the most brilliant idea I've ever had and I think I could persuade The Colonel to go for it. What do you say?'

Isobel stood up and picked up her glass. It was too late for another one of Clare's flights of fancy. 'I say we have to finish the dishes and we've had too much to drink. Let's talk about it in the morning.'

'No, I'm serious Isobel. It's the most fantastic idea. C'mon, say you'll give it a go,' Clare pleaded.

Isobel sat down again. 'You're really serious?'

'Seriously serious.'

Isobel thought for a moment. 'Well, it could only be for a couple of weeks at the most. I couldn't leave Ellen and Alex for any longer than that.'

Clare grinned, she couldn't believe that Isobel, dear, safe old Isobel, was really considering this idea. Brilliant, she thought, filling up their glasses again. 'A couple of weeks would be perfect,' she assured Isobel. 'Say we do it for one week, then swap back for one day on the weekend, just to have a break. Then we switch lives again for the second week.'

Isobel held up one finger, a little drunkenly. 'But I see a problem here. I mean, you can always look after the kids, you've known them since before they were born. But what on earth am I going to do in a magazine office? I've never been in a magazine office. I'd be useless.'

Clare waved one hand. 'Don't worry about that, there's plenty of things you can do – photocopying, cups of coffee. I don't know but the office secretary will come up with plenty.' She smiled at Isobel. 'This is going to be fantastic. Now all I have to do is convince The Colonel to accept the idea so I don't lose my tiresome job.'

Isobel squeezed her hand. 'You won't lose your job. If you ever did I'd personally come over and rap that woman over the knuckles.'

'Oh,' Clare wagged her head. 'You don't know The Colonel.'

'No, but maybe I'm about to.'

Later that night, after seeing Clare comfortably settled in the spare bedroom and peeping in at Ellen and Alex, Isobel tiptoed off to bed. The light was still on, and Phil had fallen asleep with his glasses on and a copy of the latest Tom Clancy blockbuster rising and falling gently on his chest.

Isobel picked up the book and the glasses and put them on the bedside cabinet. Then she slid into the ensuite bathroom and cleaned her teeth with the electric toothbrush Phil had given her for her last birthday. She washed her face and smoothed on some budget-price sorbolene cream. Finally she brushed her hair twenty times and tied it back in a loose plait.

She crept into her side of the bed (the left side) and sat for a moment looking around before she snapped the light off. She took in the sensible off-white walls, the framed wedding photos and Phil lying next to her dressed in his favourite baggy flannel pyjamas.

'The next twenty years,' she murmured almost inaudibly to herself.

'Z'everything okay?' Phil muttered, curling himself around her.

'Everything's fine,' Isobel whispered. 'Go back to sleep.'

Then she lay back and clicked off the bedside light, smiling. She'd decided that if Clare was serious about this sister swap idea, then so was she.

Why the hell not?

CHAPTER 6

Clare wearily surveyed the two bright little faces lifted up towards hers. 'Now, who wants some delicious toasted cheese sandwiches?'

'Yum, yum, yes,' shouted Ellen, while Alex banged both hands on his high-chair table in apparently enthusiastic agreement.

'Great. Well, you both sit there very still and do me a lovely drawing and I'll make you a sandwich.'

This mothering stuff wasn't quite as easy it looked from the outside, Clare admitted to herself as she hacked into the greasy yellow slab of cheddar cheese.

She was just three days into the first week of the 'Sister Pact' life swap and already she was longing for Sunday, when she could go home and doze on her own squashy sofa with a good book, a bad video and a big bowl of diet ice cream. Anything rather than making cheese sandwiches. Even her hastily purchased copies of *How to Have Kids and Your Own Life Too* and *The Me Centred Guide to Motherhood* hadn't helped her deal with the reality of looking after small children. The dirt, the drudgery, the Dr Seuss books.

At least The Colonel had bought the sister swap idea as a substitute for Thumper Arundell. As long as this story came up well, Clare could assume that her job and her mortgage were safe – for the moment. The Colonel in fact loved the idea, especially when she saw a photograph of the gorgeous Isobel with her handsome family. Isobel was 'Suzanne' to a tee, The Colonel saw immediately – attractive wife, professional husband, two pretty children (nicely spaced, right genders).

Of course, as Clare explained to Isobel later, their stories would have to be '*Verved*', by which she meant they had to come to the conclusion that the best possible life would be the life of a typical *Verve* reader – kids, nanny and a part-time job running a small gallery devoted to rare Amerindian art pieces.

In the end the whole thing had been arranged in two weeks flat. At the last minute, Isobel was so nervous she'd tried to back out, wailing, 'I can't leave the kids for two whole weeks.' Clare had had to jolly her along. 'I can see it all,' she'd told Isobel. 'The Colonel will be delighted by the stories, *Verve* will unexpectedly win prestigious journalism awards, we become big stars, go into feature films (written by Leo), earn a fortune (looked after by Phil) and we all live happily ever after.' Then she almost pushed Isobel out the door and on her way to St Kilda with her impeccably packed suitcase.

Now Clare wondered how Isobel was going. The thought of her sister sitting at her desk, using her coffee mug and taking her place at the weekly conference was unnerving.

'I'm hungry,' whined Ellen, smacking her textas down on the table.

'Okay, okay, it's coming,' Clare said, grabbing the almost-burning toast out from under the griller.

The lunch thing was easy enough. She hadn't yet ventured into the dangerous territory of trying to get vegetables into the kids but she could always try that next week.

'It's got green, I hate green,' Ellen yelled when she saw her toasted cheese sandwich.

'That's not green, Ellie, that's a bit of parsley it picked up off the chopping board. I can take it off. See? All gone.'

Ellen bit into her sandwich dubiously. 'This tastes funny.'

'No,' Clare said, a bit tetchily. 'It's not funny, it's delicious. I put some yummy tomato sauce on as well. It's my magic recipe.'

'It tastes yukky, I don' want it.'

Alex picked up the mood and threw his plastic bowl over the side of the armchair where the food splatted down beside the delighted dog.

'Fine,' said Clare through lightly gritted teeth. 'You don't want my toasted cheese sandwiches. What will you have instead – Yoghurt? Fruit?'

After Alex and Ellen had consumed a bag of crisps each, Clare tried to persuade them that they needed an afternoon nap, an idea that they found unconvincing in the extreme. She'd discovered with surprise that when she had sole charge of them, she felt slightly nervous, as if the kids knew more than she did. As she hopped smartly over to the fridge to fulfil Ellen's demand for a third glass of apple juice, she wondered if she was being overly indulgent. Or were you meant to give small children whatever they asked for within reason? She didn't want Phil coming home to dehydrated, starving children.

And they were used to five-star service. Isobel wrapped the kids up in a cocoon and pampered them to an absurd degree. Clare thought that Ellen and Alex would emerge from this tight maternal embrace convinced that the world owed them a nice supply of home cooked meals, hot baths and ironed underwear. They were in for a nasty shock, she thought ruefully.

After several energetic games of hide and seek, a game whose main purpose – hiding – seemed to have escaped both Ellen and Alex, Clare felt like she was going to scream with boredom. She finally plonked them down in front of the television, shoved *The Lion King* video into the machine's gaping maw and collapsed on the lounge with a mug of coffee and her favourite comfort book, the omnibus edition of *Love in a Cold Climate*.

Clare guessed it was probably the fifteenth time she'd sat through *The Lion King* since she had moved in on Sunday. Ellen wasn't just a fan of the film, she was an acolyte. But thank God for videos. Absolute life savers.

Before Phil had even left this morning, she already had the kids planted in front of *Winnie the Pooh* so she could stack the breakfast dishes in the dishwasher.

'Iso would be aghast to see them gawping at the box already,' he'd warned as he packed his lunch into his briefcase.

'What she doesn't know won't hurt,' Clare had answered vigorously.

Phil still seemed a little shellshocked by the idea of having his sister-in-law living in the house as a kind of housekeeper. However, easygoing by temperament, he was willing to put up with it if it was what Isobel wanted to do.

He was a tall and lean man, his skin faintly pockmarked by the scars of severe acne which must have made his adolescence miserable. Clare thought maybe that misery might have also been responsible for his Puckish sense of humour, which bubbled through an accountant's exterior. Perhaps the other clue to this side of his personality was his naturally exuberant wavy hair which continued to express itself, even though he kept it cropped short.

'I have this theory that if the next generation are going to be vidiots, we owe it to them to give them a flying start so they don't get left behind in the techno-race,' said Clare.

Phil had surveyed his children with a glimmer of a grin. 'Hmm, there's probably a flaw to that logic somewhere. Anyway, I think there's a built-in safety switch. You'll find they get bored with videos after fifteen minutes.'

'That's fine, I thought we could do some face painting after that. I brought some paints with me,' Clare had said, rather proud of her imaginative ingenuity. Maybe the time she spent working as a clown in that all-women circus was going to come in handy after all.

But the face painting seemed to have kept them amused for about half a minute, and then she was already desperately trying to think of something else for them to do. Not to mention guiltily aware that she really should have been catching up with the ironing, putting on some washing and doing the weekly supermarket shop.

Listening to Elton John burble on about The Circle of Life, Clare realised she was bowled over by how difficult everything was when two small children were involved. It was like being caught up in an avalanche. Everything seemed to snowball further into chaos, from the ironing piling up in the laundry to the toys littered all over the family room floor. And she was the one being buried alive.

Her blithe assumption that this childcare-housewife thing would be easy if approached with pragmatic inventiveness and a cool head had disappeared on the afternoon of Day One. About the same time that it dawned on her that these two small, unreasonable, egomaniacal human beings were really entirely dependent on her for food, drink, clothes, safety, transport and entertainment. Not even her cat was that bad. At least he looked after his own social life.

She had moved into survival mode just to get through the day. She showered at night after the children were asleep because she hadn't figured out a way to wash in the morning and still keep an eye on Ellen and Alex, who were set on a kamikaze mission to destroy themselves, either by leaping off tables, rolling down stairs or swallowing Draino.

She'd adopted instant dressing methods (leggings and a big shirt) and had given up wearing make-up, except for a smear of lipstick for self-respect. It was too difficult to do her usual artful shading and outlining with Ellen standing beside her happily squashing ninety-dollar French lipstick all over her T-shirt.

Already she felt slightly mazy with tiredness after just three nights of broken sleep. Last night had been the worst. Every time she succeeded in jigging Alex back to sleep and then put him down in the cot, he'd woken up as soon as his body touched the mattress.

Consequently she'd spent a couple of hours pacing back and forth, shivering a little because she'd only thrown on her dressing gown. Next time she would make sure she put on trackpants, a jumper and a woolly hat.

But the nights were positively peaceful compared to the clashing chaos of the days. The mornings always began with Alexander's stupendously wet and rank nappy and Ellen's lengthy, impassioned interrogations on why she needed to brush her hair or why the rain fell down from the sky or why she couldn't watch *The Lion King* again. Which of course she could – anything for a moment's peace.

Breakfast (which Clare never managed to find time to eat herself) was a three-ring circus. While she attempted to keep up with Ellen's cuisine preferences – 'I don' wan' Weetbix, I wan' pancakes! Don' wan' pancakes, I wan' corn chips!' – Alex would either be yelling for his cereal or mashing the said cereal all over his head.

Meanwhile Daisy would have planted her fat bottom firmly in the middle of the kitchen demanding to be fed and the washing machine would be beeping insistently to let her know that it had finished one load and was ready to have the second one shovelled in.

And in the middle of this cacophony, Phil would wander in carrying a tie and asking, 'Hey, does this tie go with this shirt?'

This morning she'd finally snapped irritably at him,

'Oh for God's sake, Phil, you're a grown man. I'm sure you don't need me to tell you what clothes to wear!'

Phil had looked a little hurt. 'Well, of course not, but Iso always tells me what to wear. I mean, you know, she'll tell me if I'm getting it wrong. It's just a second opinion. Women generally seem better at that sort of thing . . .' He took in Clare's stormy face and his voice trailed away.

Alex had taken advantage of her lapse in concentration to start joyously throwing globules of bran mush onto the rug from his highchair.

'I'd rather you wear whatever you want, no matter how much of a sartorial disaster, than bother me for advice when I'm in the middle of all this,' Clare had said testily as she crouched down to scrape up the cereal. 'Alex, stop that right now. And Ellen sit down and eat what you asked for. Yes, of course, you can squeeze the bread up into dough-balls. I don't care what you do with it as long as you eat something.'

'Well,' Phil had muttered awkwardly. 'I can see you're busy . . .'

Clare had felt sudden compunction. After all, Phil had been a good sport about this outlandish life-swap idea, and he was a nice guy. It wasn't his fault that he had the habit of blowing his nose loudly in the shower and wore woolly sheepskin slippers around the house at night. Everyone had their failings, she decided generously.

She'd tried a quick smile. 'I hope that didn't sound rude. It's just, you know, you can make up your own mind about what to dress yourself in.'

'Sure, sure,' he echoed, backing away hastily from the

doorway. 'I can see you're busy. I'll just lie low with the ties.'

While the kids learnt all about patriarchy from Walt Disney and the Lion family, Clare realised with apprehension that she really shouldn't put off the supermarket any longer. She was going to have to load the children into the Volvo stationwagon and set out in search of the nearest Safeways.

Just two hours later, she was finally underway, with Ellen and Alex safely strapped in the back and temporarily unable to do anything more than grizzle and throw things at one another. Clare relaxed a fraction. She was even able to smile at the memory of Phil backing hastily out the door, forlornly clutching his fistful of ties. There was no way that Leo would ever ask her to tell him what to wear, she thought.

Clare had convinced herself that one humiliating phone call had ended her relationship with Leo forever, but when he finally called her three days later, he hadn't even mentioned it. Maybe, she thought hopefully, he believed it was all a bad dream. Or maybe, a more cynical voice muttered, he was just keen to fall into bed with someone before he rushed back up north to spend another week on set.

He told her he needed to be around to do any last minute re-writes, but Clare suspected he just enjoyed the thrill of watching his script being realised. Either way, he'd hurried off so quickly that she hadn't even been able to explain to him about the Sister Pact. Or that was what she told herself. Maybe it also had something to do with not wanting to talk about motherhood again; he always accused her of being obsessed with babies and biological clocks.

Anyway, she had consulted *Manifesting Your Man* and been warned to leave well alone.

THE ARGUMENT: Be warned that while women love to return to a good argument, and worry away at it like a dog with a flavoursome bone, men do not feel the same way. This is because they're cats. If you want to make yourself desirable in the eyes of Mr Appropriate, you need to start acting in a way that he understands. For him, once the argument is finished, it's over. It is even more over if you follow it up with some enthusiastic love making. For him, it will be as if the argument never existed, particularly if he can attribute it to some external cause – indigestion, premenstrual tension, your mother. That's the way he likes to keep it.

Men don't like women who sulk or hold grudges. Of course, women love to do both those things but, in the interests of manifesting your man, resist the temptation. Once an argument has finished, let it evaporate like mist in the hot summer sun. If you must hang on to anything, hang on to the lesson of the argument so you can see ways you can stop the same thing happening again. Some people believe arguments are good therapy for a relationship. Nonsense! Do you argue all the time with your best girlfriend? Your favourite sister? Your pet poodle? If the answer is no, then why should you treat your man with any less respect and tolerance?

Clare had mulled over this passage earnestly, and had dutifully endeavoured to extract some kind of lesson from the disastrous phone argument with Leo. The best she had come up with was don't call him when you're tipsy. Either that or never make phone calls after cooking bad quiche. It didn't seem very satisfactory. Still, at least things appeared to be back on track and, with a bit of luck, she might even see him on Sunday.

Ellen was singing a quiet car song to herself and Alex was nearly asleep, so Clare turned the volume down on the Wiggles tape and reviewed the progress of the Sister Pact story. From her point of view, she thought dismally, she really needed to come up with a few more positives to motherhood. *Verve* women were almost always mothers. Or, if they weren't mothers, they still *believed* in motherhood. As a Lifestyle Concept. They didn't want to read some litany of disasters. Clare decided she would probably have to cheat a bit, put in some guff about what exquisite fun the kids were to play with or how beautiful they looked when they were asleep.

She yawned widely. Talking of sleep . . .

At last finding a spot in the supermarket carpark, she commenced her usual ten-minute struggle with the insoluble gorgon's knots that were the Safety Authority's idea of reliable child restraint. Then, clinging to Clare with one hand, she carried Alex into the supermarket and managed to squash him awkwardly into one of those trolley baby seats. It took every ounce of her upper body strength to manoeuvre the unwieldy cart, with Ellen trailing behind whining that she wanted to be allowed to ride on the trolley too.

At least it was a work out for her pecs, Clare decided. She'd had no time to go to the gym since she took over Isobel's life. Iso had left behind her daily chore schedule detailing exactly what mopping, sweeping, vacuuming, washing, folding, ironing, baking and gardening Clare should be doing every day. But if the two children had (miraculously) managed to fall asleep at the same time, all Clare wanted to do was slump in a chair and suck back a cup of coffee.

She'd realised last night she'd guzzled a shocking ten cups of coffee that day (most of them consumed cold because she never seemed to get around to drinking them in time). Then there were all the chocolate biscuits and toasted cheese sandwiches that snuck in as well, using the cup of coffee as a Trojan horse in their sly campaign to make her thighs balloon out.

It was when she saw she was almost out of supplies of chocolate biscuits, cheese and bread that Clare conceded she was going to have to go shopping with her two charges in tow. It was like taking part in some wacky game show where you were given two items which had to go with you wherever you went, and if you forgot them or let them out of your sight for one minute, you lost the game. It was easy to see why some mothers never left the house. The logistics of managing one baby, one toddler and a pram were too terrifying.

She'd wangled from Phil the small fortune he suggested was necessary to buy food for a family of four for a week. She supposed vaguely that she should come up with a balanced diet, that thing old 'Mother Hubbard', their school home economics teacher, used to drone on about all the time. At the very least, she had to provide variety: say, lamb one night, beef the next, then pork, chicken . . . at which point she ran out of genres of meat, so started toying doubtfully with the thought of tuna.

Was there *anything* edible that could be done with a tin of tuna? Her mother had regularly churned out a fish casserole recipe which involved a tin of condensed mushroom soup and potato crisps on top, but she couldn't picture herself, Clare Callaway, making – never mind eating – something as embarrassing as a tuna casserole.

She remembered Isobel's earnest strictures about children liking nice, plain, old-fashioned food – obviously her faithful standby, green chicken curry, was out.

She desperately scanned her meagre mental repertoire of recipes for plain food and came up with tomato soup (tinned) and spaghetti bolognese. Would Phil notice if he had beef bolognese tonight, pork bolognese tomorrow night, chicken bolognese the next, then lamb bolognese? And was there any such thing as tuna bolognese?

Somehow she doubted an exclusively bolognese diet could be described as balanced. Iso always blathered on about the children needing vegetables to avoid scurvy or their fingernails shrivelling or something. But how to get vegetables down the little blighters when they blanched at green cordial, let alone green, leafy, fibrous plant life?

Alex began to squirm ominously in his trolley seat, reminding Clare that she had limited time before he became bored with this disappointing outing and decided to exercise his bagpipe-capacity lungs once more.

Clare dreaded finding herself transformed into that most pitiful creature, the one she herself had always treated with such icy disdain – the woman at the supermarket checkout with the rogue child.

She began to hurtle up and down the aisles, battling the strong sideways pull of the heavy cart, which was even heavier with Ellen clinging to the edge shrieking, 'Faster, Clare, go faster!'

To keep Alex amused, she started to sing nursery rhymes to him and jigged about with forced merriment. Though he watched this frenzied performance with a basilisk look of stony boredom, Alex's face crumpled into sobs whenever she stopped, so she had to sustain her manic trolley dancing up and down the aisles while she shopped.

'Three Blind Mice . . .' she carolled, grabbing ten tins of baked beans. 'Twinkle Twinkle Little Star' kept disaster at bay while she loaded in the tuna (there had to be *something* she could do with it). And by the time she got to 'Humpty Dumpty Sat on a Wall' she was pulling litre after litre of milk out of the fridge. It was incredible how much nasty, allergy-inducing, mucus-producing cow's milk these kids chug-a-lugged in a week.

She hovered in front of the soups, wondering dubiously if tinned tomato soup could count as a meal (surely if she did wholemeal croutons . . .) when she realised that the giant-size tin was on the top shelf out of her reach.

'Excuse me,' she said sweetly to the man standing next to her. 'Would you be very kind and hand me down one of those jumbo, family-size, econo-tins of hearty tomato soup?'

When he turned to look at her, she noted with appreciation that he was gorgeous – close cropped hair, tight T-shirt, jeans that cupped his toned and taut buttocks like a pair of eager female hands. Possibly gay but worth the benefit of the doubt. She bestowed on him the full wattage of her best, regularly whitened, occasionally flossed smile as he handed her the tin.

126

But she felt as though the air had been sucked from her lungs as he took in Clare and the children and turned away without taking a second glance. It was almost, she thought in horror, as though she had somehow disappeared. She was a suburban *hausfrau* who was not to be smiled at, not to be appreciated, not even to be noticed. Standing in the supermarket aisle, with her full trolley and two young children, Clare had suddenly become the invisible woman.

As the stranger strolled casually away, Clare felt a sudden desperate impulse to stumble after him and tug on his T-shirt. 'Look, look at me,' she wanted to say. 'I am a real person. These aren't my kids, this isn't my trolley, this isn't my life. I live in the inner city, I wear hipsters, I have a cupboard full of stiletto heels, I listen to Triple J even though I'm over thirty. I'm worth noticing, goddamn it!'

Instead, she kept numbly loading in pre-cooked meals and anything else that promised to be easy bake, quick cook and one step. She was surprisingly detached through Alex's tantrum at the checkout and Ellen's refusal to get into the car until she had her banana ice cream. Which in turn led to Alex grabbing at the ice cream with one eager little hand and knocking it onto the floor so Clare had to buy both of them more ice cream which they didn't eat fast enough anyway to stop it melting all over their clothes and the car seats.

By four they were home, washed and changed again, and Clare felt like she had been run over several times by a street-cleaning machine. She even *looked* like she had been, she thought miserably, catching a glance at herself in the bathroom mirror. And Ellen was already asking for pancakes for dinner and she hadn't got around to unpacking the shopping or cleaning the car.

Clare had promised Ellen she would play another game of *The Lion King*. Ellen never seemed to tire of this game which involved prancing around on Iso and Phil's bed, which became Pride Rock for the duration of the game. Ellen pretended to hunt assorted jungle animals, which were then eaten with pancakes and sugar for dinner while Clare lay staring up at the brass light fitting and mechanically saying things like 'yummy yummy giraffe pancakes'. Even more worrying, visions of a mountain of ironing kept popping into her head, with Iso standing right behind them looking gravely disappointed. Clare had always prided herself on knowing where housework sat in the food chain of life: somewhere below having her legs waxed and slightly above going to the dentist. Now she seemed to be becoming obsessed by it.

Assuring Ellen she would play with her soon, she planted the kids in front of *Pocahontas*, and started to stack the supermarket purchases on the pantry shelves, wondering what she could whip up for dinner.

Phil had explained earlier in the week that Isobel usually had the children fed and bathed by the time he got home from work and she would then cook a real meal for the two of them. But Clare had waspishly replied that if he thought he could just wander through the door, plant a quick kiss on his children's freshly washed little cheeks and snap on the TV while she stirred the roasted-fennel risotto, he'd better think again.

So they had agreed on a new routine, having a 'family meal' at 7 pm. Clare knew Isobel would be shocked if she found out the children were eating just before bedtime but figured she wasn't around to fret about it.

Last night Ellen and Alex had refused to eat her chicken dish which, from a couple of kids who were quite happy to eat snails and drink Draino, was sobering condemnation.

She'd felt like slopping it on their plates and hissing behind Phil's back: 'Eat it, you little beasts!' Not, she realised, a mature response.

Then she'd had to beg Phil to open a bottle of red wine ('It's not the same trying to unwind over a plastic beaker of blackcurrant juice') and then he'd had the nerve to ask her if she wanted him to help with the dishes or the kids.

From the look on his face, Clare could tell he was chuffed with his own magnanimity. Probably thought he was acting out the epitome of the New Man and would dazzle his sister-in-law with his contemporary, caring masculinity. Clare wondered cynically where this attitude had been when she was flinging herself around the kitchen trying to get dinner ready while he watched the evening news. And his use of the term 'help' was risible. They were his children. Come to think of it, they were his dishes too.

'The fair thing would be to divide – washing kids versus washing dishes. I'll toss you for it,' she'd offered.

It was with some satisfaction that she'd watched Phil, laden down with two children, head off to the bathroom while she got the kitchen all to herself. She'd turned the radio to Triple J and played it loudly as she jived around the kitchen.

But by 10 pm, she was wondering how she ever had the energy to lift a dish, never mind do the twist. Alex was finally asleep but Ellen, Phil and Clare were still stuck in front of *The Lion King*.

The idea, Phil had explained, was that Ellen found her favourite video so comforting and soporific that she fell asleep watching it, whereas if they just put her to bed she would start yelling and wake Alex. But there had been no sign Ellen was even thinking horizontally. To be frank, she was frighteningly very wide awake. Clare, meanwhile, felt she would have given anything just to lie down and let her sagging, concrete-heavy eyelids blissfully drift close.

Phil had yawned and stretched. 'I think I better do some reading and turn in. I have an early meeting tomorrow. See you guys in the morning,' he'd said, giving Clare a peck on the cheek and ruffling Ellen's freshly washed hair. Without a flicker of hesitation, he'd strolled off to bed, leaving Clare stuck with priggish little Simba and his up-beat jungle pals. 'What about me,' Clare had felt like wailing. Just keeping her body upright felt like excruciating torture.

As the sleep had rolled towards her in another big wave, Clare moaned desperately at Ellen, 'Sure you don't want to hop into bed now, sweetie pie? It's very, very late.'

'No!' Ellen had said, eyeing Clare obstinately, 'I wanna watch the video. Don' wanna go to bed.'

Eventually, after one video, a game of chequers (Ellen cheated) and *Topsy and Tim's Tuesday Book*, read aloud five times by Clare in a progressively huskier voice, Ellen had dozed off.

Clare was able to awkwardly gather the surprisingly heavy little body into her arms and stagger into Ellen's room. After a few minutes of trying to turn down the bed-clothes with her teeth, she'd even managed to get her into bed. She then had the world's fastest shower and had just crawled into her own bed when Alexander started to cry. Hoping Phil would get up, she lay doggo for a few minutes. But as Alex's cries grew ever more desperate, she'd worried he might wake Ellen again, so she sighed and clawed her way up the bedhead and out of bed.

If madness really could be induced by sleep depriva-tion, thought Clare, she was going to become as batty as the mad woman in the attic.

Remembering the night before made her feel so sleepy that, by the time she'd finished stacking the groceries away, Clare decided she could pop *The Little Mermaid* on after *Pocahontas* and see if she could sneak in a quick doze on the couch while Ellen was occupied.

She was just snuggling down on the couch when the doorbell rang.

'Who could that be?' she muttered grumpily.

She pulled open the door to find Margaret, the neigh-bour-from-hell, on the doorstep. With some dismay, Clare took in the dumpy woman with a broad, plain face, today wearing a denim shirtwaister dress which seemed to have acquired a peculiar orange hue, hopefully due to some disaster in the wash and not the designer's intention. It certainly went oddly with Margaret's flushed complexion. She was wearing a pair of large red-rimmed glasses.

'Uh, hello Margaret, how can I help you?' Clare said as politely as she could.

131

'Clare, super to see you,' Margaret said, her beady eyes already darting over Clare's shoulders to assess the interior of the house. 'How are you?'

'Fine,' Clare said, wondering how quickly she could close the door in this woman's face. 'I'm afraid Isobel is not here . . .'

'Of course I know that. Isobel has told me all about this funny thing you're doing for that magazine with the odd name. I never seem to see many copies of it in the newsagent so the name always slips my mind. Anyway, I know all about it, although I did say to Isobel that I was not at all sure that it was a good thing to do for the children's sake. Kiddies like stability. Kevin and I haven't had one day away from our two since they were born.'

'I'm sure Ellen and Alex aren't at all bothered by this,' Clare said coolly, again driven to wonder who the hell Margaret thought she was. The neighbour-from-hell nickname scarcely did her justice.

'Anyway, I've just popped over to let you know about the kindie fundraising day. You know that Ellen and Katie go to the same kindergarten and I'm the business manager, well – oh, do you mind if I come in and I'll explain all?'

Ungraciously, Clare stood aside, conscious that as she walked through the house, Margaret's mind was clicking away like a camera, taking notes on everything from the untidy house to Ellen's unusual hairstyle (she'd insisted on having three ponytails).

'Would you like a cup of coffee?' Clare asked reluctantly, as she got out some play dough for Ellen and plonked it on her little table.

'Super. Lovely. But I won't take up much of your time.

I know you'll be busy, struggling to keep up with these two. I've always said they're quite a handful, not like my two who are so beautifully well behaved. I did mention Attention Deficit Disorder to Isobel once but she didn't seem to take up the suggestion. So often people are actually afraid to look the truth in the face, aren't they? But of course you're a journalist so you'll know all about that. And are you still going out with that film writer chappy?'

Clare, taken aback, said yes before she could think to say it's none of your business and I'm not entirely sure.

'Oh well, it'll all come out in the wash. I've always said that you have to kiss a few toads before you come up with a prince. And by the time a woman reaches your age, there's really not a lot of choice left, is there? The best men tend to be snapped up quite early. I know I met Kevin when he was twenty-five and we were married by the time he was twenty-eight. Probably a little sooner than I would have wanted but there was no way of saying no to him, he just insisted on getting married. I guess it was because he didn't want to let me slip through his fingers. It's just as important to men to get the pick of the crop, you know. Anyway, the reason I popped by was that I just wanted to ask what you plan to make for the kindie Bring 'n' Buy fundraising on Friday?'

Clare was thinking how fabulous it would be to have some kind of trap door so she could just push a button and Margaret would drop down into some cesspool below the house and disappear forever.

'Clare?' Margaret asked again in her penetrating voice.

Clare shook her head. 'Oh, Iso didn't mention any fundraiser. Umm, what sort of thing do you need?'

'Biscuits, cakes, pots of home-made jam, whatever your little speciality is. Of course, you may not have a speciality since you're not much of a cook. Isobel told us about that birthday dinner you gave her at your place. What a funny story! It's incredible that so many things could go so wrong with one meal! But any contribution would be welcome. We're desperate. So you'd be more than welcome to pop down to the shops and buy something and donate it to the table. Of course most of the mothers at Fast Track prefer home-made, we're all terribly conscious of additives and preservatives. But we can always make an exception. And if anything doesn't sell, it's donated to the teachers for their afternoon tea and they don't care what they eat.'

Clare felt her lips go stiff with outrage. 'I'm sure I can wrap my brain around making a few cookies for a kindergarten fundraiser,' she said crossly. 'Do you have milk and sugar in your coffee?'

'Milk, no sugar. I'm sweet enough,' trilled Margaret (somehow Clare just *knew* she was going to say that). 'You don't have any low fat? I always make a point of having both low fat and regular milk in the fridge because you really don't know which people prefer these days. No, no, don't worry about me, regular will do. But now, how are you settling in? I bet you're finding that motherhood isn't all beer and skittles. It really is the toughest job in the world, you know. And yet the only one that's really worth doing. You're actually creating a new life which is awesome to think of, isn't it? Of course, not that you've created any life, it's more babysitting really, isn't it? I know you're one of those one-track career girls who's decided there is no room in your life for children. They just take too much out of you. You just have to give, give, give completely selflessly.'

'Oh,' said Clare sweetly. 'But you work part-time don't you? That must give you a bit of a break from all that ceaseless giving.'

'Yes, of course,' Margaret said with self-satisfaction, 'And *I've* always thought that I'm giving in even more ways by bringing home my thoroughly stimulated mind. After all, if the mum is happy, the children will be happy. That's how I always see it. What an extraordinary outfit you have Ellen in. I'm sure I never saw Isobel team that shirt with those pants. It's quite a *startling* combination, isn't it?'

'Oh, Ellen chose it herself,' said Clare. 'I think it's important for her to make her own decisions about things as much as possible.'

'That explains it then,' Margaret said, rolling her eyes. 'I know for a fact that Isobel hardly ever lets Ellen choose her own clothes. It's always disastrous, poor little poppet.'

'What, depriving her of her big chance to make the cover of *Vogue*?' Clare said sharply.

Margaret raised her ample eyebrows. 'Well, we all know that mums are judged by how their children are turned out. And no wonder, you can tell so much about what's going on back at the home by how the kiddies look. A stain here, an unironed T-shirt there, it all speaks volumes, you know. You might not see these things because you're not a mother but other mothers really notice it. And Isobel is very careful about how her children look, I must say that for her. And I'm speaking as someone who has often been described as meticulous in these matters.'

'I'm sure you pay enormous attention to your kids' clothes, Margaret,' Clare said. 'Now I'd offer you another cup of coffee but I know how impatient you must be to dash off and keep organising that fund-raising . . .'

'Yes indeed. Ooops, you're right, so many people to see,' Margaret declared, glancing at her watch.

As she got to her feet and headed slowly for the door (craning her head back to take one last look at the state of the kitchen), she trod on some of the little farm animals scattered over the floor. She bent down and picked up a black and white cow. 'Are these yours, Ellen?' she asked, shaking the cow towards Ellen's face. 'You know you should pick up your toys and put them away when you've finished playing with them. I do believe you're just trying to get away with being naughty because Aunty Clare is here and she has no idea what she's doing around the house. You're a bad little girl!'

Ellen, bending over her play dough which she was shaping into a giant rat, kept her head turned away and began to hum a little tune. I know how you feel, kid, Clare thought, for once empathising with Ellen rather than regarding her as the leader of the opposition.

'Ellen is not a bad girl, she's extremely good,' she said loudly to Margaret. 'And as for the toys on the floor, that's deliberate. It's called Creative Chaos, the latest parenting technique from the Family Faculty at Harvard University. I'm surprised you haven't done a course in it.'

She ushered Margaret out into the entrance hall.

'I'll see you on Friday at the fundraiser,' Margaret said, now wedged in the front doorway. 'And I must check out that parenting technique, what did you say it was called? Of course I know all about the Family Faculty at Harvard University, but I just wasn't familiar with that particular technique.'

Clare smirked a little. If Margaret had heard of the Family Faculty at Harvard, she was the only person who had.

'Creative Chaos,' Clare repeated. 'It means it's okay for the children to make a mess.'

CHAPTER 7

Isobel crept as unobtrusively as she could into a seat at the end of the table, as far from Helen Hogan as she could possibly get while still being in the same room.

She'd heard all about these editorial meetings from Clare and, frankly, she was feeling quietly terrified. Not that she expected to become one of The Colonel's victims (unless the editor had decided to set whole new benchmarks in photocopying standards). But kindly Isobel felt that even the prospect of seeing someone else torn apart was terrifying enough.

She smiled wanly at William when he came to sit next to her. He'd been so sweet, she thought, showing her where the stationery was kept and even offering to take her out to lunch one day. Pouring him a cup of coffee, she thought what a good man he was. It was a shame Clare had no interest in him. Isobel had decided that he was perfect fatherhood material.

In fact, if it wasn't for William and Fiona, Isobel didn't know how she'd have coped with the week so far. It was extraordinary to think people dealt with offices, commuter traffic, fragile pantihose and clumsy high heels on a daily basis. And after only four days of sitting under fluorescent light, Isobel felt her skin was already turning a peculiar shade of yellow. Perhaps that was why *Verve* staff members were so lavish with their make-up.

She wasn't enjoying Clare's life at all. Every morning, she was woken by an alarm clock blaring out rock music at 5.45 am so she could clamber into dank exercise clothes and drive to the gym for a pre-breakfast workout. As she trudged drearily on the treadmill, she'd concluded that this torture could never actually be good for you. It was the kind of thing they made rats do in laboratories, but at least the rats had electric shocks as motivation.

On the first morning, a balding man in his thirties had strutted up to her when she was lying on the bench press and said jauntily, 'Welcome to the Breakfast Club!' Isobel had just blinked up at him in stupefaction. At 6.30 in the morning, when her hair was frowzy and her bare face still crumpled from sleep, the last thing she needed was conversation. And she certainly didn't intend to belong to any club made up of the kind of people who went to the gym before breakfast.

After the gym came the daily struggle to decide what to wear, followed by the even more difficult battle to keep herself looking corporate, wrinkle-free and pristine for an entire day. It was a shame that someone hadn't invented the standing up desk for working women, Isobel thought quite seriously. It would make it so much easier to keep oneself looking like the impeccable women in the catalogues. But then imagine trying to stand up all day in those shoes ...

Even getting into work was a hassle, taking the crowded tram, which was, more often than not, standing room only. This morning, looking out at a beautiful blue-sky winter day, she'd thought how much she'd love to be taking the kids down to the park, or mucking about in the garden. Instead she'd be sitting inside a virtually window-free office.

She spent her days as the general office dogsbody. It had sounded like a cinch ('After all, I'm a mother, isn't that the ultimate in dogsbodies?' she had joked feebly to Fiona during a break in the downstairs cafe). But in practice she was quickly bored by days spent photocopying, calling couriers, sorting readers' letters (trashing the nasty ones before The Colonel saw them) and trotting downstairs five times a day to pick up rounds of low-fat, extra-strength cappuccino.

Then, to finish it all off, there was the tram journey home at night, wedged miserably in the peak hour crush. Isobel couldn't be bothered cooking herself dinner every night. 'It hardly seemed worth the effort for one person. Instead she'd taken to eating bowls of stale muesli on the couch while listlessly watching junk television.

Now she was so hungry that she even started to eat one of the dreary sandwiches on the conference table platter (cheese and chicken loaf – The Colonel did not believe in indulging her staff's gourmet pretensions). Isobel wondered what Ellie and Alex were doing right now. She hoped that Clare was keeping an eye on Ellen's chest – she was prone to worrying bouts of wheezing and breathlessness . . .

She was jerked back into the present when The Colonel strode into the room.

'Right,' she snapped, sitting down at the head of the table. 'Update on circulation for the latest issue which has now been out on the stands for two weeks. Result as follows – Not too bad.'

Apparently, this was as specific as the Colonel ever got about circulation. She regarded it on the same level as bodily functions – necessary but inadvisable to discuss in detail. The idea of measuring *Verve*'s success in terms of numbers displeased her. She preferred to think of it as an icon.

She moved on quickly. 'I think we can say it was not a bad issue. Feedback says we can be especially pleased with response to the feature on Big Tick Life Transformations Through Tiny Cosmetic Tucks. So well done to Clare wherever she is.'

(Here Isobel couldn't help beaming proudly. She made a mental note to tell Clare when she saw her on the weekend.)

The Colonel continued brusquely, 'Another week, another week. Let's do the whip around and see what progress we're making.'

The staff ran through their pieces clockwise around the table. Isobel chewed on an extraordinarily boring cheese sandwich as she listened to the outline of stories about How to Transform your Coffee Table into an Art Gallery, Fifty Ways to Improve Your Lover, Fashion for a Country House Weekend ('Sleeves and Wooster') and the Tragic Truth of Female Circumcision in Third World Countries ('Sew What?!' was the headline The Colonel was toying with).

Isobel was a little horrified by the glib way everyone talked about human tragedy as another attention-grabbing page filler. It was like going through the looking glass into a world where divan covers, divorce and designer shoes were just as important as monogamy, babies and female equality.

She was also dismayed by the way the word 'absolutely' seemed to have replaced the word 'yes'. '*Absolutely*,' everyone kept saying to The Colonel, nodding furiously. Isobel discovered that even her vocabulary had become obsolete while she was doing time in her suburban isolation cell.

'Okay, coming along, coming along,' The Colonel murmured, rolling her pen between her claw-like hands. 'But we do have one problem. Fiona,' The Colonel directed the full laser beam of her little eyes down the table. 'I've read that copy on the "Breast Battle – Triumph and Tragedy from the Frontline of the War on Nature". Absolute blancmange.'

Isobel's heart went out to Fiona, who for once wasn't smiling but sitting with her head bent over her notebook.

'Don't give me an insipid story and expect to get a cover line,' The Colonel barked. 'For heaven's sake, if we're doing something on breast jobs, we want to see exactly what went right and wrong. We want to know about every pucker, bulge, corrugation or slipped nipple. And we need pictures. Big, beautiful perfect breasts. "Look What Doctor Fumble-Fingers Did to My Breasts" breasts. Don't give me crap about the women being modest. Suzanne doesn't want to imagine Quasimodo's bosom, she wants to see it. She wants to shudder a tiny bit, and then she wants to see what fabulous results she can get if only she follows the *Verve* battle plan for stylishly recreated breasts. So get me pictures.'

Fiona muttered acquiescence. (Isobel could have sworn she said 'absolutely'.)

'Right, just make sure you do. Now that's it for this week, so if you greedy lot have finished scarfing lunch you can go back to work. Oh, we do have one final bit of business – this issue's "Trials of Style" page.'

Isobel nodded; she was a keen reader of Trials of Style, a test guide that compared things which were new on the market with the old (but extremely similar) things they sought to replace. It could cover anything from aromatherapy candles to must-wear designer exercise wear, and of course it was inevitable that the 'new' stuff had to outshine the 'old' stuff. *Verve* was nothing if not a celebration of unabashed, cutting-edge consumerism.

'Okay, we need a tester,' said The Colonel. 'This time we'll do something foody. These.' She held up a plastic packet of some shrivelled black stringy pods. 'Vanilla beans,' she announced triumphantly. 'Organically grown and hand-picked by a silent order of nuns in the south of France. New, incredibly expensive and Suzanne will *love* them – a huge talking point at her next dinner party. I need someone to get hold of a couple of other types of vanilla beans, cook a few things, and then decide that the ones the nuns make are totally Must Have. I'm thinking of the headline, "Bean There, Never Done That".' She smiled modestly. 'Anyone volunteering?'

There was a lengthy pause while everyone looked studiously down at the table. No one really wanted to waste their time on Trials of Style, where they wouldn't even get their by-line on the page. Clare had managed to avoid the page for her entire career at the magazine. 'I'm a writer. I don't want to sit around tossing up about different types of throw rugs,' she'd once sniffed.

The Colonel looked around frostily. 'Here we go again. You know I can just nominate someone or we can have a volunteer. It's up to you.'

Isobel suddenly felt her hand shooting up in some kind of involuntary and embarrassing throwback to tenth grade.

'I can do it, Ms Hogan,' she faltered.

'Great, great. That's what I like to see, hands up, shoulders to the wheel. Splendid. Here's the nun beans and Gina has the petty cash so you can pick up a few other brands yourself. Don't forget, Isobel, the nuns have to win. If that's it then, we can all go back to work.'

Isobel was hurrying out of the conference, relieved to be getting back to her photocopying, when The Colonel marched up beside her.

'Isobel, got a moment?'

Then without waiting for an answer, The Colonel swung into her office and Isobel meekly followed.

The Colonel held court from behind a vast antique desk with an old-fashioned padded leather top. She was perched on the edge of an impressive chair upholstered in green leather, holes worn away in the arms where her elbows had dug in over the years. In such a vast space, her wizened little body looked even smaller. She was dressed as always in her working uniform, a simple grey Armani suit with a touch of white around the neckline, as recommended by Coco Chanel.

Flipping a strangely out-sized silver pen from one little paw to the other, she bestowed upon Isobel that warm smile she kept specially for situations she liked to think of as 'office pastoral care'.

Isobel found it scary as hell.

'Now,' said The Colonel. 'How are you settling in to our little *Verve* family?'

'Oh, fine, it's all fine. Everyone has been very welcoming,' Isobel babbled. 'And I do think it's great to see the office. I mean, I've been reading *Verve* for years, long before Clare started working here. Of course, it's always hard to get used to a strange workplace. You know, that terrible first day where you don't go to the loo because you're too embarrassed to ask the way and then when you do go you get lost on the way back and end up trying to walk into the cleaner's closet in front of everyone. Although, actually you probably don't remember that feeling, or if you did it was such a long time ago . . .'

The lucid part of her brain that was still functioning wondered with rising panic if she was ever going to be able to stop gabbling. Maybe she and The Colonel would be found here in twenty years' time, Hogan dead from old age and Isobel still blathering about bathrooms.

After four years of a relatively authority-free existence (if you didn't count that dragon of a nursing sister at the Mother and Infant Clinic) it was nerve-racking for Isobel having a 'boss', even for two weeks. Every time The Colonel called her into the editor's office, Isobel's nerves jangled. She felt like a schoolgirl about to be hauled over the coals by the headmistress for some prank. She had to keep reminding herself that she was thirty-six years old, which only gave Helen Hogan a headstart of half a century or so.

The Colonel broke in briskly.

'Excellent, excellent. Now my dear, I want you to do a little job for me.'

145

'Certainly,' Isobel said hastily.

'Clare told me you used to be a nurse.'

Isobel blinked. This was the last thing she had expected. 'Uh yes. That is, I quit about five years ago when I was going to have Ellen.'

'Perfect. It just so happens that we need someone to fill in on the problem page. "Dear Marion". The regular writer is away having a little cosmetic adjustment so someone needs to answer the letters for the next issue. I gave Clare a shot at it but it proved to be somewhat out of her range, whereas I think that you could be perfect – a mature woman, nurse, mother. Give the readers a Mum Steer, if you like,' The Colonel said airily.

'Oh,' Isobel gasped. 'I don't think I'd know what to say.'

'Nonsense my dear, just use your commonsense. And it won't have your name on it of course, so there's no need to feel self-conscious.' The Colonel gave her death's-head smile once more. 'You'll manage splendidly and it will give you a taste of what it's like to really work on the magazine. Just pass your copy on to me afterwards so I can give it the Magic Make-over. I'm sure you won't go wrong. One thousand words. On my desk by next Wednesday.'

'Oh but Ms Hogan . . .'

'Sorry my dear, no time for a chit chat. Love to but I've got So Much To Do About Nothing. Off you pop.'

Isobel reeled out of the room, almost colliding with William. He grabbed her by the shoulders.

'Ooop, sorry,' he apologised, steering her back towards Clare's desk. 'So, what on earth are you going to do with three different brands of vanilla bean?'

146

Isobel said dismally, 'At least I do know how to cook. But Ms Hogan just told me she wants me to do the answers for the problem page.'

She looked up at him in horror and saw that William had almost laughed at the sight of her sorrowful face.

'Well, if Derryn Hinch can do it, I can't see why Isobel Ashton can't have a bash,' William smiled at her, making his puppy-dog eyes crinkle up rather attractively around the edges. 'Don't look so miserable about it.'

'I can't help it. I feel miserable. I feel even more miserable than I look. The whole thing terrifies me. Rating vanilla beans is okay but solving readers' problems is something else. I'm not a psychologist and I'm not a writer either.'

In fact, Isobel realised that she hadn't written anything more elaborate than the Christmas family newsletter for years. The thought of trying to write a bona fide magazine column made her feel ill. Being at home with children had its moments but she'd never felt this nauseating fear of failing or embarrassing herself, not since the days when she was a trainee nurse. And she hadn't missed it. Forget all that stuff about facing the fear and doing it anyway, the truth is that it's always so much more comfortable just to avoid the fear in the first place. Isobel yearned for the peaceful rhythms of her life at home. Even if Ellen was pouting and Alex was screaming, it was better than this feeling that her gut was flopping about like a dying fish.

'It won't be that bad,' William reassured. 'Just imagine the letters are from your best friend asking for some sensible advice. We could even go out to lunch tomorrow and nut out some answers together if you like.'

'Oh,' Isobel clasped his arm fervently. 'Would you do that? That would be fantastic.'

She darted back to Clare's desk thinking maybe it wouldn't all be impossible after all. William just seemed so – *nice*. And she was rather proud that she'd had the guts to actually volunteer for something, even if it was just Trials of Style. Since giving up work, Isobel had developed a phobia about speaking in public. She'd never even dared to volunteer to be on the Neighbourhood Watch committee for fear of blushing and stammering whenever she had to speak in front of people.

But this time, Iso thought, sitting down in Clare's chair, she'd actually had the nerve to speak out in front of the whole table and volunteer for a job. She would have loved to be able to call Clare and tell her about it.

The place was packed to its shamrock-green walls with a dark sea of business suits. Isobel and Fiona shoved their way through the crowd to one of the few vacant tables which happened to be right next to a loud speaker. Isobel had a strong intuition that she did not want to hear fiddle music played at quite that volume but there wasn't much she could do about it.

In fact, she'd tried to weasle out of coming for an after-work drink with Fiona at all. After an afternoon spent looking desperately through the 'Dear Marion' folder, she wanted to creep home. Guiltily she remembered all the times she'd piously lectured Clare, telling her that if she didn't go out and socialise more, she'd never meet 'the right man'. Now she understood why going out after work wasn't always an easy thing to do.

Fiona, however, had laughed away her refusal, and

taken her round the corner to Fergus McFingall's, a cod-Irish pub complete with Guinness on tap, a short fiddle player in a peaked hat and a fake peat log fireplace. It was ghastly.

'So what will it be?' shouted Fiona over the noise. 'My round.'

Isobel asked for a gin and tonic and watched Fiona disappear into the throng.

'I felt bad for you in the conference today. I wanted to say something about it before now but I didn't know how to put it,' said Isobel when Fiona had returned with the drinks and sat down.

'Oh don't worry about it.' Fiona slurped her light beer. 'The old cow just needs to kick someone's head in every so often. That's The Colonel's definition of a work out. Doesn't bother me, though it means I have to go back to those women and harass them to let us take a peek under their Yves St Laurent lingerie. The journalistic equivalent of "Show us ya tits".'

Isobel blushed. Fiona was such a lovely person, she thought, but so – *frank*. 'I have to say you seemed to handle it well,' she said sincerely. 'If it had been me, I think I would have been in tears under the table.'

'I'll let you in on a secret,' Fiona leant towards her conspiratorially. 'It's the way I've figured out how to survive this business. Fake it. You just pretend to be the kind of person you'd like to be in a tricky situation. Sometimes I might say to myself, "Now how would Germaine Greer handle this situation?" Or the Queen or Jackie O or anyone else I think might help. Then I pretend to be that person. Works every time. Or helps at least,' she amended.

Isobel was intrigued. 'So what were you saying to yourself in the meeting?' she asked curiously.

'I actually said, "What would Jane Austen do?" I decided she'd probably be outwardly polite but inwardly scathing and make some cutting remark to herself about how The Colonel will probably die of fright one day when she stumbles upon a mirror unexpectedly. So I just pretended to be calm and inwardly amused.'

Isobel tried to think of ways in which she could apply this theory to her own life. God knows there were plenty of times when she felt out of her depth and wished someone else was there to handle things for her. 'So I should be just pretending that I'm an agony aunt?' she asked, hesitating.

'Exactly,' Fiona said triumphantly. 'But even better: pretend you're an expert at it. Pretend you're Dorothy Dix meets Dorothy Parker. Have fun with it. It probably takes no more imagination than you use every night to tell bedtime stories to the kids.'

Isobel thought she could give it a go. Even though, she added to herself with strict honesty, she did tell pretty boring bedtime stories. Clare's were much better.

'So is this the sort of place people come to meet men,' she asked, looking around. 'There seems to be an awful lot of them about and it looks like they're all casing the crowd.'

'Well, you can ...' said Fiona. 'It just depends on whether you have the energy.'

'Energy?' Isobel asked, wondering if there was going to be folk dancing down the track or some other physical exertions. She hoped not; her feet were killing her as it was.

'It takes a bit of energy to go through the whole chat up process,' Fiona explained. 'You have to think of things to say to a stranger with whom you have nothing in common. Then you have to flirt, look gorgeous and, at the same time, size them up to see if they're a creep or not. Hard work.'

She tore open a packet of crisps with her strong white teeth. 'I don't think I'm going to bother ever again. The whole dating thing. I mean, you get to a certain age and it just makes you feel tired to think of having to go through that process again. Hearing about his terrible mother or his authoritarian father or the awful man his sister married. You can just imagine your future unrolling endlessly before you, hours of listening to him bang on about his family or having to go to tense dinners at the sister's house. And what do you get in return? A few months of mind-blowing sex and then someone to keep the bed warm at night. I can get the sex elsewhere and my dogs and Mum's hand-knitted bed socks do a fine job of keeping me warm.'

'But isn't it about having someone in your corner?' Isobel said. 'Because, in the end, people give their ultimate loyalty to their spouse or their lover. They're the people who are really on your side. I think being single must be incredibly lonely because, when the chips are down, you're by yourself.'

'Ah, but when the chips are down we are always by ourselves,' Fiona said. 'Marriage just gives you an excuse to pretend otherwise.'

'That's so cynical,' Isobel protested, stirring her drink with the straw. 'You know, I think looking for the right man is a bit like losing your virginity. The longer you put it off the more difficult it becomes. When I got married in my early twenties, I just thought Phil was a man who I loved and he'd make a great father. That was good enough for me then. But the longer you leave it, the fussier you get. You know a lot more, you get more attached to your freedom and your independence. Someone would have to be pretty special to make you want to give up your autonomy. Or that's how I read it.'

Isobel looked around the pub with a shudder. All that noise, all those men leaning in to leer invitingly at all those women, everyone shouting at each other. It felt loud and cold and unkind. She could never imagine herself actually trying to 'meet someone special' at a place like this. And what were the chances of running into someone compatible? What was the chance that you'd end up talking about anything apart from star signs, football and the final episode of 'Seinfeld'?

'So where do you go to meet good men these days?' she asked.

'Ha!! The jackpot question!' Fiona yelped. 'Every single woman in her thirties is asking it. You can go to a place like this, which means you have to sift through the dregs who just want to work their way through their latest packet of condoms as quickly as possible. Or you can try to take up a hobby, but it's no use doing something like a reading group, which will be packed with other women, you have to take up abseiling or mountain-bike riding or some gruesomely sporty thing like that. Most people just hope to meet someone at work, which is where everyone spends most of their day anyway.'

'There's always William ...' Isobel suggested tentatively.

'Ah Will,' Fiona sighed affectionately. 'He's so nice. Thank heavens for William. The office would be a bear pit without him.'

'I think he is genuinely gorgeous,' insisted Isobel. 'So, have you ever seriously considered him? I think you two would be great together.'

Fiona shifted the coaster around on the table.

'Well ...' she said hesitantly. 'Just between us, I might have. But it seemed too difficult. First of all, we work in the same office which is always a trap. I mean, if it doesn't work out, one of you has to go and it'd be more likely to be me than the deputy editor. In fact, he's sort of my boss in a way. And I've always thought he had a thing for Clare. I think he just sees me as a buddy.'

Isobel leant forward excitedly. 'But that's fantastic. I think the best relationships are really friendships. They're the kind that endure. Are you *sure* you don't ever think how good it would be to have a man around?'

Fiona shrugged. 'Maybe, but just because you "have a man around" doesn't mean that you're guaranteed a lifetime of passion and romance.'

'Believe me, there's more to marriage than passion,' Isobel said, with feeling, thinking that sometimes she would trade all the sex in the world for one child-free weekend every month.

'So that's exactly my point,' Fiona exclaimed, banging the coaster down on the table. 'Why get married at all? You're poor, you lose your sex drive, you get bored, your dogs get sent outside to sleep and you have to spend a lot of extra time picking up after a man who doesn't even realise you're doing it so never says thank you. Is it worth it?'

'Of course it's worth it,' Isobel said. 'It's seen as a sell-out these days if you say you want to take care of another person, but I think it's the best thing you can do with your life. Or part of your life anyway,' she amended, because she didn't want to sound like some kind of domestic doormat.

Fiona sighed. 'I'm not sure I'm the type. I like to have things my way. I guess there are times when I'd like to have someone I feel comfortable with around. You know, someone who likes the dogs and who'll listen to me crap on about work. I can even take him home to the family Christmas party so I don't have to listen to all the aunts grilling me about when I'm going to settle down. But there's a trade-off, isn't there? I mean, you lose some of your independence. I hate that word compromise.'

'It's worth it,' Isobel insisted.

'So you're genuinely happy?' Fiona asked.

'Yes,' Isobel said. 'Yes, I really am.' And right then she did believe it. Her bright little house seemed like heaven compared with this dark, smoky, loud room.

'Well good for you,' Fiona stretched. 'Look, I'm bushed and I've got a big day tomorrow trying to inveigle women into letting us see their breasts. I'll split a taxi with you, if you like. The puppies will be pining for me, anyway.'

When she got home to a dark flat and an indignant cat, Isobel saw the answer machine light was flashing. Her heart gave a lurch. Breathlessly, she imagined pressing the green button to hear that Ellie had been taken to hospital with an asthma attack or Phil had been run over by a bus on his way home from work.

With her coat still on, she tottered across the room to the evil winking red eye on the machine. She pressed down the play button with cold fingers.

'Babe, pick up,' said a voice that Isobel didn't immediately recognise. 'Are you there? Just got back into town and I'm looking forward to seeing you. I'll come over tomorrow night and we can have dinner or whatever. The film is amazing. I think this one is going to be the big one. See you at the usual time. *Ciaou bella.*'

Clare must have forgotten to tell Leo about the 'Sister Pact', Isobel thought, vexed. And, short of ringing Clare to get Leo's unlisted phone number, she couldn't think how she could get in touch with him to let him know that his 'babe' was living in the suburbs for a week. Yet Clare had made her promise that, bar emergencies, there would be no contact between them until Sunday when they would meet up to swap notes before going home for the day.

Still frowning, Isobel peeled off her coat. It was only 9.30 and she wanted to make a start on some 'Trials of Style' cooking. She changed into trackpants and a thick jumper and then went over to light Clare's gas heater. After years of central heating she'd forgotten what it was like to come home to a freezing cold house.

Fetching the packets of vanilla beans out of her bag, she decided that Clare's kitchen could probably stretch to caramel custards. Letting the different types of beans infuse in three different pots of scalding milk, Isobel flicked on the oven and then made herself a mug of black tea, thinking how much she liked Fiona. Of all Clare's friends, she was the one who seemed the most down-to-earth and likeable.

Isobel fossicked through Clare's cupboards until she unearthed some ancient caster sugar and measured it out roughly (Clare's kitchen didn't seem to stretch to anything as precise as a tablespoon measure). As she was meditatively boiling the sugar and water together in a small saucepan waiting for them to caramelise, Isobel thought what a shame it was that Fiona was still single. Dogs were all very well, but a dog doesn't give you a hug. A dog can't offer advice. A dog won't get up on the roof and clear out the gutters. And Fiona was so warm hearted and easygoing, she'd make someone a dream wife. A dream mother, too.

When the caramel was honey-golden, Isobel snatched the saucepan quickly off the heat and waited till the bubbles subsided. Then she found three small china dishes from the back of a cupboard and gave then a quick rinse under the hot water tap just to be on the safe side. She quickly poured a little caramel syrup into the bottom of each and swirled them around to coat the sides. She carefully wrote down which vanilla bean flavoured milk was going in which pot, so she would remember when it came to the taste test the next day.

Whisking together eggs, egg yolk and more caster sugar, Isobel concluded that Fiona and William would be brilliant together. They worked in the same field, they had similar interests, they were both obviously home bodies. Sure, William had once made some passing reference to a dog-hair allergy but that was something that could be fixed. Desensitising shots or something, Isobel thought vaguely.

156

She divided the egg mixture into three, and poured a different milk into each of them, breathing in deeply the comforting, sleepy smell of warm milk and vanilla. She whisked each bowl, while she imagined Fiona and Will sharing a little terrace house. She could just see William cooking up the evening meal while Fiona took the schnauzers out for a walk. Then the whole family would curl about together in the living room in front of the open fire, the dogs lying on the hearth rug, Fiona toasting marshmallows, William reading aloud from *The New York Review of Books* ... Isobel could almost smell the burnt vanillery smell of the marshmallows and hear the wuffling sighs of the dogs.

Straining custard into each dish, she decided that these two people had potential that was too good to waste. If Fiona and William couldn't see they were made for each other, then Isobel would just have to help them by opening their eyes a little.

She put each dish in a baking tray and carefully poured in water so the china dishes sat in their own little bath, and then loaded them into the oven. As the rich smell of baking custard filled the flat, sending Barchester into a frenzy of mews and leg rubs, Isobel felt almost happy again.

She might have doubts about her ability to be a magazine agony aunt, but she was sure she could open the eyes of two star-crossed lovers. She'd often thought of herself as a bit of a life counsellor. After all, she'd had years of practising with Clare.

CHAPTER 8

Clare was feeling pretty satisfied with herself. She hadn't managed to whip up any recipes featuring impressive use of the bain marie method, but she had managed to bake some coconut cookies for the Fast Track kindergarten fundraiser.

Admittedly, they were a little over-cooked on the bottom but she'd bundled them up in cellophane bags sprinkled with gold stars, and tied the top with gold and silver satin ribbons. She thought they looked gorgeous.

Seeking any excuse to avoid the chore of loading two small children in and out of the car, Clare had walked over to the kindergarten, pushing Alex in his pram with Ellen clinging to one of Clare's hands and dragging her feet. It wasn't that Ellen didn't like her new kindergarten, it was just that she seemed to have an innate reluctance to do anything according to a schedule. It drove Clare nuts.

She always seemed to be scrambling behind schedule herself. And today would be no different. At least she'd given that Babyrobics the flick. Why do it? Alex hated it. So days that were filled with doing virtually nothing flew by and still she hadn't got the ironing done.

This morning Phil had wandered into the kitchen and asked, 'Are my sandwiches in the fridge?' He didn't bat an eyelid at finding her vacuuming the top of the kitchen bench.

'Sorry Phil. I ran out of time,' Clare had said, turning off the machine. 'You'll just have to buy something, or slap them together yourself. See you tonight.' She'd smiled apologetically. 'Look, I hope dinner will be a bit better than last night. Sorry again about the meal. I had no idea lamb could go that hard ...'

'Me neither,' he said, grinning. 'But it made an excellent teeth-cleaning implement for Daisy. And I liked the fish and chips. Haven't done that for years.'

She'd watched him mooch off and felt vaguely shame-faced about his bloody sandwiches, until she decided that this guilt was inappropriate (a word much favoured by her third therapist, the feminist one).

After all, if she was looking after two small children, and trying to keep the house clean – well, *reasonably* clean – it didn't seem too much for Phil, a fully functioning adult, to pack his own lunch. Especially if he was perverse enough to want something as archaic as a packed lunch in the first place.

It was amazing, she thought peevishly, that no matter how zoo-like the house became in the mornings, Phil quietly ignored the chaos. On weekends and holidays, he had always seemed such a keen father, happily helping dress the kids or patiently teaching Ellen how to weed between the plants. Clare had unthinkingly popped him in the Sensitive New Age But Boring (SNABB) box in her mind. Yet during the week he was totally focused on his own working day. He steadily went about his routine of getting ready for work oblivious to the mayhem around him: shaving methodically, knotting his tie perfectly, wiping his shoes over one more time to make them gleam. It made Clare want to spit; evidently the Ashton household had strict demarcation of responsibilities.

Clare frowned as she shoved the stroller through the gate of the kindergarten, which was standing in its garden like a gingerbread cottage.

Isobel had explained that the Fast Track teaching method would give Ellen a competitive head start for school. She would learn her letters and numbers, not to mention some basic French. Clare couldn't see the point in a four-year-old speaking French unless the four-year-old happened to be French, but Ellie seemed to enjoy it anyway.

Clare headed a little shyly toward the trestle table she could see had been set up next to the playground. She jumped nervously when Skandi pounced on her. They'd met earlier in the week but Clare was impressed that the teacher remembered her name so effortlessly.

'Hello Clare,' Skandi said energetically. Today she was wearing a green pants suit which made her look more like an elf than ever. 'Fantastic to see you at the fund-raiser. Anything to report from home?'

'Uh, no,' said Clare, feeling guilty that she didn't have anything to report (like Ellen had just whipped through *Le Rouge et Le Noir* for bedtime reading).

'Well that's fine, as long as there are no problems. You might like to spend a little more time going over Ellen's numbers at night. I noticed she was struggling a bit on Wednesday.'

'Sure, sure, we'll do that,' Clare said apologetically.

'Fantastic. A little less time in front of *The Lion King* perhaps. Ellen has told me that's her favourite video and Aunty Clare is very fun because she lets her watch it whenever she wants.'

'Oh, er, yes,' said Clare, thinking venomous thoughts about small children with big mouths.

'Well, I'll let you get over to the table. Margaret is in charge so just see her if you have anything to contribute. I must get on. I see Bradley is about to put on one of his performances . . .' and Skandi tripped daintily away.

Clare looked after her, surprising herself by feeling a little envious. Not that she would personally want to spend her days prying sobbing children off their mother's legs and dragging them away to French lessons but here was someone who seemed to know exactly what she wanted to do with her life and was happy to be doing it. Skandi probably woke up like those absurd people in mattress ads, with a big, white smile and wide open arms stretching out to welcome another fun-filled day.

'Can I go an' play?' Ellen said, impatiently tugging at her hand and looking longingly at the play equipment.

'Yes, sure. I'll be over near that table if you need me,' Clare said reluctantly. She felt half-inclined to keep Ellen with her as a shield but she knew that was cowardly. She hung back, watching Ellen trot over to the playground, but then Lexxie muttered in his sleep so she had to get the pram moving before he woke up.

She covertly surveyed the women as she bumped her way across the lawn. Isobel had told her that she hadn't made any friends at the new kindergarten so far, and Clare was not surprised. By the look of them, Iso would either have to take up tennis or develop a liking for ash blonde hair and headbands if she wanted to fit in. Clare felt sure that her non-maternal status stood out like a big neon sign above her head, flashing 'HAS NEVER BEEN THROUGH LABOUR' or 'UNWILLING TO BECOME ADULT' or, even worse, 'NO MAN WOULD TRUST HER TO HAVE HIS CHILDREN'.

She pushed the pram towards the table, which was laden with jams, chutneys, cakes and biscuits. Self-consciously, Clare fetched out her own bags of biscuits and handed them over.

'Well, they look most acceptable,' declared Margaret, who was presiding with Thatcherite authority over the table. 'Now where did you buy those?'

'I didn't. I made them this morning,' Clare said composedly, watching her glittery little bags join the other stuff on the table.

'Yes, of course. And I've always thought that anyone, no matter how domestically inept, can cook a batch of biscuits. I have no time for these packet mixes,' Margaret sniffed, writing out price stickers for Clare's biscuits in precise little figures.

Today Margaret was wearing the most extraordinary safari suit, circa early seventies, Al Grassby. To stay warm she'd teamed it with a mustard-coloured jumper worn underneath the safari jacket.

Clare felt she was gaping slightly, so hastily turned away, but not before she noticed that Margaret was giving a similarly supercilious look at Clare's own outfit. Obviously chunky black boots, black jodhpurs and a cropped jumper were not suitable wear for a kindie mum.

Standing a little off to one side, Clare had the satisfaction of seeing every one of her cookie bags sold, although she was glad she wouldn't be around when people got them home and found all the bottoms were blackened. She herself bought a chocolate cake, a pot of home-made plum jam for Phil's breakfast and a crochet bag for holding cotton wool balls in the bathroom (admittedly she got a trifle carried away at that point).

Then she stood by herself near the playground, watching Ellen play while Alex sat on his blanket at her feet trying to stuff the crochet bag into his mouth.

Clare was surprised when some of the other women smiled at her. Isobel's stories had made Clare assume that young mothers spent their time in competition with each other, telling Sheila Kitzinger-inspired fibs about how their birth contractions felt like orgasms, or boasting about toilet-training achievements.

But standing around the playground, these women seemed at least willing to be friendly. Clare found she even felt quite proprietorially proud of Alex, grinning wildly at everyone in his red hand-knitted jumper and matching tartan cap.

'What a sweetie,' one of the mothers said. About Clare's age, she had an open face and a honey-blonde ponytail that made Clare think of the cheerleaders in the teen novels she'd devoured during adolescence.

Clare was tempted to pretend that she was Alex and Ellen's mother for a flicker of time, but then figured she was bound to get caught out. Some of these women must know Iso. Besides, this bouncily healthy young woman would probably want to talk about daunting Sheila Kitzinger–type experiences.

'I'm his aunty,' Clare confessed. 'I'm just looking after Alex and his sister Ellie for a fortnight.'

'Lucky parents!' the woman said, laughing.

Clare was about to reply when she was distracted by some screeching from the playground.

'Oh no, that's Ellie,' she muttered. 'Could you keep an eye on Lexxie for me?'

The woman nodded, and Clare dived into the playground, which was like some kind of swarming Osh Kosh antheap. Under the slide, she found Ellen and another little girl rolling around in the chip bark, squealing like piglets.

'Ellen!' Clare reached in to pull the little girls apart. At the same time another pair of hands lunged in to grab the other child.

'Jessica!' a voice said.

Straightening up, with Ellen in her arms, Clare came face-to-face with a man. Evidently he was the father of the little girl.

'I'm sorry. I don't know what was going on there,' Clare said.

'Then you shouldn't apologise,' he replied calmly.

Startled, she took another look at him. It was quite incongruous to see a man among this sea of women and infants. He was unremarkable in almost every way: youngish, shortish, with light-brown hair. He did have those kind of starry eyes that seemed to twinkle all the time, Clare noted with irritation. She hated eyes like that. Or at least, she'd never been able to understand why some people had them and the rest of the people, ie Clare

Callaway, just had ordinary, old, normal, untwinkling eyes.

'She pushed me,' Ellen started to whine and wriggle.

'Did not,' said the other little girl, who was clinging to her father's leg.

'Did too,' said Ellen.

'Enough,' said the father. 'If there's anything worse than girls who brawl, it's girls who start doing that unimaginative "did not, did too" routine. I think you should both apologise to each other for not playing properly together.'

Jessie, a stocky little girl with an uncompromising bob haircut, stuck out her bottom lip mulishly.

The man bent down and said to her softly, 'C'mon princess, you know the right thing to do.'

'Okay,' the little girl muttered. 'Sorry.'

Clare, who had been impressed by the calm and yet authoritative way in which this man had handled his daughter, put Ellen down on the ground and turned her round to face the other little girl.

'Your turn,' she told her.

Ellen smiled suddenly. 'Sorry Jessie. Do you want to go first on the slide?'

The other little girl nodded and the two of them scampered away.

'Another crisis averted in high-level peace talks,' the man said, grinning at Clare. 'Would you like a cup of tea?'

Clare agreed straight away, then remembered with a pang of guilt that she'd left Lexxie with a virtual stranger.

'I just have to go and grab the baby,' she muttered.

When she'd fetched Alex and the stroller back from the friendly cheerleader woman, Clare found that Jessica's father already had two polystyrene cups of tea, a plate of shortbread biscuits and a couple of folding chairs.

'May as well make ourselves comfortable. They'll probably be playing together for the next hour,' he said, setting up the chairs and spreading out the instant picnic on the grass. 'I'm Rory Maguire by the way. And that little warrior princess was my daughter, Jess.'

Clare shook the man's hand with her firm, professional handshake.

'Hi, I'm Clare Callaway,' she said. 'And this is Alex and that was Ellen. They're actually my sister's children and I'm looking after them for a couple of weeks. You might know her, Isobel Ashton?'

'Of course I know Isobel. She's that tall, dark and rather beautiful girl?' He smiled.

'That's her,' said Clare, suddenly mortifyingly conscious of her own barely made-up face and lank hair.

'She's a bit shy, isn't she? I've asked her round to my place for coffee a few times because Ellen and Jessie get on well. Or they usually do! But I've never been able to tempt Isobel to come over.'

Clare thought wryly that this was typical of Isobel. Give her an invitation from a friendly, personable man with nice eyes and a good smile and she'd insist on staying home to disinfect the bathrooms.

'She takes a little while to get to know people,' Clare explained. 'Maybe when she comes home I can threaten to do something unspeakable, like cook her a meal, if she doesn't become a bit more sociable. If you'd experienced my cooking, you'd know how effective that could be.'

Rory laughed. He had a good laugh too, warm and well-used. They sat down facing the playground so they could keep an eye on Ellen and Jessie, who had now moved on to the swings.

'So has your sister gone away on holidays?' Rory asked, passing over a cup of tea.

Clare explained quickly about the sister swap idea. 'I've got one more week to go after this,' she said. She put Alex into his stroller and then gave him a biscuit to suck.

'I bet it's harder than you thought,' Rory commented. 'I'm a single dad so I have Jess to myself all the time. When you're doing it by yourself, you can't even have a change of shifts. It's always your turn. Still, I wouldn't be without her. But then, I guess I have to say that now.' He quirked one eyebrow at Clare.

'Of course, I absolutely love the kids,' Clare declared enthusiastically. For some reason she didn't want to seem like an unmaternal, hard-headed career woman in front of this man. 'In fact, that's the reason I wanted to do the Sister Pact story in the first place. I thought it would be fantastic to get a chance to spend two weeks with Ellie and Alex. We've always been incredibly close. And it's a real privilege to be able to spend time with them, just doing all those little things.'

'Oh I can see that you get on well with them,' Rory said. 'You waded into that fray out there like a professional.'

'They're a joy.' Clare shifted the stroller around so Alex, who was dropping off to sleep, would be out of the direct light of the sun. She tucked the blanket in around him, wondering whether she looked maternal as she did this. It was irritating, she suddenly thought, this self-consciousness about how you looked to other people. She wondered if it was just women who felt like that, or whether men ever felt on display too. More likely it was a female thing, she decided. And then stroked Alex softly on the head.

'So what do you do?' she asked. She thought that Rory Maguire was a pleasant-looking man but there was nothing really outstanding about him, except those eyes. She mentally compared him to Leo, who had a tall lean body, tangled dark hair and hollow writer's eyes. Even if she'd seen Leo in a bus shelter she would have known there was something special about him.

'I'm a landscape architect,' Rory explained. 'I run my own company which, in some moment of madness, I called Scape-Scope. I must have been pissed. Only four days a week though, so I have more time at home with Jess.'

Clare glanced down at his hands which were big and broad, with capable but perfectly clean fingers.

'So is that just an arty way of saying you're a kind of – gardener?' she asked.

'No. More a green way of saying I'm a kind of architect. We plan gardens, but we also do outdoor spaces, such as squares or city parks, and we do the landscaping round big buildings, hospitals, office complexes, that sort of thing,' he clarified.

Clare felt embarrassed by her display of ignorance. 'Sorry, you must get the gardening thing all the time.'

'Of course. Still you're a journalist, I guess I have to expect you to think in clichés.'

She glanced at him sharply and then saw that he was teasing. His eyes gleamed and he looked momentarily very attractive.

'We prefer to think of them as universal truths,' she said primly.

'Oh Rory, thank heavens I found you.' Margaret came panting up, all sweaty face and flyaway hair. 'Disaster has struck. We're just about to do the raffle draw and I've discovered the barrel doesn't spin any more. You're so wonderful with fixing things, could you come and get this right for me?'

'Sure,' Rory said easily. 'Sorry Clare, I'll have to leave you to it for a while.'

'Oh Clare,' Margaret said. 'I didn't see you sitting down there. I'm sure you won't mind if I borrow Rory, will you? You can't monopolise him all day you know,' she added archly.

'No trouble at all,' said Clare, nettled by Margaret's assumption that she would want to monopolise this man and even more nettled by her interrupting their conversation.

'It was nice to meet you,' Rory said. 'Maybe I could persuade you to bring Ellen over to play one day next week? Jess would love it. I have Tuesdays at home.'

Clare hesitated. 'Oh – maybe. I'm not sure about our plans for next week yet.'

'Okay. I'll just give you my number and you can give me a call if you're going to come. Bring the whole family. I've got a big garden with a sandpit so the little fella will probably enjoy it as well.'

While Margaret looked on with avid, beady-eyed interest, Rory wrote a phone number on the back of a bright yellow business card and handed it over. Clare took it, conscious of Margaret lapping up every move.

'And, by the way, I bought some of your delicious-looking coconut cookies,' Rory said casually. 'Margaret made a big point of telling me that you cooked them yourself. So if you come over, we can have them for afternoon tea.'

'How wonderful,' Clare said.

As she pushed the stroller home, half-listening to Ellen burble away about her day, Clare took out the business card for another look. It had 'SCAPE-SCOPE' printed on the front in bold green letters, and underneath was printed 'Rory Maguire, managing director/vice-president of marketing/cleaner'. Clare smiled and then wondered about the coffee invitation. Was it a 'cup of coffee while the kids play' type cup of coffee? Or was it a 'getting to know you better over the safe neutrality of a cup of coffee', cup of coffee?

She could have sworn that he was attracted to her; there was something flirtatious about the way he looked at her when he handed over his phone number. On the other hand, he had already said that he wanted to invite Isobel and Ellen over previously. Surely he wouldn't have been planning to make a play for Isobel, a married woman, no matter how 'tall, dark and beautiful' he thought her?

Clare knew she wouldn't be interested in a single father called Rory. She already had the infuriatingly attractive Leo, and she didn't see any reason why she'd swap him for a sandy-looking man with twinkling eyes.

Granted, Rory seemed perfectly nice, not to mention funny and intelligent, and she'd definitely liked the way he had teased her. She also liked those big capable hands. While Margaret was drawing the raffle (out of the effortlessly spinning barrel), Clare had found herself standing there staring at Rory's hands. They were so different from Leo's long, white, thin hands.

But then the very fact that he was nice was a point against him. Clare never fancied men who were too nice, any more than she wanted to drink lemonade instead of tonic water or have chicken soup when she could be having curry laksa. Nice just wasn't her thing.

And what about that little girl? Clare had read (and written) countless stories about the nightmares of step-parenting – resentful, poisonous children and vengeful ex-wives lurking in the background and siphoning off half the income. Too many complications.

Back home, Clare parked Alex, who was still asleep in his stroller, in the corner of the family room, and plonked Ellen down in front of *The Aristocats*. Then, thankfully childfree for half an hour, she went into the kitchen to make a cup of coffee.

While she waited for the kettle to boil, she wondered idly what *Manifesting Your Man* had to say about step-parenting. She fetched it out of her bag and flipped through until she found the section where the authors dealt briefly with the subject.

BLENDED FAMILIES: Of course Mr Appropriate may have children from an earlier marriage. All we can say is, hey guys, life is not perfect. Cards on the table: children are going to make it so much harder to manifest your man. For a start, you will have to address a whole different agenda. Mr Appropriate will be looking at you as a potential

171

stepmom and will be assessing your performance with living, opinionated, often blood curdlingly difficult children. It's hard to look impressive in this complicated real-life situation. It's much, much easier to look like someone he can imagine cuddling his newborn baby to a generous milky bosom. The former requires diplomacy, skill and patience; the latter just requires you to keep your hair clean and gush whenever you visit friends who have babies.

If your man has children then, as surely as Scarlett went home to Tara, you'll have to sort out a relationship with them. Expect hostility, wariness and rejection, then you won't be disappointed. If there are children, at the very least they should have come from a previous marriage (a man who has children out of wedlock is not likely to be the man you want in your life). After that, the only advice we can offer you is: Don't try to be a mom to his children. He's still a single parent even if you do get it together. In the meantime, be tolerant, be patient and butt out most of the time. Good luck.

Clare closed the book and poured hot water over the instant coffee. It was a gloomy picture. She had a nightmare image of having to try to placate that stubborn-looking little girl with her pudding basin haircut. She saw that small children could be like big thorny hedges, leaving Prince Charming sleeping undisturbed in the castle in the middle.

Picking up her mug, she mentally shook herself. What on earth was she thinking? Rory Maguire was hardly Prince Charming. If she didn't get over this tendency to think of any man she met as a prospective father for her babies, she would have to shoot herself.

Seeing that Ellen was still enthralled by the
Clare decided to sit down at the kitchen table and mai
some notes for her *Verve* story. She figured she'd have
twenty minutes before Alex woke up and started
howling. If she used the time to put in a good chunk of
work on the story, she'd reward herself with two Tim
Tams with her coffee.

Clare sighed. At this rate of chocolate-biscuit consumption, by the time Leo saw her again she'd be as big
as a house. He frequently made disparaging comments
about women he regarded as overweight. Not quite
'Look at the arse on that', but nearly as bad.

'Clare, Clare, read me *The Cat in the Hat*.' Ellen came
up, slapping a book at her.

Clare sighed inwardly. She'd come to loathe and detest
those repetitive books. In fact, dodging book reading was
one of the skills she was starting to develop. If she could
deflect Ellen's attention to the television set or her train
set, it saved Clare from having to read any more drivel
about green eggs and ham or what do busy people do
all day. The trouble with kids was that as soon as they
finished the book, they wanted to start back at the beginning again. It was weird.

'Okay,' she agreed. 'Let me just go and grab a Tim
Tam. Want one?'

Clare trudged back into the kitchen.

Funny, all her dreams of holding a baby in her arms
had never seemed to include the fact that looking after
children could be so dreadfully, so relentlessly and so
monotonously *dull*.

CHAPTER 9

William dropped a small wooden letter opener on Isobel's desk. On the handle was inscribed 'A memory from Fiji'.

'I found this floating around my house last night and thought of you,' William said.

Fiona, who was passing by, guffawed. 'What's that Will? Something to stab herself with when it all gets too much working at *Verve*?' she joked.

William flushed. 'I just remembered Isobel saying that opening the mail every morning was a slow job. Thought this might help.'

'I'm sure it will,' Isobel said gravely.

'So, are you still on for lunch today?' William asked.

'Of course, I'd love to,' Isobel said. 'And it's my shout. If it's okay with you, Will, I've invited Fiona to come along too. I want to thank both of you for everything you've done for me this week.'

William's shoulders dropped just slightly. 'Oh, uh, of course. That would be great. The three of us.'

'See you then,' Fiona said, heading towards the library.

They went to the Italian bistro around the corner from the office, a place Fiona dubbed 'home away from *Verve*'. Nick, the surly owner, had opted for minimalist decor, just roughly painted cream walls and wooden tables. But Will and Fiona assured her that the pasta, whipped up by Nick's brother-in-law, was heaven-sent.

Isobel was interested by everything, from the glass of house wine Nick thumped grumpily in front of her to her view of a depressing city street on a grey winter day.

'We hardly ever go out to eat. It's too expensive and then we have to worry about babysitters. Alex is still a very clingy sort of baby,' she explained, scanning the menu. 'I hope Clare is coping with them. Today is kindergarten for Ellen and she also has to take Alex to Babyrobics, which he really hates.'

'Babyrobics?' echoed William, blinking.

'Oh a kind of health club for babies, really good for them. Development and so on. But he's a bit frightened of all the equipment.'

'So whaddya want?' demanded Nick, snatching his pencil from behind his ear.

'Oh, hi Nick,' William smiled warmly, eliciting from Nick a vague expression of disgust. 'What do you recommend?'

'Today's special is veal in a white wine and cream sauce. The rest is the same,' Nick said indifferently.

William chose the spaghetti marinara and Fiona her usual carbonara. Isobel dithered, then settled on the veal.

'So, the problem page,' William said.

'Oh God, "Marion",' Isobel said, conscious once more of her stomach fluttering nervously. 'Look, I really don't think I can do this. I've never written anything. I think I'll just have to go into Ms Hogan and tell her that I can't do it after all.'

She miserably imagined herself having to go in and confront the terrifying Ms Hogan with a refusal. It was hard to know which would be worse: failing at the job or having to say no to The Colonel.

'Nonsense,' Fiona said. 'Of course you can do it. It's no different from picking up the phone on a Friday night and listening to Clare bang on about her problems. All it takes is commonsense advice, and you can dish that out in spades. And if there's any research called for, there's the library, or I'd be happy to show you how to use the data base.'

'It sounds fairly simple when you put it like that . . .' Isobel said.

'Have a bash at it and bring it in to me on Tuesday and we'll work on it together before you give it to Helen,' Will said.

'That's incredibly nice of you. Both of you. You really are two very fantastic people,' Isobel said, looking meaningfully from one to the other.

But before she could capitalise on the moment, the meals arrived and everyone became distracted as Nick distributed the Parmesan cheese and the black pepper.

'So how is this twisted sister act going?' William asked, neatly wrapping his spaghetti in precise spirals around the tines of his fork.

'To be honest,' Isobel said glumly, 'I'm just hanging in there. In fact, I was thinking I might suggest to Clare on Sunday that we make it one week instead of two. I miss the kids, and Phil too, of course. And I'm just a bit –

well, it's hard to explain, it's like a strange blend of tedium and overstimulation.'

'Which bit is which?' Fiona asked.

'Oh you don't want to hear all the gruesome details . . .' Isobel said diffidently.

'Yes we absolutely do,' Fiona insisted. 'Tell all.'

Isobel found it was actually a relief to be able to talk honestly about her week. She felt she'd been doing so much polite and co-operative smiling for the last five days that her face was about to fall off.

'I have to admit I loathe having to get up every morning and go to Clare's gym and then try to make myself look corporate and battle through the traffic and the car fumes to get to an office by a certain time,' she said. 'Then I spend the day feeling uptight in case I get something wrong and make an idiot of myself. And every night I go home to this quiet, dark flat and Clare's cat just sits there on the other side of the door waiting for me. It's creepy. For five nights now I've hung about, watching rubbish on television just for the sake of having some noise in the flat and then gone to bed at 9.30.'

'And that must be so different from home,' prompted Fiona, who'd been over to Isobel's place for dinner a couple of times with Clare.

'Oh sure, when you have small children your life is always busy. Not to mention noisy,' Isobel said, using her paper napkin to wipe up the wet ring that her wine glass had left on the wooden table. 'There's always someone who needs you or something that needs to be done. Clare's life feels barren. I thought it would be magic to be able to lie around in my spare time and read all the books I've been meaning to catch up with and give myself pedicures. But I find myself picking up a book, reading for a few minutes and then stopping to listen to the sound of the fridge humming.'

William filled up her wine glass again. 'I expect you're just a bit lonely.'

Isobel smiled tremulously at him, suddenly grateful to have someone tell her what she was going through.

'That's it exactly. I really miss the physical contact too, the feeling of the kids hugging me and even Phil, who's like a big, solid, warm wall of flesh in bed . . .'

She stopped, a little embarrassed.

'Oh, sorry, I think I just got carried away.'

'Chick chat,' William said with a grin. 'I'll take it as a compliment.'

'He loves it,' said Fiona, rolling her eyes. 'So I guess you haven't heard how Clare is doing?'

'I speak to Phil every day so I know everyone is alive and kicking. But Clare and I have an agreement not to make contact until Sunday, unless there's some kind of emergency. I left instructions all over the house, even notes on how to use the bread machine so she can still cook their fresh bread for lunch every day. I hope the kids are behaving for her.'

'All the better if they're not,' Fiona said. 'This is her chance to discover whether she really wants to have kids or whether it's just that she's reached the age where all her friends are joining the motherhood club and she'd like to sign up as well because she can't bear to be left behind at anything.'

They paused as Nick strutted up to the table to snatch their empty plates as if he was convinced they were about to stash them under their coats and make a run for it.

'Would you like coffee?' William looked at Isobel and Fiona.

'Cappuccino,' Fiona said.

Nick rolled his eyes as if to suggest that now he'd seen the depths of human depravity.

'I'll have a latte. And Isobel . . .?' William said.

'Oh, not for me,' Isobel said hastily. 'I'm afraid I have to get back to the office to finish that, er, photocopying. But don't leave because of me. You two stay here and have coffee and a good chat and I'll fix up the bill on the way out. See you back there.'

'Oh no, we can come too,' William said.

'No, I insist. You've already ordered. I'll see you soon.'

Isobel slipped away, pausing by the cash register to hand over her credit card and sign the docket, before hurrying out into the street. As she passed the window, she waved gaily at Fi and Will.

She only hoped Fi would be smart enough to take advantage of an opportunity when it presented itself. Or was presented by a caring friend.

Smiling smugly, Isobel strode back to the office.

When the doorbell went, Barchester dived under the couch and Isobel took a deep breath. Then nervously smoothing down her long black skirt, she went to open the door.

Leo, who was lounging against the door frame, leant forward as if to kiss her and then pulled back in surprise.

'Isobel,' he said in his dark smoky voice.

'Oh hi, Leo. Come in,' Isobel pulled the door open wider.

She'd decided that, as she didn't have Leo's number,

she would simply wait for him to turn up for his date with Clare, and then suggest that he went out to dinner with her instead of the absent Clare. Frankly anything would be better than sitting around by herself for another night. And while she didn't regard Leo too warmly, he had to be better than Friday Night Football on the television.

Leo went through, looking around for Clare.

'She's not here,' Isobel said. 'She mustn't have had a chance to explain to you about this story for *Verve* . . .'

Leo's eyes narrowed. 'Story?'

Isobel sketched in details of the Sister Pact, and told him she'd explain the rest in the restaurant. That is, if he was willing to have dinner with her instead of Clare . . . It could be part of the swap. In a way, she added in a fluster.

Leo shrugged. 'Why not? We could just go down the Esplanade.'

'Great,' said Isobel, brightly. 'I'll grab my coat.'

Walking down to Acland Street, with him slouching along beside her, Isobel shot Leo covert looks. Dressed in black with his dark hair swept back from a high pale forehead, he was quite handsome in a wan kind of way, with a sharply intelligent, thin face and long fingered hands which he moved around a lot when he was talking.

Not that he was talking now – more like maintaining a moody silence. Perhaps he was angry with Clare for not filling him in on her plans, Isobel thought. Understandably. But at least this night would give her something else to write about in her Sister Pact story, apart from the *Verve* office and going straight home to

180

Clare's flat. She was beginning to worry that she would have nothing to say at the end of two weeks except a litany of complaints.

She wondered what kind of havoc the mischievous night breeze was going to play with her hair. She'd spent hours getting it to co-operate in a French roll. Getting ready for this 'date' had been a revelation in itself, she thought, as she tripped along beside Leo. She'd realised how many years it had been since she'd tried to doll herself up for any man. She'd put on too much make-up, then had wiped it off at the last minute. She'd fretted over what to wear. She'd decided to wear her hair up, then down, then put it up again. And then she'd sat on the couch waiting for the knock on the door, too edgy to read her book or concentrate on the evening news.

When they were threading their way through the Friday night crowds, Leo suddenly came to life.

'This will do,' he said. 'Do you like Malaysian?'

Not waiting for an answer, he steered her into a busy noodle cafe with modern jazz thundering out of the speakers. Once they were settled, Isobel was still floundering for something to say. She tried to explain a bit more about 'Operation Sister Pact' but now they were here, Leo didn't seem very interested.

Still, she felt compelled to try to entertain this man for no real reason except they were out to dinner as a couple and she had always subconsciously believed that it was the woman's job to keep the conversational ball rolling along.

Of course it had been a long time since she'd had to play Sheherezade. It was so easy with Phil. If they ever ended up in a restaurant, they exchanged easy, muted conversation – gossip about mutual friends, trivia about the kids, old jokes from a decade past, remarks about the other people in the restaurant. It was as comfortable for Isobel as being alone. In fact, they probably could have sat there quite happily in silence except Isobel was so conscious of not looking like one of those sad married couples who no longer talked to one another.

Now she felt she had to amuse this stranger. She hadn't liked Leo when Clare had brought him over for a meal one weekend. He struck her as too confident and full of himself, making no secret of the fact that he found his own life the most interesting thing in the room. And she could never forgive people who heard that Phil was an accountant and dismissed him as uninteresting from that moment on. It made her feel fiercely protective. He wasn't just an accountant, she told herself, he was a – a very important accountant who dealt with major companies.

She'd also been convinced that Clare's new boyfriend found her dreary, a boring mother-of-two whose idea of a great film would probably star Meg Ryan. Or perhaps that had just been her own paranoia. Clare seemed to have a knack of finding men with scarily impressive jobs and the ability to talk for at least ten minutes at a stretch without using any words under three syllables. They made Isobel feel inadequate.

But, like an old show pony hearing the band strike up once more, she smiled and urged him earnestly to tell her all about his film projects. She'd read years ago in a women's magazine that the way to make a man think you were interesting was to appear to be interested in

182

him. This had turned out to be true (unlike many things you read in women's magazines).

Leo talked fluently for most of the meal, only pausing long enough to slurp down a large bowl of hawker noodles. And he even turned out to be amusing, telling funny, malicious anecdotes about film sets and people in the film world who even Isobel had heard of.

When he talked about his plans for the future, he did so with a kind of ferocious passion that Isobel found fascinating and yet daunting. She'd never wanted anything that badly in her life, except the wellbeing of her children, and didn't everyone feel like that?

'So, do you ever talk about anything other than film-making?' she finally asked him, half-jokingly.

He smiled. 'No. Sometimes I talk about making television, just for a change, but I prefer film. Television is just what I write to pay the rent. Films are going to be my life's work. I could talk about films for a week and not get bored, although I guess I can't necessarily promise the same thing about the person on the other side of the table.'

He began tearing a piece of roti bread into tiny strips. 'I've been obsessed by films since my dad took me to see *Citizen Kane* when I was still a kid. I thought it was the most amazing experience I'd ever had. I'm going to get into directing eventually and if I could write and direct just one film as good as *Citizen Kane*, I think I could be content for the rest of my life.'

'You don't strike me as someone who'll ever feel especially content,' Isobel said thoughtfully. 'I mean, with your work that is. You'll probably clamber up one mountain and all you'll be able to think of is the one that's ahead. And the one after that. I think that would be an exhausting way to live your life.'

He shrugged. 'It doesn't feel exhausting to me. I'd say thrilling. In fact, that's what attracted me to Clare. She's got that same driven quality.'

'Clare?' said Isobel, wondering if they were talking about the same Clare. 'I've never thought of her as particularly ambitious.'

Leo raised his eyebrows. 'Of course she is. As soon as we met she was telling me that one day she wanted to take over *Verve* as editor, and then maybe go on to edit something big like *Vanity Fair*. She's really on a mission. I love that about her, that sense of purpose right from deep inside her gut. That's how I feel about filmmaking and I know Clare feels the same about her writing.'

Does she? Isobel thought to herself. As far as she knew Clare had never expressed any special ambitions to claw her way up the magazine hierarchy. She suspected Clare might have been doing a bit of judicious self-editing for Leo's consumption. But of course everyone did that early in a relationship. The whole unvarnished truth only came out down the track. Isobel remembered the early days with Phil when he managed to somehow convince her that he loved watching British costume dramas, thought giving her foot massages was fun and was keen for her to go on with her nursing career.

So now she just nodded at Leo. 'Clare is a fantastic writer. Still, it must be hard with two ambitious people in one relationship.'

'Why?' Leo asked. 'We think it's perfect. Means we're both busy so one of us isn't hanging around whining about needing more attention or "quality time". We just get on with our lives and spend time together when it suits both of us. It's the dream relationship.'

'And do you ever think about having children one day?' Isobel probed daringly.

'Oh kids,' Leo grinned. 'There's plenty of time for that for me. Maybe not for Clare but that's something she'll have to figure out. I personally think with her kind of career she'd be better off not having any kids at all. She could go a long way if she didn't have anything holding her back. Underneath it all, she already realises there's more to life than having a couple of amnio babies and ferrying them around from sports practice to ballet classes. Why else has she stayed single for so long?'

Annoyed, Isobel remembered all the things she'd disliked about Leo when she'd met him. His arrogance and his habit of making her own life seem very small. Sports practice and ballet classes indeed. (And what was wrong with that anyway?)

Leo tossed a piece of bread in his mouth. 'And, as for me, I'll wait till I'm set up financially. I know that by the time I get to LA, the money is going to be outrageously good. I want to own a couple of houses at least before I worry about whether I'm going to have kids.'

Isobel frowned even more. A couple of houses! She and Phil would be lucky to finish paying off their house by the time they hit sixty. Especially as they planned to send the children to private schools.

Isobel sat silently as the waiters handed over the dessert menus. But Leo was positively jovial when she decided to have banana fritters for dessert after already eating two different appetisers and a main course.

'You're so unlike Clare,' he exclaimed. 'She's always

picking at her plate and wanting to order steamed fish, hold the sauce.'

Isobel, who figured he was hinting that she was guzzling her food, reluctantly passed on the chocolates that came with coffee.

There was an embarrassing hiatus when the bill came and Leo left it in the middle of the table after checking the amount. When he made no move to get out his credit card, Isobel said hesitatingly, 'Er, the bill . . .'

He looked at her quizzically. 'I thought you'd be able to read it for yourself, it's fifty-eight dollars.'

'Oh, do you want me to pay?' Isobel began to quickly fumble for her purse.

'Of course not,' he said in surprise. 'We'll split it. Thirty bucks each.'

Her cheeks burning, Isobel reached in her bag, knowing she would not have enough cash and would have to put it on her credit card where Phil would find it in a month's time. She decided it was a bit rich that Leo was so insistent on going halves when he'd been boasting just a moment before about all the fabulous money he would be making soon.

Isobel thought that, back in the days when she was dating, men still paid for dinners. Obviously things had changed. But as she tossed her credit card on the saucer, and insisted on paying for the lot, she remembered how Clare had once lamented that relationships were expensive.

'Sometimes I think we kicked ourselves in the shins financially with feminism,' she recalled Clare saying. 'Every time I get a boyfriend and have all those movies and dinner and romantic little weekends away, it costs me an arm and a leg. Even if the bloke is earning twice as much as I am, I still pay my own way. It's almost enough to make me want to learn to cook so I can save some bucks by dishing up meals for him a home. Except then I'd still be paying, anyway.'

Isobel also remembered her own response. 'Equality has been the death of division of household chores too,' she'd grumbled. 'Men used to mow the lawns or take out the rubbish. Now women are able to do all that stuff but they still get stuck with the toilet bowl and the ironing. So we do the lot.'

Well, ain't that the truth, she thought now, scribbling her signature on the credit card docket that the waiter had left on the table.

'What are you smiling at in that Mona Lisa way?' asked Leo softly across the table.

Isobel was startled to feel a clutch of excitement in her stomach at his bold eye contact. The old stranger danger, said a detached small voice at the back of her mind.

'Nothing. Shall we head off?' she said quickly.

They wandered along the Esplanade for a while, then Leo announced: 'Hey, Luna Park is open. Do you want to go?'

Isobel, who was secretly longing to get home to bed, felt she would look suburban if she refused.

'Sure!' she cried, trying to inject her voice with devil-may-care gaiety.

It must have been more than two decades since she'd last gone to the amusement park. But she'd swear the park hadn't changed in all that time. It was still greasy and grubby and smelt of bad hamburgers, fairyfloss and sweat. The tawdry fairy lights strung across the power poles flickered in a wan attempt to conjure up a carnival atmosphere. The meagre crowd seemed to be made up of drug pushers and their customers, taking advantage of the many dark corners. Either that or sullen looking adolescent couples, the girls wearing spandex boob tubes and microskirts, the boys with thin ponytails and big boots.

Leo dragged her straight across to the Big Dipper. Isobel followed him apparently willingly. But the truth was she thought going on a rollercoaster was about as fun as an episiotomy.

For a start she was terrified that the carriages were going to bounce right off the track and they would all die. Then there was the fear that, even if there was no fatal accident, she might still scream or cry or even throw up all over her own lap out of sheer terror. She had never been good at daredevil experiences, unlike Clare who, as a child, was always the one pestering to go on the big slide or the fast pony, while Isobel preferred to be left in peace to read her books.

But she couldn't say any of this to Leo. He was lounging back, looking cool and yet just a bit crazy, like any self-respecting, self-conscious young movie writer.

He turned and gave her an encouraging grin. 'Here we go,' he said, picking up her sweaty hand, with a rather endearing childlike simplicity.

Isobel wondered if she should scribble some last minute words of maternal advice to Ellie and Alex on the back of her ticket. The problem was that she couldn't think of anything meaningful to say except perhaps, 'Never let someone persuade you to get on an old, rickety and appallingly maintained rollercoaster.'

The ride rattled off with a lurch and Isobel convulsively clutched the safety bar across their laps with one hand, while she clung on to Leo with the other. She felt the carriage accelerating and her long hair was torn free from its twist to stream behind her. They trundled to the top of the first hill and from the crest she could look down to see the lights of the fairground park below and the onyx-glitter of the nearby dark ocean. Then, with a rush, the carriage tipped over the peak and hurtled down the slope and she didn't notice anything more, except an explosion of speed, exhilaration and terror.

When the ride finally trickled to a stop, she turned to Leo with a glowing face.

'That was amazing! I haven't done anything like that for years. I actually loved it,' she said.

'I could tell from the way you were screaming,' he replied, smiling. 'You nearly squeezed my hand off.'

They clambered out and Leo bought her some fairy-floss as a second dessert which made her laugh as she ate it, it was such stupid stuff. Then they sat under the canvas awnings at a grubby coffee stall drinking strong cappuccinos.

'So, were you trying to ask me back there what my intentions really are towards Clare? Or are you just going to keep beating around the bush?' Leo leaned in towards her, his eyes mocking.

Isobel thought that he looked quite friendly now. It was as if sharing the rollercoaster experience had made them buddies. He was even teasing her.

'Of course not,' Isobel retorted. 'I'm only interested in what Clare wants, not what you want.'

'Right this minute, I'd say Clare is a little stuck in the

baby-chase mode,' Leo said, leaning back, nonchalantly. 'In my experience, it's common in women in their thirties. In fact, that's probably what this whole crazy life-swapping Sister Pact thing is about. Trying out the lifestyle. That's why I'd never trust a woman in her thirties to handle contraception. There are too many little "accidents".'

Isobel felt cross again at his complacency. As if Clare was just begging to be allowed to bear any man's children. Which she most certainly wasn't (was she?).

'Really,' she said testily, 'I hope you are not going to give me that little speech about how every woman just wants to sink her hooks into a man and how every man has a fear of commitment. Because from the experience of my friends, it's the other way around. It's the men who can't wait to settle down and play houses and keep us cooking meals for them. I can tell you that Clare has had more offers of cohabitation than she could shake a tea-towel at. Men are desperate for commitment. It's the women who are the choosey ones. Probably because having guaranteed regular sex isn't such a big deal for women.'

'That's not what the women I've slept with say,' said Leo, gleeful that he had prodded her into a reaction. 'But you must admit it would be a bit off-putting when you know the person you're sleeping with is counting down the hours to infertility.'

'Personally I hope any woman who's desperate to have a baby is sensible enough to take the sperm-bank option, rather than lowering her standards to whatever man she can get. After all, the quality of the genetic material is crucial,' Isobel said acidly. 'And, by the way, I hope you remember your appalling smugness when you're fifty and all the young fertile blonde-haired girls are turning up their noses at you because you're a pot-bellied, boring, old fart who takes three hours to come.'

She stopped, blushing at her own outspokenness, but Leo just laughed.

'But they won't be, because I'll be rolling in money, incredibly famous and part of the sexy film industry. I'll be going through 23-year-old wives faster than Rod Stewart. I'll probably even have the same bad hair and dress sense.'

Isobel smiled, despite herself. 'Well I just hope that your 23-year-old wives walk out on you with the same alacrity as they do with poor old Rod. It will be gratifying to think that you never have the pleasure of going through life with someone who is your intellectual, emotional and chronological equal.'

Leo grinned at her cheerfully.

'You should really learn to lighten up a bit, Iso. I was teasing. My hair will never be as bad as Rod's. And anyway, what are you so pissed off about? You should be triumphant. You've got the lot – the kids, the ever lovin' partner, the house with vegie patch. You should feel sorry for people like me.'

'Oh I do,' Isobel assured him. 'I really do. Who needs Hollywood when you have a vegie patch? But I really have to get home. I'm not used to staying out past midnight and pretty soon I'm expecting to turn back into a mouse.'

'Okay Cinders,' he hauled her to her legs, which still felt a little wobbly from the rollercoaster ride. 'I'll take you home. But before we go, I have to buy a ticket to the Hall of Mirrors. I want to see what I'm going to look like when I'm a pot-bellied, boring old fart.'

CHAPTER 10

It was Sunday morning, and Clare and Isobel were lying in the women's sauna at Clare's gym. They were on the same bench, feet to feet, so if they wanted to look at each other they had to raise their heads uncomfortably and peer through the swirling steam. This was not really a problem, however, as both Clare and Isobel found they were not keen on having much eye contact, or one of their usual intimate and rambling conversations.

In fact, both Isobel and Clare thought a bit guiltily that they couldn't wait for this 'debriefing' charade to be over so they could get the hell out of there and go *home* for a day. Clare was thinking dreamily of real coffee and a leisurely Sunday newspaper. Isobel imagined Ellen and Alex's ecstatic faces when she walked through the door.

'I won't stay long,' Isobel said, staring up at the damp ceiling through the mist. 'I'm dying to see the kids.'

'Oh, absolutely,' said Clare, who had her eyes closed. 'I can imagine your life must feel so strange. I mean, without having them around you all the time.'

Isobel smiled. 'This week, whenever I used your car, I kept looking in the backseat thinking they would be there. It felt so weird. You do get used to being with them all day.'

'Don't you just,' said Clare feelingly.

In the ensuing silence, Clare ran her hand uneasily over her naked belly. Surely all this inattentive gobbling of spaghetti bolognese and left-over fish fingers must be showing up by now ... She had arranged to see Leo tonight before she went back for another week of pretending to be Ms Stay-at-home Mother-of-two. She didn't want him to think she was turning flabby and bloated, in body or mind.

But she was half-wondering if this might be the last time they were together. Their patchy, stop–start relationship seemed so tenuous that it might hardly exist. Curiously, the thought didn't bother her as much as she thought it might. After a week with the kids, Leo was as distant and two-dimensional as a cartoon character. But perhaps things would be different when they were face to face. He had always been able to draw her back in with that husky voice and his expression of cool amusement. That trick he had of narrowing his eyes and just letting the mirth glint through. It got her every time.

'So,' Isobel interrupted Clare's thoughts. 'Tell me how everything went. The kids behaving? Ellen having any problems with her wheezing? Are they eating well?'

'No problems at all. Especially now I've worked out how to get Phil out of his armchair to do a few more things around the place,' Clare said. 'Although, I'm sorry, I had to stop taking Alex back to that Baby-robics. I don't know how you can bear it, he hates it.

I've tried him out on swimming instead, and he seems to like that.'

'Swimming?' Isobel lifted her head so she could peer at her sister over the tops of her toes. 'Well, I don't know, there's the risk of ear infections . . .'

Clare lifted her head in turn and smirked at Isobel. 'Oh Iso, they really should have called you Cassandra. Your local pool assures me they're scrupulous about hygiene standards and they even have special swimming classes for babies. You might join him up when you get back. He looks unbelievably cute in his little swimmers.'

'Yes, I expect he does,' Isobel said tersely.

'What about you?' Clare asked, lying back down. 'How's old Barty-cat? Are you surviving The Colonel of Wrath? And Leo phoned me this morning and said you went out to dinner. How was that?'

'Everything was fine. Bart seemed happy enough in a feline kind of way, although I'm sure he missed you. Helen Hogan was not so bad. The downside was that she asked me to fill in as "Marion" for the next issue, which is scary as hell. I did a rough draft on Friday afternoon but I know it's terrible. I'm dreading having to hand it over to her next week.'

'So she's giving you a crack at it too?' Clare said. 'The Colonel didn't seem to appreciate my forthright style, but I'm sure you'll do a much better job.'

Isobel grimaced to herself. She didn't even want to think about 'Dear Marion'. This was meant to be her stress-free day at home. 'Dinner with Leo was quite an experience too,' she changed the subject.

Clare held up her hands in front of her face so she could examine her fingernails through the steam. Two were now torn. Housework, she thought, was hell on your nails. 'In what sort of way?' she asked idly.

'Oh you know, he was full of stories about the film industry, which were fascinating. Of course I don't know as much about it as you do so I found it all intriguing. Then we went to the amusement park and went on a rollercoaster. It was a very strange way to end an evening, but quite exciting.'

'A rollercoaster? I don't think we've ever done that. Maybe you should take it as a compliment.'

'I think I can see what you see in him. He can be quite engaging,' Isobel said cautiously. 'But do you think there's any future in it for you two?'

'Probably not,' Clare said, irritated. She really did not want to be having this conversation now. She was going to see Leo tonight and try to figure out if there was any future in the relationship. Until then, she didn't want to have to speculate about it.

'I'd hate to see you get hurt over him, Clare-bear,' Isobel said, using the old nickname from their childhood. 'Why don't you start cooling it off? Then if you break up, that will make it hurt less. And if he can't get by without you, then he'll realise it much faster if you're not around as much.'

'You sound more and more like a self-help book every day,' Clare said a bit waspishly. 'But I guess you're right, although now I'm wondering if it isn't all over anyway. But let's stop talking abut Leo, that would gratify him too much.'

She sat up on the bench. 'Okay, let's put cards on the table instead. What do you *really* think of life as the single career woman?'

Isobel sat up too so they were sitting side by side on the bench. 'Cards on the table?' she said slowly, wrapping her towel around her swimsuit. 'I admit it but – you were right, I hate it. I found it lonely and isolated and rather boring going back to that flat alone every night.'

'Although sometimes that can be very peaceful,' Clare said. 'Just having your own space and doing what you want with it . . .'

'It hasn't felt peaceful to me, more like deserted. I keep thinking that if I fell over and broke my legs getting out of the shower no one will find me for months. And then there's *Verve*. I thought it would all be very glamorous, and it is in a way, but it's also shallow. All that talk about "lifestyle" and skincare. Don't you find that?'

Clare was a little hurt by this dismissive verdict on her life and her work. She shrugged defensively. 'Maybe. But that's what the readers want.'

'But everyone seems so enthusiastic about such trivial things. And, even though I thought it would be heavenly to have an empty sort of life, with lots of free time, I just feel I've discovered that most television is absolute junk.'

'You should have been getting out some decent videos. That would have made it much more enjoyable. And we do tackle some big issues at *Verve*. Maybe it was just a quiet week,' said Clare who, to her confusion, was now defending the lifestyle she usually criticised.

'Maybe. But what about you, how are you finding motherhood?' Isobel asked.

'A bit like being in Alcoholics Anonymous. You just try to get through one day at a time,' Clare said.

'Of course Ellie and Alex are very easy children to get on with,' Isobel said.

'Oh yes,' Clare agreed carelessly, 'but I think all small children would be similar – exhausting. Like yesterday morning, I decided to take the kids down the street. I wanted to try this new tuna casserole recipe. Anyway, you know what it's like, even something as simple as that turns into half a day's work ... A nightmare of straps and buckles and pushing and dragging Ellen and then there was no room in the shop for the pram and there's steps everywhere. It's all so much *effort*.'

'I suppose so,' Isobel said. 'Although you do find that all that becomes second nature after a while.'

Clare swept on. 'I've never done so much cleaning in my life – cleaning up the spilt food, cleaning up the bathroom, cleaning up the wet beds, cleaning up their snotty noses. Being with kids all the time is like living in some kind of whirlwind. I realise now that whenever you come over to visit me, you arrive in this sort of whirlwind. You whirl around the flat for a few hours and then you drive off and the whirlwind is still in the car with you. You never get out of it. Meanwhile, I can just breathe a sigh of relief and relax back in the tranquillity.'

'Or you could look at it another way and say that you're stuck by yourself while I go off to be with the family that I love,' Isobel pointed out sharply.

Clare disregarded that. 'And Phil!' she exclaimed. 'He's impossible! How do you put up with it? Whenever the kids need something, he seems to assume that I'll be the one who does it for them while he sits on his tush in front of the news or reads the paper.'

'That's a bit harsh,' Isobel objected.

'You really have to train him better,' Clare barged on. 'Make him see that he has to pull his weight around the house. After all, they're his kids too. I've made a few changes which I think will make all the difference. Like, none of this split shift dining, we all sit down to one meal at seven o'clock. And at least we now have a couple of glasses of wine with dinner, like civilised adults. I must say that makes the night shift much easier to take.'

Isobel couldn't help feeling riled. Here was Clare, who couldn't even keep one little flat clean, telling her what to do with her family. 'Well that sounds great,' Isobel said sarcastically. 'So you have my kids eating absurdly late at night and my husband drinking.'

Clare folded her legs up so she was sitting cross-legged. 'Don't get huffy. It won't hurt them for a few weeks and it's saving my sanity. Next week, I think I can get Phil even more involved. I reckon he just needs a bit of encouragement to be more proactive, and some reassurance that he's doing a good job. But enough of that dreary domestic stuff. What about the office, what's the goss?'

'Nothing much,' said Isobel, sulkily. She was going to tell Clare all about her romantic scheme for Fiona and William but now she thought that Clare might step in to wreck all her hard work out of sheer dog-in-the-manger petulance. Instead, she told Clare about her week spent opening letters and fetching cappuccinos.

'I had a bit of excitement,' Clare broke in. 'I met a man. A nice man. Did you ever meet a guy called Rory Maguire at the kindergarten?'

'Oh sure, he's Jessie's dad. We've talked a few times. He's a single father, isn't he?'

'Exactly,' Clare said triumphantly. 'And he invited me over to his place for coffee next week.'

'Oh, he's invited me over a couple of times. I think he's just a very friendly person,' Isobel said. 'You shouldn't read too much into that.'

'Oh, I'm not reading anything into it. But I did think he has nice eyes. Don't you think his eyes are nice?'

'I can't say I noticed,' Isobel said curtly. 'But I really don't think he's your type Clare, much too *ordinary* for you. Even if you started something you'd probably be dumping him after a month because he wasn't being challenging enough. And that wouldn't be fair to him, or to his little girl. You should think about the other people involved.'

'Woh, what's got into you?' Clare said in surprise. 'What am I, Mata Hari? Anyway, I wasn't saying I would be starting a relationship with this guy or anything, it's just a cup of coffee. I just wondered what you thought of him.'

'I think he seems very sweet and you should leave him alone. He's probably got some shocking personal habits you couldn't stand, like wearing Y-front underwear or reading Dick Francis novels or being thoughtful to his girlfriends.'

'Oh forget it, let's not talk about him if it's going to make you cross,' Clare snapped. 'So, if you're not happy, perhaps you'd like to call off the second week.'

'Perhaps you would,' Isobel said.

'Not at all,' said Clare. 'I'm happy to finish what we started.'

'Of course I am too. I don't like leaving jobs half done,' Isobel said.

Clare, interpreting this as a personal slur, started to gather up her things.

'Want to do the plunge pool before we go?' Isobel asked.

'No, let's skip it,' Clare said coldly. 'I want to get down to the Esplanade and have a coffee and watch the real world go by.'

'Great. I want to go home and see my family.'

They hurried off to get dressed and, eventually, parted without even a peck on the cheek.

Isobel's hands were trembling with excitement as she tried to get the key into her own front door. Before this week, she had never been away from the children for longer than one night. Now she hadn't seen their little faces for a whole week.

As she pushed open the door, she heard the sound of throbbing disco music and children giggling.

'Hello? I'm home,' she called.

'Mummy!' Ellen shrieked, catapulting through the door which led to the family room.

'Hello my precious, how are you?' Isobel asked, sweeping her up in her arms.

Ellen struggled to get free. 'We're doing a exercise vid-yo cos it's raining outside. Clare got it for us from the vid-yo shop and it's got dancing music,' Ellen explained importantly, tugging her hand to lead Isobel back into the family room.

'Really? That sounds fun. I can watch you do it.'

Phil, looking unusually sweaty and dishevelled, met her at the door carrying Alex.

'It's great to have you back,' he said warmly, giving her a one-armed hug and a quick kiss on the mouth. 'At least we can have a decent dinner tonight.'

'Well I really missed you too,' Isobel said, smiling into Alex's beaming face and gently pinching his fat, peachy cheeks. 'I'll go and put the kettle on for a cup of coffee and Ellie can show me her exercise video.'

'Daddy 'n' Lex was doing it too,' Ellen assured her.

Isobel raised her eyebrows as she took Alex into her arms. 'Was Daddy? Well luckily I'm here now so Daddy can get on with putting that sealant on the roof that he's been meaning to do for ages.'

'The boss is back,' Phil said, smiling. 'Although I might just have a cup of coffee first. It's been quite a few years since I did star jumps and my knees are wanting to discuss that with me for a while.'

Isobel and Phil sat up at the kitchen bench with their coffee, watching Ellie put herself through a four-year-old's idea of an aerobics routine.

Isobel gazed at her hungrily. 'I can't tell you how much I've missed them,' she told Phil. 'How's it all been?'

'Just another week really, although Clare's cooking has to be eaten to be believed. I mean I never knew you could burn spaghetti bolognese, and last night she did the most peculiar thing with tuna I've ever tasted. But we soldiered on, no small thanks to the local fish and chip shop.'

'The kids look fine,' Isobel said, watching Alex who was using the video cassette box to beat his favourite red wooden train. 'I half expected to come back to some kind of battlefield but they seem perfectly normal. Ellen doesn't even have one of her colds.'

Phil helped himself to another chocolate biscuit (Clare had ensured the house had a plentiful supply of those, if nothing else).

'They both seem relaxed. Clare's been great with them, face painting and swimming at the pool and all that stuff. It's been Club Med for kids.'

'Although they're not exactly neat. Did Clare even do Ellie's hair this morning?' Isobel asked, frowning.

Phil grimaced. 'Oh that was me. Clare slept in this morning. We took turns this weekend to do the early morning shift. I tried to do Ellie's hair but she kept pulling away so in the end I guess I gave up. Decided she could get away with the casual look. Does it look really terrible?'

'Oh not exactly terrible but it's a little bit messy.' Isobel brushed her fingers briskly together over the plate to get rid of biscuit crumbs. 'But don't worry, I can fix it up in two minutes. I see you've gone for that bright colour combination in the clothes again.'

'I think it looks sassy,' Phil said. 'I've never really understood why you can't wear red trousers and a purple jumper. Especially if you're four years old and no one will ever let you get away with it again till you go to university.'

'No reason at all,' said Isobel, 'at least she won't get lost in the dark. And did I hear you say "sleeping in"? That sounds like a civilised arrangement. What happened to you having to catch up on your sleep ready for the big, important working week ahead?'

'Oh, I got to sleep in on Saturday,' Phil explained. 'It's only fair.'

Isobel raised her eyebrows at him but held her tongue. Fair!

When he had headed out to look at the roof, Isobel washed up the mugs while she looked lovingly around at her family room and kitchen. After Clare's cramped little flat, it looked so spacious and light-filled that she felt like sticking her arms out like Julie Andrews in *The Sound of Music* and twirling about a few times. Home . . .

She dried up instead, reflexively noting the peels of onion skin in the corners of the kitchen floor. She'd have to tidy up a bit after she'd spent some quality time with Ellen and Alex, otherwise the house was going to be a pigsty by the time she came back next weekend. There was quite a lot of pleasure, she admitted to herself, in being back in an arena where she felt so totally competent.

She now felt bad that she'd been so short with Clare. So Clare had made a few changes to the children's routine. Was that the end of the world? And maybe a normal bloke like Rory Maguire was exactly what Clare needed to settle down. He was the sort of man that Isobel was always urging Clare to consider, wasn't he?

The kids did look well. A little untidy, but plump and clean and obviously coping effortlessly with their mum vanishing for a week. She supposed she should really be delighted that they were so independent.

'Come and dance, Mummy,' invited Ellen, jiggling around while the tiny woman on the screen said tinnily, 'That's it, ladies, you're looking good.'

'You come here and let me fix up your ponytail first. Then we'll have lunch and wait for a gap in the rain so we can take Alex down to the park. You really do need to get out and have some fresh air,' Isobel told her.

Phil stuck his head round the door. 'Oh, by the way, your parents are coming to dinner. They just invited themselves as usual, and I didn't have the heart to say no.'

'Well, is there any food in the house?' Isobel asked, crankily. Now she'd have hardly any time to tidy up, never mind even thinking of that big mountain of ironing she could see peeping around the corner of the laundry. And she had been so looking forward to spending time with Ellie and Alex.

Phil looked a bit sheepish. 'Maybe not. Clare seems to run a hand-to-mouth kind of kitchen. And, in fact, it's mainly hand-in-packet-of-chocolate-biscuits-to-mouth.'

Isobel sighed. 'Well I was going to suggest we just order in Chinese but I guess you'll all need a proper meal anyway. I'll go to the supermarket and pick up some things on the way back from the park with the kids. How's the roof looking?'

'Nearly fixed,' Phil voiced floated back as he vanished from sight.

But just as she'd bundled the kids into their outdoor clothes, the doorbell rang. Isobel impatiently yanked open the front door and found Margaret on the doorstep.

'I just happened to see you walk in when I was out the front planting the bulbs,' Margaret said, sidling past Isobel and into the family room without waiting to be invited. 'I couldn't resist the temptation to pop over and see how it was all going.'

Isobel trailed after her back into the family room. 'Fine, great to be back. Would you – um – like a cup of tea? I'll just put Alex and Ellie out in the garden to play where Phil can keep an eye on them. They're in their coats because we were about to go down to the park . . .'

'Lovely,' Margaret said. 'My goodness, this place looks very *lived in*, doesn't it? I expect that's your sister practising a bit of Creative Chaos.'

'Creative chaos?' echoed Isobel blankly. 'Maybe, or maybe it's just that she couldn't be bothered tidying up.'

Margaret, scenting discord like a bloodhound, plumped herself down at the kitchen table and prepared to get confidential. Isobel noted with annoyance that her neighbour was still wearing her gardening clothes, rust-red drawstring trousers and battered shoes. A fine shower of dirt was sifting down underneath the table.

'I'll just put the kettle on,' Isobel said, mentally adding 'wash kitchen floor' to her list of chores. 'So how was the kindergarten fundraiser? I'm sorry that in all the excitement I forgot about it so I didn't leave anything for Clare to bring but she tells me she cooked some biscuits anyway.'

'Oh yes,' Margaret said, helping herself to one of the chocolate biscuits from the plate on the table. 'Clare was an absolute star as a matter of fact.'

Isobel felt envy seeping into her like black ink. How typical of vivacious Clare to be able to go into a situation and charm everybody. If it had been Isobel, she knew she would have been standing shyly up the back all by herself, or stuck talking to Margaret all day. Whereas Clare had obviously gone in and wowed everyone with her stylish clothes and exotic hair and interesting job. Isobel felt like a peahen.

'Really?' was all she could think of to say.

'Really,' Margaret said emphatically. 'She made these dear little biscuits and packaged them up so cleverly, they positively flew off the table. Just between us, I had a close look at them and they were singed on the bottom, but I wasn't going to tell anyone about that. All the more money for the kindie.'

Isobel came back to the table with a couple of mugs of tea. 'I hope that's not too strong for you. So did you make a lot of money?'

'Stacks,' said Margaret complacently. 'Even if I do say so myself. Skandi was delighted, and of course so was I. It's so gratifying when one's hard work pays off. And did Clare tell you about Rory Maguire?'

'Well, she did mention something ...' Isobel said vaguely, unable to believe that Clare would have confided in Margaret.

'All down to me,' Margaret said triumphantly. 'I knew Clare was just stuck in that dead-end relationship with that film man and I've always thought that Rory looks a bit lonely. He's constantly coming over for long chats with me whenever we meet up at kindie, obviously pining for a bit of female company. Of course I'm very, very happily married so there's no point him looking longingly at me. But I did happen to see Clare at the fundraiser and it occurred to me that she would be perfect for him.'

'I see,' said Isobel. 'Although, do you think Clare is really his type?'

'Yes of course. I always think a man will put up with all sorts of things as long as his most basic needs are being met, if you know what I mean.' (At this point, Isobel could have sworn that Margaret managed a leer, a facial expression little seen outside the world of literature. Having seen it, Isobel hoped it would stay that way.)

Margaret then sipped her tea and droned on. 'Anyway, I dragged Clare over to introduce her to Rory and they got along like a house on fire. Spent the rest of the afternoon together. She was all over him in fact; I finally had to rescue the poor man. But I really think we might have something there. Wouldn't it be fun if they got together and Clare ended up being a step-mum to poor little Jessie? Then you two would both be mums at the same kindergarten.'

'Yes, that would be – fun,' Isobel said. With a hollow feeling, she imagined what it would be like to have Clare around at the kindergarten all the time. Isobel thought that she would continually be playing second fiddle as Clare's boring big sister. She told Margaret, 'I'm not sure that Rory is actually looking for a mother for "poor little" Jessie. He seems very happily self-sufficient to me.'

'Nonsense, I can see beyond that tough facade. He needs a good woman, every man does. I only hope they invite me to the wedding as I set the whole thing up. Registry office I guess, given their respective past histories. But tell me all about *Verve* magazine. Did you feel strange being there? I expect they found it a bit odd trying to think of things for you to do, not having any special skills.'

'I had a great time,' Isobel said baldly, determined not to give Margaret any more details. 'Look, I hate to rush you away, Margaret, but I have to pick up a bit of shopping. My parents are coming to dinner.'

'I always make sure we go over to Mum's house, that way she has to cook,' Margaret said. 'But then, it's always easy to whip up something quickly if you know your way around a kitchen the way I do.'

Sure, thought Isobel, remembering Margaret's favourite 'signature dish' – a supermarket-roasted chicken with a tin of apricots dumped over the top. Margaret's 'Chicken Gloria' had become a standard joke in the Ashton house (when they weren't having to face up to the actual prospect of eating it at one of Margaret's dinner parties).

'Look,' Margaret went on heedlessly, 'I was going to ask you about the kindie Christmas concert. You know the money we've raised is going towards it and I'm working out the budget now. We have to hold it the first week of December before term finishes, so that's hardly any time at all to get things organised. I was wondering if I could put you down for something. Nothing too up-front, I know you're a behind-the-scenes kind of person, but maybe scenery? Or costumes?'

Isobel felt embarrassed that she'd forgotten all about the concert too. Stepping out of her life for just a week had made everything at home recede and seem so much smaller.

'I'll do whatever you want. Just see where there's a gap and plug me into it,' she said. 'Now, sorry, but I really do have to get to the shops before they close.'

It took another twenty minutes but eventually Isobel was able to shoe-horn her neighbour out the door. Rushing Alex and Ellen into the car, she just had time to pick up a leg of lamb and some vegetables before the supermarket closed. The advantage of the roast dinner was that she could put on the meat and potatoes and leave herself with a spare hour or so to get the kids bathed and dressed in their pyjamas before their grand-parents arrived. With a bit of help from microwaved vegies and packet gravy, the busy supermum could have squeaky clean kids and a home-cooked meal on the table for the whole family before the evening news was over.

She was watching Ellen and Alex wallow about in their favourite blueberry flavoured bubble bath when Phil wandered in carrying two glasses of red wine.

'I thought we might have a pre-June 'n' Jack drink,' he said, offering her a glass.

Isobel half-smiled. She knew where this new habit had come from. Before Clare came to stay, Phil had always treated wine as a dinner-party accessory. Opening the bottle was a kind of Pavlovian reaction to the doorbell. This was a throwback to his family, where his father, a parsimonious tax accountant, used to cite his Methodist religion as the reason he hardly ever opened a bottle of wine unless they had guests. However Isobel suspected that his objections had more to do with saving money than gratifying any alcohol-averse deity.

Phil, the oldest of three, had inherited many of his father's characteristics, including his passion for figures, golf and what his whole family referred to irritatingly as a 'goodish night's sleep'. But whenever Isobel thought she detected that Phil had also inherited his father's excessive frugality, she tried to snuff it out. She thought of it as meanness. She had a very different attitude to that of her mother-in-law, a devoted housewife, who seemed genuinely happy to be drinking her own home-made lemonade and darning socks to make them last (albeit uncomfortably) that extra couple of years.

'Great idea,' Isobel said now, reaching for her glass of wine. She set it down on the bench and picked up the bottle of shampoo to wash Ellen's hair. Meanwhile Phil sat on the floor, leaning up against the towels hanging on the rail, and watched Ellen pretend to be a seal while Alex pounded a rubber whale with one flannel-covered fist.

'This is nice,' said Phil. '(Yes, you are a seal, Ellen, I can see your shiny wet fur). It's really cosy to have you here, even if it is only for one night.'

'Well it's very relaxing to be back,' Isobel said, dolloping some shampoo onto Ellen's head and lathering it up, despite her protests. 'For the first time in a week I feel I can just let go. But I hope that it doesn't confuse the kids more than ever to have me reappear and then leave again.'

'I'm sure they'll cope. They loved having their Aunty Clare here. Thought it was one long picnic.'

'Is that a reference to the food she was giving them?' Isobel asked, tipping a beaker of warm, clean water over Ellen's head.

'You don't want to know,' Phil assured her. 'So, what was it like on the other side of the fence? Did it make you regret that you're not a career woman?'

Isobel shook her head emphatically. 'It's been a hellish week. Nerve-racking. Clare's office is full of the most scarily impeccably groomed women, all yakking on the phone about whether women are going to be wearing mauve or lilac nail polish this season. It made me feel like a humdrum housewife.'

'But it's not as if you were ever trained as a journalist,' Phil pointed out reasonably.

Isobel took the flannel off Alex and started to use it to scrub him thoroughly. 'I guess not. But it did bring home to me how much self-confidence I've lost, just

210

staying home all the time. Even catching the train was a bit terrifying. Everyone busily shoving their way to somewhere.'

'I've always said you should get out more.'

'Oh yes, you've always said,' Isobel snapped, while Alex whimpered in protest against her energetic washing. 'But when you're looking after two tiny children it's very hard to "get out more". Apart from the fact that it takes all my time to keep up with the kids and the house and the cooking, whenever I do have some time off I feel about as lively as an oyster. The last thing I feel like doing is trotting off to self-improvement classes.'

'I didn't mean that,' Phil said mildly. 'I just meant something you could enjoy. Or even do with the kids – maybe join one of those new pram-pushing walking groups or something like that.'

'Pram-pushing? Well that sounds fun. As if I don't get to push enough prams in my day. Of all the patronising ideas . . . they should start a university for women stuck at home with babies, not some bloody pram-pushing group. We do still have brains, you know.'

'Of course I know that,' Phil said. 'All I'm saying is there must be something that you would enjoy doing and you should do more of it, whatever it is, when you have the time, if you want to.'

'I'm sorry. I'm being a bitch, aren't I?' Isobel said contritely. 'It's just that I was really looking forward to coming home.'

'Are you disappointed? It's just the same as when you left.'

'Maybe that's the problem. You all got along perfectly well without me. I might as well never have gone, or maybe never come back,' Isobel stopped in confusion.

'It was only a week,' Phil said. 'Everything would come apart at the seams if you were away for a month.'

'I certainly won't be going away for a month,' Isobel said, reaching for the clean towels she'd left on the bench. 'Two weeks is too long.'

As he was drying Ellen, Phil asked, 'So did you enjoy anything about last week, apart from getting a break from us three?'

Isobel didn't bother to contradict him. He was blatantly fishing for a compliment. Instead, she thought about his question while she held Alex in her lap and rubbed his tummy in slow circles, which made him giggle.

'Not much, although maybe it was quite enjoyable to spend all day with a bunch of people calling me by my real name instead of just hearing "Mummy". The worst thing was that the editor asked me to write the agony-aunt page for the next issue of the magazine. I'm petrified I'll just make an idiot of myself. You should see the way The Colonel rips into people in meetings. She seems to use public humiliation as an incentive method, and next week it could be me.'

'Of course you'll be able to do it,' Phil told her. 'You've always written fantastic letters. I'm sure you'll be wonderful with this agony-aunt thing. It's just a matter of sitting down and working away at it.'

Irritated, Isobel picked up Alex and took him into his bedroom where Phil had already laid pyjamas out on the bed. Why did men always feel they could offer advice on everything, even when they had no idea what they were talking about? she thought pettishly. Phil followed her into the room carrying Ellen.

'Oh, not these pyjamas for Alex. They're too small now. I'll grab some more,' Isobel said shortly. The door bell rang and she sighed. 'Mum and Dad are here already and I haven't even started to do the vegies. Can you go down and let them in while I quickly finish up here?'

'I can do the kids while you go and spend a few minutes with your parents if you like,' Phil offered.

'No, it'll be much faster if I do it. Just get the door will you?'

As Phil walked out the door, Isobel felt terrible. He was just trying to be helpful. Why did she feel so cantankerous with him?

After dinner, Isobel persuaded Ellen and Alex into their beds, promising Ellen that she would be there to get her breakfast before she headed back to her 'new work' for one more week while Aunty Clare came back to take care of Ellie and Alex.

'Good,' said Ellen sleepily. 'She promised to teach me to dive.'

'That will be lovely. Just be careful to start with little dives first,' Isobel said.

'And I can do my own fish fingers in the microwave.'

'Can you?' asked Isobel grimly.

Jack and June Callaway had, as usual, ensconced themselves in the two squishy armchairs in the family room so Phil was perched on the hard sofa-bed couch.

'So have you had enough of this silly idea with Clare?' asked June, smoothing the skirt of her mauve rayon dress neatly over her knees.

'Not at all,' said Isobel, who was standing at the kitchen bench slicing some of her special chocolate cake to have with coffee (thank heavens she had frozen half a cake just a few weeks ago). 'We're going to swap back for one more week. And in the October issue of *Verve*, the problem page will have been answered by me. The editor asked me to fill in.'

'I can't see the sense of it. You've got your lovely home here and two darling little kiddies – why are you going off to that magazine? We don't understand it, do we Jack?'

Jack Callaway was watching television with the sound muted. One of the little things that annoyed Isobel about Phil was the way he switched the television on as soon as he walked into the room. He'd left it on now, ostensibly so they wouldn't miss the late evening news, to which he and Jack shared an addiction.

Jack was a tall, skinny man with stooping shoulders. Although only three years older than his energetic wife, it now seemed as if there was an age between them. His eyes, as if strained from years of peering at bottle labels, were pale and tired behind thick lenses. His hair was sparse and limp, whereas hers was iron grey and thick, coiled in a big bun at the nape of her neck. While she moved her big strong body with the sturdy motion of a Clydesdale, he trailed behind her like a thin wraith. When they sold out of the shop, it was as if his purpose in life had ended, and he was content to fade gradually away like an old photograph.

June had always henpecked him from morning to night, even during their days at the shop. Isobel and Clare used to wince whenever they heard their mother snapping at their father, 'Why didn't you pack a handkerchief? I reminded you three times!' or 'I told you that shirt doesn't go with those pants. Why do you think I left out the blue one?' Both sisters had vowed never to marry a man as weak as their father, or ever to become as critical as their mother. Isobel, when she caught herself prodding Phil into doing some household task, often wondered if she was just following in her mother's footsteps, like all the psychology books predicted.

'Do we Jack?' June repeated tetchily, tapping him briskly on one cardiganned arm.

'Do we what?' Jack asked.

'We don't understand why Isobel is going in to do Clare's job while Clare stays home and looks after the kiddies. It just seems foolish to us.'

'Yes,' Jack agreed meekly.

Isobel carried over a plate of chocolate cake and her own glass of red wine. It must have been her third glass for the evening, and she was feeling tipsy.

'I hope this will do for dessert,' she said, nodding at the cake as graciously as she could manage. 'I only got home at lunchtime so I didn't have time to make anything else.'

June reached for a piece. 'And what Clare thinks she's up to we don't know. She has a good career with that magazine, it's a dream job. Why she wants to mess around with it like that, we really don't know.'

Phil leapt in. 'But June, this swap thing is a story for the magazine, so it's part of Clare's job. And Iso is going to be in the magazine herself with this page she's been asked to write. I think it's quite a feather in her cap.'

Isobel sat down beside Phil and took another swallow from her glass of wine. 'You should approve Mum, you're the one who is always so big on women having careers. Or you should be. You put a lot of work into having one of your own.'

'It wasn't actually a career,' June corrected. 'It was a family business, wasn't it Jack? Plenty of flexible hours so I could be home with you and Clare whenever you needed me. Of course, I think it's right that you're staying home with Ellie and the baby. It would be silly if you were going off to work in some hospital and getting exposed to goodness knows what kinds of germs.'

'Oh, unlike you at the pharmacy,' Isobel cut in. 'The truth is, Mum, that your job was the priority in your life. Clare and I were always second.'

Everyone looked taken aback at Isobel's outburst, particularly herself.

'That's not true. My girls always came first. Why do you think we worked so hard at the shop? It was to provide for you,' June protested.

'Oh why don't you just be honest for once?' Isobel said. 'Motherhood was way down on your list of priorities. You didn't really have any idea of what we wanted. I remember you always gave me bug catchers and science books when what I really wanted were dolls and ballet classes. I'll never forget when I was ten and I wanted rollerskates for my birthday and you gave me a junior microscope instead.'

There was an embarrassed silence.

'Well I'm sorry, we just thought we were doing the right thing. That microscope was really quite expensive,' June said eventually.

'Oh well, pity I didn't want it. You always had this preconditioned idea of who we were meant to be. I was the brainy, serious one, Clare was the arty one, and if

216

we ever tried to step out of those boxes, you just squashed us back in.'

'Isobel . . .' Phil said gently.

Isobel suddenly became aware that everyone was regarding her with bemusement. She blushed and took a forkful of chocolate cake.

'Sorry, sorry,' she muttered, chewing furiously. 'Just a bit tired after a big week.'

'Of course I loved being home with you girls,' June said, leaning forward so she could try to catch Isobel's downcast eyes. 'Of course I did. It's just that it took two of us to run the shop. It was a two-man business and we were determined to send you girls to a private school if we possibly could. Give you some of the advantages that we didn't have. But, yes, I did like working too. Well, you and Clare should understand that. You both enjoyed your jobs.'

'I guess so,' muttered Isobel, forking down another chunk of cake.

'It wasn't the done thing then, was it Jack?' June ploughed on. 'The working mum. There were some raised eyebrows among the other women sometimes, I can tell you. Is that why you were embarrassed, Issie? I thought you might have even been a bit proud to have a mother who was ahead of the times.'

'No, no, I wasn't embarrassed. And I know you thought you were doing the best thing for us. Look, let's forget I said anything at all.' Isobel took another flustered sip of wine, and then decided she'd better lay off the alcohol. She didn't think she'd ever spoken to her parents in that tone of voice in her life, and she could see that Phil was looking at her warily. He was probably wondering what had happened to the placid woman he'd married. In fact, Isobel was wondering that too. She knew in her head that she had signed up for life to be the dutiful daughter, the sensible wife and a conscientious mother. But right now, in her heart she didn't feel like mothering anyone. Husband or kids or, heaven help her, parents. She remembered Clare saying that life at home with small children was like Alcoholics Anonymous. Just one little day at a time . . .

Phil cleared his throat. 'Isobel's really getting into this magazine business. You should have seen the stack of them she brought home with her.'

Isobel swallowed her mouthful of wine. 'William, the assistant editor, told me that the best way to improve your writing is to read heaps of other people's work,' she explained. 'The style just percolates through into your own writing. So I'm going to sit up tonight and plough my way through a whole stack of *Vanity Fairs* and *Harper's Bazaars*.'

'Whatever for?' asked June. 'It's not as though you're going to be a magazine writer. You were never any good at English at school. Science subjects were your strong point.'

Isobel sighed. She might just as well never have spoken. 'I do have to finish this page for the magazine, so I will have to write something next week, even if I never have to pick up a pen for the rest of my life,' she said evenly. 'Now how about some more coffee?'

'I'd love some,' said Jack loudly.

'Goodness, you've got two arms and two legs, haven't you?' June snapped. 'Help yourself.'

'I'll get it,' said Phil, springing to his feet. 'I need the exercise anyway. I was doing aerobics with Ellen this morning and my muscles are killing me.'

'Precious poppet,' said June fondly. 'Whatever will she think of next?'

Phil poured out more coffee. 'Actually, it was Clare's idea. She picked up some aerobics tapes along with *Teletubbies* and *The Wiggles* at the video shop.'

'That Clare, you never know what she is going to come out with next. Original she is. But then she always was, wasn't she Jack?'

'Yes she was,' Jack said.

'Not like you, Isobel. You're more the planned, organised type,' June said.

'Yes, Mum, I'm really into planning,' Isobel said bitterly. 'Lucky me. It means I spent all of last week at the magazine tiptoeing around trying to do the right thing and petrified of making a fool of myself by getting something wrong.'

'There's nothing wrong with that. You just like to be in control. You've never liked surprises, never,' June said, reaching for another slice of chocolate cake. 'I mean, you are who you are. This cake is delicious. Next time you're making it, Iso, make one for us too and pop it in the freezer.'

'Isn't that the late news?' asked Jack.

'Yes, it is,' Phil said with alacrity. 'I'll turn the volume up.'

Clare knew that it was never a good idea to talk to Leo after sex. This was because he usually fell into an immediate post-coital coma.

The sex between them had been its usual stupendous, animal self but she'd felt strangely unmoved by him tonight, and now she was impatient to find out if she was wasting her time with him. Of course she knew it was a lousy time to initiate a 'let's talk about us' discussion. She'd read *Men are from Mars, Women are from Venus* and knew all about the importance of letting Leo go into the privacy of his psychological 'shed'. But she had to say something. She couldn't just let things keep stumbling along like this.

'Leo, are you awake?' she whispered.

'Ynghy,' he muttered, shifting about irritably.

'Sorry, am I too heavy?' asked Clare anxiously.

'If you just move over a bit more . . .' Leo muttered.

'Sure. If God had any sense he would have made our arms detachable so we could just take them off when we want to lie on our sides. I mean, when you're in bed with someone there's always the problem of The One Arm That Gets in the Way. If not the Two Arms . . . Leo, have you gone to sleep again?'

'Not yet,' he sighed.

'I didn't mean to wake you up. It's just that we haven't talked about last week and I just wanted to see how it had gone.'

'Last week?' he muttered.

'Oh, you know, dinner with Iso. Just wondered if you wanted to tell me how frantically you missed me,' Clare said lightly.

Over a long dinner at their favourite Moroccan restaurant, they'd actually canvassed Leo's week fairly thoroughly. Clare had learnt that the film was nearly finished and Leo was irritated about a last-minute change to the ending but gratified that his hero's key speech had gone in uncut. He was also talking to several producers about his third screenplay and someone had already suggested that he might like to start speaking to agents in America. Clare had demonstrated all the appropriate enthusiasm, horror, gratification, interest and excitement at these revelations.

But somehow they never seemed to get around to discussing her week. Perhaps, on reflection, that was a good thing. An in-depth chat about fish fingers and finger painting would hardly fit in with Leo's image of her as a hot magazine writer on the make. However, she was also conscious of just how much time she spent with Leo talking about himself. Once again she'd wondered if there could be any future in a relationship that was so much like a soliloquy.

'So you took Iso out for dinner,' she prompted him.

Leo yawned, and reached over to the bedside table for a cigarette. It was a habit Clare loathed and she'd have to spend the next morning frantically trying to air the smell out of the flat before Isobel came back. But relationships were all about compromise. As *Manifesting Your Man* put it, 'If you're not prepared to change your life one little iota, then find yourself a deserted island and set up camp. The tree that doesn't bend is going to break.' Or something like that.

'Yeah, we went out for dinner,' Leo said, before pausing to light the cigarette. 'It wasn't too bad actually. Your sister is a really good listener, really focused, and she asks some sharp questions. And of course we talked about you all the time.'

'Did you?' Clare said, feeling pleased.

'Of course. I think she was fishing around to see what my intentions towards you are.'

Clare waved some cigarette smoke away from her face in the semi-dark. 'What did you tell her?'

'I told her my intentions towards you were exactly the same as yours towards me. Strictly dishonourable.'

Clare shifted her leg that had been twined over his. 'I'm glad you enjoyed dinner. I always said you under-estimated Iso.'

'But you know the most surprising thing was watching her eat. It was great to see a woman eating like that.'

Clare had rarely heard Leo sound enthusiastic (if you set aside Orson Welles, his Mum's roasts, his own films and his diatribes on class distinctions).

'What's so special about the way Iso eats?' Clare asked peevishly.

'She just hoed in. Three courses. She eats like a man, without any of those hang-ups that women have today. Very sexy.'

Clare felt a sour squelch of jealousy and sternly told herself not to be stupid. So he liked the way Iso ate, so what?

'I'm really glad you got on so well,' she said flatly.

'Of course I just did it for your story. You know I'm crazy about you, babe,' Leo said, giving her a cigarette-flavoured kiss on the mouth.

Clare noticed that Leo still couldn't bring himself to use the 'L' word. For months now she'd been determined that she wasn't going to be the first one to use it. And she wasn't going to do her usual thing and split hairs by saying 'I'm in love with you', rather than 'I love you'. No, this time Leo would have to go first.

Manifesting Your Man had been quite clear about things like that. The authors had assured her that Mr Appropriate needs to feel he's in charge and setting the pace. Any other way is 'emasculating'.

'I had the week from hell with the kids,' Clare changed the topic. 'I mean, you know I love them, but staying at home full-time with two small children is enough to drive you round the twist. I never thought I'd ever miss The Colonel, but strangely enough I did.'

'I told you,' Leo said complacently. 'You're much too switched on to settle for something like that. You've got first-rate talent if only you'd really start to use it.'

'Of course I do,' said Clare, wondering what the hell he thought she was doing with her talent now.

'That's what I told Isobel. You and I have that in common. We're both ambitious.'

'Oh yes, we are,' agreed Clare, automatically. 'But especially you. You're a man possessed.'

He snorted. 'I suppose that's your way of saying obsessed. You should count your lucky stars. If things had turned out differently, I might have been taking Harley Davidson motor bikes apart in your living room when I wasn't going out to get another tattoo. And besides, you're the one who's always making jokes about coming to the Oscars with me.'

Clare ran her fingers lightly down his bare arm. She'd decided it was time to press him and find out if there really was any future. She fished around for some way to bring up the topic. 'So is that your ultimate dream in life?' she said finally.

'Not at all. I just want to make films,' he said. 'Pure and simple.'

'I'm sure you will.' Clare hesitated, 'Your personal life doesn't figure in there at all? You don't think about having children or big family Christmases . . .' her voice trailed away.

Leo grinned at her in the street light filtering through the wooden blinds. His eyes narrowed.

'Oh no, the baby question. C'mon Clare, you've just spent an entire week with sprogs. Did you get any work done? Did you have any creative ideas? Did you come home full of energy?'

'Not exactly, although a two-hour nap this afternoon made a big difference.'

'But if the kids were your own you wouldn't have had the two-hour nap. You'd be too busy taking them down to the bike track for family bike-riding sessions. You don't really want kids any more than I do. You think you do because all the women's magazines tell you that you do, but you don't. And if you do find Mr Sperm and get knocked up, I'm telling you it will be the biggest mistake of your life. You're much too fond of your lifestyle and your waistline. Would you really give it all up just to have some kid suck you dry like a leech and then walk out of your life seventeen years later with a drug habit and an attitude?'

Clare, with a sinking feeling, wondered if this could be true. After all, having a baby was a bit like playing Russian roulette – you never knew what you were going to get. Maybe the joy of your life, or maybe someone who would hack you to death with an axe when he turned eighteen so he could get his hands on the family fortune. But she wasn't going to give Leo the satisfaction of admitting he could be right. 'It doesn't have to be like that,' she insisted.

'It might be though. It often is. Kids are parasites, and like most parasites they are not particularly mindful of their hosts – they'll take what they want and move on. In the meantime, you'd have no money, no career path and no decent holidays. C'mon Clare, dare to be different. You know you want more out of life. What about all your plans to become an editor, move to Los Angeles, take over from Rupert Murdoch . . .'

Clare hooted. 'I never said I wanted to take over from Rupert Murdoch, give me some credit. But you're right, I do want more to life than the knowledge that I've reproduced my DNA a few times. In fact, I can't see any point in reproducing my DNA. Some kid just inherits my knock-knees and appalling eyesight . . .'

'And your great mind. Don't forget you have a first-class brain,' Leo said.

'Do I?' Clare asked, suddenly very happy.

'Of course. I wouldn't be here if you didn't. I've always been totally upfront about the issue of kids, you know. I won't even think about them for years.'

He yawned. 'Can we just go to sleep now? I've got a television episode to finish tomorrow and you've knackered me. It's fantastic to have you back, even if it is just for one night.' He leant over and gave her a long, loose kiss, to which she responded without feeling much of anything. Then he flopped onto his back and soon his breathing became deep and regular, while his legs twitched occasionally, a sure sign that he was nearly asleep.

Clare lay still and watched the striped shadows of the blinds move across the ceiling. She couldn't help loving the way Leo could suddenly turn on the charm and make her feel like the most fabulous woman in the world. But then no man could be more emphatic about the fact that he didn't want a committed long-term relationship. Of course, he could change his mind; people did all the time. And it wasn't as if babies were not portable – babies could go to Hollywood too.

But then there was her career. This elusive thing that she had been looking for since she had left university. The Right Thing. It was going to be the thing that told her who she was, and gave her a reason to get up in the morning.

However, she knew she wasn't ambitious in the same way as Leo. He lived his work. In his own mind, he could not succeed as a human being if he did not succeed as a filmmaker. Clare didn't feel like that, certainly not about writing for magazines. When she saw a six-month-old copy of *Verve* in the dentist's waiting room, greasy with fingerprints, she didn't feel inspired with pride. Not in the same way as The Colonel, who would probably want to wipe it lovingly clean and frame it.

Besides, she'd figured out that if you go up the chain, you have to put in the extra hours as well. Clare couldn't imagine wanting to do any job so much that she was willing to work fourteen-hour days and give up her weekends as well.

She thought that at least Phil had got that part right. He took his job seriously – goodness knows he probably even enjoyed it, knowing Phil – but he made sure he had a whole other part of his life there for his children. And that probably made Phil a more balanced person than Leo, she thought. Maybe there was more to Phil in some ways because he was willing to take on the irksome restrictions and the frightening responsibilities of having a family. The same went for someone like Rory Maguire, who worked four days a week so he could spend more time being a dad to the formidable little Jessie.

'The thing is,' Clare said aloud, 'I'm not sure that the point to this whole existence isn't in relationships. I mean, if there is a point. We'll all be dead in a blink of an eye. The stories I write won't matter; even the films you make won't matter. So as far as I can see, the only possible point must be in relationships.'

She sighed. 'Which means I need to have a few more of them while I still have time.'

She thought about that for a while and wondered if it was true that you really only matured in relationships, through the love and pain and petty irritations of living closely with other people, whether that be a lover, a child or even a sister. If so, it was no wonder that she some-times felt about five years old. She could count the number of close relationships she had on one hand.

She paused. 'Leo, are you awake?'

He said nothing.

'Leo, did you hear all that. What do you really think?' She poked him in one thin rib.

'I think you sound a bit like a new-age loony,' Leo mumbled. 'Anyone can give birth. Only someone excep-tional makes it to the top in the global village. Forget the easy stuff, go for the challenges. That's where it's at.'

Clare rolled over. 'I guess it depends where you think the challenges are.'

Leo didn't answer. He really was asleep this time.

CHAPTER 11

'And now kids, *Mulan* time!' Clare said, pressing the 'play' button with a flourish. She waited a few minutes, and then when the children were well and truly zoned out into videoland, she sidled off into the kitchen to make herself breakfast in peace.

She wondered how her mother had ever coped without a VCR. The day before she'd gone to the video shop to stock up on fresh material and taken advantage of their excellent 'Ten Kids' Vids for the Price of Five!' offer. Admittedly, taking out twenty videos may have been a bit excessive and she had felt rather foolish carrying them all out of the shop. But she figured that was still only three a day for the rest of the week, which would just give her time to make a few notes and get through some housework. Besides, videos were almost educational tools, weren't they? Broadening horizons, developing language skills, introducing the important cultural concept of American hegemony . . .

Finishing her muesli, Clare put on the kettle for a cup

of coffee and picked up the newspaper, determined to put the thought of ironing out of her mind.

Looking back at suburban domestic life from the safety of her flat on Sunday, she'd decided in the second week she would become ruthless about domestic short cuts. No more soaking the whites in bleach as per Isobel's instructions; no more decanting the sugar, flour and rice into neatly arranged jars; and definitely no more ironing. It was time to jettison Isobel's unrelentingly high domestic standards and put housework back in its box (and shove it underneath a bed and forget about it as much as possible).

She decided she should use the time to make some notes for her Sister Pact story, so she got out a notebook and dutifully scribbled down, 'housework . . . videos . . . instant coffee . . .' and sat back, biting the top of her pen. Then she idly wondered what *Manifesting Your Man* had to say about first dates. It was a long time since she'd read that chapter.

FIRST DATE: First dates are absolutely crucial. They are the key in the ignition, the gate in the door, the first blossom in your bridal bouquet.

Yikes, thought Clare, that was enough to put you off the whole concept of dating, right there.

Manifesting Your Man went on obliviously.

The way you handle a first date is vital. Here are five golden rules that you break at your peril:
1. Look Fantastic. Scientific research has found that men get 90 per cent of their information visually, so you have

to look gorgeous. You can probably make up the other 10 per cent with a good perfume.

2. Let Him Do The Talking. We guarantee you that he'll have a good time if you nod your head, open your eyes very widely and breathe, 'How interesting,' every five minutes.

3. Start Small. Always make the first date coffee or a drink. Just whet his appetite. Any more and his palate will be jaded. Any less and he won't have enough time to see how good you're looking.

4. Make Him Pay. Forget whatever the feminist movement has told you about going Dutch. Men, like most of us, value what they pay for. The more it costs, the more valuable they think it is. Just assume in your ladylike way that he is going to pay and thank him prettily. He'll be sure to think he got his money's worth.

5. Do Not Have Sex With Him. Repeat DO NOT HAVE SEX WITH HIM. Remember, according to the *Manifesting Your Man* technique, sexual congress does not take place till after an emotional commitment has been made, either verbally or with a large diamond. Why should Mr Appropriate see you as special if you're prepared to cast yourself away so lightly?

Clare found herself toying with Rory Maguire's small yellow card as she read, tapping it on the edge of the table. It was Tuesday morning already and she hadn't called him yet to confirm if she would be coming over for coffee that afternoon.

She was in two minds. After Sunday night, she was really beginning to think that her relationship with Leo may well be running out of steam, but that was no reason to rush off after someone else. She remembered

Isobel telling her prissily that she should do this man a favour and leave him alone. That decided her. Picking up the yellow card she walked across to the wall-mounted phone.

He answered on the second ring, sounding out-of-breath and flustered.

'No Jess . . . Hello?'

'Oh hello, Rory. This is Clare Callaway.'

'Oh Clare, hi.' She thought she heard his voice cool perceptibly.

'I'm sorry, have I rung at the wrong time?'

'Not at all. Jessica was just asking me for the nine hundreth and sixty-second time if she could get a pet mouse. I was telling her that they smelt.'

'Apparently rats are much better, less smelly,' Clare offered.

'Well for God's sake don't tell her that. I think Michael Jackson had a pet rat and look what it did to him.'

'I'm not sure it was an actual rat, more a song about a rat,' Clare said. 'But I take your point. I was just thinking that it would be fun to come over for coffee as you suggested. That is – if you're still home this afternoon?'

He seemed to hesitate before he said, 'Yes, we are. Jessica would be thrilled to see Ellen.'

'Great. Well, we'll be over around four, if that's okay with you.'

'See you then.'

Rory hung up before Clare did so she heard the sharp click of the phone. He definitely had not sounded as friendly as he had on Friday, but then some people just had unfortunate phone manners. After all, he was a landscape architect – he probably had a great bedside manner with plants.

That afternoon Clare stood outside an Edwardian bungalow that could have been a carbon copy of Isobel and Phil's. Except, while theirs was painted in tasteful cream, this one was splashed with vivid Mediterranean blue with sea-green trim. Quite – eye-catching, Clare thought.

The house was set on a huge block. Unlike Isobel's garden full of lavender and lilies, Rory had crammed his front garden with an elaborate system of fish ponds, fountains and streams, surrounded by lacy, drooping trees. The water was splashing dreamily in the quiet of a suburban weekday afternoon, and it looked utterly peaceful. Clare could even see fat fish through the water lilies.

When she pushed the gate open, a small Jack Russell terrier bounced up the side driveway, yapping foolishly and leaping in the air as if his feet were on springs.

'Woof,' announced Alex, with great delight.

'That's right, Lexxie, good boy. Woof, woof says the dog,' said Clare, bending down to pat the excitable little dog.

The front door smacked open and Jessica tumbled out.

'Ellen, Ellen. Come and look at my sandpit an' my swing an' we've made scones,' Jessica sang, running down the three front stairs to Ellen.

Crouched down patting the dog, Clare looked up to see Rory Maguire framed in the doorway. He looked decidedly unsmiling, to Clare's bemusement. What had happened to the cordial man she'd met last week? She began to regret the effort she'd put into getting ready for this meeting, choosing a soft woollen V-necked jumper in pistachio green (feminine) which she wore with jeans (casual) and high-heeled boots (sexy). She'd even used make-up and the hair dryer, things she hadn't touched for more than a week. Now it looked like she'd been making a bit of a fool of herself. He might have wanted Ellie to come over and play with his daughter, but he didn't seem to have any interest in seeing Clare again.

She followed him through the house, making nervous small talk about the ponds in the front garden. Apparently an electric pump was the secret to keeping the water running through the system.

She scarcely noticed the house, expect to register that he'd painted the walls in bold colours, deep purples, teal greens, mustard yellows. Out the back, in the big open-plan living area which again reminded Clare of Isobel's house, the walls and ceiling were pale blue with swirls of white. The wooden floor was covered in woven green, gold and blue rugs so the whole room was reminiscent of the seaside with a blue sky arching overhead. Bonnie Raitt played softly on the stereo and Clare couldn't see a television set.

Rory got out some toys for Alex to play with and then set up a coffee tray on the table on the back verandah, so they could sit in the winter sunshine and watch the two girls running hysterically around the lush garden, chased by the small terrier. The back garden was as fantastical as the front, with grottos, archways, topiary animals and a playhouse for Jessie in the shape of a turreted castle. There was even a cave somewhere, Clare was assured. Just a small, safe one.

'And don't worry about Spoddy, he wouldn't hurt a fly,' Rory said.

'Spoddy – er – the dog?' Clare guessed.

'It's short for Dog-Spoddy,' Rory explained.

'I see.' Clare laughed nervously.

The atmosphere was constrained and it didn't improve when Rory took a bite out of one of Clare's fundraiser cookies and then had to pick the bits of charcoal out of his teeth.

He took a swallow of coffee then said curtly, 'Look, I should say up front that Margaret has told me all about the magazine article.'

Clare look up in surprise. 'Has she? What do you mean "all about the magazine article"?'

'Well, I mean that when we met last time you implied that you were really just doing this story so you could spend time with Ellen and Alex, but that's not true, is it?'

'Of course it's true. In a way.' Clare glanced sideways at the garden, acutely uncomfortable.

'What about the fact that you were about to lose your job and this story was the only way you could keep it?' Rory asked. 'Margaret got talking to me at the fundraiser and told me all about it. She said you don't actually like spending so much time with the kids and this is all a bit of a chore for you. She also just happened to mention that you're in a long-term relationship.'

Clare snorted. 'It's none of Margaret's bloody business.'

'No, but she seemed to know what she was talking about. Was she right about the magazine?'

'Sort of. She was right that my job was on the line

234

unless I came up with a story, and that I suggested this one.'

'And what about the boyfriend?'

'I don't see why I have to sit here and be interrogated. I just came over for a cup of coffee,' Clare protested.

'I'm sorry, you're quite right. I didn't mean to interrogate you,' he said, very courteously. 'It's just that I like to know where I stand. For example, there's no way I want to find me or Jess turning up in some superficial article in a half-witted women's magazine. I mean, of course, if you're looking for material I'd be quite happy to talk to you "off the record" but there's no way I want to see my name in print.'

Clare didn't know whether to be more miffed at this man or at the tattle-tongued interfering Margaret. Either way, she wasn't going to give Rory the satisfaction of letting him think that she had come over to spend time with him.

'It would be really great if we could talk off the record,' she said sweetly. 'Naturally you won't turn up in the article, although I assure you it won't be "half-witted" or superficial.'

'I guess I should apologise for that,' he said, a bit shame-faced. 'I'm quite sure nothing you write would ever be half-witted. That was below the belt.'

'Oh well, I'm a journalist. I have to be able to take it as well as dish it out,' Clare said airily. 'So, tell me what it's like to be a single father?'

Rory hesitated, scanning her face to see if it was a serious question. Apparently satisfied that it was, he answered, 'Hectic, fantastic, exhausting. I guess all the things you would expect. I never actually intended it to be this way. I mean I didn't fight for custody or anything. Jessie's mum just took off when Jess was three weeks old. We weren't married and I've never heard from her since.'

'Not even a phone call?' asked Clare, shocked.

'Nope. I'm not even sure if she's still alive, to tell you the truth. She was a bit wild; maybe I was too. But a lot's changed in four years. It has to when you find yourself with a three-week-old baby on your hands. Sort of alters your perspectives drastically.'

'It must be odd going to places like the kindergarten, where it's all women,' Clare suggested.

Rory shrugged. 'I guess I'm used to it. I used to take Jessie to the local "new mothers' group" and it was full of women and new-born babies, everyone breastfeeding like mad. Well, almost everyone . . . I guess the time I'll see other dads is when I can persuade her to start playing football, which shouldn't be long now,' he added, affectionately watching his small daughter hurtle around the garden.

'Well I think you're very brave,' Clare said, then cringed when she heard the cliché come out of her mouth.

He raised one eyebrow. 'Of course it doesn't take bravery, it takes an impossible amount of patience and the superhuman ability to deal with sleep deprivation.'

He stood up abruptly and went over to the balustrade. 'Jess, Ellen, do you want a drink? And there's some scones about to come out of the oven too.'

The girls ran panting up the stairs and fell upon the food like wolf cubs. Clare fetched Alex from the sunroom and sat him on her lap where he sucked happily on a scone. She looked over at Rory. He was wearing faded jeans and a very blue shirt, which brought out the colour of his eyes. His big, capable hands were wrapped around a mug of coffee and he looked enchanted as he watched the girls mashing scones, jam and cream all over their faces.

'Look, sorry about the biscuits,' Clare said suddenly. 'They were crap, weren't they?'

'Absolute crap,' Rory said smiling. 'Still, it's money to a good cause. It's all going towards the Christmas concert, they tell me. Jess is going to be Rudolph the Red-Nosed Reindeer, aren't you Jess?'

'That's great, Jessie,' Clare said. 'Ellie, do you know what you're going to be yet?'

'A sheep,' said Ellen, a bit sadly. 'I wanted to be a' elf but Miss Skandi said I had to be a sheep.'

'A sheep!' Rory said. He had the knack of talking to small children without putting on a funny high-pitched voice. Clare had noticed that this was quite rare, especially in men. 'That's fantastic,' he continued, talking to Ellen. 'Lucky you. You get to wear a woolly coat and if you're really lucky you can have spots too.'

'Sheep don't have spots, silly,' Ellen informed him.

'They do if it's a Dalmatian sheep,' Rory said gravely. 'Maybe you can ask your mum to let you be a Dalmatian sheep.'

'Could I be a Dalmatian sheep, Clare?' Ellen asked eagerly.

'I don't see why not,' Clare said. 'But we'll have to talk to Mummy and Miss Skandi about it.'

Ellen beamed at her ecstatically and then, still sticky with crumbs and cream, the two little girls took off down into the garden. Alex nestled into Clare's lap and began juicily sucking his fingers. He would need a nap soon. Clare tilted her head back and let the pale sunlight soak into her bones.

She thought that she liked Rory's colourful house and his easy way with his daughter. Maybe Isobel was right about good-hearted men. They really were so much easier to like. But then, he obviously regarded her as a hard-bitten, manipulative hack, working for a shallow women's magazine, so the liking wasn't a two-way street. And anyway, she'd always told herself that settling for a nice man would get boring in the end. Like dying your hair sensible chocolate brown when you really wanted to be drop-dead platinum blonde.

'Would you like another cup of coffee?' his voice interrupted her thoughts.

'No, I better get back. I'm going to make lasagne for dinner so I need to allow myself some time to cook it.'

'Isn't it a bit late for lasagne? You have to cook the bolognese for at least a couple of hours,' he asked casually.

'Do you? Bugger. Oh well, I guess it will be canned tomato soup again. I'd better go, anyway. Ellie, meet you out the front,' Clare called over the balcony.

Climbing reluctantly to her feet, she carried Alex to his stroller.

'Thank you for coffee, it was very – relaxing,' she told Rory, as he walked her to the door.

'That's a pleasure. Sorry about the prickly start. I just had this feeling that I was going to end up being used as a guinea pig when all I'd wanted was a friendly coffee.'

'Don't worry, you're safe,' Clare assured him. Standing at the front door, Clare noticed that, when she had

238

high heels on, they were nearly the same height. She also noticed again the stars trapped in Rory Maguire's eyes. Like David Essex used to have, she thought absurdly.

'Well, nice to see you again,' she said lamely.

'Likewise. Good luck with the story.'

Clare turned away, bumping the stroller past the fish ponds and down the cobblestone driveway. Ellen and Jessie came running up the side of the house pursued by Spod, and Clare managed to persuade Ellen that she'd see Jessie again at kinder on Friday so there was no need to make quite such a drama over the parting.

As she clicked the gate shut, she waved one last time to Rory, who'd taken Jess inside and was closing the front door.

Of course, Clare thought, when she went back into her real life, Rory and this strange, fabulous house would seem utterly incongruous. She lived an inner-city life, full of restaurants and book shops and ludicrously expensive coffee. She might as well not have a kitchen at home for all the time she spent there. Rory came from another world, a place of Christmas concerts and home-made scones. Obviously he was never even a contender for Mr Appropriate. There was nothing appropriate about him. They had nothing in common. Clare expected she'd never even see him again, unless she ran into him at the kinder on Friday.

In fact, she thought, tit-tupping down the street in her high-heeled boots, she really hoped she wouldn't.

CHAPTER 12

When Phil Ashton glanced inquiringly into Clare's bedroom three days later, he observed that the bed had sprouted legs, all of which were waving in the air like the fronds of some convulsing sea anemone. On keener inspection, he detected that the legs belonged to Clare, Ellen and Alex, who were lying on their backs on the bed kicking their feet in the air and squealing with laughter like three little pigs. Or, more accurately, two little pigs and one rather large one.

Phil coughed politely.

'Um, good morning . . . I just wondered where everyone was. There's no one in the kitchen but Daisy,' he remarked.

Clare's legs swung back down to the bed and she sat up, hair mussed and face flushed.

'Sounds like a bad Victorian music-hall number. Or is that a tautology?' she remarked jovially. Then she tugged her pyjama top down and looked faintly embarrassed. 'Sorry Phil, I've just been trying to get in touch with my inner child. I figured if you can't beat 'em, join 'em. And it did occur to me that it's Wednesday, the kindergarten's closed for spring cleaning so the kids and I don't have any big plans for the day. There's really no need to rush about trying to get us all ready by 8 am when you walk out the door.'

Phil finished knotting his tie.

'Oh ... so do you want me to feed Daisy while you're – umm – busy here?'

'Oh yeah, great, Phil. She must be chowing down on the tiles by now. And could you put the kettle on? I'm dying for a cup of coffee.'

Clare smirked to herself as Phil headed off down the corridor. He was really coming along quite nicely, she thought complacently. He now regularly pitched in with household chores without feeling the need to send out a national press release proclaiming what a great guy he was for stepping into the kitchen or changing a nappy.

She stretched. 'Okay, you two, feel like a bath now? And then we can talk about what's the plan for today. I was thinking we might go down to the pool for a swim after lunch.'

Ellen yelled 'goody' and ran ahead to the bathroom. She didn't generally have her bath in the morning but last night she'd been so sleepy that Clare had put her straight to bed after dinner without bothering with the usual wash. Clare swung Alex into her arms, a deliciously warm and heavy bundle. He gave her an ecstatic grin and babbled earnestly while gripping her nose.

It was only now that she'd started to gain confidence around the children that she had begun to relish their physical presence. She loved the fragile bones at the nape of their necks and the way Ellen casually leaned against her when she was sitting, or trustingly took her hand as they walked down the street. Last week, she hadn't noticed such small pleasures. She'd been too busy worrying how she could keep the kids distracted so they wouldn't burn the house down.

She ran a big soapy bath while she drank her coffee and idly taught Ellen to count to ten in German on Alex's toes.

'Come in the bath too, Aunty Clare,' begged Ellen.

'I'll just get Alex out of his nappy first. You hop in, Ell's Bells, and see if you can make the bubbles froth up so high they touch the ceiling.'

Sitting in the warm water, dutifully, if sketchily, rubbing a flannel over Alex, Clare made her plans for the morning. Maybe *Pocahontas* while she quickly tidied up. And then she could write up her Sister Pact notes and then a trip to the park. She might even be able to persuade Ellen to play by herself on the swings so Clare could sneak in a quick half hour of reading.

She was tempted to take along *Manifesting Your Man* and re-read the rather depressing chapter on compatibility which she'd looked at last night. According to the authors, 'Opposites might attract but they had a world of trouble living together.' Clare wondered if that really meant that a career-minded inner-city woman could never be contented with a suburban family man with his own fish ponds. But people could change, couldn't they? She wriggled away from the thought impatiently. What did it matter, given that it was obvious that Rory Maguire had so little interest in her in the first place.

Clare decided she'd take a new thriller to the park instead. She was fed up with *Manifesting Your Man*.

Perhaps it was time to bin it and move on to the next promising title. She'd heard some interesting things about *What Your Mum Didn't Know and Your Dad Didn't Tell You*. Or was that *What Your Mum Didn't Tell You and Your Dad Didn't Know*?

With June and Jack, Clare thought, fishing the kids out of the bath, it could have gone either way.

After a late lunch (fresh fruit, frozen peas and fish fingers, a combination she found the children revered), Clare loaded Ellen and Alex into the Volvo for the trip down to the local public swimming pool.

She'd discovered that the indoor toddlers' pool was bliss. It was as steamingly hot as a big bath and she would emerge feeling sodden with relaxation. It was, Clare had decided, a great way to play with the kids and indulge herself at the same time.

Ellen was able to float around in her new yellow inflatable ring, while Alex clung firmly in Clare's arms, kicking his feet about and cooing contentedly.

At first, Ellen was reluctant to let go of the edge but Clare had tried a technique she'd once seen her Aunt Lois use to teach a dog to swim – chuck the dog in deep water and then yell 'well done' when it stayed afloat. Clare tried to use the same theory by gently pushing Ellen away from the wall and then lavishing enough exaggerated praise on her to distract her from bursting into tears.

'That's it, Ellen, kick your legs about really hard. When you're too tired to speak, that's hard enough,' Clare called encouragingly, as she lifted Lexxie up out of the water and then down again while he crowed with excitement.

When Ellen announced she needed to have a pee-pee, Clare was reluctant to get out of the hot water and stand shivering on the cold cement or pick up warts on her feet while she waited for Ellen to do her stuff. Might as well continue the lesson in independence and send Ellen off on her own, she decided. The door to the female changing room was only three metres away.

'Well, you know where the toilets are. We can see the doors from here. Off you go and Alex and I will be right here when you get back,' she told Ellen.

When Ellen was slow to return, Clare didn't even notice at first. She was encouraging Alex to float on his back, with her hands cradling his head.

But when nearly ten minutes had gone by and there was still no sign of Ellen, Clare looked up and felt a clutch of anxiety. She began scanning the people hurrying to and fro across the concrete but there was no sign of a small, pot-bellied girl in pink and green floral bathers.

Suddenly she was terrified. Ellen could have fallen in the big pool and no one might have noticed. She could have been kidnapped by some lurking paedophile. With the purest sense of panic she had ever experienced, she imagined having to face Isobel and Phil if anything happened to Ellie. Clare scrambled out of the pool carrying Alex, and began to hurry towards the changing rooms. Behind her the yellow ring bobbed forlornly in the empty toddlers' pool.

She rounded the corner into the women's changing room, almost cannoning into a girl in businesslike Speedos, goggles dangling from one hand. There was no one else in the changing rooms and after quickly looking in the corners behind the lockers, Clare went next door to the bathroom area.

'Ellen, Ellen are you in here?' she shouted, looking into empty cubicles.

She banged each of the doors frantically, as if Ellen could be hiding behind one of them. A middle-aged woman in a giant sized T-shirt and spandex leggings who was washing her hands at the basin asked her if she was all right.

'It's my little girl, Ellie. She came in here to go to the toilet and I can't find her,' Clare said, by now half-gasping with smothered sobs. In her arms, Alex, shocked by her distress, began to wail as well.

'Oh goodness, you poor thing,' the woman said. 'I haven't seen her in here. And I've been in here changing for a good ten minutes.'

'Oh my God,' Clare muttered, terrible visions passing through her mind. Ellen grabbed; Ellen frightened; Ellen alone and wondering why her world wasn't looking after her any more.

Clare spun on her heels and half-ran back out into the pool room. She scanned the toddler's pool, the big pool, the high diving board, looking for a little body in pink and green. She even stumbled over to look into the large pool, terrified that she was actually going to see Ellen spread eagled on the bottom.

'The police,' Clare muttered to herself. She had to call the police. She began to rush around the side of the pool, trying not to slip on the wet concrete, Alex heavy and dragging in her arms. She had to get to the office where there was a phone so she could call the police to report Ellie's disappearance. Then they could come and search the place with sniffer dogs or whatever needed to be done. Beginning to shiver in her cold bathers, Clare struggled to keep the tears out of her eyes. She had to stay calm.

'Clare!' She felt two warm hands grip her upper arms. She looked up through a tangle of wet hair and saw Rory, with Jessica standing beside him. Both were fully dressed, dry headed, and Rory was carrying a big swim bag. They'd obviously just arrived.

'Clare, what's wrong?' Rory stooped slightly so he could look into her distraught face.

'It's Ellie,' Clare gulped. 'She went off to go to the loo and she hasn't come back and they say she was never in there.'

Putting it into stark words just made it seem even more shocking, and Clare dissolved into tears.

Rory was still holding her arms and now he squeezed them. 'Don't worry, she won't have gone far,' he said easily.

Clare, listening to his calm voice, almost believed him.

'You go and find the pool attendant and tell him what's happened,' he said, his steady voice slicing through the fog in Clare's brain. 'They'll put an announcement over the loud speaker and then everyone will be looking for her. Maybe someone has already found her and they're taking care of her. She might even be in the office at this minute. I'll keep looking. Are you right with Alex?'

Clare nodded dumbly, relieved that someone was telling her what to do. Of course, the loud speaker. She hurried off in search of a pool attendant, clamping her mouth shut to control her trembling lips.

Rory, picking up Jessica, had headed off in the other direction.

'Clare,' he called after her. 'What's she wearing?'

'P-pink and green bathers. That's it,' Clare said, tears welling up in her eyes again as she thought of Ellen's thin little arms and legs.

'Right. Don't worry, this will be sorted in a jiffy,' Rory smiled at her encouragingly.

Clare searched frantically until she spotted a pool attendant in the crowd. She was spilling out her incoherent story when someone touched her arm.

'Are you Clare?' a nervous teenager asked her.

When she nodded, the teenager said awkwardly, 'Uh, there's a man in the men's who says you should go in there. Says his name is Rory and he's found her.'

'Oh, thank God.'

Forgetting that she was just wearing a swimsuit and nothing else, even forgetting Alex in her arms, Clare really did run across the concrete this time. The entrance to the men's changing room was right next door to the women's. Clare barged in, ignoring the men hastily reaching for their towels in the changing room.

'Rory?' she shouted.

'In here,' he said from the bathroom area.

He met her as she came round the corner, Jessie clinging ferociously to one of his legs.

'She's over there, wedged in the corner behind the basins. I can't persuade her to come out,' he said softly. 'I think she's just frightened and she needs to see someone she feels safe with.'

Hardly even stopping to acknowledge him, Clare pushed past. She heard a faint sob and finally saw Ellen, a tiny, bedraggled figure against the wall behind the handbasins, her swimmers still down around her knees.

'Oh, sweetheart.' Clare knelt down on the concrete floor and gently coaxed Ellen away from the concrete wall and into her arms alongside Alex, who continued to sob in sympathy with his sister.

Clare tucked Ellen's head in under her chin. Then she said as calmly as she could, 'Ellen, are you all right? What happened? Did – did someone touch you?'

'My bathers got stuck,' Ellen whispered.

'What, what?' Clare bent her head so she could hear the thread-like voice. 'What happened?'

'My bathers got stuck on my legs and I couldn' get them up,' Ellen said.

'Oh gorgeous, that's just because they are wet. You should have come out and asked me.'

Ellen shook her head emphatically. 'I couldn' come out because my bathers was *stuck*,' she gulped.

'Is she okay?' asked an elderly man wearing voluminous swimmers and a rubber cap. 'I heard a child crying when I came in but I couldn't see where it was.'

'She's fine, thank you,' said Clare. 'She just went in the wrong door by mistake and then she got in a tangle with her swimmers.'

'Oh dear, well, never mind dear, Mummy is here now.'

This time, Clare didn't correct the error. She smiled at the man and gathered Ellen in an even tighter hug, feeling suddenly how precious and vulnerable she was.

'I'm sorry Ellen,' she said softly. 'I should have come in with you and shown you the right door. I was being a lazy sod. I hope you'll forgive me. Now don't worry about your bathers getting stuck, that happens to everyone sometimes. See, we'll just give them a good tug and up they'll come. Will you come back out into the pool and get warm? You're freezing.'

Ellen kept her head bent down.

'Please, sweetheart?' Clare said. 'Jessie's here so you can play with her. And your yellow ring is out there in the pool and I bet he's getting pretty lonely without you.'

Ellen looked up at that. 'Awright,' she whispered.

Rory, who had been waiting by the door, came over and silently lifted up Alex, leaving Clare free to pick Ellen up in a tightly reassuring bear hug. Together they headed out of the changing rooms and back into the toddler's pool, which to Clare felt blissfully warm on her chilled body. It evidently felt the same to Ellen, because she soon revived.

After getting changed, Rory and Jessie joined them, and the two little girls played squealing and chasing games while Rory and Clare leant up against the side of the pool. Alex, earnestly experimenting with vowel sounds, bobbed around in front of them in Jessie's floating ring, which had a built-in seat.

'Thank you,' Clare said to Rory, finally but fervently. 'Thank you for finding her.'

'It was just a hunch. I knew the two doors were side by side,' he said, shrugging. 'I'm just sorry you both had to go through it. You looked absolutely frantic.'

'When I realised she hadn't come back, I think it was the worst moment of my life,' Clare said. 'And all my own stupid fault. The dumb thing was I even watched her walk through the door. I just didn't register that it was the wrong door. I should have gone with her.'

Rory smiled at her, his eyes friendly again. 'We can't

be perfect all the time. And everyone is allowed to do ten really dumb things every year. It's so you remember that you're human.'

Clare smiled back. 'And I suppose it also helps you to be kind to other people when they do really dumb things.'

'Exactly. You're coming along nice at this parenting stuff. Learning to accept that you're deeply flawed is the most important part.'

They stayed in the pool till they were wrinkling up like prunes. Then Rory said he was going to take Jessie over to the big pool for a diving lesson, but Clare and Ellen agreed it was time for a snack. Something about panic makes you incredibly hungry.

'So will I see you again?' Rory asked, as Clare stood at the edge of the pool, wrapping Ellen and Alex up in their big beach towels.

'Oh sure,' Clare said casually. 'Maybe at kindie on Friday? And of course I'll be at the Christmas concert. I wouldn't miss seeing Ellie be a sheep for the world.'

'Hopefully I'll see you before then,' Rory said.

Unsure exactly what he meant (date? coffee? chance encounter at the local Seven-Eleven?), Clare nodded.

In the shower she resolutely pushed aside the thought of the piles of washing building up at home.

'Can we have party pies? They're my very favouritest,' Ellen begged, tugging at her hand.

Clare groaned inwardly at the thought of yet more junk food. She knew that if Ellen and Alex were tucking into hot pies, she'd be unable to resist. Then she remembered, with a zing of jealousy, Leo's irritating monologue about Isobel and her sensuously enthusiastic eating habits. Well, if he liked eating, she could show him a thing or two about eating. If anyone knew how to eat, it was someone who dieted a lot. Besides, astoundingly, despite not going to the gym for a whole week, when she got on the scales on Sunday night she discovered that she actually hadn't put on a scrap of weight.

She said to Ellen, 'If you stop banging those locker doors and find me Alex's shoes, we'll go to the canteen and get party pies.'

'Yum yum bubble gum,' observed Ellen, dancing on her toes with impatience.

Sitting at a white plastic table, Clare watched as Ellen smeared party pie from one ear to the other. The trouble with Leo, she thought, was that he wanted sexy, voluptuous, sensuous eating, without the big hips that came with it. That was men for you: they didn't want to listen to women whine about their boring diets and gnaw away at the edge of their dessert with a teaspoon. But they didn't want their woman to look different from the anorexics on TV either. No wonder so many women treated their dieting and overeating like a secret love affair to be indulged behind their boyfriend's backs. She wondered if Rory would be like that, making unflattering remarks about any woman whose hip width exceeded the size allowable to soapie starlets. She thought not. He seemed to have too much of a sense of the ridiculous.

In fact, she got the feeling that Rory wouldn't give two hoots how depressing the back of a woman's thighs looked in the fluorescent light of a department store changing room. He'd probably be too busy telling her about the next fantastical thing he'd dreamed up for his eccentric garden.

She suddenly hoped she'd get to see it again some day.

CHAPTER 13

Isobel had refused to take on all of Clare's habits (she drew the line, for example, at experiments with colonic irrigation). But she'd readily agreed to take Clare's place drinking coffee with William and Fiona on Thursday mornings. It was a weekly nine o'clock rendezvous in the downstairs cafe.

Isobel saw it as an ideal opportunity to open Fi and Will's eyes to the potential in each other. She'd noted with chagrin that nothing had come of her leaving them alone at the lunch table last week. They'd both re-appeared quickly back at the office, and when Isobel asked William what they'd talked about, he said type-faces. And apparently meant it.

So Isobel wanted to use this morning to show them what lovely people they both were. She wondered how she could inch the conversation round to relationships and how, so often, the person near you is the one who can turn out to be 'the one' if you only have the wit to see it.

As Chapel Street coffee bars went, this was a tired and cheerless specimen. On one side, chairs were lined up against a counter which displayed an array of noxious-looking, fluorescent-iced cakes that no one had ever been observed to order ('or survive' as Fiona pointed out darkly). Posters for theatre shows that had interested no one in particular five years before were still stuck, peeling and plaintively pointless, on the walls. A handful of round tables were scattered haphazardly across the dull wooden floor.

Iso, Fiona and William were huddled around a table of such modest dimensions that occasionally their knees bumped together quite painfully. William always paid for the coffee because he said that he was (almost) their boss and needed to pump them on the sly for useful information about other members of staff. Isobel felt quite relieved when Fiona convinced her that he was joking.

'I'm dreading the editorial meeting today,' groaned Fiona as she savagely poured an extra teaspoon of sugar into her cappuccino on top of the three she had already shovelled in. 'Last week was an almighty cock-up. Those bloody women refused to show off their mangled boobs for that Tits in Bits story, so I basically have to start the whole thing again and find new victims. The Colonel of Wrath was livid.'

'Well, I know you did the best you could,' William comforted her with a spray of pastry flakes. (He was eating a toasted ham and cheese croissant). 'Just close your eyes, keep your head down and it will blow over. It always does. Besides,' he added reverently. 'We are working for one of the few remaining legends in publishing history, a genuine figure from the old school of journalism. We won't see her like again.'

'Well halle-bloody-lujah,' muttered Fiona.

'If it looks too bleak, you could always conjure up a medical emergency and skip the meeting. By next week you'll have found more women and she'll have forgotten all about it,' suggested Isobel.

'Oh no, may as well swallow the medicine in one gulp,' Fiona said. 'Not that you have to worry, Isobel. She just loves you at the moment. Not only did you finish "Dear Marion" ahead of schedule, but I believe The Colonel was describing it as sensible and yet sophisticated.'

Isobel flushed. 'The only reason I finished it early was because it was making me feel sick with nerves. I kept having this ominous sense of it hanging over my head so I thought I'd better just get it over with. Although, when I went in to hand it to Ms Hogan, my heart was beating so hard I thought it was going to burst right out of my chest. I'm just relieved that she thought it was okay.'

'Okay!' Fiona said. 'She wanted to ask it out on a date.'

Isobel smiled modestly. 'In the end writing it wasn't so bad. I enjoyed being able to sit down and focus on one job from beginning to end. Most of my time at home I feel I never actually finish a job properly before I have to rush on to the next. And of course I can't take all the credit. William helped me with the whole thing.'

She glanced over at Fiona. 'William is so generous, don't you think? He really didn't have to make time to help me but he did.'

William chipped in modestly. 'All I did was tweak around the edges. You had it all written.'

'And that's without even mentioning all those bloody crème caramels and cookies,' Fiona continued, apparently oblivious to Isobel's hints about Will's virtues. 'The whole office has been gorging itself. I swear I even saw Skye-the-stick-insect having one of your apple tarts, although I was probably hallucinating at the time. And now I hear you're lined up to do "Trials of Style" for the next issue as well, even though it's about handcreams and every woman in the place was itching to get her dry and roughs on three free tubes of the stuff.'

Isobel gave her coffee an unnecessary stir. 'Ms Hogan did ask me if I would do it, which I thought was good of her. Although I was tempted to suggest that she should try using them herself . . .' she said.

'Oh Lordy,' snorted Fiona. 'Nothing could save those shrivelled-up old talons except a couple of transplants. And then they'd have to start by giving her a heart.'

Isobel giggled immoderately. 'You really are so funny, Fiona,' she said. 'Isn't she Will?'

Fiona regarded her with mild surprise, while William just twisted the conversation back to the previous topic. 'It was all your own work, the problem page,' he told Isobel. 'You should be proud of yourself.'

'More like relieved,' Isobel admitted. 'I was beginning to think that I wouldn't be good for much of anything by the time I finished ten years at home with the kids. It can strip away your sense of competence in the outside world. And the way people react when they ask what you "do". As soon as you say you're at home with children, you're completely dismissed.'

She shook her head. 'But there I go griping on about

me again. When what I really wanted to talk about was you two.'

'Well, I think I envy your life in a way,' Fiona said, slowly drawing patterns in the top of her cappuccino. 'I mean, it's not as if you'll be at home with the kids for the rest of your life. And having that time out of the workforce, concentrating on something as important and yet elemental as children, that must be quite an experience. Even if underappreciated.'

'Oh yes,' Isobel said hastily, casting a look at William and hoping he was registering the fact that Fiona was reasonably keen on the idea of motherhood. 'And you'd be a wonderful mum, Fiona. You're amusing, warm, down-to-earth . . .'

Fiona snorted. 'It's funny how people with children always go around telling other women what great mothers they'd be,' she said. 'When I'm in my more cynical moods, I think it must be a way of conning other women into joining them doing hard labour.'

'But you do want to have children . . .' Isobel pressed her.

Fiona blushed a little. 'Maybe, if the circumstances were conducive. But I don't see it as my right or anything. If it doesn't happen, it doesn't happen.'

'So how's the second week of the big social experiment going?' William asked, changing the topic again to Isobel's irritation. 'It must have been tough to see your children on the weekend and then leave again.'

Isobel picked up a sachet of sugar and started flexing it a bit crossly between her fingers. Honestly, getting these two to talk about the same thing was more difficult than persuading small children to get into the bath.

'Not as bad as I thought it would be,' she said. 'The house was still there, the kids were still healthy, the sky hadn't fallen in. And by the end of the day, it was a bit exhausting to have them jumping all over me. Now I understand what it's been like for Clare for the last four years. She always has that look of anticipation on her face as she walks out the door, leaving me with tired, crotchety, insomniac babies while she heads back to eight hours of blissful, uninterrupted sleep.'

'So you're glad you have another week "off"?' Fiona asked.

'That makes me sound like a terrible mother. Of course I can't wait to go home on Sunday, but I have to admit there'll be things I'm going to miss.'

Isobel had torn the sachet so white sugar granules spilled onto the table. Now she started tidying it up.

'Sitting down and writing that "Dear Marion" page was so ... *satisfying*. Like exercising a muscle I didn't even know was cramped,' she said, sweeping the sugar back into the torn packet. 'And this week it finally dawned on me that it can be quite peaceful not having to watch out for the kids all the time. I don't have to be on my guard in case I've forgotten to pack the snack bag or a change of clothes. I can just pick up my handbag and walk out the door without excusing myself to anyone. It's hard to explain what a luxury that is. We're thinking of having another baby, but sometimes the thought of another few years of buckling babies in and out of the car is unbearable.'

'I'm sure you cope wonderfully. You're the kind of person who just gets on and deals with things as they come up. It's very impressive,' William said, lightly touching Isobel on the shoulder.

Isobel laughed. 'Will, I think that you're trying to flatter me.'

He smiled ruefully. 'More like trying to flirt with you, but I don't seem to be very good at it. It's never very effective.'

'I'll still take it as a compliment, but it's misdirected. I'm the married woman here,' chided Isobel, feeling uneasy with Fiona sitting there listening to this. 'This time next week I'll be wearing trackpants, spooning bran mash into the baby and losing intellectual arguments with a four-year-old.'

William leant forward. 'But there's nothing wrong with doing that. In fact, I admire you for it. You're so *feminine*. Not just gorgeous and smart and a nice person, but also so very – womanly, for want of a better word. I think a lot of women these days are running scared from that side of their nature. They don't want to be nurturing. Unlike you.'

William's face swam moonily towards her. Isobel leaned back fractionally.

'Oh Will, you'll never get your girl by telling her how nurturing she is,' she said lightly. 'You get her by telling her you're so grown up you don't need looking after seven days a week. In fact, you are so mature that you might even be able to nurture *her* occasionally. Just for a change. That's a novel offer that a sensible woman would find irresistible.'

Fiona stood up abruptly, her spoon clattering down onto the table. 'I'd better go up,' she began to chatter, gathering her bag together. 'I want to be able to say at the meeting that I've already written up the little story on that socialite who once shook the hand of Princess Di in a charity ball line-up and now believes she receives psychic communications from the People's Princess whenever she puts on her pearl choker.'

With a tight smile at both of them, she blundered out the door. Isobel, not knowing whether to be angry with herself or William, also began to get her things together.

'I have to go up too,' she explained. 'I've decided to make sandwiches for the editorial meeting. The ones we had last week were so appalling.'

As she got into the lift, Isobel felt guilty about Fiona, feeling responsible for her downfallen face and sudden departure. On the other hand, she admitted to herself that there was the tiniest warm glow somewhere in the back of her mind. Isobel certainly had no desire to take William up on his tentative advance, if that's what it had been, but she had forgotten how gratifying it was just to be approached.

Poking her head in the office, she saw that Fi's desk was empty, so acting on instinct she headed for the ladies' loos. The *Verve* bathroom, outfitted by the New York designer, was a vision of *faux* oak panelling, brass fittings and rounded edges. Fi had explained to Isobel that it was meant to remind the women of being in the bathroom of a luxury cruise liner ('The *Titanic*!' Fi had joked). Now, sure enough, one of the wood-panelled cubicle doors was closed.

'Fi?' Isobel said tentatively.

'Out in a minute,' Fiona said brightly, but Isobel was sure her voice sounded more muffled than usual.

'Look Fi, I'm sorry about all that,' Isobel said bluntly.

'You know that there's nothing between Will and me, he was just carrying on. Being nice. I hate to think of you being upset.'

The cubicle door banged open and Fiona came out, her face flushed and eyes red as if she had been crying a little.

'Don't bullshit me, Iso,' she said. 'Of course I know there's nothing between you and Will, but that doesn't mean he doesn't fancy you. And he definitely doesn't fancy me.'

'Oh no, you can't say that . . .' Isobel began.

'Of course I can,' Fiona cut her off. 'And it's not that I even mind normally. We're good mates, he's a great guy to work with, that's it. But then you raised certain ideas in my mind and I guess I just got to thinking . . .'

'I'm sorry if I was wrong,' Isobel said awkwardly.

Fiona splashed her face with cool water and then looked at herself in the mirror. 'It's not that I even mind being single,' she said looking into her eyes. 'In fact, most of the time I prefer it. Me and the dogs, we're a functional family. It's just that something can come along and throw your equilibrium. Make you wonder if there should be other things to life. It's so much better not to start thinking of all that stuff in the first place.'

'I'm so sorry,' said Isobel. 'Please don't look sad.'

Fiona smiled at herself in the mirror, more a baring of teeth than a true smile. 'I'm fine and dandy,' she said, turning to Isobel. 'Like I said, most of the time I prefer being exactly the way I am. And most people can't say that, can they?'

After the editorial meeting, in which Fiona, William and

Isobel all avoided each other's eyes and looked a little embarrassed, Helen Hogan called Isobel into the editor's office.

Isobel was now becoming almost immune to this experience, her heart only doing a couple of flops instead of executing an Olympic Gold Medal–winning series of flips, half-turns, twists and an entry in pike position.

'Isobel, my dear,' The Colonel said, showing her to the burgundy-coloured leather couch she kept in one corner. 'Let me start by thanking you for the sandwiches. Delicious and delectable. A very thoughtful "parting gesture". I would never have thought of putting chicken with avocado. And what was giving the beef that delicious flavour . . .?'

'Er, the mustard?'

'Mustard! What an extraordinary idea. Must Have Mustard. Now my dear, I just wanted to say it's been a pleasure to have you around the office . . .'

'Gosh. It's been rather fun for me too,' said Isobel gaily.

' . . . and I must also say,' continued Hogan smoothly, 'that I find your attitude refreshing. Or should I say your *lack* of attitude. I've watched the way you deal with people around the place. You've only been here two weeks and already you're the office confidante. A kind of Work of *Aunt*, if you like.'

'Uh, thank you,' said Isobel, miserably conscious that she had made a complete hash of things with William and Fiona. Somehow she'd left Will feeling foolish and Fiona out of balance. Not exactly a stirling recommendation for an office agony aunt.

'Your sister has been coming along nicely since she

joined *Verve*,' The Colonel continued confidingly, 'but I think I can say to you that sometimes her attitude is not quite what we would like to see. I really sometimes feel that Clare would be happier writing *Remembrance of Things Past* than working at this magazine. She is not always a *team player*.'

Isobel bridled. 'Clare is a wonderful writer.'

'Your loyalty is a credit to you. Here's to the Loyal Family. But I just wanted to say that I appreciate people who are willing to get the job done without grandstanding. And in recognition of your work, I would like to present you with a small cash bonus.'

'Oh there's no need ...' Isobel exclaimed, still smarting.

'But of course there is. Money Makes the World Go Round. And you will also, naturally, be paid as a freelance writer for the piece you do on swapping lives with Clare. Did she tell you that she came up with a really catchy headline – "Flipside"? Perfect. I'm now thinking of the cover line. Something along the lines of "Sisters Role Over and Let Us In on the Secret – Whose Lot is the Happier One?"'

'Well, that sounds – perfect. And thank you for the bonus, this is really unexpected.' Isobel took the envelope and couldn't stop herself from surreptitiously squeezing its satisfyingly spongy thickness. She couldn't remember the last time she had money all of her own. She could use it to buy something for the children – toys or new winter shoes or worming medicine or a tranquilliser gun ...

Dismissed, Isobel closed the editor's door behind her, wheeled around and did a half-skip. She looked across at William, who mouthed, 'The money?' and did a double thumbs up when she nodded. Fiona, too, was miming a victory sign. 'You deserve it,' she murmured.

Isobel went back to her desk still grinning. It was nice to have friends, she thought, even borrowed ones. She hadn't realised how isolated she had let herself become in her post-natal life. No wonder she'd come to depend so much on Clare's friendship – all her other friends from work and school days had been allowed to fade away.

Perhaps, she thought, smiling over at Will and Fi, she shouldn't try to manoeuvre other people's lives so much. Having friends could be just about letting them be happy being themselves, like Fiona had said. The thought crossed Isobel's mind that maybe the same went for your children and your husband. And even agony aunts.

But that thought was too big to tackle right now. Instead she covertly opened the envelope under her desk. Five hundred dollars. Bugger the kids' shoes, for once in her good-girl life she was going to spend the money on herself. She would go shopping on Saturday (her last day of freedom as she was already beginning to think of it) and have a chic haircut and generally plunge into an orgy of self-indulgence.

It would stand as her last gasp of selfishness before she trudged back into life as Isobel 'Mummy will have the burnt chop' Ashton.

CHAPTER 14

Clare deftly manoeuvred the pram through the big glass doors at Henderson Blake, the city accounting firm that counted Philip Ashton amongst its partners.

'Hi there,' she said to the immaculately over-groomed 18-year-old behind the long reception desk. 'Clare Callaway to see Phil Ashton.'

'Just one moment, Ms Callaway. Is Mr Ashton expecting you?' asked the receptionist.

'No, he's not.'

The receptionist attempted to raise two meagre eyebrows which looked too plucked into submission to attempt anything as daring as growing hair ever again. 'Then can I tell him what it's in connection with?' she asked pertly.

'You can tell him,' said Clare, 'that it's in connection with his children. Thank you.'

The girl took a wide-eyed look at Alex in his pram, and a second look at Ellen, who was wearing her new cowboy suit, and picked up the phone. Her lips (matte, not gloss) barely moved as she murmured into the receiver.

Clare smiled to herself. How to start a rumour.

A few minutes later, Phil appeared through some frosted doors looking flustered and pink-faced.

'Clare, what's the matter?' he asked quickly.

'Hi Phil, nothing. I just thought it would be nice if we surprised you and took you out to lunch.'

'Yes Daddy,' echoed Ellen, who had been picked up in his arms. 'We're going to eat pizza.'

'Pizza, umm, that would be – delightful,' Phil said. 'I just wasn't expecting you.'

Clare grinned. 'We thought we'd come in on the off-chance. Ellen was keen to have a ride on the train and I thought we could check out the new museum. But we'd love to have lunch with Daddy first. I figure they don't see much of you during the week.'

'I'd love to do that,' Phil said. 'Ellen, that was a wonderful idea. Just wait here and I'll get my jacket.'

Phil disappeared back through the frosted doors, still carrying Ellen, who had insisted on seeing where Daddy worked. Clare smiled winningly at the receptionist and murmured in an artless girlish confidence: 'Men!'

The woman, eyes now as big as saucers, was obviously itching to pick up the phone as soon as they had gone.

In the nearest Pizza Palace ('All You Can Eat for $6.95 Plus Our World Famous Pasta, Salad, Garlic Bread and Sundae Bar!'), they ordered a family-size pizza with plain cheese and tomato topping and a couple of glasses of the house red. Clare delved into her backpack to find Alex's little container of mushed up lamb and vegetables.

She passed it over to Phil. 'He might eat some pizza

but, just in case, you may as well feed him this disgusting gloop.'

While Phil spooned in the mush and played aeroplane games with Alex, Ellen told him how many snails she had found on the path in the backyard this morning. She also counted to ten in French and sang 'Santa Claus is Coming to Town' very loudly and without remembering many of the words.

'Wonderful!' Phil applauded by clapping Alex's starfish hands together. 'Bravo, Ellen.'

'You'd better have some pizza before it gets cold or I eat the lot,' Clare warned Ellen. Clare had been enthusiastically demolishing a huge wedge. She couldn't believe what an appetite she had these days – if only Leo could see her chomping away now, she thought wryly, he would scarcely be able to contain his excitement.

'You must be hungry too,' she said to Phil. 'Stick Alex in the stroller and I'll give him his bottle and a crust to gnaw on while you eat.'

Phil smiled at her. 'Thanks for coming in. I've often thought Ellen must wonder where I go every day when I leave the house for this place called "the office". At least she knows now that my desk is covered with photos of her and Alex.'

Clare gave him a derisive look over her wine glass. 'Well you had better take advantage of this window of opportunity. Once she's a bit older, she'll figure out Daddy has one of the most boring jobs in the world and she won't want to know anything about it.'

'Oh, unlike Lois Lane, girl reporter, over here with her ground-breaking investigative stories,' Phil teased.

'Speaking of which, next week you'll be back into the thick of things. Looking forward to it?'

'In a way,' Clare admitted. 'This,' she said, nodding slightly at Ellen and Alex, 'was truly much harder work than I expected. But I can't say that *Verve* is the love of my life either.'

Phil bit into another slice of pizza. It was surprisingly good. 'I thought the two weeks went well,' he said. 'The swap, I mean. I was a bit concerned about how the kids would take it, but if anything they seem really relaxed. And what do you think you've learned from the experience?'

'Where do I begin?' Clare answered, rolling her eyes up to the ceiling. 'For a start, I realise that I've always thought about babies and women, and I forgot to think about the role of men in all this.'

'I think that's pretty clear,' Phil said.

'No, seriously. I think there's a clash between our romantic ideal of "the couple" and the way families work. It seems to me that you're so busy when you have small children that you don't have much time to be a couple. It's more like "pass the baby baton" when you cross paths. And then the dads seem to get a bit marginalised too. Like at kindergarten, with all those women and children. Where are the men?'

'Out earning the money for the exorbitant fees?' Phil quipped.

Just then the waitress came to clear the table, so Clare ordered another two glasses of wine. Phil passed Ellen the paper placemat which could be coloured in with a couple of pens from his breast pocket and she immediately set to work, scribbling and humming a little song to herself, which could have been called 'Variations on Two Rather Flat Notes'.

'Getting back to that marginalising thing, it does happen,' Phil continued once he was sure that Ellie's attention was absorbed in her drawing. 'I think it actually starts out with the mother and the baby being so wrapped up with each other. As the man, you just feel a bit – extraneous. It's the mother the baby really wants all the time. It sounds silly, but it can be a bit humiliating when this little baby rejects you because it always wants someone else. Especially when you're also having to put up with sleepless nights and sacrificing things you value – like leisure time, freedom, quite a bit of money and time. You just have to keep telling yourself that the baby has no idea what it's doing.'

'But then, that's just when they're a baby,' Clare said. 'It must be different once they grow up and you can start doing all those manly things, taking them to the football, playing backyard cricket, teaching them how to ride bikes or kill wild animals with their bare hands ...'

'Don't you mean crying in front of them so they know it's okay for men to emote too?' Phil grinned. 'The truth is that the man is still excluded a bit. Or I am. Iso is the one who's home with them so she's much more expert and they tend to go to her first. And it naturally annoys her when I'm slower at doing things or when I do them wrong. She's always saying, "Oh here, let me." I guess I'm just not very good at that stuff.'

'She should learn to let go. Make life easier for herself for a start,' Clare said. 'To be honest Phil, when we started talking about this Sister Pact story, it was because she was getting really exhausted and run down.'

'What else can I do?' said Phil, nettled. 'I already support her to stay home full-time.'

'Crap Phil, you mean you want her to stay home with the kids because you don't believe in full-time childcare. But you have to realise that she is *working*. In fact, it's probably the kind of tedious repetitive work that you're glad you don't have to do all day and all night. So it's up to you to make sure she gets a break, like a morning off on the weekend or a chance to sleep in. Otherwise she's doing the job seven days a week, and looking after you as well.'

'Okay, but she's the organised one, she always leaps up to do things.'

'Phil, you know she's got the biggest martyr complex this side of Joan of Arc,' Clare said. 'It's up to you to save her from herself. Just tell her you're taking the kids out for the day or that you want her to stay in bed on Sunday mornings. You're perfectly capable of looking after them.'

'Of course I am,' he said doubtfully. 'But things just always seem to go so much more smoothly when Iso's in charge. She doesn't even like the way I dress them.'

Clare shook her head. 'Then that's just bullshit. Who cares how you dress them? And when you say you do things wrong, don't you just mean you do them differently to Isobel sometimes? Is that the end of the world? Having seen you in action, I think you're great with the kids. That was a genius idea to put the blue food colouring in the bath last night. They loved it.'

Phil blushed, pleased. 'You really think I'm good at the fatherhood stuff? It's hard to tell sometimes. I mean, there's no 360-degree feedback program.'

Clare laughed at him. 'You see, Phil, there's your problem. 360-degree feedback problems shouldn't exist anywhere, but especially not in fatherhood. But, just between the two of us, you're great at it. Of course Iso is fantastic too. The problem is that she's just so determined to be perfect that she tries too hard and railroads you.'

'She's wonderful with them,' said Phil, loyally. 'But it's interesting, the more time you put into the kids, the better you are at it and the more you get out of it. These last two weeks have been a bit of a revelation for me.'

It was at that point that Alex chose to launch a chewed chunk of pizza crust at Phil, catching him square in the middle of his white-shirted midriff. Although he tried to look nonchalant about the red sauce mark, Clare could see that he was seriously chagrined. Phil was almost fanatical about looking clean and tidy for work.

Alex, perhaps realising the heinous nature of his crime, looked piteously at Clare and held out his arms.

'I see what you mean about getting more out of it. You're beginning to relish the rich tapestry of parenthood,' Clare told Phil, unbuckling Alex from the stroller for a cuddle.

'Yeah,' he said with a reluctant smile.

'Just keep your jacket on this afternoon, no one will see it,' Clare advised him. 'Now,' she looked at Ellen. 'What about we see what other kind of food we can throw at Daddy ... do you want some chocolate ice cream for dessert, Ell's Bells?'

'Yes please,' said Ellen happily, interrupting her hum. 'Could I have some chocolate and some vanilla and some strawberry?'

'Sure,' said Phil. 'But only one scoop of each. And no throwing. What about you, Aunty Clare, how about "the legendary baked cheesecake"?'

Clare groaned. 'Oh no, Phil. For two weeks now I've been stuffing myself like a Christmas turkey.'

'Good. You were just a bag of bones before. Honestly Clare, how do you think you're going to get yourself a bloke if you don't have any flesh on you? Men love curves.'

'I already have myself a bloke, so you must be wrong there.'

'Oh Leo,' Phil said dismissively. 'Another one of your collection of novelty men. I was thinking of someone normal and down-to-earth. Preferably someone who's fonder of you than of themselves.'

'Leo's not that bad,' Clare felt compelled to say. 'Admittedly we're going through a bad patch right now, but if I had someone who was a really decent human being, I'd probably get bored.'

Phil shook his head. 'No, you'd probably just get appreciated. Then all you'd have to do is get used to that strange sensation.'

Clare touched his hand. 'You're a good guy Phil. It's almost enough to make me think that Isobel is right and I should be looking out for Mr Nice. In fact, I might even have met him ... I *will* have the cheesecake. But only as long as you order the Jumbo Size Royal Banana Split and give Lexxie some of your banana.'

'Deal,' Phil said promptly. After they'd given the dessert orders, Phil asked, 'What do you mean you might have met him already?'

Clare blushed a bit. 'Well there's this single dad at

kindergarten . . . You might know him: Rory Maguire?'

Phil shook his head. 'I haven't had much to do with the new kindergarten yet. Too busy working to pay those fees. So tell me about this bloke. Do you think you're ready to take on a single father?'

'Maybe not,' Clare admitted. 'He's got a daughter who's Ellen's age, called Jessie. He's a landscape architect, lives just around the corner from you guys and he's one of those honest, good-hearted kind of guys. He was the one that helped me find Ellie at the pool when I lost her yesterday.'

'Ah, that one,' Phil said. Their desserts arrived and he began spooning bits of banana into Alex's mouth, which opened like a bird's as soon as he saw the spoon coming his way.

'So is he interested?' Phil asked casually.

'I don't know. He might be, although I'm not sure that he approves of my job,' Clare said, tackling her cheesecake.

'Forget that. I'll let you in on a high security secret. Men don't really care about women's jobs, not in the same way that women fuss over what a man does,' Phil said. 'So when are you seeing him next?'

'Not sure. I thought I might run into him at kindergarten this afternoon, but Ellie really wanted to go to the museum so we decided to do that instead.'

'Well call him up,' said Phil promptly. 'Ask him out.'

'Isn't that against all the rules?' Clare said doubtfully.

'Stuff the rules. There are no rules. And take it from me, men love to be asked out occasionally. Do you know how exhausting it is to have to do all the running?'

'I guess so,' Clare said hesitantly.

'Go on, what have you got to lose?'

'Only the upper hand,' Clare said.

'I loathe talking about upper hands and rules. If you like the guy, let him know it. If he doesn't like you back, you may as well find out. Save you a lot of hassle.'

'Okay,' Clare said, crunching through the biscuity crust of her cheesecake. 'I'll do it. I'll ring him when we get home.'

Which is what she decided to do later that afternoon, after sitting Ellen and Alex in front of a Jane Fonda exercise video. Nervously she went over to the phone but at the last moment wondered if she should consult *Manifesting Your Man* on the best way to ask a man out on a date. Yes, she decided, it was definitely better to get some advice first. And while she was at it, she may as well make herself a cup of tea and have a Tim Tam.

Sucking chocolate off her fingers, she flicked through the early chapters of the book until she came to the section called 'Who's Zooming Who?' She was less than reassured by finding the authors advising her to 'make the first phone call or advance at your own peril'.

He'll never forget that you chased him and, while some relationship might follow, always at the back of his mind will be that small voice asking him why you had to come looking for him, rather than vice versa. Never forget that men are the hunters, women are the gatherers. According to the laws of evolutionary psychology, which are just now being understood by sociologists and scientists, men are programmed to go out there and win their prey, whether that prey be culinary, career or sexual. Meanwhile, women are programmed to find good fathers for their babies, preferably someone with status, money and power (all of which will help keep the woman safe while she gestates and then raises her young). So you can see how it works. Follow the laws of your in-built genetic programming, and act according to the laws of nature to manifest that man into your life in record time. But if you flout those laws, you can be sure that he'll feel there's something not quite organic about this relationship. Mr Appropriate is much more likely to stick around if you let him do what comes naturally and make the running.

Clare hesitated for a while. Could there be any substance to this psycho-waffle? But then, remembering what Phil had said, she decided she'd just have to disregard the authors of *Manifesting Your Man*. After all, she reasoned, the book had scarcely helped her 'manifest' Leo on any permanent basis. Reaching in her purse for Rory's card, she marched over to the phone and forced herself to call. He wasn't home but he'd left his mobile number on the answering machine so she called that in turn.

'Hello,' he answered cheerfully.

Her mouth went suddenly dry. 'Oh hi, Rory, it's Clare,' she croaked nervously.

'Oh Clare, great to hear from you. I didn't see you at kindergarten this afternoon. Is it because you're ill? You sound like you have a cold.'

Clare cleared her throat. 'No, no, I'm fine, no cold at all. Ellen just felt like going to the museum so I thought I'd give her a treat. My last week as acting mum and all that.'

'They say the new interactive stuff is amazing.'

'Um, yes,' Clare had no desire to talk about the

274

museum and just prolong her misery. 'Look,' she blurted. 'I was wondering if you might like to come out with me, to dinner or something?'

'I'd really like that,' he said simply.

'Well, great. What about tomorrow night? Phil is home so he will take care of the kids at this end.'

'A genuine, old-fashioned Saturday night date. I haven't had one of those in years,' Rory said. Clare could hear the smile in his voice. 'I can get my mum over to look after Jess. Mum's always urging me to get out more. Just between us, I think she wants to get rid of me so she can get Jess to herself for a whole night. Anyway, I'll come over and pick you up at your place. Or rather Isobel's place. And I'll book somewhere. Say eight o'clock?'

'Perfect.' Clare gave him the address and then hung up, feeling inordinately pleased with herself. But she made the mental note that she would definitely not include a description of this date in her Sister Pact story. Unless, of course, it turned out to be a fabulous success and they fell madly in love and all the *Verve* readers would be driven green with envy.

And even then, she was not sure. After all, Clare didn't want to be shown up in the magazine as the kind of woman who had to go around asking men out on dates. No matter what Phil said.

CHAPTER 15

When the mid-morning Saturday tram rattled past her window, Isobel cranked open her eyelids a millimetre and then closed them rather quickly.

Her farewell drinks with the *Verve* team at Fergus McFingall's had involved more than a few glasses of the robust house chardonnay. She seemed to have hazy memories of attempting some vaguely Irish dancing, with her skirt hitched up around her thighs, while Fiona skipped around opposite her, gleefully shouting exclamations she thought were suitably Irish such as 'T'be sure, T'be sure!', 'Bring another round of Guinness!' and 'I loved *Angela's Ashes*!'

It had been, Isobel had to admit, gingerly touching her head, quite a night.

She had been left with the warm and gooey conviction that people at the magazine would genuinely miss her. Being a maternal figure wasn't such a bad thing in the workplace, she thought sleepily. During the course of two weeks at *Verve*, almost everyone seemed to have decided she would be the willing recipient of their confidences. It was like having access to her own daytime soap opera, except the players didn't use quite as much make-up or meaningful eye contact.

She had also been touched that the staff were so gratifyingly enthusiastic about her cooking, unlike her own family, who tended to either throw the food on the floor (kids) or swallow it without taking their eyes off the television screen (Phil and/or kids).

But this was it, her last day of freedom before going home to pick up the reins she'd reluctantly dropped two weeks ago.

Already she could feel nagging dutiful thoughts sidling sneakily into her mind – had she paid next term's subscription for Babyrobics? Should Ellen be taking up a musical instrument yet? Had Clare managed to discover and then decimate her precious hoard of frozen home-made emergency casseroles?

She would have to start cooking as soon as she got home to stock up again. She always liked to keep a full freezer, just in case Phil's mum ever looked in there (she never had but you never knew where she was going to peer next).

She forced herself to think about the day ahead instead, her indulgence day, which would be spent blowing the *Verve* pay packet. And tonight, she would be cooking a dinner party for two. When Leo had rung her two nights before to ask how her second week was going, she had impulsively offered to cook him a home-made meal as a parting gesture to thank him for his last minute co-operation with the story.

She wondered uneasily if she should be whipping up

some exotic and sophisticated Vietnamese or Sri Lankan dish but then decided to stick with her original plan, a homely feed of roast lamb followed by bread and butter pudding. She was loathe to make a fool of herself by botching a new recipe in front of him.

She swung her legs out of bed and rushed across the bare cold boards to the bathroom. Life was really so simple without children or husband. She could lie in bed for three hours, or get up and clean the flat like a dervish. She could read Jackie Collins or stand on her head naked against the wall or eat deep-fried ice cream, all without explaining or justifying herself to anyone. It was a strange feeling, but not altogether unpleasant.

On the other hand, she reminded herself, as she stood under the shower washing her hair (Isobel could never let a hairdresser wash her hair if it wasn't already squeaky clean – it didn't seem *nice* somehow), if she lived like this all the time, she would get terribly self-centred and inflexible.

The single woman's life would make her lose her ability to compromise with and tolerate other people's foibles. Particularly of the male variety. After a few years of solo living, Isobel knew she couldn't go back to television channel surfing, fart jokes, shower trumpeting and social commitment amnesia. So it was a good thing that she was forced to keep flexible by winding herself around the lives of two small children and a spouse, she thought. Otherwise, she could turn into the kind of person who started screeching whenever someone disturbed the arrangement of their art books on the coffee table.

Besides, she missed the sweet, easy familiarity of life with Phil, and of course she yearned for Ellie and Alex.

Every time she walked past small children in the streets, she longed to be back with her own two, who were so much more beautiful, remarkable and interesting than any other children she saw.

Vigorously drying her hair with a towel, Isobel decided that it was reassuring to know that the habits she had developed as a 'homemaker' had functioned in the real world too. Looking after young children had taught her to just get on with the task at hand quickly without fuss. That had apparently been a hit at the magazine. She still remembered The Colonel's parting words with a thrill of pleasure.

'My dear, if you ever find yourself looking for a job, come to me. I'd love to have you back on my team, because you're a real team player. Shoulders to the wheel,' The Colonel had said, blinking her shiny little black eyes. 'And I just know that Suzanne would *love* your work.'

Isobel smiled at the memory, even though she doubted she'd ever take up this flattering offer. It did make her start to think about possibilities other than rushing home to try to conceive a third baby at all costs. Maybe she could go back to nursing part-time, or even do a course in something ...

Outside it was a superb day. Sunlight bathed the left-over drifts of leaves and the air was soft, almost as if the weather had decided to fast forward through winter to the benevolence of spring.

Isobel, in her most comfortable shoes, hit the city department stores and played shopping. First she leisurely tried on wads of expensive clothes and then stuffed them back into the arms of the sulky salesgirls.

She noticed that two weeks at the gym had started to give her definition in muscles she hadn't even known she had. Then she headed for the book section, where she stroked the smooth spines and read through half-a-dozen magazines thoroughly.

Then it was down to business. She put herself in the hands of one of those 'make-over' women who glide around behind department store cosmetic counters. This purse-lipped fifty-something, who looked like she applied her own make-up with a paint spray gun, uttered that ominous phrase 'What are you using on your skin at the moment?' and then proceeded to tell Isobel that she was plagued by dry bits, oily bits, scaly bits and untoned bits, all of which could be remedied by spending $500 on essential products which, as far as Isobel could tell, were all variations on petroleum.

As the efficient hands daubed at her face, Isobel let the spiel wash over her, the soothing incantation of words such as *younger-looking*, *radiance*, *smoother*, *anti-oxidant*, *tightening and toning*, *firming*, *illuminating*, *resurfacing*, *renormalising* (renormalising? she thought).

In the end, to go with her expertly embellished face, she bought a new moisturiser and a lipstick to join the tribe of little tubes waiting for its newest sibling in her bathroom cabinet.

After lunch, she paid a hairdresser a small fortune to shear four centimetres from her hair so when it dried it would lift and curl at the ends. Feeling like an escapee from a shampoo commercial, she bounced her hair as she walked back up to the tram stop, liking the feeling of it tickling her shoulders instead of being lashed back in the usual sensible, child-proof ponytail.

Then, tired but buzzing with post-purchase endorphins, she went home with her bags of new toys – including a new pant suit in a floaty, flattering, dark-blue fabric; some stuff which a sales assistant assured her would 'melt away' her cellulite; the new vibrant lipstick ('It lights up your face with an inner glow,' promised the make-over woman); a couple of latest-release books and homecoming presents for Ellen and Alexander.

When she reached the flat, she opened all the bags and distributed things around her on the floor while she ripped off the price tags. Barchester relished this Christmas-for-One, pouncing in and out of the plastic bags and batting the tube of lipstick around on the floor until Isobel had to stretch under the couch to retrieve it.

She was shocked by all the dust and cat hair and (empty!) condom packets under there. Really, she thought wincing, she should give the flat a thorough spring clean before Clare and her slovenly housekeeping standards returned. On the other hand, she reflected, it seemed a waste to do all that work, given that Clare was going to come back with her aforementioned indifference. Isobel realised that she was beginning to appreciate that there might be possibilities in cutting corners. Especially as this afternoon was her last opportunity to sit down to read one of her delicious new books, knowing her peace was not going to be shattered by the sound of a child crying. Sheer indulgence.

By five o'clock, after a short but sumptuous afternoon nap, Isobel was in the kitchen spiking the joint with garlic and sprinkling roasting potatoes with rosemary, salt and pepper.

Once the meat was on and the pudding was waiting

in its pan of water, Isobel had a long bath, carefully keeping her expertly painted face from the water. Afterwards she slathered herself in one of Clare's arsenal of body moisturisers. She put on her new pant suit and touched up her mouth with the lipstick, which she had to admit did add a certain vibrancy to her face, although she suspected that such a vivid shade of magenta would do that to anyone.

Leo thumped on the door half an hour late. By that time, Isobel was beginning to fear that her lamb would be cooked through and she would have to serve the pudding as a side dish with the main course.

He was dressed in his usual top-to-toe black and looked even paler than usual, perhaps as a result of long hours spent hanging around in the dark annoying the editor and director of his film.

As soon as he sauntered through the door, Isobel hustled him off to the Clare's little dining table, in one corner of the living room. Telling him to open the bottle of wine he'd bought, she hustled back into the kitchen to carve the meat. Leo seemed startled but gratifyingly impressed by the hearty plate of food she thumped on the table in front of him.

'Amazing. Just like Mum's,' he said, reaching for the mint sauce and gravy.

'Speaking of Mum's, where did you grow up?' Isobel asked curiously, following with her own plate.

'Oh, you know, western suburbs, little wooden house, two bedrooms, outside loo.' He looked pugnacious.

Isobel refused to gratify him by exclaiming over his childhood plumbing arrangements. 'And I take it your mother cooked a good roast?' she asked.

His face softened. Obviously it was still cool to think fondly of your mum's food. In fact, the thought crossed Isobel's mind that perhaps the fashion for comfort food had brought women's traditional cooking skills into new repute. Provided, of course, the food was reinterpreted by a man and dished up at exorbitant costs with a bowl of olive oil and some peasant bread on the table.

'By the way,' she added, passing the dish. 'Would you like some olive oil for your bread?'

'Fantastic,' Leo said with his mouth full.

Leo eagerly scoffed down the first plateful, seconds and even a smidgen of thirds before leaning back in the chair groaning and loosening his thick leather belt. 'That was totally amazing. You're a fantastic cook,' he said, eyeing her respectfully.

'You know, I have to say it again. It's incredible how different you are from Clare,' he continued. 'She hardly knows her way from the kettle to the tap and you can churn out this fantastic food. If I see her tomorrow, I bet we'll be eating pizza. In fact, knowing her cooking, I hope we'll be eating pizza.'

Isobel lifted one shoulder. 'I guess she's never been interested in cooking. I don't think I was either but when you have a husband and children, you have to learn. You can't order takeaway Chinese every night or ask them to live on bowls of muesli and low-fat milk like Clare does.'

'It's interesting though, isn't it, the differences between siblings,' Leo mused. 'I mean, here's two women raised by the same parents but you're totally different. You have the kids and Clare is a dedicated career woman. She's always doing that "does my bum look big in this?" routine whereas you don't seem to care.'

Isobel flinched. It was strange, she thought, that even while she could see Leo's drawbacks (arrogance, insensitivity, complacency), she still felt an unaccountable urge for his approval. 'I think I just heard you say I have no brains and a big backside,' she said.

'Not at all.' Leo wiped a piece of bread around his plate to sop up the last of the gravy. 'I honestly think it's fantastic to meet a woman who isn't emaciated. Not that Clare is emaciated, of course, but you know what I mean. And you have plenty of brains, it's just that you don't express them by running around wearing a power suit. Of course, I also think it's fantastic that Clare is so into her career,' Leo said smoothly as he picked up the empty plate and passed it to her. 'Did you say bread and butter pudding? I love bread and butter pudding. With cream?'

'Double.'

After the meal, they sat on Clare's sofa, drinking freshly brewed coffee and glasses of some dubious port that Leo had unearthed from Clare's motley stash of liquor.

Leo sighed happily, taking another home-made chocolate truffle from the plate on the coffee table where his Blundstone boots were propped.

'Now, this is enough to make me think it's worth getting married. Glorious for a man to come home from a hard day in the editing suite to find all this waiting for him.'

'Your outlook on marriage is a trifle anachronistic,' Isobel observed lazily, leaning back into the squishy embrace of the couch. 'Isn't the man rushing home from work to put on the dinner himself, because his partner has been out working even harder?'

'Oh yes, of course.' Leo airily waved his hand. 'But you can still dream about all this,' he said vaguely indicating the coffee pot, the chocolates, his feet on the table and Isobel herself. 'It's a fantasy.'

'But that's hypocritical,' Isobel objected. 'You say you love women who are ambitious but now you're wishing you had some little wife at home cooking lamb roasts for you. Of course, if that's what you want, you don't need to be married – just hire a housekeeper. She or he wouldn't even have to live in.' Isobel was beginning to enjoy this debate. Leo had a knack of stimulating conversation, even if it was powered by irritation, she thought looking across at him.

'I can't get quite all of it,' Leo drawled. 'For instance, I don't know if my housekeeper would look quite as luscious as you do lying there on that couch. And before you leap to your feet and slap my face while crying "fie, sir", I am actually agreeing with you. I *could* get all this from a housekeeper.'

'So what's your point?' asked Isobel, sipping some port while a pleasant fuzzy sensation lapped at the edges of her mind.

'Well, I'm actually feeling so well-fed that I'm not sure I'm capable of making any points,' Leo said solemnly. 'But I think my point is that women have nagged themselves out of marriage. I mean, take your average modern woman. She wants to share all the cooking, share the household tasks, share the childcare and get multiple orgasms in bed on top of all that. What's in it for the bloke? He's better off paying for someone to do the household chores and running a girlfriend on the side. Gets less nagging, more shagging and someone who's still happy to go down on him.'

Leo topped up his port glass again and raised it to her. 'But then I see someone like you and I think that maybe it could all be worth it. If I could find a woman like you – beautiful, smart, cooks, great breasts – maybe marriage could be a viable option. But then, you're the exception that proves the rule. I mean, you tell me, why should any man in his right mind get married these days?'

'Or any woman for that matter,' Isobel retorted, thinking that this man really was an annoyingly sexist jerk. 'The woman has to clean up after two people instead of one, and little things like red roses and special dinners go flying out the window as soon as the wedding certificate marches in the door. No wonder women get so hysterical about their weddings; they know subconsciously that they have to cram in enough romance to last a lifetime.'

'That's a bit harsh,' Leo protested. 'I know plenty of men who are romantic husbands, poor bastards. It's a shame if your husband has forgotten how lucky he is. He should be getting down on his knees beside the dinner table every night to thank God for what he's got.'

Isobel giggled suddenly. 'Or to pick up the spaghetti that the kids have thrown under there. But we're getting off the point. What was the point? Oh yes, marriage and why people do it. What about children?' she asked triumphantly. 'Your picture of the lone, happy, lazy, satiated bachelor leaves out reproduction altogether.'

'Oh I told you, that comes later,' Leo said dismissively. 'When the man turns about fifty and hears the grim ticking of his own mortality. Until then, I think you're better off with a fastidious cleaner and a laid-back girl-friend. And I do mean laid back. Much more efficient than trying to combine the two in a wife.'

Isobel put down her coffee mug, her hand a little unsteady. 'So Clare is the "laid-back" girlfriend in this scenario of yours?'

'Sure. Look, I'm mad about Clare, but that's the deal. She knew exactly where we stood, even if she wants to move on to Mr Sperm. As for me, I think my next romance might be with a married woman. They're inde-pendent and together. None of the "where is this rela-tionship *going*?" bullshit you get from single women.'

Leo filled his glass again. 'Not that I mean Clare, you understand. But are you happy as a wife? Do you just love getting that dinner on the table every night? Personally, I think it's a waste. You're beautiful, you're intelligent and you spend your day looking after two little kids.'

Flattered, despite herself, Isobel shook her head. 'I think looking after kids is the best use you can make of your brains. Children are only little for such a short time. And I hate to say something so drearily clichéd, but what could be more important?'

Leo leant back and in doing so his head came closer to Isobel's. She could even smell the port on his breath.

'You're right,' he said softly. 'What could be more important? I certainly never complained about my mum staying home. When we ran home from school in the rain, she always had a hot bath waiting for us. It was fantastic. Still,' Leo turned his head slightly so he could look intently at Isobel, 'it does seem a waste. I can't believe your husband doesn't appreciate you. You have a first-class mind, you know.'

'Do I?' asked Isobel, suddenly suffused with a warm glow.

'Absolutely.'

Then he leant over very gently and kissed her.

Isobel was knocked for six by that kiss. In her defence, she had consumed more than her usual modest glass of wine, and she was already a little overcome by all those references to her beauty and her fabulous breasts.

And it had been many years since she had been kissed by anyone but Phil. Come to think of it, she was not sure she kissed Phil much these days either, not like before they were married, when they could spend hours wrapped in head-swimming clinches. All that had somehow faded away into cheek pecks and conjugal hugs. And this kiss from Leo was quite a kiss, starting soft and sweet and ending up deep and greedy and consuming, with all the dark glamour of forbidden fruit and the thrill of the unknown.

Before Isobel even had time to remember that she had a conscience, she was flat on her back on Clare's sofa with Leo on top of her and one hell of an erection pushing firmly against her new dark-blue, floaty-fabric pants suit.

Now all she had to do was decide what she was going to do about it.

CHAPTER 16

Now you might have thought that at that moment Clare, stranded in the suburban sprawl and somnolent from viewing *The Lion King* for the twenty-seventh time, would feel a frisson of uneasiness. Some sixth sense that all was not well in her world. A lurking eddying of the ether.

But Clare was feeling mellow.

It had been a delicious day. Because the sun was shining so benevolently, Clare had suggested to Phil that they take the children to the beach where they could pretend it was a cool summer's day.

So one big family, they'd piled into the stationwagon with kids, dog, buckets, spades, towels and a picnic cooler. This last item Clare had hastily filled with fruit, a packet of frozen mixed peas and corn, peanut-butter sandwiches and bottles of fruit juice. Phil, meanwhile, pushed and pulled the kids into their sunsuits, in case they were determined to go into the sea. He also smeared non-chemical sunblock cream on their milk-white, tender limbs because Isobel insisted they wear it summer or winter. 'Ellen will go down on her knees and thank me one day,' she always said.

Phil commented to Clare that she seemed to be able to get things packed very quickly. A day out hardly seemed like a drama at all. Of course, he added judiciously as they tootled seaward, he realised they wouldn't be eating the kind of nutritious and delicious picnic that Isobel would have produced, but it didn't matter.

They found the long thin sliver of beach at suburban Edithvale was almost deserted and they had what Clare later described as a storybook day – the sea was clean and mild; the dog didn't scoff the sandwiches and throw up in the back of the car; the children didn't whine more than was absolutely necessary to express themselves.

Instead, Ellen and Alex briefly showed off their new swimming skills to their suitably admiring Daddy, then they all, including Daisy, dug big holes in the sand, constructing primitive sandcastles which they jumped on, knocking them down.

And whenever she could, Clare nursed to herself the luscious thought that tonight she had a Saturday-night date with a potential 'Mr Appropriate', someone she thought she actually liked. Maybe even quite a lot.

She'd already decided to wear a dress for a change. She was sure that every time Rory had seen her she'd been wearing leggings or pants (except that one time when she was wearing nothing but a wet swimsuit of course). Clare had even had a quick shuffle through Isobel's wardrobe and found the perfect thing, a flowing knit dress in a soft maroon colour with a deep scooped neck. It would look casual but flattering, feminine but simple. Clare was already looking forward to going home and starting her Getting Ready for a Date rituals.

In the meantime, she relished this time with the kids and Phil. Lunch was a matter of delving into the picnic cooler whenever anyone felt hungry, and they finally headed for home late in the afternoon, when the sun was turning tarnished gold and they were down to the last clean nappy for Alex.

The children dozed in the car but woke up when they reached home for a bottle of milk (Alex) and *The Lion King* (Ellen). After that they fell fast asleep again, and were tipped, still sandy and briny, into their beds.

Clare rushed to start getting ready to go out. She was in the shower washing her hair when Phil knocked hesitantly on the door.

'Uh, Clare?' he said shyly.

'Yes?' Clare bellowed back over the noise of the shower.

'It's Rory Maguire on the phone for you.'

'Oh. Could you tell him I'll call him back?' Clare said, her heart sinking a little. A phone call at 7.30 pm before a date was not a good sign. Unless he was ringing to ask if she preferred yellow roses or something in a box from Tiffany's.

Wrapped in her terry-towelling dressing gown, oblivious to the fact that her hair was drying in fluffy disarray, Clare marched into the family room. While Phil made sympathetic faces at her over the kitchen counter, she called Rory.

'It's Jess,' he said without a preamble. 'She has a temperature. I was thinking that I could leave her with Mum, which is why I put off calling you. But it still seems to be going up and I just can't leave Mum with the responsibility.'

'Of course I understand. I hope it's nothing serious,' Clare said.

'It's probably not, but you have to keep an eye on temperatures. Look, I'm sorry to ruin your evening.'

My evening, thought Clare, a bit piqued. No reference to *his* evening being spoiled, of course. 'Not at all. All the best with Jessie,' she said formally.

He thanked her and rang off, without making another tentative date. So that, Clare thought, is probably that. He was most likely just being polite about the whole thing in the first place.

'Cheer up,' said Phil encouragingly. 'There's plenty of other evenings. Why don't I put one of Iso's casseroles in the microwave? We'll open a really good bottle of red and watch some TV. How does that sound?'

'A riot,' Clare said. He really was a kind man.

They ate an excellent boeuf bourguignon, with crusty bread left over from the picnic. Phil sacrificed one of his really fine bottles of wine and it slid down like warm satin. By the time she had nearly finished her half of the bottle, Clare was hardly conscious of feeling disappointed at all. And the food was delectable. If only she'd known about all those casseroles earlier . . .

After eating, they sat on the family room couch in front of the blank television. Phil opened a second bottle, not quite as good as the first, and they sat talking quietly about the day. What Alex did with that dead seagull, what Ellen said when the old lady lost her bikini top in the sea, whether Alex had really said 'Dad' or the rather more likely 'Duh'.

It was, Clare imagined, the kind of conversation married people had all the time: effortless, companionable.

Very peaceful, she thought sentimentally. And really, Phil was such a sweet man. She couldn't imagine someone like Leo spending a day playing toddlers' games on a beach. And what about the way Phil had come home with a tub of Dairy Bell Ice Cream the night before and remembered that her favourite flavour was Caramel with Toffee Chip? There was no way Leo would have bothered. Even if he had brought ice cream over – which was unthinkable – he would have bought whatever suited him best ('Clapperboard Chip!' Clare thought, giggling immoderately with the aid of too much red wine).

Also, she decided, cocking her head to one side (or at least letting it flop over), Phil was quite handsome in a wiry-haired sort of way. And – what was the word – *honourable*. Not a word you heard a lot of these days but it definitely suited Phil. The Honourable Philip Ashton. A truly decent bloke. Bit like Rory, she thought hazily, another truly decent bloke, staying home with his feverish little daughter. What a shame he obviously didn't feel she was a truly decent woman. Bloody shame.

Feeling sorry for herself again, she drained her glass. When Phil regretfully waggled the empty bottle around in front of her, she said a little unsteadily: 'Well, I guess that's the sign that I should head off to bed. I think all that fresh air has gone to my head.'

'What about the dishshes?' Phil asked.

'Oh forget 'em. You can do them in the morning,' Clare said, waving one hand expansively.

They both leaned forward and stood up and someone, possibly Clare, stumbled and someone else, possibly Phil, reached out to steady her, and then, before either quite knew what was happening, they had their arms around each other and they weren't letting go.

The honourable Philip Ashton was, of course, horrified to his very core. He loved Isobel and firmly believed in fidelity in marriage. How did he come to be in this position?

But, to explain rather than excuse, it had been a long time in the wilderness for Phil. He and Isobel only really made a determined effort to make love when she was fertile. If he was really honest with himself, he knew Isobel didn't find him deeply exciting in *that* way, although he'd often thought things would be better if she was a little more enthusiastic herself.

Now, here he was with a woman who seemed to like him and enjoy his company. He felt himself crushing her tightly to his chest so he could feel the softness of her breasts and the firm bump of her pubic bone.

'Oh God,' he groaned. 'What are we doing . . .?'

Clare didn't answer. Right now, she was concentrating on leaning in to kiss this man who evidently found her so wildly, thrillingly desirable. If anyone was thinking (which no one was), there may have even been just a tiny element of victory for Clare. After a childhood spent being beautiful Isobel's plain younger sister, here was this man, yes, Isobel's man, who wanted her so much he could hardly speak.

In the words of Robin Williams, *carpe diem*, thought Clare Callaway foggily, standing on her toes.

Thirty kilometres and a socio-lifestyle mile away, Leo squirmed his clever fingers up Isobel's top and down her new pant suit until Isobel wanted to scream with pleasure.

Phil had never been a very imaginative lover and she had been too shy and, maybe, too squeamish to figure out what she should ask him to do differently. Besides, men were meant to be the sexual experts weren't they? And how could you ask for something if you didn't know what it was you wanted to ask for? Certainly, desire had never been so immediate, and yet so white-hot and molten. She'd forgotten the excitement of making love with a stranger, and she didn't think she had ever known that sex could be this frenzied, this reckless.

Maybe Isobel would have had the strength to pull back from the brink even then, especially if she had considered the fragility of the little family raft she'd lashed together with such hope and determination, if Leo hadn't put his mouth somewhere that no one else's mouth had ever been.

Barchester got such a fright when Isobel started to screech with joy that he took off and hid under the bed and refused to emerge for another two days. (Clare thought later it was because he was sulky with her for having gone away and she was rather flattered.)

Leo almost purred. Already he could imagine how it would feel to have his hands tangled in Isobel's long, thick hair and to be plunging into her like there was no tomorrow.

Clare leant in to Phil, her face turned up, her eyes closed.

She sensed his face, anticipated the kiss. She even thought fleetingly how soothing it was to be wanted, after the coolness and cruelty of Leo, and the elusive ambiguity of Rory Maguire.

But then, for one fatal second, she flicked open her eyes, and saw her brother-in-law's face, as familiar to her as her father's.

'Oh my God,' she muttered, pulling back.

At her words, Phil too opened his eyes and looked down at Clare, his unfocused eyes slowly sharpening and then giving way to a look of profound guilt and embarrassment.

'Bloody hell,' he said succinctly.

Isobel was so swallowed up in sensation that she hadn't even bothered to think about putting something down to protect the couch, which she would usually have been meticulous about (so much easier to simply pop a towel down rather than having to change the sheets all the time).

She wriggled like a fish and screamed like a banshee and sank her teeth into Leo's ear like a tigress. It was stupendous.

She wondered fleetingly if it was possible to actually spontaneously combust from sheer excitement. And when Leo wrapped his fingers into her hair and brutally pulled her head back as if her neck was going to break, it was the most heart-stoppingly, darkly erotic moment of her life.

And then he paused and smiled at her, positively wolf-like with his teeth bared and his eyes gleaming.

Isobel heard the crackle of condom wrapping but

closed her eyes. She didn't want to think about that. If she started thinking, everything would come rushing back in on her. Right now she was concentrating on not thinking one tiny little thing.

'I'm going to bed,' Phil told Clare.

'Me, too,' she said. 'I'm going to my bed,' she added hastily.

Just then Alex woke up and gave one of his short sharp cries. They almost bumped into each other in their desperation to get out the door to attend to him.

'I'll get him,' Phil said. 'It must be my turn.'

Clare didn't argue. Still feeling hot with shame, she disappeared into her bedroom and closed the door tightly. She couldn't believe what had just happened.

Neither could Leo. He knew he was attractive to women, but this was definitely a Saturday-night bonus. He looked down at Isobel, who was apparently asleep, lying back on the couch with a big strawberry flush spreading across her chest, her full, slightly floppy breasts spilling sideways, and her long hair in disarray.

Leo reached over for another home-made chocolate truffle. Really, amazingly delicious he thought with satisfaction.

Isobel opened her eyes just in time to see him complacently popping one in his mouth. With his mouth full and his teeth stickily brown with chocolate, he smiled his wolfish smile at her.

Bloody hell, thought Isobel, *what have I done?*

CHAPTER 17

At five o'clock on Sunday morning, Clare sat at the kitchen table feeling like a snake in the grass.

And what was worse, she knew she was a snake so there couldn't even be any sneaky melodramatic pleasure in her self-castigation. She still couldn't believe she had almost snogged her own brother-in-law. It was unthinkable. Almost as bad as incest. And a betrayal of good, kind Isobel, who even be now would be sleeping the sleep of the innocent. Clare wondered how she was going to look Iso in the eyes when they met in a few hours time.

Miserably she reached for her copy of *Manifesting Your Man*, which she'd left sitting on the kitchen table. She remembered there was a whole chapter towards the end on 'Avoiding Mr Inappropriate'. The authors were quite firm.

There are all kinds of Mr Inappropriates, which is why this book has given you the keys to attracting the right man into your life. Obviously there are men who you should avoid like doggy doo-doos – the violent man, the financially mean man, the man who won't come home to meet your folks, the man who never introduces you to his friends or work colleagues, the man with a serious criminal record. More on the borderline is the man who never tells you you're beautiful or who watches too much sport on television. He's a man who might just be saved by the guidance of a strong woman. Then there are the taboo men, men you should not even consider, such as your best friend's husband or boy-friend for example. No matter how charming this man may be, it is extraordinarily unlikely that he will be your Mr Appropriate. Men who mess around with their wives' best friends are hardly ever appropriate.

If you do find yourself fatally attracted to such a man, treat him like a forbidden treat – say chocolate cheesecake when you're on a diet. Reward yourself when you ignore him or avoid him (buy yourself that new scarf or pair of shoes). And punish yourself if you find yourself flirting with him or joining him out in the garden to look at the moon. You could give up having facials for a month or stop eating cookies (which might be good for your figure as well!). This kind of carrot and stick approach will soon get you over any adolescent crushes on the taboo man.

Clare started speculating on what penance could be severe enough to make her feel okay about nearly kissing Isobel's husband. Perhaps she could switch to a macro-biotic food diet. Or go to work in Zaire with the ebola virus. Or, even worse, force herself to work at *Verve* for another decade and volunteer to fill in for the gardening writer. Or . . .

'Clare?'

Oh God no, Phil was awake already. Please God, she thought, don't let him walk in and say he's fallen in love and wants to leave Isobel for me. Don't let him want to run away and abandon his family.

'Clare?' Phil sat down at the table beside her. His hair was appealingly tousled, his flannel pyjamas crumpled as if he had tossed and turned all night.

Clare knew she had to tell him where he stood right from the word go. 'Phil,' she said solemnly. 'I love Iso.'

'So do I,' he replied.

Phew, she thought, what a relief.

'What we nearly did last night was still a despicable thing. Unbelievable,' Clare said.

'I know.'

'Yes, well, I mean, it was really, really bad.'

'I agree.'

Clare told herself she was not even the tiniest bit peeved that Phil was not hurling himself at her feet and telling her she was a goddess and begging her to run away with him. No, she was relieved that he too had come to the only sensible conclusion and saved her the trouble of turning him down.

And he looked terrible too, eyes bloodshot, hands trembling, skin pale. Now she just needed to make sure that he agreed with her about the best way to handle their folly.

'I think the only thing we can do now is decide it never happened,' she suggested carefully. 'Isobel need never know anything about this. She'd be devastated. It would be terrible for us to salve our own consciences by making confessions which would only devastate her.'

'As far as I'm concerned, nothing happened.'

'Nothing did happen really.'

'Nothing.'

'Nothing.'

There was a long, long pause.

Clare wondered in a detached way how she could ever have been even fleetingly attracted to this man with his Harpo Marx hair and those ridiculous faded flannel pyjamas. She must have been the victim of too much booze, too much sun, too many hormones, too much *Lion King* exposure. Not to mention Rory and the whole anticlimax of last night. Story of my life really, she thought bitterly. Anticlimax.

She jumped up hastily from the table. 'I'll put the kettle on then I'll get dressed before the kids start to wake up.'

'Yes, I'll get dressed too.'

Daisy had to scuttle smartly out of the way as they both raced for the door at once.

About ten o'clock that morning, Isobel stood outside her own front door feeling sick to the bottom of her heart. For a moment, she didn't even feel she had the right to use her own front door key to get into the house.

Isobel had always been a believer in monogamy. It made sense to her – so much easier to keep things clear cut and under control. Now she'd betrayed Phil and her children and herself. Yet, even filled with black shame, Isobel knew she had no intention of telling Phil what she'd done. Her only thought was a fierce determination to keep her family together. And then do whatever it took to earn her own forgiveness.

Taking a deep, wobbly breath, she let herself into her own house as gingerly as any stranger unsure of her welcome.

'Mummy!' Ellen was a flying whirlwind of arms and legs and pigtails and chocolate-smeared mouth, leaping into her arms.

'Mummy's home! Mummy's home!' Ellen chanted.

Clare appeared from the family room carrying Alex, who honked with happiness at the sight of his mother and held out his dimpled little arms. Soon Isobel was carrying both of her children and pretending to stagger under their combined weight.

'Welcome back to your life,' Clare said.

'Thank you. I've left yours back at the flat.'

The sisters looked at each other and exchanged big jolly smiles and both failed, for perhaps the first time in their lives, to pick up that there was anything seriously wrong with the other.

'I love your hair like that, and that colour lipstick looks amazing on you. You look really gorgeous,' Clare babbled. 'Glowing. It's fantastic to see you again, I've missed you. But don't just stand there, come through, let me make you a cup of coffee. Or maybe you'd like to make it yourself? It's your house after all.'

'No, I'd love to sit down on the couch with the kids while you make the coffee. Where's Phil?'

Clare looked away quickly. 'Oh, he had quite a few chores to do outside in the garden and then he had to nip down to the hardware store to pick up some stuff. He should be back any minute.'

'I can't wait to see him, I've missed him much more than I thought I ever could.'

They finally settled around the kitchen table to drink their coffee, while under the table, Ellen laid out her new seashell collection in an elaborate pattern that was only slightly spoiled when Alex tried to eat one.

'Home-made biscuits, Clare?' Isobel said, picking up a gingernut. 'Don't tell me you've been so overcome by proxy motherhood that you've taken up baking?'

'Nope, I didn't lower my standards that far,' Clare said. 'These were actually given to me by Karen Elliott, one of the women from kindergarten. She just dropped in to say hi during the week. She's a really great woman. Maybe you should get to know some of the other kindergarten mums. Not that I want to tell you how to live your life,' Clare added hastily. 'I'm sure you know what you're doing far better than I do.'

Isobel shook her head. Once she might have secretly agreed with Clare on that, but now she couldn't afford that old complacency. She didn't think she'd ever feel so sure of herself again. 'You're right about the other mums at kindergarten,' she said. 'I've been thinking how lazy I've been about making friends and getting out of the house since we moved here. Maybe worse than lazy. Maybe I've been plain old snobbish.'

'Iso, you're not lazy or snobbish, you're just a bit – self-contained, sometimes,' Clare said very kindly.

Isobel would have none of it. 'Or I just started to get too entranced by that picture of myself as the Lone Mum, housebound, proud and defensive,' she said with brutal honesty. 'So do I take it that you still hate suburban life?'

'It got better,' Clare admitted. 'Like you always said, it can get very tedious, but the kids are a joy. You're doing a great job with them, Iso. You and Phil. But what about the single woman's life? I spoke to Fi and she said you'd gone great guns at the magazine.'

'Not at all. I just did menial work. And wrote that problem page which The Colonel re-wrote totally and then went home miserably every night to an empty flat. I'm sorry that I ever made light of your problems, Clare, I can see now how difficult it must be not to have a family around you.'

Clare was puzzled. As far as she was aware, Isobel had never made light of her problems. 'Well, my life does have quite a few pluses,' she said. 'Like not having to do hours of housework or push prams or play *The Lion King* game till you want to scream.' Clare poured herself another half a cup of coffee. 'So, we'll both be glad to get back to our own lives then,' she said.

'Oh yes, very. I won't miss your life at all,' Isobel agreed.

'No, no, nor me yours. But it should still make a great yarn for the magazine,' Clare said.

They drank their coffee rather quickly.

'So I guess I might be seeing Leo tonight,' Clare remarked. 'Even if it's just to finish the whole thing off once and for all. Phil told me you were planning to make a home-cooked meal for him. Did that ever happen?'

Isobel found herself completely absorbed in watching the children attempt to stuff seashells down Daisy's ears. 'What? Oh Leo, oh yes, last night. It was okay. He seemed to like the food and that was it really. He went home.'

She certainly wasn't going to admit that he went home half-naked, half-tanked and very furious. When Isobel had sat up on the couch and looked at him, she'd felt nothing but amazement and disgust. She couldn't believe that this grinning man had persuaded her to risk everything she valued. That family wheel, of which she was the hub, now seemed infinitely fragile and precious. Something wonderful that it was criminally stupid to risk by misbehaviour.

Leo had had a little trouble believing that Isobel meant it when she said he had to leave – right now. In the end she'd hustled him out the door so fast that he was still hopping to get his second leg back into his black jeans. And she threw his leather jacket out the living room window and yelled at him that he had better run down fast to get it before someone pinched it.

Her last sight was Leo standing on the pavement shaking his jacket up at her and yelling, 'Bitch!'

Then she'd got in the shower and scrubbed herself for half an hour, trying to blot out the knowledge that she'd discovered something about herself that she didn't like. She'd always known she wasn't perfect, but she'd been comfortable in the idea that she was probably better than most. Not any more.

After the shower, she wrapped herself up in her big blue dressing gown and made herself a comforting mug of hot milk. Sitting at the table, as far as she could get from the couch, Isobel realised with dread that throwing Leo out of the flat was not a very politic way to handle the situation. If he felt vengeful he might tell Clare what had happened and that would be frightful.

But it would be unbearable if Phil were to find out. Phil, who now seemed so thoroughly desirable and true-hearted. Isobel was humiliated at the idea that he could ever find out that she'd been rolling around on a couch with some stranger. Just the thought of it made her shudder. What price now for calm, bossy, in-control Isobel?

Trudging off to bed, she had decided that she'd just have to trust that Leo would be so reluctant to reveal his own ignominious part in last night's events that he would keep quiet. Or maybe, if he had any better nature, he'd think twice before saying something that could ruin her friendship with Clare and probably her marriage as well.

After a long sleepless night, she felt nothing but relief as she threw her clothes into a bag and left Clare's flat for good, rushing home to the place she belonged.

If she could still belong there.

She jumped when Clare said softly again, 'Leo.'

'What did you say about Leo?' Isobel croaked.

'I said I don't think there's any future for me and Leo,' Clare repeated. 'Having spent some time away from him, I don't see what I was so entranced by. I mean, yes, he's attractive, he's smart, he's fantastic in bed, but his brain is mostly away somewhere else. He just likes having a woman around in the wings for regular sex and occasional conversation.'

Isobel felt loathe to comment. 'Well yes, there is that . . .' she muttered.

'So why am I wasting time with him? Maybe you were right all the time, it is better to find someone who is a decent human being – someone with integrity – and stick to him like a limpet.'

'Like Phil,' said Isobel fervently.

'Yes,' agreed Clare. 'Like Phil.'

'But do you still want to have kids,' Isobel asked, 'having spent two weeks with them?'

Clare threw her hands up in the air. 'To be honest, I don't know! I've loved being with Ellie and Lex. But, you know, whenever I imagined having kids, I thought about having a baby or a cute little toddler, at a pinch. But now I look at Ellen and Alex and try to imagine their future – maybe Ellie as a sulky, bulimic adolescent chucking up her vegetarian dinner every night, or Lex with spots hunched over a computer screen and listening to Death Metal music. Kids don't stay cute and funny for ever. So then I think maybe parenthood isn't the promised land after all.'

Isobel gave her a little punch on the shoulder. 'Yes, thank you very much for sharing that vision of the future with me,' she said. 'So when do we get out of here?'

And then quite suddenly they both began to giggle hysterically.

When Phil arrived home with a bag of nails he didn't need, Clare made her excuses to pack her bag and go, hugging each of the children fiercely before she left.

'I'll see you all soon,' she said.

'We'll look forward to it,' Phil said formally.

Left alone, Phil wrapped Isobel up in a big bear hug. Isobel put his unusual effusiveness down to her long absence because, normally, Phil's idea of a welcome home was a peck somewhere in the vicinity of her right ear.

'It's so completely wonderful to have you home,' he told her.

Isobel hugged him back at first tentatively, and then enthusiastically. Gazing up into his face, which looked both dearly familiar and yet strangely new at the same time, she swore to herself that if she could somehow forget all about last night, she'd start again with Phil. She'd appreciate him differently. She wouldn't be so smug and self-righteous. She'd leave him room to be as human and fallible as she'd discovered herself to be. If only she had the chance to start again.

'It's fantastic to be home,' she told him. 'I never thought I'd enjoy seeing all the usual clutter but right now it looks like heaven. I'd trade in Clare's neat flat for this any time.'

'Well we don't want you to go away again, at least not in a hurry. It really didn't feel like home without you in it.'

Isobel smiled up at him, pure affection, pure relief. 'Well that's good to hear. I was starting to worry that it didn't make any difference whether I was here or not, apart from the standard of the menu.'

Phil tightened his arms. 'Never think that,' he said seriously. 'It was like the heart of the place wasn't here. Look Isobel, I know I don't say it often enough, but I do love you.'

Isobel wrapped her arms up around his neck. 'I don't say it often enough either, I love you too. I've missed you like crazy.'

'We're lucky, aren't we?'

'Incredibly lucky. The day you walked into the casualty department with blood running down your arm was the luckiest day of my life. If I don't count the days when Ellie and Alex were born.'

'Ah,' Phil said, grinning, 'in that case I'll never let you tease me about being a hypochondriac ever again. Any other man would have just stuck a couple of bandaids on the cut and told everyone it didn't hurt a bit.'

Isobel was serious. 'Well then I guess I'll just have to pay attention to what an exceptional man you are.'

'About time. Now come and sit down on the couch

and tell me about it,' Phil hustled her over to the sofa, keeping hold of one of her hands as if he didn't ever want to let it go. 'Now you've seen how the other half lives – any regrets at all?'

'No major ones,' Isobel replied, thinking silently that there was only one major one. And that was something she would have to deal with.

Phil breathed deeply. 'Well I know you must be itching to unpack and start straightening things up around here, after two weeks of wear, tear and Clare. So I'll walk the kids down to the shops to round up some bread rolls and ham for lunch while you get settled.'

'Oh no, Phil,' Isobel said. 'I can unpack and look after them at the same time. It's no bother. You're doing things with the garden. And you know how slow Ellen is when she walks. I can put them in the car and nip down to the shops to get lunch while you finish whatever you were doing outside.'

'Iso,' he said firmly. 'I really like to spend some time with them. It's the sort of stuff I miss out on all week. And there's no rush, you know. It's Sunday, and we pass the playground on the way. I'll put them in their outdoor gear right now. I want to do this.'

'Oh,' said Isobel, somewhat startled. 'Well in that case, the unpacking isn't all that urgent. It can wait. And who cares about straightening everything up anyway? The place looks like home with a bit of clutter about it. I'll come with you for the walk.'

Now it was Phil's turn to be startled.

Then he held out his hand and she took it.

'With lipstick that colour,' he told her, 'you'll be more than just a mother and a wife. You'll be a road-safety asset.'

CHAPTER 18

Clare forlornly scanned the rows of plastic folding chairs which had been set up in the kindergarten. They all faced the kitchen end of the room which had been designated 'the stage' for the concert, although that just meant clearing away the boxes of blocks and reading books to leave an empty space on the floor. A giant banner suspended from the ceiling said in wobbly letters, 'Fast Track Christmas Extravaganza!'

It was a weekday afternoon but the place was packed, mainly with the usual contingent of women and babies, but also a fair sprinkling of dads and mums in business suits who had obviously sneaked away from the office to see their child's first concert performance.

Just when Clare was despairing of seeing anyone familiar in this mass of beaming parental faces, she spotted Isobel's hand waving.

'I've saved you a seat,' she mouthed at Clare, patting the chair beside her.

Apologising and dodging, Clare pushed her way down

one of the rows to where Isobel and Phil were sitting, holding hands. Alex was curled up on a seat next to Phil, fast asleep. Over four months down the track, Clare could now peck Phil on the cheek with scarcely a qualm. She could even see that one day she would forget all about the terrible night of The Kiss that nearly was. And the sooner the better.

Clare gave Isobel a quick, affectionate hug. Even in the fluorescent lights of the kindergarten, she could see that Isobel was looking radiant.

'God, Iso, you look even more gorgeous than ever,' Clare said. 'I do love it when you wear your hair out like that. I'm glad you've started to do that more often.'

'I wish I could say the same about you,' chided Isobel in a comfortable, big-sisterly way. 'You've filled out a bit but you look very tired. Have you been doing too much?'

'Huh,' said Clare, with a snort. 'You might say that.'

The year was ticking over into summer but already the weather was hot so Clare was wearing a loose, sleeveless summer dress. Isobel thought to herself that its pistachio green colour just made Clare look even more pale.

'Well, doesn't this look festive?' Clare said, quickly changing the subject.

Phil smiled. 'The kids have been working on their Christmas decorations for months,' he told her, across Isobel.

'Well, it certainly looks like Santarama,' Clare said. 'Still at least it helps us get into the mood for a Christmas concert this early in the month.' She reached into her bag. 'Oh, I forgot these,' she said, flourishing a large manilla envelope. 'The Flipside pictures.'

Isobel laughed as she leafed through the big glossy

photographs and then passed them on to Phil. They showed Clare wearing an apron and looking harassed in the kitchen, while Isobel sat mournfully home alone by the phone with Barchester on her lap and the phone on the hook.

'Well, at least you got to keep your job, which was the most important thing,' Isobel commented. 'And it's amazing what hair and make-up people can do. We both look very glamorous.'

'Not bad,' Clare said, squinting critically at her own photographs. She thought she looked a bit puffy in the face. 'Fiona's comment was, "Great to see that whichever way you go, single or married, you're going to be miserable".'

There was a flurry of activity at the front and they focused on the stage for a minute, thinking the concert was about to start. But it was a false alarm. One small child in a shepherd's costume had come wandering out of the kitchen/dressing room, and had to be corralled back in by one of the teachers. A friendly chuckle passed through the audience.

'So how is Fiona and everyone else at the office?' Isobel asked when the fuss died down.

'Just the same,' Clare said. 'Everyone's worn to a shred doing stories on the new make-up colours for autumn and whether it's ever stylish to be seen at an Australian ski resort. And I have a bit of suspicion that Will and Fiona might be "seeing each other". You know, out of hours. They haven't actually said anything, but they just seem to be eating the same kind of food and seeing the same films and turning up looking sleepy on the same mornings. Fi won't admit a thing but I'm definitely suspicious.'

'Well – that would be wonderful, wouldn't it?' Isobel asked, a bit tentatively. 'That is, if that's what they both want, it's wonderful.'

'Of course,' said Clare, although secretly she was just slightly put out, and a bit ashamed of feeling that way. Talk about dog in the manger, she scolded herself.

'Have you started writing your Flipside story yet?' Isobel asked.

'No,' Clare confessed. 'I've been flat out at work. But you don't have to worry, The Colonel has decided it's a back-to-work, early autumn kind of story after all so she won't be running it till well into next year. If you can do it before the end of the month that should be okay.'

'That's a relief. I can put it off for another week. And then you'll help me with it, won't you?'

'Of course, what are sisters for?' Clare said lightly. 'Besides, don't forget that The Colonel will write most of it for us anyway.'

At this point, the concert really did start and the proud parents were treated to an hour of ecumenical Christmas delights, which managed to interweave Rudolph the Red-Nosed Reindeer with 'Silent Night', and Santa Claus with shepherd's crooks, all without any references to the baby Jesus for fear of offending the non-believers in the audience. Clare and Isobel screamed with delight when Ellie came on in her sheep costume, covered in big blue dots, right down to the one on her nose.

'She looks brilliant,' Clare whispered. 'You are clever.'

'It was your idea,' Isobel whispered back.

Clare didn't say anything, but she remembered very clearly that it had been Rory Maguire's idea. She hadn't heard anything more from Rory, despite leaving a message on his answer machine to say she hoped Jessica was feeling better. Through Isobel, she'd heard that the little girl had ended up with pneumonia and had been in hospital for a short while but was fine now. In fact, Clare had just spotted her prancing around the stage as a very lively Rudolph. But any little spark of attraction that had existed between Clare and Rory had evidently fizzled out in the face of sickness, distance and time. Clare hardly thought about him any more.

The finale was a rousing and less than tuneful chorus of 'Santa Claus is Coming to Town', followed by the arrival of Santa himself, distributing bags of (sugar-free) Christmas lollies and dried-fruit snacks. The kids went wild with delight, gathering around him so he seemed to be wading knee deep in small children.

Clapping, Clare remarked to Isobel, 'I don't see the dreaded Margaret anywhere. Don't tell me that's her in the Santa suit?'

'Oh no,' whispered Isobel. 'Didn't I tell you? She got the sack.'

'No!' Clare said in shock.

'Oh yes. It turns out she was filching supplies from the kinder for herself, everything from envelopes and pens to finger paints and toys for her kids. Skandi had suspected someone was doing it for some time and finally caught her red-handed in the act.'

'How shocking. But why on earth was she doing it?'

'Who knows?' Isobel said. 'It wasn't as if they were poor. Maybe it was just some kind of mental aberration. Anyway Skandi didn't press any charges, just gave her the sack and said she wouldn't be taking the matter any further. I've never even seen Margaret since and Phil tells me they're putting their house on the market and moving. But I'm going to go over there and see her. I'd hate her to move away without saying goodbye. After all, anyone can make a mistake in life.'

'Oh yes,' Clare marvelled, gleefully delighted. 'But who would have guessed it?'

When the concert was over, and Ellen had run through the crowd to show Phil and Isobel her bag of Christmas lollies, Phil offered to look after the kids if Isobel and Clare wanted to get some tea and have a chat before Clare had to get back to work.

Standing in the short queue, waiting to reach the urn, Isobel said to Clare, 'I must tell you my fantastic news. Well, two bits of fantastic news. I've applied to study a psychology degree and I've been accepted, starting next year! They've agreed I can study part-time until Lexxie is at school.'

'That's great,' Clare said. 'You'll be so good at it. They say most of the course is as boring as the Queen's Christmas message but it will all be worth it in the end. I think you'd be a fantastic psychologist.'

'I hope so. I don't take anything for granted, but I'm going to work at it,' Isobel said. 'And we've definitely shelved the plans for a third child. We think two children are going to be enough. I'd rather have time to enjoy being with Phil and the kids.'

'Oh yes,' Clare agreed with her.

Isobel continued, 'But the other amazing news is that The Colonel rang this afternoon and asked me to become the new "Marion". Apparently the woman who used to do the column wants to retire permanently and The Colonel has offered me the chance to take over. Except it's going to be called 'Dear Isobel'. Isn't that a hoot? And I can do it from home to fit around the kids and make $1000 a page. As The Colonel said, it's the opportunity of a lifetime.'

'Oh Iso, I'm thrilled for you,' said Clare. 'I thought The Colonel was looking terribly mysterious and pleased with herself every time she looked at me today. I'm so happy. It's perfect.'

And she meant it. Any latent rivalry that had existed between the sisters seemed to have evaporated.

They got cups of tea and took them back to their seats. They could see Phil through the windows, helping Alex slither down the slide.

'So how does Phil feel about all this?' Clare asked, as they watched him and sipped their tea.

'He's been amazing, completely accepting about me going back to study right from the beginning,' Isobel said. 'And he was very proud about the magazine column. I think he was more pleased than I was. He's practically looking after the kids single-handedly a lot of the time too, so I can have more time to myself.'

Isobel watched through the window as Phil took Alex back up to the top of the slide to start sliding down again.

'He is a dear man,' she said tenderly. 'And I think in the end he'll love having a working wife. I can't wait to be able to give him the odd romantic weekend away or those custom-made golf clubs he's always wanted. I'm lucky to have him.'

She sighed with surprising heaviness and then turned to look intently at Clare. 'So what about you? What's your news?'

'Oh,' Clare sipped her tea casually. 'I guess my big news is that I'm pregnant.'

Isobel gaped at her. 'No, you can't be.'

Clare smiled wryly. 'Well yes, it seems I am capable of it after all. We all know that the diaphragm isn't a hundred per cent reliable, and I guess I've just become a statistic. I promise you it was an accident.'

'So how pregnant are you?'

Clare's hand unconsciously strayed towards her belly. 'Just over sixteen weeks. It must have happened just after I got back from your place. Leo and I had one heck of a fight, followed by one heck of a making up before we finally broke up for good.'

Isobel frowned at her. 'But, you witch. You've known all this time and you haven't told me. I can't believe it.'

Clare looked a bit shame faced. 'It's not that I wanted to keep it from you, Iso. I just decided to have tests first to make sure the baby was okay, then I was going to make up my mind what I was going to do. I'm sure I would have told you either way, but those tests all take such a long time. Believe me, I've been dying to tell you. It's been torture not talking about it.'

'I should hope so.' Isobel was still almost angry, until she paused and recollected that there were other secrets drifting between them, secrets that Clare would never know about. She picked up Clare's hand. 'I just can't stand the idea of you going through all those tests and things by yourself. What did you have, CVS, amnio? But everything's fine? You will even have been for your first ultrasound by now.'

Clare smiled at this torrent of questions. 'I decided on CVS and everything is fine, at least as far as they can tell me. And yes, we've had the ultrasound. I even asked if it was a boy or girl. They think it's a girl.'

A girl. Isobel took this in, still amazed that five minutes ago she had not even been aware of this baby's existence. Now she had a niece. Almost. She mentally counted over the months in her mind. The baby should arrive at the end of autumn, perfect timing for some bright-coloured, woolly, knitted clothes. Isobel decided she'd start brushing up on her old knitting skills.

'So – umm – Leo, does he know yet?' she asked nervously.

Clare looked down. 'Yes. Just before he headed off to LA to meet with a whole bunch of agents and become the next William Goldman. He said it was my choice and if the child ever wanted to get to know him later in life, he'd be contactable. But he doesn't want to be involved. Which is fair enough. Keeping the baby is my choice. And it's not as if I want to be in a relationship with Leo. Once we got back from the Sister Pact I couldn't stop seeing how little affection there was between us and I thought, at my age, I don't need this.'

'I don't know what to say about it all,' said Isobel. 'Of course, if you're happy, Clare-bear, I'm happy for you.'

Clare shot her a look. 'You don't have to say it. I know how gruelling it will be and it won't be all teddy bears and misty eyes. I'm not some sixteen-year-old who thinks it will be like having a doll or a dog. But I hope that you and Phil might help by being a kind of extended nuclear family for us. I was thinking of asking you to be her godparents.'

'Of course we'd love to. Anything we can do to help,' Isobel assured her.

'I'm still bamboozled. There's so many things to think about – money, childcare, responsibility . . . It's huge.' Clare took a deep breath. 'But now it's happened, I'm going to make the best of it. The Colonel knows and she's been great. Says I can take maternity leave with pay, then do work from home or put in flexible hours or whatever works best with the baby. Which is funny really. I once thought that the worst punishment in the world would be to work at *Verve* for another decade but now that's exactly what I'll be doing.'

'Oh, it's not so bad, especially if you make your own sandwiches for the editorial meeting,' Isobel joked.

'Never,' said Clare firmly. 'If I'm about to start eighteen years of sandwich making for this kid, there's no way I'm going to be making any more than I have to now.' She sighed. 'It's such a pity that William isn't gay, after all. Wouldn't it be perfect to have a marriage of convenience with a gay guy? He'd even be able to cook and wash nappies.'

'I think William is probably very happy with the way things are right now,' Isobel said. 'And you can always use disposables. I think we should drink to this baby. It's about time we had a little Callaway in the family.'

They toasted each other with their polystyrene foam tea cups, sharing a sense of excitement and apprehension. A feeling of stepping out blindly into a void.

'I better go out and find my family and take them home,' Isobel said finally. 'Thanks for coming to the concert. It meant the world to Ellie. Gosh, she's going to be so excited when she hears that you're having a baby. Although heavens know how we're going to explain the fact that Aunty Clare doesn't have a husband. She's still very straight about these things.' Isobel laughed, allowing herself to feel delighted that next year she would be holding Clare's baby. Clare's daughter. She started to gather her bags together. 'We'll see you this weekend so we can celebrate properly? I'll make something with lots of dairy products in it. This baby has to have strong bones.'

'That would be lovely. Would you do me a favour and tell Phil about the baby?' Clare asked. 'I'd hate to see his face if he looked all disapproving.'

'Of course he won't,' Isobel answered staunchly, 'but I'll tell him anyway. And you'll have to tell Mum and Dad soon too, you know. They'll be hurt that you left it so long.'

'I know,' Clare sighed. 'I've been putting it off till I was sure I knew what I was going to do. But I'll go over and see them this weekend some time.'

'I think they'll surprise you,' Isobel predicted. 'I think they'll be thrilled.'

'We'll see,' said Clare.

When Isobel went out to join her family, Clare sat alone for a few minutes, trying to summon up the energy to get up and head back into work. She'd been feeling lethargic for weeks. Although it was getting better, she still hadn't hit that rush of energy that everyone assured her happened in the second trimester.

'Clare,' said a voice.

'Rory,' she said, before even looking up into his familiar face.

'I was just outside with Jess on the play equipment and I bumped into Phil. He said you were in here.'

'Well, here I am,' Clare said. 'I was actually about to

head back into work. Thursday is one of our busy days.'

'Before you go . . .' Rory hesitated. 'I'm really sorry we never got to have that dinner. Things just fell apart. You've heard that Jess got pneumonia? Well, of course you have because you left that nice message on the answer machine. Anyway, once it was all over and she was home safely, I didn't know whether you'd want me to call you or not.'

'So you thought, or not,' Clare said, smiling faintly.

'I guess so. When in doubt, always take the cowardly option,' he said, grinning back. He sat down beside her in the seat that Isobel had vacated. 'How have you been? Still working at that – what was it – "half-witted" magazine? And did that story ever come out?'

'I think you forgot to mention superficial,' Clare reminded him. 'And no, not yet. We'll be running it some time early next year but I'll make sure I send you a copy. Although I'm afraid that you won't get a mention. I should confess right now that I never really wanted any background material from you and Jess, I just thought you'd be a nice person to have coffee with.'

Rory grinned. 'I was hoping that might be the case because that's why I invited you over. Cravenly using my daughter as an excuse, I'm afraid.'

Clare thought that he looked older then when she had seen him last. As usual he was wearing jeans, this time with a blue rugby top, but she saw faint shadows under his eyes. Perhaps the experience of having Jess in hospital was still with him. Come to think of it, that must have been a terrible time in his life. Perhaps he had even thought he was going to lose his daughter.

'I'm sorry about that answer phone message,' Clare

said simply. 'Looking back, it was a dumb and cold thing to do. I mean, your daughter was in hospital. The least I could have done was drop over and see you in person, maybe brought a casserole over or something.'

'Oh no, heaven forbid. I tasted your coconut cookies and barely lived to tell the tale,' Rory teased her.

Clare smiled at him, remembering all over again the peculiar easy warmth of this man and feeling melancholy that their lives had wandered off in different directions. That is, if they had. Right now Clare still felt so numb by the extraordinary direction that her own life was taking that she found it hard to imagine ever having control over it again.

'Look.' Rory picked up her hand.

Odd, Clare thought, how many people were picking up her hands today. But she liked the look of her hand lying engulfed in Rory's large practical paw. It felt safe.

'The truth is I have been a coward,' Rory went on. 'First I hid behind Jess to get you out on a date, and then I hid, a bit, behind her illness to get out of a date because I was worried about how something this big would impact on the rest of my life. But I'm going to be brave now. I'd love to see you. Maybe you could come over to dinner some time? I'm a fantastic cook, even if I do have to say it myself because Jess takes me for granted. And I'd love to cook for you.'

A man who cooks, Clare thought. She wondered what *Manifesting Your Man* would have to say about that. But she'd never know. She'd thrown it into the bin about the same time she brought herself a pregnancy testing kit at the supermarket.

'That sounds very tempting,' she said to Rory, meaning

322

it. In fact, right now she thought how wonderful it would be to curl up beside Rory, put her head down on his pillow and fall asleep for years. Then she resolutely took her hand out of his. 'But I'm afraid I'm very busy at the moment. In fact I'm probably going to be very busy for about another year or so. There's something I have to do. Would it be all right if I called you some time next year to see if the dinner invitation is still open?'

He looked at her quizzically. 'Are you serious?'

'Perfectly. This is just something I need to do by myself for a while.'

He smiled at her. 'Well, please call. Of course, I can't guarantee that the chef will still be in the kitchen . . .'

'I guess that's a chance I'll have to take,' Clare said. 'But I will definitely call,' she promised – meaning it.

She walked out to her car, feeling the hot sun warming her cold bare arms.

Leaning against the driver's door for a moment, Clare decided that, all things being equal, the future would probably turn out to be just about as good as she would allow it to be.

Then she got into her little car, and roared away.

EPILOGUE

LIFE ON THE FLIPSIDE – Two sisters role over and let us in on a secret. Just whose lot is the happier one?
Verve magazine, March issue

When *Verve* feature writer Clare Callaway told us that her sister had the easy life, we wanted to hear more. (Apart from anything else, it gave us an excuse to sit down for a few minutes with a latte, always a welcome excuse around this busy office.) Clare claimed her sister, Isobel Ashton, a stay-at-home mother of two, really had it made. She hadn't worked full-time for five years and all she had to do all day was take care of her two gorgeous children, Ellen, aged four, and baby Alex, eleven months.

'Bliss,' said Clare, who's a busy career girl.

But not so fast. Doesn't everyone say looking after small children is the most demanding job in the world? We decided to put it to the test. We dared Clare to try her hand at Isobel's home work. And while she was at it, Isobel could see what life was like working in the whirling dervish that is *Verve* headquarters. Like good sports, Isobel and Clare agreed to swap lives for two weeks. They discovered that life on the other side of the fence was very different to what they had expected. But yes, Virginia, there is a way you can have it all . . .

Says supermum, ISOBEL, about her two weeks as a career girl:

'I thought I had it all – fabulous husband with a partnership in his firm, beautiful Edwardian house with open-plan kitchen and two delightful children, Ellen and Alexander.

'But I have to admit that I always looked at my sister Clare's life with more than a pang of envy. As far as I was concerned, she had quite a few things too, not least of all a job on my favourite magazine!

'So when she suggested swapping lives for this story, I leapt at the idea. Here was finally my chance to do what a lot of women have dreamt of – to live my sister's life. I could see it all . . . the glamorous job, the apartment in chic inner-city St Kilda, the fabulous parties, the even more fabulous chance to sleep in the morning after. We had two weeks to see how the other half lives. And I couldn't wait.

'Looking back, I think I found out a lot more than how the other half lives. Or loves. I also found out how a cappuccino can be a mood-altering substance and why television can be the single woman's best friend.

'Of course, working at *Verve* was wonderful. Although if everyone hadn't been so nice, I'm not sure I could have coped with a workplace where the coffee mugs are colour co-ordinated with the desk tops and everyone seems to not only *know* the A-list, but be *on* it as well.

'Having been out of the workforce for five years (before

that I worked as a nursing sister in a large hospital), I wasn't prepared for the nine-to-five regime. Getting woken up by an alarm clock, having to look chic by 7.30 in the morning, coping with public transport, battling the crowds for a salmonella-laden chicken sandwich at lunchtime, saving all the shopping and cleaning for the weekend. All that working girl stuff is really hard work. To be frank, even getting a pair of pantihose to last me through the day was hard work.

'Then there was coming home to Clare's empty flat with no one to talk to about my day except her very charming but rather reserved cat. When you've had a long day in the office, knowing there was nothing at home but a microwave and television set did feel lonely. I began to eat bowls of cereal for dinner. I changed into my pyjamas at 7.30 pm. The television became my best buddy. I used to put it on just to hear the sound of voices in the house. It was either that or start talking to myself.

'So let me tell you the things I loved about my sister's life. In no particular order – sleep, reading, watching any TV program I felt like, going to bed any time I chose, never having to hear the words "we should be weeding the garden". I even loved the chance to try out writing skills I never knew I had. It was like eating exotic Japanese food, scary at first but rewarding and refreshing. The things I loathed were the loneliness, the silence and the fear that if I slipped over and broke both my legs getting out of the shower no one would find me for weeks.

'After it was all over, it was fabulous to be back with my family, but I couldn't let go of the taste of freedom. I'm now keen to do some paid work and go back to study, as long as I can fit it in around the children's lives. I've realised I have to pack more into my life because, while you may only have young children for ten years, you're not going to get those ten years back again. So I've joined clubs, I go to a motherhood support group once a week and I make sure I spend real, twosome, romantic, appreciative couple time with my gorgeous husband, Phil.

'Oh, and I've also realised I don't have to iron the sheets. I'm making more space in my life for me.'

CLARE, our smart and sassy, career-minded feature writer, says:

'It wasn't that I hated my life. I have a fabulous job, as well as an interesting love life and a beautiful flat which I share with my cat and the bank. But I couldn't help looking at Isobel and thinking how much easier things were for her.

'I thought how dreamy it was to have someone else paying the bills. How wonderful just to get up when you feel like it. What an indulgence to have no schedules. And then there's the children. I've known Ellen and Alex since they were hours old and they're wonderful kids – lively, funny, beautiful. So if all Isobel has to do is look after her gracious old house and take care of the basic needs of these two very special little people, I thought her life must be heavenly.

'She's often said she feels tired or frazzled, but as a thirty-something single woman who was confronting the fact that I might never have children, I secretly believed she should be a lot more grateful for the good things that she had.

'Then came experiencing the flipside. How can I describe being plunged into full-time stay-at-home mother-hood? It was like being thrown off the end of a pier into a rough, dark, icy sea. Everywhere I turned there was toiling motion, chaos and a feeling of being out of my depth. The housework was never ending, the cooking was constant, the working hours stretched up to eighteen hours a day, seven days a week.

'I learned to my amazement that little children don't have to sleep. I learned that you can spend hours in the kitchen making some healthy treat for dinner and then be forced to look nonchalant when they spit it out on the floor. And like Victorian ladies, kids can easily make their way through six changes of clothes in one day.

'I now know that the most grating sound in the world is a baby crying. And although Ellie and Lexxie were gorgeous, they could also be as tedious as the most tedious job in the world. Think of anything involving paper hats and production lines and I'll bet you that looking after kids can be more boring at times. And at least on a production line, you might have another adult to talk to and a tea break.

'But most of all I think I learned about control. How to give it up. When you're a single woman, you figure you can control most things. You've got potions to smooth your smile lines, push-up bras to lift your breasts, aerobics classes to slim your thighs. You can decide when and where you want to see your lover. And if you're feeling a little down, well, there's always a Ralph Fiennes movie, an early night or a family-size block of milk chocolate.

'But with children there's no such thing as control. You don't know what they'll do next, what they'll need next or even when they'll sleep next. It's all about relinquishing mastery. Even living as part of a family takes away your ability to run your own life. Suddenly I had to consult three other people before I knew what I was going to do with my time at any given moment of the day or night. It was like wearing shackles.

'Not that it was all bad. There were times when the kids were so funny and so delicious I wanted to eat them. There were times when I sat around the family dinner table, with a big bowl of spaghetti bolognese in the middle, and the kids were laughing with their dad and I thought, this is how it feels to be part of a unit. Belonging. And even if the house was a shocking mess, it was a warm, living kind of clutter created by children playing.

'But no, I'll never say my sister has the easy life again. Now I know she doesn't. I know about the hours, the exhaustion, and the effort required sometimes to smile sweetly and say all the right, reasonable things when the children are whining and fussing and showing off.

'And bringing up children is such an awesome responsibility on every level, from your duty to keep them safe and nourished to your obligation to make them positive, optimistic, well-balanced human beings. If they'll let you.

'I guess now I do want it all. I want to be a mother, I want to have a great man, I want to keep pushing myself in my career. Oh, and now I also want a great nanny. And a size FF push-up bra.'

Editor's note: Verve is thrilled to confirm that Isobel, a fully trained nursing sister as well as a mother of two who has also studied psychology, has joined the magazine permanently to write our problem page. Look out for Dear Isobel's page in next month's *Verve* and send all your letters to the usual address.

Clare, one of our very special team of in-the-know

feature writers, will soon be going on maternity leave. It's a secret between us girls, but she's having a baby girl called Sadie. Of course, Clare will continue to write for the magazine as well as being a mother because, like all *Verve* women, she knows it is possible to have everything. As long as you are smart enough to pay someone else to make your fresh home-made pasta. We wish both Clare and baby Sadie well for the future.